THE
RETRIBUTION

by

Mike Wardle

Previously published under the title: *A Time of Giants*

Burning Chair Limited, Trading As Burning Chair Publishing
61 Bridge Street, Kington HR5 3DJ

www.burningchairpublishing.com

By Mike Wardle
Edited by Simon Finnie and Peter Oxley
Cover by Burning Chair Publishing

First published by Vivid Publishing, 2019 as *A Time of Giants*
This edition published by Burning Chair Publishing, 2022

ISBN: 978-1-912946-22-8

Author's Note

Some of you may question the historical accuracy of the references to a few of the locations in this story. My intention was never to be historically inaccurate here, but rather to allow greater ease for the reader to identify the continents and places within. In particular to North and South America, I appreciate that this story is set in a time where these names were not yet used as a reference to their respective locals. Again, the intention is to take you on an adventure, to transport you to a different time for a moment and allow you to ride alongside the characters and their individual journeys with ease.

I hope you enjoy reading the story as much as I enjoyed writing it.

Mike Wardle

MIKE WARDLE

Prologue - 1741

It had been a hot and humid day in the port. Simon Blake stood outside the main entrance to the Stevenson Transport building, watching the busy movement of the markets in the square before him. He leant against one of the large, stone pillars at the front of the imposing building that had been purposely constructed to allow access to the port square, as well as to overlook Guanabara Bay, which harboured the many cargo and merchant ships in Rio de Janeiro.

His office was attached to a towering warehouse that stored shipping cargo ready to be distributed across South America. It was one of the largest buildings in Rio, second only in size to the Government Fort, which stood on the opposite side and was used for gala balls, state business and the settling of legal disputes.

Ironic, having a courthouse in a land where judgement is decided with a sword and musket, not a trial by jury.

Simon had been the head of the Stevenson Transport Company's South American operations for ten years and had developed a reputation for being a shrewd businessman with excellent connections throughout the Americas.

As a result of Simon running his section of the company with such consistent proficiency, Jacob Stevenson, the owner of Stevenson Transport, rarely had to make the voyage across the Atlantic. Yet, in the ten years of his tenure, Simon had never received a message from Jacob quite like the one that had been delivered earlier that week. One of the Stevenson cargo galleons had arrived three days ago carrying on board a sealed letter written in Jacob's own hand.

This was not unusual, as Jacob would often send letters with expressions of gratitude, or to provide updates on other business channels within the company. However, this recent letter was different from previous ones. It had a tone of urgency and was as cryptic as it was brief:

> *Blake, my most trusted.*
> *I am sending you the key. We must keep it hidden from them.*
> *The answer is in the borders of the sea.*
> *Keep it safe, my friend. Our world depends on keeping it hidden.*
> *Keep it safe.*
> *Jacob*

Something of immense importance was arriving on the next ship. Simon had thought of little else since he had read the message.

What could this key be; and what, more importantly, does it open?

He repositioned himself against the pillar, glancing up at the dark afternoon sky and over to the wharf, where a slave ship had anchored. It had only docked a couple of hours earlier and already the air was filled with the stench of rotting flesh and human defecation.

A death ship.

The *Grey Cloud* was a prominent and feared slave ship with a particularly violent crew who called themselves the "Scarlet Bandeirantes" and was led by an even more violent captain by the name of Jackson Bell.

"Bandeirantes" was a term that had been given to raiding parties who trekked through the new Americas enslaving natives and plundering gold and diamond mines. The Scarlet Bandeirantes called themselves expeditioners, but everyone knew what they really were: murderers and thieves of the worst kind. They did not abide by the laws of any government and were determined to throw the world into a fiery chaos.

In addition, the Scarlets were renowned for slaving and raiding the West African coastal villages for their human plunder. The captives were then shipped across the Atlantic to be sold for labour in the Brazilian sugar plantations, cattle properties and gold mines that were now flourishing in this new world.

What a monstrous way to make a living: to steal people from their homes and chain them in the hold of a ship.

It was common for dozens of these unfortunate captives to perish on the journey across the Atlantic, to be thrown overboard to float on the waves until their bodies were picked apart by sharks. He hated the black trade and cursed the slavers who lined their pockets through human trafficking.

Simon had heard that many people in England, his homeland, were now opposed to slavery and were fighting to make the trade illegal but, as far as he could see, making any real changes would be a long way off. He knew of a number of British galleons that had taken down slavers but there were far too few of them with the courage needed to make an impact.

His gaze shifted across the town square and past the markets, where he counted four slaves standing on the gallows in front of the Government Fort, their arms bound behind their backs and a hangman's noose tightened around each neck. The town square was large, with the gallows fifty yards from where he stood, and though the smoke from the market fires blurred his vision, he could see that one of the slaves was crying.

A fresh shipment of Africans had been moved off the *Grey Cloud* two hours earlier and now watched in horror from a holding pen, some crying, some staring silently in anger and all of them weakened and starving. They would soon be sent to the fattening houses, where they would be forced to eat to increase their strength and raise their value at auction, but for now they would watch and learn what the consequences were for slaves who tried to escape.

Simon pushed himself off the pillar and began walking into the markets and across the square towards the tavern. "The Monkey and Rat" was the name carved crudely into a wooden sign above the entrance to the ground floor, which was now beginning to fill with people. A lingering crowd was gathered in front of the gallows to watch the hanging, while others filtered through the markets, desensitised to an event that had become more and more frequent in this part of the world.

Rio had grown at a rapid rate in both population and infrastructure and had become the capital for Brazilian, European and British trade, which in turn meant greater slave numbers entering through ports up and down the eastern coast. Hangings had become a common spectacle, used to teach others a lesson and quite often the poor souls condemned to the rope had not even tried to escape but were plucked out of a death lottery and hanged in front of a new shipment of slaves as a warning.

As he neared the tavern, he encountered the familiar sight of drunk men spilling out onto the front veranda, accompanied by the town whores and young slave girls. In the corner sat Jackson Bell with several of his crew – some were laughing, some groping the women on their laps. Jackson showed no emotion as he stared through the doorway at the four dark figures on the gallows; he did not see slaves as people, but as commodities. He turned his head towards Simon, who was making his way past the deck of the tavern towards the gallows.

'Waste of good product – hey, Blake – this hanging business?' he called out, loud enough for everyone in the vicinity to hear. 'At least they are not mine though… right?'

Simon knew it was a statement rather than a question, which thankfully did not warrant an answer. He remained silent as Jackson spoke again.

'But … I do like to watch their dirty little bodies swing around from time to time.'

The men and women on the deck of the tavern laughed wholeheartedly as Simon walked past them. He had no interest in getting into an argument with the Scarlets during a drinking session. They enjoyed fighting, boozing and fornicating above all else and it looked as though they had all been back and forth from the tavern to the brothel for hours. He did not want to give them a reason to fight as well.

Simon turned and looked back at Jackson, who had lit a cheroot and was puffing smoke from the corner of his mouth. Simon raised his right index finger to the front brim of his hat and pulled it down slightly as a gesture of recognition.

'Jackson.' His voice was calm and strong as he nodded, looking over the rest of the crew before continuing towards the gallows. He did not look back but could feel the stares of the Scarlets burning into the back of his shirt.

They would all love to see him dead, none more so than Jackson but, because of his position in the Stevenson Transport Company, his death would attract too much attention from London to be worth an attempt on his life and so, for now at least, he was safe. He continued walking through the markets and stopped at the fishmonger. The smell of fish in the afternoon heat was better on the nose than that of a slave ship and an overripe tavern.

Beside the stall, he saw a young boy bend to the ground and re-emerge with a rock in his right hand. He turned towards the British soldiers who stood guard around the gallows. The boy looked around to make sure his escape route was clear and, as he did, he locked eyes with Simon.

'Leave it, boy,' Simon muttered. 'Unless you want to be up there next to them.'

The boy's face told the whole story: the wickedness and brutality of the situation. He reluctantly dropped the stone and scurried away, quickly disappearing into the market crowds.

Standing on a raised partition on the left of the gallows was the recently appointed Jasper Cole, a British national employed as a government liaison officer, who worked in the Government Fort and commonly oversaw the hangings and other "state affairs".

As Cole read through his list of the names of those who had committed the so-called crime of attempted escape, Simon immediately imagined a fat toad croaking loudly upon a high, wooden stump. Jasper Cole was a short, fat and powerfully ugly man, with swollen cheeks covered in warts. His hair was thin, long and stringy, as if it had only ever grown in certain places on his head. He had a reputation for mixing in unsavoury social circles and had a moral compass that only ever pointed towards the highest bribe.

'Do you have anything to say?' Cole croaked at the four doomed souls.

One of the four, a woman, cried out something in her native tongue, as if she had understood that Jasper's words signified the final stage of the proceedings.

'In English?' Cole replied, playing up to the crowd, almost amused, almost cheerful. He did not wait for another response and, with a nod, the sound of the wooden cogs clicked underneath the gallows and the floor fell out from under the slaves. They fell towards the ground in an ironical moment of freedom, only to be violently jerked back from their freefall as the ropes around their necks found their tension.

They swung in desperation, a cruel three feet above the ground, until the last of them gave up and stopped fighting. Simon heard the cries coming from the holding pen, the sighs from the market crowd and the cheers from the tavern.

What a vile business that is. This place is about to explode.

He reached inside his jacket and felt Jacob's message, safely tucked away in his inner pocket. *'I am sending you the key. We must keep it hidden from them.'* He thought about the words in the message and made a silent promise.

Whatever it is, Jacob, I will do what must be done. I will keep it safe.

From his high vantage point, Cole looked out to the watching crowd, which now included the whole of the marketplace. His small, dirty frame seemed to puff up as he commanded the attention of the entire square. He opened his mouth wide, his yellow, rotting teeth showing through the rising smoke of the markets, and he addressed the waiting crowd.

'Let it be known that any who try to escape their duties will see the gallows, and any who know of an escape and who fail to notify the authorities, will be afforded the same fate: hanging from the neck until they are dead.'

Part One–Exile

1741

Chapter 1

The Stevenson Country Estate was one of the richest properties outside London. It spanned a total of one thousand acres and was used to breed and train the best racehorses in Britain, as well as to accommodate the wealthy and, at times, royalty, at numerous balls and hunts. It boasted many extravagant rooms, lush gardens and expansive forests. Stevenson Transport had been prominent in England for many years, and when it had been time for Jacob to take over, the Americas had been colonised and the shipping of goods to and from the New World had expanded the company into an empire.

Annette Stevenson had come from immense wealth and, with the approval of both families, had been married to Jacob at an early age. She sat upright in her chair, listening to the sounds from the garden around her and not so much to the conversations of the society ladies around the table. A high tea had been proposed the week before by one of her friends. The Stevenson Estate, with its breathtaking gardens, was the most suitable location for such an event. A marquee had been erected on the lawn and servants bustled back and forth with assortments of pastries, biscuits, fruits and tea.

'Annette, my dear,' one of the ladies asked. 'Has there been any thought of whom Sasha will marry?'

'Ah, indeed,' another chimed in. 'There are many young suitors in London who come from well-established families, my nephew being one of them.'

'I agree,' the first lady replied. 'I also have a nephew who will come of age around the same time as your Sasha. He will be ready to take over the family's cotton plantations by then.'

The usual chatter.

No matter where the conversation started, it would always find its way to the topic of suitable marriages for her children. She had three. At sixteen, Brenton was the oldest and destined to take over the company in due course. Sasha was fourteen and her youngest, Penny, was twelve. Penny sat next to her mother. She loved the social engagements and mimicked the fine movements, postures and tones of fashionable ladies.

Annette looked towards her and smiled at her playfulness. 'And who will you want to marry then, my dear?' she asked, mischievously. Penny's eyes widened as if she had been anticipating the question and had her answer at the ready.

'I should like to marry a handsome man with a fine, social upbringing, please, Mother.' She had responded with the youthful certainty of a child, encouraging the ladies around the table, and they giggled with delight.

'And you shall, my dear,' one of the ladies said as she leant over and patted her on the head.

Penny looked back at her mother, satisfied with the answer she had given and the response it had evoked. 'And what type of man will Sasha marry, Mother? One who will be able to handle her wild spirit, I dare say.'

Another chuckle came from the ladies' circle as they all looked at Annette in anticipation of her response. She threw her daughter a sharp look and smiled without answering.

Eventually the pause in the air was too much for one of the nosier women. 'Where is Sasha, Annette?' she asked. 'We rarely see her on these occasions.'

Annette smiled again, but was more embarrassed this time. She had to agree that it was a fair question. Sasha was wild at heart and preferred riding her horse like a man through the estate forest than attending a high tea where she was forced to act like a lady. Her thoughts were again interrupted by Penny.

'There she is, Mother.' Penny pointed across the gardens towards the hill, which overlooked the flat lands towards the stables. Sasha was kneeling in the grass, leaning on her hands, looking down at the men working below.

'Whatever is she doing?' one of the ladies asked.

'I'm not quite sure,' she lied. Annette knew exactly what her daughter was doing and who she was looking at: the stable boy, Caleb.

One day, that boy is going to cause trouble.

Chapter 2

Sasha leaned on her hands and watched the men working below. They had begun to build a new holding paddock where her father's horses could be shown. It was attached to the main stables, which meant that his guests could easily wander down to watch the prized racehorses cantering around the yard, admire their form and, ultimately, envy her father's mares and stallions.

She had counted around twenty men in total working on the fence, which was to be much larger than the others on the estate, with posts the width of a large, black alder tree. It was demanding work and, while she had taken the time to count the workers, her gaze had been predominantly fixed on one.

Caleb had been born on the estate and was the same age as Sasha. He was born poor, into a working-class family, and his parents had both died when he was young. She had known him all her life and yet they had shared very few conversations. Her mother and father did not approve of their daughters having direct contact with the servants and, even though she spent most of her time in their home in London, she had always felt a sense of excitement when the family visited the estate, thus providing her the opportunity to watch Caleb.

He was strong for his age, as strong as any of the men, and at only fourteen he had a tall muscular frame, light blue eyes and a blond mane, which glistened like spun gold in the afternoon sun.

Sasha realised, of course, that he was her inferior and that it was foolish of her to spend the time she did watching him, but she liked to bait him – taunt him even. On the rare occasions when they spoke, she would make demands and talk down at him. Yet, she was confused by the strange exhilaration she felt whenever he was near her. She had heard her father and the managers of the estate praise his strength and hard work, as well as his natural ability with horses – her father almost sounding proud of Caleb.

Brenton, her older brother, never liked hearing Caleb being praised and would often challenge him to race their horses across the estate or to duel with the practice swords. Brenton always ensured he won the race by riding a prized stallion, while Caleb had to make do with a cart horse. Caleb would never allow himself to win when they practised fencing. It would have been such an insult to Brenton that he would have made Caleb's life hell, though it was obvious to all who observed that Caleb was the stronger, faster and more skilled of the two. Though they were of a different class, they always seemed to get on well enough, as long as Brenton continued to win their contests.

Sasha's thoughts were disrupted by the sound of her mother's calling, but she pretended not to hear. The thought of sitting upright for hours talking about London suitors with the society ladies made her stomach turn. She had only three days left on the estate before they returned to London and back to her schooling.

She and her little sister went to a prestigious girls' school in London, a school that moulded girls into ladies who would be acceptable in the highest social circles. She enjoyed school when she was allowed to read but hated the deportment classes – how to sit, how to be polite in front of a man, how to curtsy, what were appropriate topics for discussion and what were not. She had come to the conclusion that any subject requiring a woman to think for herself was not part of the curriculum.

She heard another call but from a different direction this time. This time it was her brother, and she welcomed the sound of his voice.

'Sasha, instead of sitting in the grass like a rabbit all afternoon, would you rather go for a ride through the forest?'

'Despite the fact that you just insulted me, Brother, I would take any chance not to go down to that group of bores around the table.'

'You can avoid it as much as you want, Sasha, but you will have to marry one day. There is no escaping it. Father will want to align the family with a profitable partnership.'

'What a wonderful life a woman is allowed, Brenton – to be paraded as a bargaining tool in Father's negotiations to increase company profits.'

'This company will be under my control one day, Sister, and you should not be so quick to feel sorry for yourself.' Brenton flicked his head up as he looked down at the flatlands. 'Look at them working down there.' He motioned to the men building the fence. 'You will never have to live like that. You will never want for anything.'

Only for my own freedom and happiness.

'Come, I will arrange for horses to be readied with fishing rods and a picnic. We can ride to the far lake and do a spot of fishing. Surely that is so unladylike that it should cheer you up.'

She nodded and jumped up with excitement. 'Yes! I think it just might.'

She would not have permission to go off by herself but knew that she would not be stopped if she was with her older brother, the heir to the family empire. And what was more, she would have the rare chance to talk to Caleb, perhaps even have a conversation with him, without the watchful eyes near the estate.

'Bring our horses,' Brenton ordered a servant boy after he and Sasha had made their way down the hill. 'And let the kitchen know that we will need a picnic. Pack a horse with fishing rods and fetch Caleb to ride behind us. We shall be riding to the far lake. If Father asks, we will be home in time for dinner.'

Chapter 3

Every muscle in Caleb's body ached. He had become strong and hardened from constant labour. He had muscular arms, broad shoulders and tough hands but even they were now splintered, cut and raw. The workers had been tasked to build a new show pen, where wealthy merchants could view Jacob Stevenson's stallions and stock from the ridge near the mansion. Caleb imagined Stevenson and his associates sitting in their elevated position, sipping expensive brandy, smoking the finest cigars and discussing the form of the horses.

They had been working on the fence for a week now and all day every day he had been dragging the large logs off the wagons and lifting them into the holes they had dug in the ground. The logs had been specially cut by a sawmill in London and were far bigger than any of the other fence posts on the estate. Horses were needed to pull them into position, as they were too heavy for even two men to carry. Once the logs were moved next to their respective holes, Caleb would squat down and heave them upwards, using his whole body to push the tree-sized posts into position. One after the next, hour after hour, for days he had been lifting and pushing the fence posts into each hole. Only when it had been too dark to work safely did they stop. Then he had to tend to the horses and carry out his usual tasks on the estate.

He had been born in the servants' quarters and had worked on the estate his whole life. He knew the land better than anyone, yet knew very little of the world outside it. He had only been to

London a few times to pick up supplies and cargo from one of the Stevenson ships and remembered wanting to board the giant merchant ship and see the ocean, but he had been told that it was not his destiny. He would work on the estate until he died.

His parents had both died from fever when he was only a baby. He had been too young to remember them, and yet he missed them greatly when he observed the other children on the estate with their families. He felt very alone at times when he saw those families sitting down for dinner or walking to church each Sunday.

He had his lodgings in the male quarters and had lived there since he was six years old. He was treated well enough but had grown up far quicker than most boys, having started work as soon as he was able to carry a bucket to feed the horses. At fourteen, he was not paid a wage but was fed, clothed and kept warm in the winter, for which he was repeatedly told to be thankful.

He had never learnt to read or write but could break and ride a horse better than anyone else on the estate. Jacob Stevenson and his son Brenton would often come down and watch him work with a new horse. Caleb loved that part of his job because he was always the first in the saddle of a freshly broken horse. Once Jacob was satisfied that the horse was worked enough, Caleb was no longer allowed to ride it. Not many people would know that a prize stallion, which could win the county cup and was worth two hundred pounds, had been broken and first ridden by a poor stable boy on the Stevenson estate.

He hated that his life was planned out for him, that he would never become more than he was at that moment. With no family, no education, no real possessions and no money, what else could he expect? He was the property of the estate, of Jacob Stevenson, and there was no way that would ever change. He would never know what it felt like to be free.

Caleb squatted down and braced himself for a heavy lift. He wrapped his arms around the end of the post and felt the sting from the raw flesh on his hands and forearms as they scraped against the grain of the wood. He gritted his teeth and pushed hard on his heels. As the log began to move, he felt the splinters in his hands push deeper into flesh. He grimaced, pushing hard with his legs. He lifted the log to waist height, quickly squatting back down, unfolding his arms and catching the log, having repositioned his body underneath. He made one last push with his legs and groaned as he forced the log upwards, extending his arms and pushing the post forwards, guiding it into the hole. It met the bottom with a thud and stood erect, proud and locked into the earth.

'Better you than me, Caleb,' one of the men said. 'Your young legs have more energy than mine. Don't worry. Only about twenty more to go.' The other men started laughing around him as he knelt hunched over on one knee, sweat pouring down his cheeks as he inspected the new cut that had opened in his palm. Then he heard Brenton's voice behind them.

'Actually, we will be needing Caleb for the rest of the afternoon, so it will be up to one of you amusing gentlemen to lift the rest.' Caleb and the others spun around to see Brenton and Sasha. They were both on their horses, alongside another horse packed with fishing rods and a wicker basket. Because of the noise of the cart horses and the constant banging of nails being hammered into wood, the men had not heard Brenton and Sasha ride up behind them.

Immediately, the workers stopped what they were doing and stood upright and alert. They kept their heads bowed, knowing not to raise them unless they were addressed by the future owner of the Stevenson empire.

'I beg your pardon, young master,' said the man who had made the joke, still with his head bowed.

Brenton looked over at Caleb. 'We need you to follow us to the lake, Caleb. Sasha and I would like to leave at once.'

'Yes, sir,' Caleb responded, relieved that he did not have to lift another log, at least for a while.

Sasha looked at his bleeding hand. 'Will that hand need

attention, Caleb?'

He looked up at her, his blue eyes piercing through the blond hair hanging over his face. They held each other's gaze and he felt a sharp tingle.

'No, miss,' Caleb answered. 'It's fine.'

'Very well then,' Brenton said as he tapped his heels into the flanks of his horse, motioning it forward. 'Let us be on our way before we lose too much of the afternoon.'

Caleb nodded, all the while keeping his eyes on Sasha's. She was the most beautiful girl he had ever seen. He had always thought so. She had never truly acknowledged him, yet this had not been the first time they had locked eyes, as if it were a competition to see who would look away first. Of course, it was always he who looked away so as not to overstep the boundaries.

He waited for Sasha to pass before making his way to the cart horse. She was an older mare, not a thoroughbred like Brenton's and Sasha's horses. He climbed into the saddle and rode on behind them.

Chapter 4

Jacob Stevenson stood next to the large fireplace in his office, contemplating the latest update from William Finch, the General Manager of Stevenson Transport, British Operations, and Wendell Prince, General Manager of the United Colonies. He reached into his dark green, velvet coat and pulled out a smoking pipe and tobacco pouch. The fireplace hissed as he packed his pipe tightly.

'The New World has supplied us with many bountiful pleasures,' he stated as he leant down, reached into the fire with a lighting stick, brought it to his pipe and lit the weed. 'But the best tobacco is coming in from Brazil. Profits are on the rise in British operations you say, William. How many of our ships are in operation?'

He looked across the room at Finch and Prince, who were standing at attention. Both men stood in the middle of the large office, surrounded by dark, polished wood, tall shelves filled with books and leather sofas positioned around a large, oak coffee table. Decanters of wine, brandy and sweet sherry were arrayed on the table.

'For God's sake – at ease, gentlemen. You are not in Her Majesty's Navy anymore. Pour yourselves a drink and relax.'

Jacob had three general managers, whom he relied heavily upon to run his company. Each man had a different territory. Simon Blake oversaw the South American operations; Prince, the United Colonies; and Finch looked after Britain. Both Finch and Prince had been officers in the Royal Navy, a fact which served Jacob well. He preferred to hire men from military backgrounds because they were educated, competent and would take orders easily.

Simon Blake had not been from a military background but had a far more interesting history as a captain of the Royal Courier Service. He had led a team who would deliver secret and confidential documents across England and Europe. These men were trained in weaponry, map surveying and survival tactics. They were often hunted for the information they were carrying. Jacob trusted Simon above anyone else in the company, perhaps the world. He looked over at Finch and Prince. Both men seemed to relax, as ordered. Finch spoke first.

'We currently have twenty ships in operation across the Atlantic, sir. Another eight ships are in Liverpool for scheduled maintenance and two are being repaired in Lisbon as a result of altercations with profiteering vessels.'

'Slavers?' Jacob asked.

It was Prince's turn to answer. 'We believe so, sir. They were intercepted three days' sail off the Portuguese coast. They were empty slaving ships on their way back to Africa.'

Jacob grunted in frustration. Occasionally, slaving vessels would try and turn a quick profit on their return voyage to West Africa by commandeering a merchant ship. If successful, they would sail north to Portugal and sell off the cargo. Then they would return to their original course and sail towards Africa with a full purse. He puffed out a cloud of white smoke that drifted behind him as he walked towards the window.

'How much damage?'

'Substantial, sir,' Prince replied. 'The cargo is safe and in good condition and is being stored in a Portuguese warehouse, which we own, but the galleons are back in the shipping yard and both are heavily damaged. A mainmast on one of the ships has been snapped and there are multiple cannon-shot holes to the exterior of the second and third decks. They will not be ready to sail for another month, sir.'

Jacob had reached the window and was looking out at the day. His office was built on the first-floor corner of the house and served also as a brandy room for his many esteemed guests. He had particularly asked for large windows in the office, and for it to be built in the corner of the house so he could look out and see his stables and wider lands.

'Any lives lost?'

'Three, sir. All from the one cannon shot.'

'Have the families been compensated?'

'Already done, sir,' Finch chimed in.

Jacob nodded as another puff of white smoke rose from his pipe. He scanned the landscape of the estate through the window, his gaze moving across the manicured gardens and down to the stables, where the men were heaving large posts into the ground for the new show pen.

'What news from Simon Blake and our Brazilian operations?'

Again, Finch spoke first. 'South American profits are steady, Jacob. However, we have growing concerns that the region is becoming increasingly unstable. Rough bands of thieves raid the mines and farms all the way up the east coast and further inland. The Portuguese government takes no real interest in the loss of British cargo. The region is not policed well at all.'

'That is why I have Simon there. We cannot afford not to have trade in South America, and Simon will weather the Brazilian storms.'

As he finished the sentence, Jacob felt his muscles tense. Very rarely in his life had he felt anxious, yet the message he had sent to Simon eight weeks earlier had been the most important message he had ever written. It held information about what was to be sent next: the key that he could not let fall into the wrong hands.

Seven years ago, Jacob had built his flagship, the *Retribution*, an English galleon, which was as large as it was feared. He had created it as a floating fortress, able to carry cargo and weapons together. It carried a hundred guns and three hundred passengers and crew. That crew, mostly ex-Navy, could not only run the ship, but defend it well if needed. The *Retribution* had earned itself a reputation for being a giant of the sea and was the only ship on which he would sail when travelling abroad.

He had taken a voyage to Portugal three months earlier to oversee the purchase of a new warehouse. It had not been an easy task for a British company to gain permission to purchase commercial property and have business operations on Portuguese land. It had cost him double what the warehouse was worth, along with multiple payments to Portuguese government officials. The purchase, however, was well worth the cost and gave Stevenson Transport a presence in one of the most active trade ports in the world.

Lisbon had established itself as a stronghold for trade and slaving and, as a result, attracted and fêted trade leaders from every major port in Europe. It was in the parlours, taverns and brothels where many business decisions were made. More often than not, deals were made in dark corners with no signed documents, but retribution was swift if an arrangement was broken. Stevenson Transport had become a giant empire, revered within Britain and the new Americas; but Jacob knew that, to build such an empire, occasionally one had to deal in the shadows.

It was on the return journey to England that the *Retribution* had come across a battle between a Spanish galleon and a slave ship. Both ships had been badly damaged and would soon see the ocean floor. Under Jacob's orders, the *Retribution* had flanked the slaver and blown it out of the water with ease. After the battle, they had gathered what was left of the Spanish crew and set sail for home, leaving both ships to disappear beneath the surface of the Atlantic. It was during the journey home that the Spanish captain, who lay mortally wounded, passed to Jacob a gift of immense value. With his last breath, he had handed Jacob a parchment that showed the coordinates of where a lost fortune had been hidden.

THE RETRIBUTION

It was a well-known story. Over a century earlier, the Tierra Firme Fleet, loaded with Spanish silver, had encountered a violent hurricane, sinking many in the line. The captain's story told of three ships not sunk, but whose crews had mutinied against the Spanish Crown and sailed south down the Brazilian coast.

The dying captain had explained that the wealth of this hoard was immense and was intended to replenish the debt caused by the expensive Spanish war campaigns.

'Do not let this map fall into the wrong hands, Jacob,' he remembered the captain pleading. 'The man who has this wealth will have unimaginable power, and that is not what the New World needs. Keep it hidden. Keep it safe.'

The words echoed loudly in Jacob's mind as his gaze shifted from the workers to the stables. Three riders galloped out into the fields towards the forest, his son Brenton in the lead and his daughter Sasha chasing him across the lower fields.

Foolish boy. You should be standing in here learning the business, instead of encouraging your sister to ride like a man. Sasha was wild at heart and the strongest willed of his three children. She was already beautiful and had the shape of a woman at only fourteen. *A dangerous combination.*

The third rider he saw was the orphan, Caleb, who had been born and raised on the estate. Jacob had known the boy his entire life and had always valued him as a hard and skilled worker. From an early age, Caleb had exhibited a physical presence and a natural ability with horses – strengths that Jacob had been quick to recognise. Lately, however, the boy had started to cause him some disquiet.

It is because, beneath his acceptance of routine and his obedience, he is as wild as the stallions he breaks. A dangerous situation to have a boy the same age as my defiant daughter ride off into the forest with her.

He had noticed the way they looked at each other. Suddenly, his thoughts were interrupted.

'Jacob?'

He turned away from the window to see the men still standing behind the coffee table, unsure if he had heard their last words. Prince spoke again.

'Sir, is there anything else for now?'

Jacob reflected on what had been reported – a typical update, with even the battle-torn ships and the deaths of merchant sailors becoming a common occurrence on the Atlantic. His thoughts, however, had been dominated by the secret message sent to Simon Blake. He took the pipe from out of the corner of his mouth.

'No, thank you, gentlemen. That will be all for now.'

Chapter 5

Brenton puffed his chest as he got off his horse. 'Another win for me then, Caleb, hey! What an afternoon of triumph it has been. First, I caught the most fish. Then I shot that squirrel from at least thirty yards and now I have won the race back home. You know, for a renowned horseman, I thought you would be able to beat me at least once in all this time.'

Caleb climbed off his horse. 'You have always been the better rider, Brenton, sir,' he parried as he took the reins of Brenton's stallion and led both horses into the stables. He had always pulled his horse back so that Brenton would win. Not so much that it became obvious, but just enough to make Brenton believe he could lose until the last moment, when he would pull back and let Brenton streak away.

'Perhaps I can race you next time, Brother.' Sasha entered the conversation.

'Please, Sasha, you should not say such foolish things. Perhaps you would have a small chance against Caleb, but you are a girl and could never match my speed on a horse.'

Sasha shot Brenton a look of disdain.

'Well, perhaps I should then. Caleb, would you race me?'

Caleb stopped walking the horses and turned around.

'I don't think it would be a good idea, miss.'

'And why not? Are you too afraid to lose to a girl as well?'

'If your father found out, I do not imagine he would be impressed, miss.'

'I am not worried about my father.'

'It is not you I am worried about either, miss. Let me take these horses and I will come back out for yours.'

'Don't bother, Caleb,' she huffed as she rode past him and into the stables. 'I am quite capable of looking after myself.'

'Well, then,' Brenton chimed in on a cheerful tone. 'I will leave you to it and see you at dinner, Sasha. Caleb, remember to wash the dirt out of the hooves when you clean them.'

'Yes, sir,' Caleb replied, exhausted. It was getting dark as he led the horses into the stables, and he still had to lay out fresh straw in their stalls before he could eat and rest. Sasha leant against a post with her hands behind her back and watched Caleb while he worked. The stable was lit dimly by lanterns hanging from hooks on the walls. She could see his muscular frame through his ragged shirt as he leant over to toss straw into an empty stall.

The flickering light from the lanterns turned the straw into golden spikes and made Caleb's blond hair shimmer in the shadows.

'What do you want to be when you get older, Caleb?'

Caleb paused for a moment. The question had surprised him, firstly because he had not realised that Sasha was still standing there, and secondly because of the nature of the query itself. He had never been asked such a question in his whole life. He desperately wanted to be more than a stable boy but knew he could never amount to more. He was not destined to be special, rich, powerful or free.

'I am not sure what you mean, miss.'

'Please, Caleb. We have known each other our whole lives.' She walked closer to where he was working. 'You can call me by my name. At least when we are alone.'

Caleb stood up straight and breathed out heavily. He was exhausted, and his body ached. He turned around to look at her.

'I am not sure what you mean … Sasha. I do not think about such things.' He dismissed her and turned back to his work.

Sasha walked over to a lantern and watched the flame dance inside the glass casing. 'I often think about such things.' She looked back over at Caleb and giggled to herself.

'I think you will be working on this estate, breaking in horses, until you are so old, you will have to be taken care of.'

Caleb stopped and looked at her. 'You find teasing me amusing, Sasha?'

'I just think you should think about your future here, Caleb. That's all. I would think you would need to have children to look after you when you are old and weak. Otherwise, if you have no children to take over your work and look after you, what reason would my brother have to keep you around?'

Caleb felt the blood rush to his face. Why was she still there tormenting him, crushing him under his doomed future?

'Who would you marry?' she taunted him. 'Or, more importantly, which girl do you want to take to your bed, Caleb?'

He did not know how to answer. Was she tricking him? Was she enjoying poking fun at him to see if he would react? He would never break. He may be the property of the Stevenson Estate, but he had reserves of strength deeper and more powerful than anyone he knew. He turned his back and walked into the stall to spread the straw.

'It is late, miss. Should you not be getting back for dinner?'

She ignored him and persisted with her game. 'What about the daughter of Mrs Shelby of the Cooper Estate? It is the next estate along and I believe the daughter is four years younger than we are. Would you bed her?'

'I have never even met her.' He had given up with the pleasantries and was trying to end the conversation.

'You do not have to in this day and age,' she continued. 'Brenton is being set up already with one of the daughters from the Washington family, as it makes a strong alliance with their sugar interests overseas. That will not happen to me, though,' she railed. 'I am going to choose my husband, regardless of what my father decides.'

'Ha, I would like to see that.' Caleb laughed and, as he did, he realised he had just forgotten his place. Sasha also noticed his change in demeanour, but it seemed to only encourage her further. She walked into the empty stall with intent. They looked at each other through the warm light for what seemed like an age, until she broke the silence.

'So what? You don't think I can make my own choice of whom I let into my bed, whom I marry and whose children I bear?'

Caleb looked at her. *You are as beautiful as you are wild, and any man would feel lucky to marry you.*

'I don't know, Sasha. All I know is it is time for you to go to dinner.' He turned back once again to face the wall, pretending to tie a rope on the back beam, hoping desperately the torment had ended and Sasha had left.

He heard footsteps behind him and, as he turned around, he came face to face with her. He backed away until he was against the wall, but she moved with him until her body was against his. She was tall for her age and their bodies, now pressed together, seemed to match perfectly.

He looked around in panic for anyone who could be watching. They were alone and he returned his gaze to see that she had not looked away. He stared back at her and, for another long moment, they looked at one another in silence.

He could feel her breath against his cheek and the curves of her body pressed tightly against his. He had never felt the way he did in that moment. The soreness in his body seemed to disappear and was replaced by a burning desire to wrap his arms around her waist and pull her in to him. He could feel his manhood ache and swell. He tried to fight it but the longer they stared at each other, the greater the swelling. He could see that Sasha also realised what was happening and her face seemed to light up as she broke her gaze from his to look down at this new development.

She looked back up at him with an expression of appreciation, triumph and joy. Her hands moved slowly up his arms to the top of his shoulders. He built up the courage and grabbed her hips with his hands, squeezing her against him. She let out a deep breath, closed her eyes and moved her mouth up to his.

Caleb closed his eyes and let himself become lost in the moment. Nothing as significant as this had ever happened to him before. Her lips, soft and wet, found his. Her hands moved up from his shoulders and around to the back of his neck, grabbing a handful of his long hair and pulling his face to hers. He could feel her tongue slide into his mouth and massage his own. All the world had faded around them; all the world had disappeared. They were the only two people that mattered.

He felt her hand move from his neck and across his chest, down over his stomach, towards the top of his hips. It continued down over his pants and across his manhood, causing every muscle in his body to tighten. He moved his hands down past her hips, grabbing her buttocks and pulling her tightly into him. His head was swimming, yet clear, as if he had been lost and found in the same moment. Then, suddenly, they were torn apart by the familiar ringing of the dinner bell echoing loudly through the stables.

Sasha broke from the kiss and quickly backed away from him. She was breathing heavily, with a look of desperation on her face, and Caleb saw she was not impressed with the interruption. She said nothing. She just stared at him from across the lantern-lit stable.

She was looking at him differently now: as an equal, as someone who was special to her. After a long silent moment, without a word, she smiled at him and left.

Chapter 6

Jackson Bell sat in the darkest corner of The Monkey and Rat, smoking a cheroot, billowing white smoke from behind his yellowed teeth. He and his crew had been in Rio for a week now and he had grown restless. He twirled the top of a bone-handled knife and watched the point drill its way into the wooden table.

Jackson sat backed into a corner, the position he adopted wherever he went. He always thought it better to see them coming and fight his way out than be knifed from behind. Though he had knifed men in the back before, he had no intention of suffering the same fate.

He drank from his cup of ale and caught his reflection in the knife as it angled into the light. He could see the scars on his face, the largest running from his right eyebrow to his jawline, a memento from a knife fight with a man who had once tried to take what was his. It had not ended well for the other man, Jackson recalled, with his intestines spilling out onto the tavern floor and his cock cut off and stuffed down his throat. Jackson smiled to himself as he recollected the fight.

Across the table sat Adder, his first mate and second-in-charge of the *Grey Cloud*. They had been in many battles together, yet were still both relatively young men. Jackson did not know exactly how old he himself was, but he guessed around thirty-two years of age, with Adder being younger still. Adder was as violent as he was grotesque. You could scarcely see a patch of skin on his body that did not bear either a scar or tattoo.

The body of a great warrior, and my most ruthless soldier.

'We have lost too many slaves this shipment, Jackson. Not enough of those rotten bastards survived the journey,' Adder said.

Jackson breathed the white cheroot smoke out from his nostrils. It was true. Many more than usual had died on this voyage, leaving barely enough to pay the crew and replenish supplies. Slaving was a lucrative trade, but human cargo could easily be wasted if not managed properly. Much of the food supply had gone bad two weeks out from Brazil. He needed to decide whether to keep feeding the slaves or kill them off.

He did not want to dismantle his crew. They were loyal and fierce and soldiers of his revolution, soldiers who fought to take down the rich and allow chaos to create its own rulers. Fat, useless inheritors with family money had ruled his world for long enough. He would see it burn, so strong men could rise from the ashes and take their place as the rightful leaders, as in the days of old, when power was earned and not given.

No. He had plans for his crew and could not risk them losing faith in his leadership. At the same time, killing too many slaves would leave him with too little profit – another way to lose the respect of his crew.

Jackson had come up with another idea. He had ordered Adder to bring him one of the female slaves from below deck. He had slit her throat and hung her up to bleed out. He then cut through her stomach and discarded the entrails over the side of the ship. His crew watched in horror as he spent an hour flaying the human flesh, piling it up on a table on the deck.

'Bring up the cook!' he had yelled. When the cook arrived on deck, Jackson had pointed at the bucket filled with human flesh. 'There is your fresh meat. Stew it and serve it.'

They were surprised at the enticing smell that wafted out from the galley and throughout the ship. When it had been served, not one man had hesitated to feast. They had laughed, drunk and sung while they devoured the stew. They had cheered Jackson for his cunning and for discovering a way of supplying fresh meat throughout an entire voyage.

In the two weeks before arriving into port, they had killed and eaten five women to feed both the crew and slaves. Jackson did not intend to eat the profits on future voyages but was content knowing that they would never starve while they had slaves on board.

'We need to go back to Angola, Captain. The men understand that we had some bad luck this voyage, but their pockets will soon be empty again and they will want a plan to fill them.'

'It will be six months before they see their pockets filled again, Adder. We will need a different strategy this time.' He continued spinning his knife into the table. 'It is time to start our revolution.'

He drank from his cup and wiped the froth from his mouth. He looked up at Adder, who stared back at him with a slightly confused look.

'I have worked and captained slaving ships across the Atlantic for ten years now and what has it given me? A lucrative trade, yes, but the power in this world is still controlled by those who do not deserve it. Boys receive their inherited fortune and pretend to be men. They make decisions that others must live by. It has to stop. We must create chaos in order to bring down those who seek to control us. Only when there is chaos will real men rise to greatness as they seize control. These are the men who should lead the New World. We are those men, men who will take what is ours and stand up to defend it against those who would try to deprive us of it. Men who are willing to go beyond the borders of their souls to build a new world where real men are truly free. We raid Angola and all along the African coast for black slaves, but we are still slaves ourselves.'

'Jackson, we are free men. We do as we please.'

'We are not free. Not yet. But we will be, Adder. There are whispers in the night that a great fortune is hidden in this land. Fortune enough to raise an army. Enough to build cities. Enough to challenge those who have held us under their heels for so long.'

'I have heard those tales also. The lost ships of the Spanish Treasure Fleet. Jackson, it is just a story that was made up to attract workers to the gold mines.'

'No, Adder. It is real, and it will fund our revolution.'

'Forgive me, Jackson. How can you be sure it is real?'

Jackson raised his cup to take another drink. He looked past Adder to the short, fat man walking towards their table. He was a leech of a man, a weak coward who fed his greedy ways off the backs of stronger men. He reached the table and pulled out a chair to sit down. Jackson could smell the weakness coursing through the pathetic body that sat in front of them and helped itself to a cup of ale.

'Adder, you remember Jasper Cole, the government liaison man.'

Jasper Cole extended his small, fat hand towards Adder. As Adder met him for the greeting, Jackson Bell calculated that his first mate's hands were three times the size of Cole's.

The difference between a warrior and a swine.

'I expect to be compensated well for the information I am about to divulge, gentlemen. I am risking much just by being here,' Cole said as he drank from his cup.

'You are risking enough just sitting at this table, Jasper.' Adder replied. 'You have risked leaving here with your balls no longer attached to your body, should you displease us.'

Jackson could see that Adder wanted to kill Cole. Though this look was typical of Adder's general temperament, Cole was needed for now.

'Tell me then, Jasper. What is this great news you bring me?'

Cole poured himself another cup of ale and Jackson could see Adder's shoulders tense. Adder had yet to learn patience and politics. Though Jackson hated the games that had to be played, he knew the need to play them was only temporary and would no longer be necessary once he had created his new world order.

We will bow to your game and play the fool. Then, one day soon, you will all feel the blades of our swords.

'Well, straight to it then, hey?' Cole replied. 'I have been told by a credible source that the coordinates for the lost fortune of the Spanish Royals have surfaced.'

Jackson's knife stopped twirling as he let it fall onto the table. 'How have you come by this information? How can I trust that it is the truth?'

'Ah, you see, Jackson, I am not skilled with a blade, nor do I care for manual labour in the mines. No. My weapon is information itself. It needs to be credible or what do I have left to fight with? I have my own sources, whom I reward whenever they give me worthwhile information, and I think we can all agree that information about the lost Spanish Treasure Fleet is quite worthwhile, yes?'

'Where are these coordinates?' Adder grunted, tired of Cole and his scheming nature. 'Jackson, let me go and kill the man who has them and I will bring them to you. I will not fail you.'

'Not so hasty.' Cole cut Adder off, which clearly served to further displease him. 'The coordinates were in the possession of a Spanish Royal Navy captain, probably a descendent of one of the outlawed Treasure Fleet crew themselves. His galleon was sunk after a fight with a slaver; and the remains of the crew, including the captain and his coordinates, were saved by the intervention of the *Retribution*.'

'The *Retribution*!' Jackson breathed heavily as he said the words. 'Stevenson has these coordinates now?' He picked up his knife and rammed it into the table. 'One of the very men that makes the rules of this world now has a map to further his empire? I will not let him find it. He cannot find the treasure, or he will own us all.'

'I agree,' replied Cole, staring at the not-so-inconspicuous sight of a bone-handled dagger lodged in the table. 'If Jacob Stevenson finds the treasure, he will become more powerful than King George himself. He could take over the New World and run it as he sees fit. He, himself, would become a king.'

'What else do you know, Jasper?' Jackson spoke now with urgency. His worst fear had come true. He would not let the Stevenson Transport Company become the New World regime.

'The *Retribution* is sailing here. It will depart London a week from now, without Jacob Stevenson. I am inclined to think that the coordinates are on board.' Cole's voice was now quiet, so as not to allow anyone but the other two men at the table to hear.

Jackson took another deep breath. The *Retribution* rarely sailed to Brazil. It was mainly used for larger transports in Europe and to the North Americas. This event was significant and added weight to Cole's story. Had Stevenson truly come across the coordinates for the treasure hoard? Had he sent his strongest, largest ship to give this information safe passage across the Atlantic?

'Simon Blake,' Jackson muttered as he looked up at Adder. 'He is bringing the coordinates to Simon Blake.'

Adder nodded in agreement. 'Then we kill Blake before the *Retribution* gets into port. We finally kill off that bastard once and for all.'

'Not the best idea, in my opinion.' Cole returned. 'More than likely the coordinates will be encrypted and will need to be deciphered. You will need Blake alive to do this.'

Jackson turned the possibilities over in his mind. He wanted Blake dead as much as Adder did, but his life was now far too important to waste. He knew what had to be done. He looked around the tavern to make sure what he said next would not be overheard. They were out of range of anyone else's hearing and the music and constant tavern chatter served to cloak their whisperings.

'We will intercept the *Retribution* and take her down before she can reach port. If the coordinates reach land, they will be lost to us.'

Both Adder and Cole looked at him as if he were mad, but it was Cole who broke the silence first.

'The *Retribution* is as strong as she is armed. It is near

impossible for a ship to take her on the open seas.'

'Not ship,' Jackson replied. 'Ships.'

Again, both men looked at him, perplexed. This time, it was Adder who spoke.

'Jackson, we have only the *Grey Cloud*. Where will more ships come from and who will be willing to take down the *Retribution* and risk being sunk?'

Jackson smiled back at Adder.

'We will take over another ship, a slaver heading up towards the Caribbean. We will give the crew a choice to fight with us or die, then and there. We will intercept the *Retribution* with two ships and box her in. We will attack and, when she is too crippled to fight, we will board her, and I will slowly cut the truth out of every crew member on board. Two galleons are leaving in the morning. We follow them up the coast and take the slower of the two. We have at least six weeks to get ourselves another ship and intercept the *Retribution* off the coast of Rio.'

Adder's eyes lit up. 'It looks as though we are about to start the revolution, then.'

Jackson nodded at the two men sitting in front of him. 'Buy the provisions and gather the men. We leave at dawn.'

Jackson sat back in his chair and watched Adder leave to carry out his instructions. He thought about Jacob Stevenson, about Simon Blake and all the others who had deprived him, and men like him, of their true calling.

It will not be long now before you all bear witness to the revolution.

At that moment, Simon Blake entered the tavern.

Chapter 7

Caleb lay down on his bed and closed his eyes. He had finally finished his work in the stables and had found the remains of a cold rabbit stew left in a pot for him in the kitchen. The others had eaten at least an hour earlier and had picked out all the meat, leaving a watery gravy, a few pieces of carrot and some stale bread.

This was a usual occurrence when he finished his work late, as the other men considered him to be a child when it came time to eat, and a man when it came to work. As he lay there in his bunk, he knew he should be tired. His hands were hardened from years of work but even they had been torn apart from working on the holding pen. Yet he lay there with a quiet energy, staring into the dark, his head swimming with thoughts of what had happened earlier that night.

He had always been fascinated by Sasha and felt a sense of excitement whenever she was around. Tonight, Sasha had looked at him as if he was special and had asked him questions, rather than giving him orders. Not many people in his life had ever afforded him such a luxury. In more recent times, when the Stevensons would visit the estate, he had realised he had other feelings for her. He noticed the physical changes in her and admired her beauty, which seemed to have grown each time she visited. He had felt a strange closeness between them, yet, until this evening, it had seemed like only a dream.

Tonight, however, had been the most eventful night of his life. He had felt things he had never felt before. He was seized with embarrassment when he remembered the look on Sasha's face when she discovered he could not control his physical desire as their bodies pressed together. Yet she did not look back at him in disgust, but instead returned a look that showed her own pleasure.

He had seen by the way her eyes flickered and the corner of her mouth moved that she had not expected it to happen either; yet she seemed interested and pleased that it had.

If only the dinner bell had not rung. What would have happened?

His body no longer ached in pain. Rather, it ached from the feeling that was surging inside his stomach, inside his chest. More than this, he felt something he had never truly felt before, something foreign. He stared into the darkness, trying to pinpoint what it was. What was it that had made everything in his life change, and seem better? Why did he feel alive in a way that he never had before?

Was this love? Perhaps. No, it was something else.

As he stared up at the dark ceiling, he found himself smiling and, in that moment, for the first time in his life, he felt hopeful.

Chapter 8

The Monkey and Rat tavern was as dark as it was dingy. As he stepped off the deck and through the tavern door, Simon Blake gave himself a moment for his eyes to adjust to the dimly lit bar room. There was no mistaking where he was as his senses were assaulted by the smell of pungent tobacco smoke clinging to the fermented air. He could feel the temperature in the room rise as he made his way through the crowded tables towards the bar, which extended nearly the length of the tavern before it took a sharp left turn to accommodate more tables at the back of the room.

As his eyes adjusted, he quickly scanned the premises for anyone who could be considered unusual or dangerous, an old habit but a valuable skill he had acquired and mastered from his days as a Royal Courier. To be able to walk into a room, immediately identify a dangerous situation and formulate a quick exit plan was a skill that had kept him alive, and others with him, for many years.

On his way to the bar he had seen a group of off-duty British soldiers crowded around three tables. One was educating the others on what women were wearing in London, while another signalled to a barmaid for another round.

He could hear chatter from a group of tables behind him, which were occupied by merchant sailors and traders. He overheard men at another table talking about the gold mines up north becoming increasingly dangerous due to raiding parties and, ahead, he could see a table of farmhands who had finished their shifts on the various plantations in the area.

He reached the bar and placed a coin on the counter. To his left, the ladies of leisure led the next paying customers up the stairs and into the rooms on the second floor. He was handed a mug of ale and slowly walked down the room, following the line of the bar, until he found an empty table where he could sit. It was much darker at this end of the tavern, with the windows situated back towards the entrance and only candles to light up the area.

He sat down and took a mouthful of ale. Not the finest he had ever tasted but he had grown used to it, as well as many other things, since being posted in Brazil. Raiding parties, slavery, theft and murder were only too common in those parts and he saw no reason why it would change. In fact, it would get worse before it would get better.

He reached inside his jacket and felt the letter in his pocket: the letter from Jacob Stevenson, sent in secret only a few weeks ago. His thoughts had been consumed by the message and yet he still had no inclination of what this key unlocked. What he knew for sure was that something of such apparent importance would not stay a secret in Brazil for long.

He drank from his cup again and noticed that, sitting to his right in the far corner of the tavern, faces barely lit with a single burning candle, were Jackson Bell and Jasper Cole. Cole was a British liaison who worked with the Portuguese government on British trade agreements in Brazil. Though his role was important, he himself was not and could have been replaced quite easily by someone with a stronger value system. Yet even a man whose judgment dragged as low as Cole's should not have been conspiring in dark corners with a Scarlet, let alone Jackson Bell himself. He did not trust Cole and had always known about his secret dealings in the dark to advance his own station in life.

As he looked at the two men an old, familiar feeling swept through him – one of rage and fire. His thoughts wandered back to the first time he had killed a man and the look of regret and fear of damnation he had seen in the dying man's eyes.

He had been sitting in a tavern not unlike the one he was in now. He was a young Royal Courier, fresh out of training and on his first mission. The nature of the documents he was carrying was unknown to him. He knew they would have been encrypted and sealed in case he was ambushed and killed and the documents taken from him. The thieves would then have had to decipher the code to unlock the message in the manuscript. Couriers were never given the decipher code so if taken, or even tortured, they would have no knowledge of how to break it.

The tavern he was at that night was on the outskirts of Liverpool and he had two days hard ride ahead of him to reach his destination. He had stopped for a bowl of hot stew before returning to the trail when he had been confronted and surrounded by three men outside the tavern. He knew immediately that there would be a fight.

Whether they were hired to intercept the documents or just common thieves looking to steal his purse and clothes, he would not wait to find out. He reverted to his training and lunged at the man to his left, initiating the first move. He moved quickly, darting close and upwards, pushing the ball of his right hand up and under the chin, causing a cracking sound as the man's head flew backwards, his jaw and teeth shattering into his own skull as he fell to the ground motionless.

Simon had pulled his right arm back towards himself as his left drew out the flintlock pistol tucked into the back of his belt. Raising it, he spun towards the other two men. He made the judgment call on whom to shoot by the way they had reacted to his initial blow. The first of them had stepped backwards, while the second had reached inside his coat.

The second man became the next target as Simon aimed calmly, firing and hitting him in the middle of his chest, sending him to the ground instantly. He dropped his musket on the ground and pulled a short sword from his right hip, simultaneously using his right hand to draw his long sword from his left hip. He had been trained to fight with swords in both hands so that he could move and parry at any angle, giving him the ability to counter with the opposing side of his body.

It was over quickly.

The third man had drawn his sword and they began to circle each other. This time Simon knew to wait for the attack to come to him; though, as he had predicted, it was sluggish with no thought of the next move. The man had reacted with fear, lunging at Simon, spearing his sword forward and aiming at his stomach. Simon had easily deflected the attack with his left hand and had stepped inwards, allowing his right-handed long sword to plunge into the man's chest.

His attacker's momentum pushed the sword completely through his body as he stood in front of Simon, skewered, his eyes filled with regret and disbelief at the realisation that this was his end. Simon remembered well the look on the man's face when he had pulled out his sword and let him fall to the ground.

Without a moment's hesitation, he had sheathed both swords, picked up his musket, mounted and set off at a gallop south towards his London destination, not in panic but with controlled haste. He remembered how easy it had been and how calm he had remained, with no regret for the three fallen men who had tried to take what was not his to give. He had felt satisfied with his reaction and proud that his cargo was still intact and en route. He had not hesitated and, therefore, he had prevailed. They had hesitated and lost. They had died because of it. A lesson learned early and a rule he had followed since that night: those who hesitate will likely die first.

His thoughts were interrupted as Jackson Bell rose from his chair and slowly walked towards him. Simon calmly reached into his jacket, where he carried a loaded pistol. He cocked the hammer and loosened the position, ready for a quick draw. He assessed Jackson as he neared the table. He carried two loaded pistols tucked into the front of his belt, a long sword hanging off his left hip, a knife in his right boot and another, with a long bone handle, attached to a strap around his chest.

Jackson was proficient with all the weapons he carried, and Simon knew if there was to be a fight, the pistols would be drawn first, then the long swords and, if needed, the knives would be last.

That is how he will fight. That is how I would fight.

He readied himself.

'I thought I might invite myself over, Blake. I am not sure I have the patience to sit over there and wait for my invitation, eh?' As he sat, Jackson put both his hands slowly on the table as a sign of a peaceful meeting. Though Simon knew he could not trust him, it was clear that Jackson had not walked over to start an argument. He reciprocated by releasing his hidden grip on the pistol in his jacket and placing both his palms on the table.

'Well, then.' Jackson continued. He motioned to one of the tavern barmaids but did not turn away from Simon's gaze. 'Whiskey and two cups. I feel like toasting.'

'You are celebrating then, Jackson?' Simon said as he returned Jackson's stare.

'I have much to be thankful for, Simon. The difficult decision is what I should toast to.'

'How about you toast to the doomed souls you have dragged in chains across the Atlantic?'

Jackson smiled back at him. 'Well, they are paying for the whiskey, so I suppose they deserve a toast.'

'I hear they do more than line your pockets these days. I hear they fill your stomach as well.' Simon's words were cold. 'I could not believe that even you would reach such depravity.'

'Easily said coming from a man who spends all his time in one place. It must be nice to have the markets and the tavern and all the British soldiers you need just beyond your doorstep, Simon.'

'Only a fool would blame others for the choices he makes, Bell. Envy is an ugly sentiment … even for you.'

'You think I envy you, Blake?' Simon could see that he had

struck a nerve, as Jackson's fingers started curling along the table in front of him. 'I don't envy you. I pity you. When was it exactly that you lost your balls, Blake? Was it when you started working for Stevenson? I was told you were a man of the sea and iron once, a man not afraid of a fight. Do you have to submit your spine to the company as well as your freedom?'

Simon stared calmly at Jackson and did not react to his insult. He was not afraid of him, unlike everyone else. He wanted to fight him but knew that there was a good chance he could lose. Jackson was younger and faster than he was and had received far more practice in recent times. Simon was a businessman now and had not had to use a weapon in years. However, he would not show weakness to an outlaw, and was not afraid of the repercussions should it lead to a fight. He answered the question calmly.

'Perhaps it was around the same time as you gave up your honour and killed that little girl. Do you ever think about her, Jackson? What her life might have been like if you and she had never crossed paths?'

Jackson sat upright, with his eyes widening, and Simon could see that he knew exactly what he was referring to. There was a well-known rumour about Jackson Bell from a time in London many years ago. Jackson had loved a young girl from a reputable family. His love had not been returned and, when he proposed to her, she had reportedly refused him. She had been found dead in her bedroom three days later, stabbed repeatedly.

While the London authorities searched for Jackson as a suspect, they discovered that he had embarked on a London-based merchant vessel by the name of the *Grey Cloud* that very morning. Coincidentally, the *Grey Cloud*, shortly after, moved away from transporting London cargo and started transporting slaves from the West African coast to the new Americas. It had never returned to an English port.

'I have killed many in my life and none keep me awake at night,' Jackson finally replied.

'And that makes you a man of iron, does it? Killing young women and those who can't fight for themselves?'

'Women are born to service men. You have become soft, Blake, as this world is becoming soft. I, however, will stay the course and live free from the debilitating rules of your world. And anyone who stands in my way will endure the fury of a truly free man. How about it? Have you found your balls yet, Simon?'

'Your words won't bait me, Jackson. Just stay out of the way of Stevenson Transport. Stick with the other slavers who, like you, have a rare talent for inflicting human suffering. And stay out of my way while you are at it. Our patience is wearing thin with the slave trade. It will not be around forever, and those who have profited from it will finally feel the noose around their necks.'

The two men glared at each other until Simon's gaze was redirected to a skulking Jasper Cole, attempting to exit the tavern unnoticed. He looked over at Simon, who smiled back at him, a smile that let Cole know that he knew he was up to no good. Cole quickly turned away and scurried out of sight.

'I have decided what I will toast to.' Jackson announced as he raised his cup to the whole tavern. 'To the men of the New World, whose freedom is earned and not inherited and who will do what is needed to keep that freedom.'

A huge cheer erupted in the tavern as Jackson stood and finished his drink, all the time keeping his gaze on Simon. He placed the drained mug heavily on the table and leaned in closer to him. He spoke again, this time his voice much lower, almost a whisper.

'And to those who stand in our way, know that your deaths are coming … soon.' Jackson leaned back off the table, turned and walked out.

Simon sat a while longer, pondering what had just occurred. *Why was Jackson Bell meeting with Jasper Cole? What did he mean by 'soon'? Had he learned about the message from Jacob? Jasper is well connected and received information from all over the*

Atlantic, but how could he have known about the letter? What were the Scarlets planning?

Again, he had the familiar feeling that this unstable region of the world was about to erupt. He had numerous contacts in Brazil, many of whom had also been Couriers and now worked for him. They knew the land well and could disappear quickly if necessary. Should this secret of Stevenson be too dangerous, he would have to be prepared to leave in an instant.

Perhaps that is the very reason why Jacob had sent it to him, he thought. Did he want him to give up his position in the company and go into hiding? The words of the message entered his head.

Keep it secret. Keep it safe.

He sipped his cup of whiskey for the first time since it had been poured and made a secret prayer.

Give the Retribution speed and safety across the Atlantic. What it is carrying cannot fall into the wrong hands.

He finished his cup and walked out.

Chapter 9

Adder stood on the quarterdeck of the *Grey Cloud*, his gaze focused on the mainmast, efficiently checking the rigging and ratlines. It was a fearsome beast, fast and strong and big enough to take on a Spanish galleon – the perfect ship for their trade. He felt most at home on this ship. It is where he was important, respected and feared.

Jackson Bell had made him who he was. Before, he was nothing. He had nothing. He was just a poor sailor on a merchant galleon. He remembered how he had hated the captain and the rest of the crew on that ship, who looked at his scarred face and avoided conversation as if he were a beast. It was one fateful day that changed his life. A ship had sailed in behind them. The *Grey Cloud*.

He had heard of this ship and knew its crew to be particularly vicious. Panic overcame the captain when he realised they could not outrun the pursuing ship, and the white flag was raised in surrender. Their captain ordered his crew to lower any weapons and stand on the main deck in plain sight.

Adder and the crew had been made to line up like cowards. They waited to be boarded or killed when the cannons from the *Grey Cloud* fired. The first shot smashed into the belly of his ship, splintering wood and inviting sea to flow into the hull. The crew ignored their orders and took up arms, but their captain's cowardice was their doom.

The *Grey* was upon them, its grappling hooks latching onto their rails and dragging them in, allowing men to leap over the side from the *Grey* and onto his ship. He remembered the fearlessness of the *Grey's* crew, how they worked as a team, cutting their way through his ship's terrified sailors.

Adder did not have a sword, only a wooden mallet. He launched into a man, who had reached back with his sword, and used the mallet to batter the front of his skull. He felt the vibration of the impact jolt through the handle and into his arm. He heard the crack of the man's skull and felt a spray of blood and bone hit his face.

It was the first time he had killed a man, and the feeling was exhilarating. He would not go down begging like the other dogs. He would die with passion and fury so his attackers would know they had been in a fight. He picked up the dead sailor's sword and braced himself for the next fight.

There were three in front of him, two on either side, and he realised he was now surrounded. He was going to die, but he would not go quietly. The sound of a whistle carried across the air, and the surrounding warriors hesitated, then reluctantly lowered their weapons. He looked around and realised the fight was lost. All his crew had either been killed or apprehended, and only he held a weapon in his hands; only he could still fight. And fight he would.

'Put it down, son, and you will be spared.' The voice came from behind him and, as the circle opened, a figure emerged through the smoke. He was a formidable man: tall, strong and unforgiving.

'You just killed my third sergeant-at-arms. I should tie you to the bow and drag you along the shoals for the crabs.'

Adder said nothing, but held his stance.

I will not lie down like a dog. I will fight.

The man in front of him stared at Adder for a moment and spoke again. 'What should be done, then? To you and the rest of the crew?'

Adder looked over at his captain, on his knees, with the remainder of his crew.

'Lay down your sword and kneel, damn it! That is an order!' his captain yelled.

Adder looked over in disgust and, for the first time on this ship, addressed his captain as he had always wanted to.

'You should die on your knees like the dog you are, you coward. I will fight to the end and be happy I was never like you.'

Jackson Bell of the *Grey Cloud* spoke again. 'Do you believe a man should be in charge of his own fate, boy?'

Adder did not answer him, but braced himself for the fight ahead.

Jackson looked up at the sky, pondered a moment and then looked back down at the ship.

'Interesting. Well, we will see about that. Give this man and his cowardly captain a sword. Whoever lives gets to sail on the *Grey*.'

It had not been much of a fight. Adder's captain had wanted to see if surrender would save his life, but Adder knew only blood would suffice. He surprised himself by how quickly he moved towards the man who had been his leader for two years. He hated him and now had the chance to show it.

It was over quickly. He thrust his sword forward, and his captain parried to the left, but Adder anticipated this. Even a man unskilled with a sword could have parried his obvious attack, which is exactly why he had chosen this opening. Adder's captain shifted his weight too far to the side and left himself open. Adder's next move was to crouch and swing the blade low across his opponent's thighs. He swung fast and hard and cut deep, and his captain dropped to his knees almost in the same motion.

The coward screamed and begged for mercy, but Adder swung the blade fast across his throat, opening his windpipe and nearly cutting off his head.

This was my proof that mercy is for the weak.

The crew of the *Grey Cloud* cheered and laughed while the

dying captain floundered on the deck, gasping for air like a hooked fish until he died.

'What is your station on this ship?' the tall figure asked.

'I am a deckhand,' Adder replied.

'It just so happens we need one of them.' He turned to his men. 'Strip the ship of anything useful and check the food and rum stocks.' He pointed his sword at Adder. 'Take this. Kill the rest of these cowardly bastards.'

Adder had welcomed the order. He had been reborn that day, as he cut down the remainder of his old crew. With every thrust of the sword, and every scream he silenced, he felt more and more fulfilled. He was put to work on the *Grey*, but it was different to the servitude he had experienced on his last ship. This crew worked as a team and shared in the spoils of battle. They were there by choice, and any man could leave at any port. They were free to choose their fate. He had learned the *Grey's* captain was Jackson Bell, a name well-known to him and, for once, was relieved stories told of the *Grey Cloud's* fearsome crew and captain had turned out to be true.

Jackson explained to Adder that they would miss the man he had killed and that he had now become his replacement. 'You cannot begrudge a man who kills another in a fair fight,' Jackson had said. 'It was done the right way. He died well, and now you take his place on the ship for as long as you need to. The rest of your crew died because they were weak. There is no room for weakness in this world. You are strong and must never give up fighting for what should be yours. If you do that for yourself, for me and for the other men on this ship, I will make sure you never want for anything again. Here on the *Grey*, we live how men should ... how men deserve to live.'

Adder had fitted in well with the crew and had spent many years since sailing on the *Grey Cloud*. He had found a brotherhood of men who enjoyed the freedom to be violent and who craved the exhilaration of a bloody encounter as much as he did.

The captain was easily the fiercest and most ruthless of them all. As soon as Adder thought he had seen every possible way a man could die, Jackson would find another, more creative, way to kill a defeated opponent; almost as if he enjoyed the theatrics of it. Jackson's reputation for violence had preceded him and had become part of folklore across the Atlantic. The crew of the *Grey Cloud* was always given a wide berth when they entered a port. Even military men seemed to turn and head in the other direction when they saw the crew walk through the streets.

He loved the respect he had earned and the status of first mate given to him by Jackson, a reward for his seamanship and his repeated efforts to be the first to board another ship to fight.

Adder lowered his gaze from the mainmast and scanned the docks in the port. He saw the slave yards and holding pens.

Money in the pocket.

But he cared not for money. He cared for the life that the *Grey Cloud* represented: a life of freedom, spirit and brotherhood.

Adder watched the tavern doors as Simon Blake left The Monkey and Rat. He felt the blood rush to his face as his whole body filled with anger. How he would have loved to sneak up behind him and slide his knife into that bastard's ribs. But Jackson had forbidden it. He knew his captain had a plan for Blake and, once he had served his purpose, Jackson would kill him.

Damn you, Blake, you dog. Soon you will die, but I hope it is me who closes your eyes.

Chapter 10

Sasha rode beside her brother and father towards the estate's new holding pen. Her father's prized horses had arrived that morning and were exploring the terrain of their new home. Though she knew little about horses compared to her brother and father, even she could tell the quality of the stock and the superior breeding that had given the stallions their strong hind quarters, tall proud necks and shimmering coats.

Her father had been very pleased with his latest acquisitions and had invited important families and associates to visit the estate for an initial inspection. Carriages had been arriving all morning and every guestroom in the mansion was now occupied with London's elite. The lakes, as always, were well stocked with fish. A hunt had been arranged for the afternoon's entertainment and a gala ball would be held that night.

As they neared the stables, Sasha saw Caleb spreading sand around a smaller, separate pen that had been built for breaking in the animals. Her chest tightened and she felt butterflies in her stomach. She replayed the moment in the stables two nights ago, when Caleb had held her like a woman, and she felt the passion and love that she could no longer deny. She had thought of nothing else and had found herself smiling and giggling over the course of the last two days. She had not had a chance to talk to Caleb since then and was desperate to see him again.

Her father would be furious with her if he found out, but the feelings that had swept over her were far stronger than the fear of being caught. Something had been awoken in her and its influence could not be dismissed. Her father led them towards the pen where Caleb was working.

'Caleb, how have they been since their arrival?'

Caleb immediately stopped working and turned to face her father, though keeping his head down. 'Fine, Mr Stevenson, sir. They seem to have taken to their new lodgings well.'

'Glad to hear it,' Jacob replied. 'You will start breaking them in as soon as all my guests have left. For now, I need you to make your way to the top stable and prepare the horses for the hunt this afternoon.'

'Yes, sir,' Caleb replied.

He mounted his cart horse. Sasha had not stopped staring at him the whole time, and their eyes found each other's as he rode past. She could not bear it any longer. She had to speak to him and tell him how she felt, to ask if he felt the same way.

'I have had enough of riding today, Father.' Sasha looked over at Jacob and Brenton. 'I think I will retire to the house.' She turned her horse around and cantered away.

Caleb had already reached the top stables and was saddling the horses when Sasha rode up to him. 'Caleb. I need you to follow me quickly. Get back on a horse and meet me at the waterfall below the ridge.'

Caleb looked at her, perplexed. 'Sasha, I cannot follow you. Your father will have me hanged if he finds out what we did.'

She ignored his refusal and replied in haste. 'Follow me to the waterfall now, before it is too late. There is something I have to tell you and it cannot wait.'

Sasha kicked her horse hard and galloped towards the forest past the eastern fields. A riding path led her down through the woods and along the creek. She rode hard, knowing that she did not have much time before she would be missed. She arrived at a stone bridge next to the waterfall, reined in her horse, dismounted and listened desperately for the sounds of a second rider.

The noise of the waterfall made it difficult, but eventually she heard a horse galloping towards her. Caleb rode into the clearing. 'Sasha, what is going on? Are you all right?'

'No, Caleb, I am not all right, and I won't be until I say what I need to say to you.'

He climbed out of the saddle and walked towards her. She stared at him hopelessly. She knew what she felt was real. She had not planned it, but she had to tell him how she felt about him. How she had always felt about him.

'Do you feel it, Caleb? Tell me you feel the same.' Her voice was desperate now.

Caleb looked back at her. 'What do you want from me, Sasha?' She sensed anger in his voice now as he continued. 'What hope do we have? You are the daughter of a rich man and I belong to the estate.' He paced along the edge of the creek in frustration. 'We come from different worlds, Sasha. They will never accept us.'

'I know.' She could barely say the words as her eyes welled with tears. 'But I love you all the same.' Her comment stopped him in his tracks. The crashing sound of the waterfall behind them wiped out any other noise.

'Did you hear me, Caleb? I said, I love...'

'I heard you, Sasha.' His reply cut her off before she could finish.

'Well?' She walked towards him until there were only a few feet between them. 'Do you feel it too?'

He looked at her with the same hopeless stare. He had tried desperately to ignore it, but he could not hold back his feelings for her any longer. He nodded at her. 'Yes, Sasha. I have always loved you.'

His response made her smile as tears began rolling down her cheeks. She flung her arms around his neck and they kissed passionately.

'Sasha!' A deep voice cut through the air and broke them apart. She froze as a feeling of terror shot through her body. She spun around to where the voice had come from, though she had already recognised it. They had been too close to the waterfall to hear the men ride over the bridge.

There were two men who worked in her father's transport business, William Finch and Wendell Prince. Alongside them was her brother, Brenton. All three had stunned looks on their faces. There were three others whom Sasha had never met, but assumed they were either military officers or businessmen who were affiliated with her father's company in some way. In the middle of the group, looking down from the bridge, was her father. He was wild with anger, his face burning red and his upper lip raised to show his clenched teeth. His eyes fixed on her in a steely gaze as everyone waited for his next words.

She looked at Caleb who was standing tall, almost as if he were preparing himself for a fight. It suddenly dawned on her the trouble she had put him in. She had to try and save him. She looked back to her father.

'Father, please. This was not Caleb's doing.'

'Don't dare speak another word, girl.' Jacob's voice cut her off abruptly and again no one spoke. The only sound was the waterfall as they all waited for her father to speak again. She was terrified of what he was going to say next. She wished her mother were there, so she could plead her case of true love. Jacob finally broke the silence.

'Seize the boy! Lock him in the cellar until I decide his fate!'

Sasha looked over at Caleb in horror. He looked back at her. His look was not of fear but of sadness and anger. She tried to read his face and wondered which was for her and which for her father.

Finch and Prince rode across the bridge and down to the edge of the creek bed, pulling their hunting rifles from their saddles. 'Get on your horse, son,' one of them ordered.

Caleb looked at Sasha. It was hopeless now. His life was made forfeit. It no longer mattered what he said or did.

'Remember me, Sasha. I will love you forever,' he whispered as he looked into her eyes. 'Love only needs a moment to change our world.'

Caleb walked over to his horse as Sasha fell to her knees in despair. She sobbed as she watched the two generals escort Caleb out of sight.

'Brenton.' For the first time, her father looked away from Sasha and across to her brother. 'Take your sister back to the house immediately.'

Sasha mounted her horse and bolted back towards the estate before Brenton could catch her. She did not look back to see if they were chasing her. She knew that they had not bothered, as there was nothing she could do now, and there was nowhere she could run.

As she rode towards the great house, and to her mother, she screamed out loud into the sky at the mess she had made, at the danger she had put Caleb in, and the sickening thought that she may never see him again.

Chapter 11

Jacob paced around his office, smoking his pipe and going over in his mind what he had just witnessed on the bridge. Annette stood next to the coffee table, watching him stride violently up and down the room. Finch and Prince had also been summoned.

How can she be so irresponsible? How can she defile her family in such a way? That his daughter would belittle herself by fraternising with a common peasant was unfathomable. Jacob had worked tirelessly to ensure the Stevenson family was well-established and extremely wealthy, a well-connected family whose reputation ensured the marriage of its offspring to those in the highest tiers of society.

What if it had been noticed by any of his guests who were arriving intermittently from London, that his eldest daughter was sharing her body with the estate's common workers? He closed his eyes tightly, trying to erase the image of what he had observed down by the waterfall. He shuddered to think what may have transpired if he had not been suspicious and followed his daughter.

He could see Annette, standing motionless by the table, also trying to make sense of the situation, but it was William Finch who spoke first.

'If I may say, Jacob, and to you as well, Annette, the only people who saw the incident are those who work within the company. This will be kept quiet and will not have an impact on young Sasha's reputation.'

Jacob nodded and looked over at Annette. She saw that he

wanted her to speak and she attempted to be a voice of reason. 'Caleb is a handsome young man, Jacob,' she began, 'and Sasha is quickly becoming a woman. Forgive her for this mistake. We should have known having Caleb here at this age would cause trouble. Your daughter is very much like you, headstrong and curious, and you know this was her doing and not Caleb's. The boy is too reserved to be the architect of something so brash.'

'I know the boy did not start all this,' Jacob admitted. 'However, even he should have been smart enough to stop it from happening. What do I do with him now? I cannot allow him to remain on the estate, and I cannot have him arrested for fear that Sasha's conduct will be exposed. But an example must be made of him, so Sasha learns the consequences of her foolishness.'

'Can I make a suggestion, sir?' Prince spoke. 'The *Retribution* sails for Brazil the day after tomorrow. The boy is capable and would make a fine addition to the crew. We could dispatch him under Captain Andrews' charge, where he can serve out his days working on the merchant routes. He will never cross paths with Sasha again, and he will still add value to the company.'

Jacob stood, silent, then nodded his head and spoke. 'It is an acceptable idea, Wendell. Add Caleb to the ship's crew for its next departure. From now on, Sasha will be watched closely and you,' his voice reeked of bitterness as he spat at Annette, 'you will eradicate these impulsive ideas that she has adopted concerning women and their place in the world. She will return to the London apartment tomorrow night. For now, she will do her duty and attend tonight's ball. Tomorrow she will learn her lesson.'

Annette looked back at him, displeased that she had been blamed for her daughter's attitude. 'And how will she learn this lesson, Jacob?'

Jacob walked over to his window and looked out over the estate.

'Tomorrow at noon when our guests have all left, I want all

employees of the estate summoned to the courtyard. Make sure that Brenton and Sasha are there also. Caleb is to be flogged.' He looked over at the other two men in the room. 'I am sure with your naval experience that both of you have used the lash to whip out insolence on a ship on more than one occasion. Since the boy is now an employee of the *Retribution*, he will endure a sailor's punishment. One of you will take the cat and see it done.'

As he finished, he looked at Annette, who had closed her eyes and dropped her head. A lashing from the cat-o'-nine-tails was a harsh and gruesome ordeal, often ending in death. A whip with nine tails and sharp knotted ends would fan itself across a man's back, tearing through the flesh. He had to set an example and, though he would now lose a good worker, he would also be able to teach Brenton what it meant to take the necessary steps essential for sustaining order. Caleb would feel the lash and, if he survived, he would be put to work on a ship far away from his daughter.

Yes, that seems fair.

'It is settled then,' he continued. 'Please, everyone, try to enjoy tonight's ball. Some of our guests have travelled far to be here, and I will not have this unfortunate business ruin the evening.'

As his wife and two general managers left the room, his gaze shifted to the far wall above the fireplace. There, a large painting of his flagship, the *Retribution*, hung above the mantelpiece. He emptied the ash from his pipe.

It will not be the only secret on board the Retribution. If you survive tomorrow, Caleb… you will sail to Simon Blake with the key.

Chapter 12

Caleb sat against the far wall of the cellar. Iron shackles, chained and bolted into the stone behind him, bound his hands behind his back. Barrels of ale and wine lined the dimly lit walls and the stone floor he sat on was cold and hard.

He had heard of occasions when insolent workers had been locked in the very same room, but he had never been here himself. The chains around his hands were meant for thieves or men who had become violent or drunk. He had been none of those things. He had worked hard his whole life and had done whatever had been asked of him, efficiently and without protest.

Sasha loved him, and he her, and how was that a crime? Why couldn't they choose to love each other? He cursed the world and his position within it. Why did the rich hate the poor so much? Why wasn't he good enough for Jacob Stevenson? Why wasn't he considered good enough for Sasha?

The only entrance into the cellar was through a large oak door. It was bolted shut and muffled the chatter on the other side. The kitchen staff had been making a considerable effort to stay quiet but Caleb knew that they were talking about him, with a gasp here and a "tut" there as they gossiped about the unthinkable sin he had committed.

'The fool,' he heard a voice say.

'What will happen to him?' one of the women asked in a raised voice.

'Probably thrown out onto the streets, I imagine,' the first voice replied.

Suddenly, the whispers stopped as he heard a louder voice in the kitchen.

'Open the door,' the voice commanded.

The words made Caleb freeze. He knew the voice well. All went quiet, until the silence was broken by the sound of the gliding of the iron bolt and the creaking of the oak door as it was flung open, allowing the light from the kitchen to stream in.

The first two men who entered the cellar he had already met earlier that day. They were Jacob Stevenson's general managers, who had led him at gunpoint from the waterfall and into the chains which now bound him.

The third man who walked in he had never seen before. The man was younger than the other two and had tanned skin with sun-streaked hair. He looked strong, able and hardened by a life spent in the wild.

A sailor. Most likely a captain if he was in the company of the other two. What business would he have here?

His trail of thought was cut short by the sight of the fourth figure who walked into the cellar. It was the owner of the voice that Caleb had heard from the kitchen and which he knew very well. It belonged to Jacob Stevenson.

The four men stood silently. Caleb had his head bowed and looked at the stone floor in front of him, waiting to be spoken to.

'Look up, boy.' Caleb was surprised that the order had not come from Jacob but from William Finch. Caleb knew little of Finch apart from the fact that he looked after the company in Britain and had once been a British Naval officer.

So this is how it will happen.

He would be questioned by the officers who had more experience in extracting information and delivering punishment.

He looked up at the men and scanned the steely looks on their faces. They were the looks of cold businessmen who stare with calculation and without emotion. The sailor had a different look from the other three and Caleb saw sympathy in his eyes, as if he already knew his fate and felt pity for him. He had not yet dared look directly at Jacob for fear that, if he did, it would unleash a raging bull, and he would be beaten to death where he sat.

William Finch spoke again.

'Caleb, I only have three questions for you. I strongly recommend you tell the truth, for your sake, son.'

Caleb looked at Finch and nodded submissively. He had never told a lie in his life and now seemed like a hopeless time to start.

'Did you at any time violate the girl's honour?'

Caleb's mind immediately reverted back two nights when the ringing of the dinner bell had cut short their moment of passion in the stables. He looked directly at Finch, shook his head and made his answer short and quick.

'No, sir. We kissed is all.'

'How long has this been going on?' Finch asked his second question.

'Twice, sir. Once today and once two nights ago when I was clearing the stables.' He could hear Jacob's breathing grow heavier and waited for the inevitable onslaught, but it did not come, and Finch spoke again.

'Last question. Was it you who pursued the girl?'

It was a loaded question. They had all seen Sasha walk up to him and kiss him by the waterfall. They had all seen her tears and heard her cries as he was taken away. They already knew the answer but were looking for a reason to blame him. They were testing his honour. He had never told a lie in his life but he knew he was about to for the first time. He could save Sasha from punishment if he took the blame. He had not pursued her, but had not stopped it either, and this made it his fault as much as hers. In a way, taking the blame was not a lie.

'It was my fault, sir.'

Finch raised his head to acknowledge that he knew Caleb was now doing the right thing by Jacob's daughter.

'I did not stop it when I should have. It is my fault, Mr Stevenson, sir.' This time he looked over at Jacob, who nodded his head as if to thank him for accepting the blame and not bringing more shame on his daughter.

The four men looked at each other and nodded, seemingly satisfied that they had got what they had come for. Finch looked back down at Caleb.

'Caleb, you will be taken away from here and you will never see Sasha again, nor ever again set foot on this estate. Before you leave, as your punishment, you will receive fifty lashes in the estate courtyard tomorrow at noon.'

Caleb's heart sank. The news shattered him as if he had been kicked by one of Stevenson's prized stallions. He had known of many who had died as a result of being lashed by the cat. His head began to swim and a feeling of nausea overwhelmed him. He felt as though he was in a dream. He wanted to wake up and find that none of this had ever happened. He wanted his parents to be alive and come and save him. He would probably die from fifty lashes and terror began to take over. He went to speak but choked on his words and they came out as a muffled whimper.

'Lashes, sir? Will I survive that many?' Now terrified, he looked at Finch.

'You may, Caleb,' Finch stated. 'You are a strong lad, so you have a reasonable chance if you are cleaned and sewn straight away and do not take to the fever afterwards.'

Finch spoke again, though this time it was not to Caleb. 'Jacob, do you mind if I have a word with the boy alone?'

Jacob nodded, then motioned to Wendell Prince and the sailor to leave the room. The young sailor opened the cellar door and followed Prince out.

Caleb looked up in desperation as Jacob turned and began walking towards the exit. He whimpered at how unfair his situation was. He had lived and worked on the estate his whole life and now his master was going to kill him like a feral animal. He no longer cared for pleasantries. His life had been forfeited and he wanted to know why. He fought back the nauseous feeling that had crippled his ability to speak as he watched the closest thing to a father walk away from him. His eyes started welling up with tears.

'Why, Jacob?' he yelled.

The sound of his words filled the room with anguish and desperation. As he spoke them, Caleb realised that this was the first time in his life that he had addressed Stevenson by his first name, something that he would never have dreamed of doing.

Jacob stopped, paused, and turned around to face him. They both knew very well why he was going to be lashed. They both knew also that the question had not been about the punishment but about Caleb himself. He could hardly see Jacob through his tears now, as they started streaming down his face and the salty taste of hopelessness crept into the corners of his mouth.

'Why do I not get to choose my own life?'

Jacob looked back at Caleb, his face now rid of anger and replaced with absolution.

'Because that is not your world, boy.' It was the reply that finally broke Caleb's spirit. Jacob walked away and, for the first time since he could remember, Caleb began to cry, dropping his head and sobbing uncontrollably, his tears falling onto the cold stone floor. He was lost. He was truly alone and was now doomed to die a painful death.

'I will be delivering the lashes, son.'

Caleb looked up at Finch, surprised at what he had just heard. Suddenly, a glimmer of hope entered his mind. Maybe he could convince him to hold back, even miss.

'Mr Finch, sir, I don't want to be lashed. I never intended to cause any trouble.'

'I believe you, Caleb. But what has been done cannot be undone, and I take orders from Mr Stevenson, just as you do.'

'Have you lashed many men before, sir?'

'I have lashed my fair share of men, yes.'

'Do I have to get that many, sir? Is fifty enough to kill a man?'

'That is what I want to talk to you about. My orders are fifty, and so you will receive exactly that many. Also, I cannot go easy or pull back the whip or Stevenson will know. He has seen this done before, many times.'

'Am I going to die?'

'The men who survive have something to live for, Caleb. They have hope and that makes them fight.'

Caleb's heart sank once again. It was hope that had got him into this situation. Hope had been torn away from him, along with Sasha. He had given up on the notion of hope.

'I have nothing to live for, Mr Finch.'

'Yes you do, Caleb. You will be taken on board the *Retribution* to work on the greatest merchant ship that sails the Atlantic. It will be a new life for you, where you will learn a new trade in a much bigger world outside of this estate or under Jacob's watchful eye. You will go on a great adventure under a great captain. A man can change his fate on the seas. Surely that is worth fighting for.'

Caleb thought about the time he had once seen a merchant ship and recalled his desire to sail. He nodded at Finch in agreement.

'One last thing, Caleb. When the lashing starts tomorrow, the pain will be shocking. You must remember to try to control your breathing. I will finish as quickly as possible. Good luck, son.'

With that, Finch turned and walked out of the cellar. Caleb sat there in his chains, scared and alone. He had never felt more alone than he did at that moment.

He thought about his parents. He thought about being at sea on *the Retribution* and his new life, if he could survive long enough. He thought about Sasha. He closed his eyes and let the tears roll down his cheeks in the darkness of the cellar.

I am so scared. I do not want to die. Please let me live.

Chapter 13

Caleb realised he had not slept when he saw the door swing open at the end of the cellar. How could he, knowing what was about to happen to him? Wendell Prince and two soldiers walked into the room. All three men were armed.

As they walked towards him, Caleb's whole body started shivering. He backed himself against the wall as the men approached him.

'It is time,' Prince said quietly. 'Give him water to drink and bring him up.'

One of the soldiers knelt down and brought a bowl of fresh water up to Caleb's mouth and he drank, savouring this small moment of peace.

The other soldier unlocked the bolt in the wall, freeing the chain and releasing Caleb from the stone behind him. Still in shackles, they led him out of the cellar, through the kitchen. The sky was grey and a fog had settled on the estate. He walked behind Wendell Prince, with the soldiers beside him, each holding one of his arms. There was no escape. Even if he could manage to break free of the soldiers' grasp and run, he would not make it six yards before Prince aimed his rifle and shot him down.

They made their way through the gardens along the eastern wing of the mansion where, as children, he and Brenton had charged around the poplars, playing with their wooden swords and pretending that they were in a great battle. How he wished he could be back in that moment and out of the chains binding his hands.

They turned the corner of the building to face the front of the mansion. The scene in front of the house caused Caleb's legs to weaken and his stomach to cramp. A large crowd had gathered at the front of the house. All who worked on the estate had been assembled to watch. They had been made to create a tunnel for him to walk through and, as he reached its beginning, he saw William Finch standing at its end. He had removed his jacket and was wearing only a white shirt, as if he had purposely dressed for a hard day's work. In his right hand, curled around itself like nine long, thin snakes, was the cat.

Caleb whimpered at the sight beyond Finch, where two large posts had been erected the night before. His legs lost their strength and he buckled under the weight of his own body. He winced as he fell to his knees, and he heard the collective sigh of all assembled. The two soldiers tightened their grips under his arms and heaved him back to his feet.

William Finch turned around to look at him. 'Caleb,' he called out from across the courtyard. 'You can either walk or be dragged. Find your courage, boy.'

Caleb put a step forward and found some strength in his legs again. As they made their way through the tunnel, he looked at the faces he had known all his life, the faces of the men he had worked with every day, the kitchen ladies who had always treated him well, the house staff who had always been so kind.

The looks on their faces were not of anger but of sympathy. He could see some of the ladies crying for him and saw the men nod at him as if to wish him farewell as he passed them by. They made their way past the main steps of the mansion, and Caleb looked up to his right to see those who were standing on the landing.

There were about twenty, he estimated. Many he had never seen but he could tell that they were guests and colleagues of Jacob's who had decided to postpone their departure from the estate in order to witness the event. He wondered what lies they had all been fed to justify his flogging. Theft? Disobedience? Laziness? Anything but the truth.

Why leave after a weekend of hunting, business and gala balls when you can finish it off watching a boy being whipped to death?

He hated them – all of them. He looked at each one of them, lined up to watch. Annette was the first on the left. She stood tall and proud but was breathing heavily, as if her dress had been fastened too tightly.

Brenton was standing beside her. As they met each other's gaze, Brenton gave Caleb a nod, which needed no words, but said "tough luck and goodbye".

Coward. Standing up there like a young emperor. You have done nothing to deserve what you have – nothing but be born.

As he looked to Brenton's left, he saw Sasha. He could never have imagined a look that spoke of such sadness and hopelessness as the one she gave him in that moment. He could not look at her and moved his gaze across to Jacob.

They stared at each other, and Caleb felt himself grow wild. His eyes burned like fire and his muscles tensed with fury and rage. As Jacob recognised the hatred in Caleb's eyes staring at him, his blank expression turned to one of surprise.

Caleb felt his senses heighten as his anger pumped adrenaline through his whole body. He felt strength like he had never felt before. He looked back at Sasha one last time. Tears rolled freely over her cheeks and her mouth moved in a silent whisper.

I love you.

He stared back at her with the same fury he had offered Jacob and saw her look also change to one of surprise. He no longer cared for love nor hope. What had they given him? No – now he only cared about his hatred for the Stevensons and the pain the rich inflicted on others without remorse or consequence for themselves. He had found his strength in his hatred, and that was what he would take with him to the whip. He turned away from her without remorse, resigned to never again seeing her face. She cried out to him, but he did not look back.

THE RETRIBUTION

You no longer have power over me.

As they reached the two posts, Caleb saw that leather straps were bound around the top of each of them. The soldiers unshackled his hands from behind his back, tore off his shirt and tied each of his wrists with the leather straps. He felt the cool air creep across his bare skin as his arms were pulled above his head so that the muscles in his back were stretched and completely exposed to the crowd.

The western hills of the estate rolled out in front of him, shifting like dark shadows in the midday fog. He glanced to his left to see the horses in the newly built holding pen, all gathered along the fence line as if they had also been instructed to watch him die.

His view was interrupted by William Finch, who walked around to face him, the cat in his hand and a circular piece of leather-bound wood in the other. 'Bite down on this or you will break apart your own teeth.'

Caleb opened his mouth and let Finch place the wood in his mouth. He leant in close to Caleb and whispered in his ear. 'It will be over soon, one way or the other. Remember to breathe and, after each lash, picture yourself sailing on the Atlantic. Muster your focus and strength and fight through, Caleb. Get ready.'

Finch walked around him and out of his view. Caleb felt his heart pound in his chest and his breathing became erratic.

Breathe. Control your breathing. Hold onto your hate and breathe.

For a moment all went quiet as he looked over the peaceful landscape of the western fields. Then ... he heard the sound of the nine tails fly back and an instant later, he felt it.

First was the thud against his back, followed by a white-hot flash of pain shooting into his spine, across his shoulder and up into his head. He screamed, biting hard on the leather between his teeth as he felt the skin on his back peel open in the afternoon air. The pain was unrecognisable. He had never believed such pain could exist. He thought about the *Retribution* and the Atlantic like Finch had advised.

He tried to breathe but there came another thud, followed by another searing flash of pain which tore him away from his thoughts, racking his body. He felt the skin along his left shoulder blade tear open. He screamed at the pain that now consumed him. He could not think about anything but the pain as the cat lashed across his back, again and again. He let out yet another scream and realised he was out of breath.

As another lash found its mark, he could scarcely let the scream out. He had lost control of his breathing and his vision became blurred. The dark hills in front of him were now fading shades of grey and black and becoming indistinguishable. Another lash hit, then more, and more again. He could no longer see and knew he was about to die.

You have amounted to nothing and you will die as nothing.

In that moment, he thought of Jacob Stevenson standing on the stairs above, watching the blood coursing down his back. Hatred filled him again and he found the strength to take a breath. Air filled his lungs and a glimmer of life crept back into his body. His vision began to return. The cat again cut across his bloodied back and his vision was lost once more. The wood between his teeth fell to the ground as his head dropped. His legs had given up on him and he hung there, suspended between the two posts.

Breathe. Just one breath.

It did not come before the next hit and, as he let out one last cry, the light in his eyes faded. The world had gone dark and everything in it was silenced.

This is death.

Then he thought no more. He hung motionless in the cold fog while William Finch delivered the remaining lashes. He hung in silence as they curled over the top of his back and around his shoulder. Darkness had won, and all thought of life had faded.

This is death.

Chapter 14

Annette Stevenson walked from the great house towards the servants' quarters. She had never witnessed a lashing before, though there had been times when workers on their estate had been reprimanded and arrested, even hanged for their crimes, but never was any of this conducted in sight of her or her children. Her husband had forbidden it and had kept their family away from that violent business.

Today had been different. Jacob had made an example of Caleb to teach everyone on the estate a lesson. She watched it destroy her daughter's tenderness and harden the softness in her son. She would need to mend her children as only a mother could but, before that, she had to see if the boy had lived. He had been taken to the servants' quarters to be cleaned and stitched and that was her destination now.

She stopped at the door for a moment, putting her hand over her mouth to try and stop herself from crying. She had watched how the people had covered their mouths and turned away in horror at what they had seen, and she had seen the anger in their eyes at what they had been forced to witness. Annette had not been able to rid her mind of the sound of the whip and Caleb's screams. She would never be able to forget the look on her daughter's face before she collapsed in her brother's arms. It was a look of disbelief and utter sorrow and the memory of it was making Annette feel sick to her stomach.

She truly believed now that her daughter loved the boy and he loved her in return.

It is an impossible world we live in.

She composed herself and knocked on the door. It swung open to show a surprised housemaid, who had not expected to open the door to the lady of the estate.

'Hello, miss,' she mumbled.

Annette could see the redness in her eyes and the tracks her tears had made down her cheeks. The maid opened the door and welcomed her into the room.

She hates me. She hates the name Stevenson and all who carry it. And why shouldn't she, after seeing what had just happened to one of her own?

The room was large but simple, accommodating the kitchen and dining room with a sizeable table that could easily sit twelve people around it. Annette imagined the workers sitting down after a hard day and swapping insults about her family.

A stone fireplace, with a pot hanging over hot coals, was set halfway along the room. A rabbit stew, Annette guessed – hearty, warm and enough to feed the servants. Not the poached pheasant with bleached greens and decanted wine that would have been served on her table. A door swung open at the end of the room, and the butler of the estate and manager of servants walked in.

Gerald had been running estate operations since her husband had purchased the land. There was nothing he did not know about the goings-on in the mansion and the lands surrounding it. He was a loyal member of staff and was relied upon heavily to oversee the logistics and budgets of the numerous events held on the property.

Gerald entered the kitchen holding a large bowl. He wore a plain white shirt and had discarded the formal vest, jacket and tie which was his usual attire. Annette shuddered as she inspected the dark red stains covering his shirt. Watery blood rolled down his exposed forearms and onto the floor. He walked over to the kitchen bench and poured the contents of the bowl into the sink. Annette watched the crimson liquid flow down the drain.

'Mr Gerald, sir.' The maid who had opened the door to Annette grabbed his attention.

'Miss Annette.' Gerald stood up straight. He was the only paid member of staff who addressed the Stevensons by their first names. He had become more family than help and took great pride in his duties. But even he was shocked.

'Gerald...' Annette swallowed hard, dreading the answer to the question she was about to ask. 'Is he alive?'

'Only just, miss. He is unconscious, but he has a heartbeat. We have cleaned the lacerations as best we can and are nearly done with the stitching. It is now up to him.'

'I want to see him.'

Gerald looked at her, surprised. 'Miss, if I may suggest, it is not a sight–'

'I want to see him, Gerald.' Annette cut him off before he could finish and knew, as a result, that there would not be a rebuttal. Without saying another word, Gerald bowed his head and lifted his arm towards the doorway, motioning her into the room. The smell of blood, whisky and sweat was overpowering as she entered.

In the room were William Finch, Wendell Prince and the captain of the *Retribution*, Andrews. The captain was leaning over a motionless body lying face down on a table. He had a long needle in the shape of a hook, which he was raising and lowering as if he were a conductor leading an orchestra. Finch and Prince were holding the skin together as it was being stitched. All three men were covered in blood. It flowed freely over the back of the motionless body, across the table and dripped onto the floor.

'Will he live?' She had not asked anyone in particular. All three men looked up in surprise. They had not noticed her walk into the room and had obviously not expected to hear her voice, here of all places.

William Finch, the man ordered to carry out the lashing, broke the silence. 'He will most likely catch a fever. It will probably last up to a week before it breaks. That is, if he can last that long. But for now, he is alive.'

As she moved closer to the table, she felt ill at the sight in front of her. Caleb's back had been torn to shreds. Even now, after proficient medical attention from three experienced naval officers, his back looked as if it had been destroyed. She covered her mouth to keep from being sick, as tears rolled down her face.

'Perhaps you should wait for news in the house, Mrs Stevenson,' Finch spoke again.

She ignored the comment and picked up a wet cloth. She started washing the dried blood around Caleb's ribs. The three men did not protest and went back to their work. She cleaned along the side of his body, dabbing ever so gently around the stitched cuts. As she wiped the blood away, she examined the horrific damage that had been done. The whip at some point had marked his right shoulder in the shape of a fork, as though a snake's tongue had wrapped around his arm.

She dabbed around his shoulder and picked up the blood-filled bowl. As she walked back towards the kitchen, she turned back to the men. 'Captain Andrews, I am told that Caleb is to join your crew on the *Retribution*.'

The captain stopped sewing and stood at attention. 'Yes, miss. We set sail for Brazil the day after tomorrow.'

Annette nodded back to acknowledge him. 'I want you to spend, use and do whatever is necessary to bring Caleb back to health. Is that understood?'

'I understand, miss. The sea air and the salt water will do him well. We also have on board a physician who is the best I have seen. If there is a place for him to heal, trust me when I say that there is nowhere better than on board the *Retribution*.'

She had not met the young captain often and did not know if she believed what he was saying, or if he was just telling her what she wanted to hear. Either way, she appreciated the comment and nodded once more before she turned around and left.

She placed the bloodied bowl on the kitchen table and walked out of the servants' quarters. She cried as soon as she knew she was alone, her heart breaking for the poor boy.

After some time, she calmed herself and wiped her face. She regained her composure and took a deep breath.

Now. To my daughter.

Chapter 15

Brenton sat on the leather sofa in his father's office. He stared at the blood-stained cat-o'-nine-tails curled on the coffee table in front of him. He wanted to throw it in a barrel and burn it, or run down to the waterfall and throw it in the creek so it could never be used again. He had witnessed men being hanged before. He had seen men die, but had not seen it happen to someone so familiar and so close to his own age. He loved his sister and felt utter sorrow for her now.

The office was more dimly lit than usual, with only the burning fireplace providing any light. For once, he was pleased at the lack of light. His father had always made a concentrated effort to teach him to be a man of principle and responsibility. Jacob had taken his familiar stance near the window next to his desk. He puffed on his pipe with one hand and held a glass of brandy in the other. He stared out into the darkness in silence for what seemed like an age.

'Do you understand what happened today, Brenton?' His father's voice was quiet and calm. 'Do you understand that I took no pleasure in what happened to Caleb? I was fond of the boy. He was strong, talented and hardworking. I never wished to cause him suffering or pain.'

Brenton said nothing, keeping his eyes on the whip as his father continued.

'I know that this foolish tryst was conjured up by your sister. I know that Caleb had little choice in the matter. She would have persisted and made his life intolerable until eventually we would have ended up in the same place we find ourselves in now.'

He puffed on his pipe, the smoke drifting from his nostrils. He turned to face his son. 'I had to whip Caleb to teach Sasha a valuable lesson. A woman only has her reputation to protect herself in this world. A stable-whore will always be a stable-whore, no matter how much wealth she is to inherit. Sasha needed to see what happens when she does not think rationally, when she does not consider the consequences of her actions.'

Brenton continued to stare at the bullwhip but nodded to signal that he understood.

'Yes, Father, I understand.'

'No, Son, you do not.'

The response forced Brenton to break his gaze upon the whip and look up at his father.

'There are things happening in this world which are far more important than what transpired today,' his father continued. 'Things you are yet to discover and situations you are yet to understand. Your duty as a Stevenson and the future chief officer of this company is to look at the bigger picture, so you can act swiftly to keep the balance. The world is governed by power and those who control it. Those who have this control have a responsibility to govern the rest of the world with order and peace.'

Jacob walked over to the sofa opposite and sat down to face his son. He poured a glass of wine from a decanter and held it towards him. Brenton took the wine and drank. It was sweet and rich and a welcome taste in his dry, parched throat. He took another sip as his father spoke again.

'There are men in this world who seek to gain control, evil men who are not interested in peace or order, only power; and who, if successful, will tear the moral fabric of the world apart. Their selfishness will spread to murder, thievery and chaos. They want to see the world burn around them and people like our family burn with it.'

'Who are these men, Father?' Brenton was relieved that, for

the first time since seeing Caleb lashed, he had been able to concentrate on something else.

'They are everywhere, Son. They are faceless until they emerge. They are men who care nothing for the order and rules that the governments of this world have worked so hard to establish to create peace. They are unable to build their own success and so they seek to tear apart anyone else who has it.'

Brenton was now intrigued. 'And how do we stop them from taking what is ours if we cannot see them?'

'We do it by maintaining the balance of power, by maintaining control. As you saw today with Caleb. And, as hard as it was to watch, if I had not made that decision and their behaviour was allowed to go unpunished, we would have allowed the balance to shift. Do you understand now, Brenton?'

He did. He had been waiting to take his place in his father's business his whole life and he was not going to let anyone take it away from him. It was his birthright, and he heard his father's warning.

Jacob finished his brandy and placed it on the table next to the whip. As he did, Brenton realised that there was something different in his father's office. The large oil painting of the *Retribution* was no longer hanging on the wall above the fireplace. For years, Brenton had run into his father's office to see him staring up at that painting. It had been hanging on the wall since he was a boy. He thought it strange that it had suddenly been removed. Again, Brenton's thoughts were interrupted by his father when he watched him pick up the lash on the table and hand it to him.

'Now that we have done what was necessary, you can get rid of this.'

Brenton nodded and took the whip. He walked out of the office, through the foyer and out the front door. As he reached the bottom of the steps, he quickened his pace. The feeling of the blood-stained whip in his hand had made him feel ill. He wanted it gone.

He made his way to the stables, running now as fast as he could. He thought about how he and Caleb used to race each other on foot and on horseback. He hated that he would never see Caleb again, but he understood why his father had done what he had done.

Brenton reached the stables and ran inside. The lanterns were still lit and he scoured the area until he found a wooden barrel. He carried it out to the front of the stables and dropped the whip into it. He held one of the lanterns he had unhooked from inside and stared down at the blood on the whip. He threw the lantern down, smashing the glass and letting the oil spread through the bottom of the barrel. Flames leapt in the air as they curled around the whip.

He stood there until he could smell it scorching. He closed his eyes and listened to the hissing of the leather as it peeled off the wooden handle. He heard the breeze in the trees around him. As he remained standing in the darkness, he slowly realised there was another sound coming from inside the stables. Not of a horse, but of someone crying. He went back inside and looked into one of the stalls, where his sister was sitting in the straw, crying, her face buried in her hands.

'Sasha.' His tone was soft and calm. He loved his sister and hated seeing her cry. She had always been so strong and sure of herself, full of life and curiosity. He could see that her heart had truly been broken.

She looked up at him with tear-filled eyes, and his heart sank for her. She looked at him hopelessly for a second and buried her face back into her hands, sobbing uncontrollably.

'He hates me, Brenton. I saw him look up at me as they led him past the stairs. He was angry at me.' She stopped to try and breathe, but stuttered and gasped as if she were drowning. 'He hates me and why shouldn't he? Look what I have done.' Her hands were still covering her face as if she were too ashamed to show herself to the world.

'Sasha,' he started again. 'Caleb is going to live. He will be sent to work and sail on the *Retribution*. This is a new life that he would never have dreamed of. I understand that he has gone through terrible pain but, in a way, Sister, you have set Caleb free. You have given him a chance to see a much larger world beyond the stables of the estate. You must see the good in this situation.'

She lifted her head out of her hands and looked at him. 'And what about me, big brother? What good comes out of this for me? I love him. I don't care about rank or station. I love him and I will never see him again.'

Brenton thought about how he should respond. What she said was true. It would be highly unlikely that she would ever see Caleb again. Her father would make sure of that. Though he did not wish to lie to his sister, he decided, given her current state of unhappiness, that it would be the best course of action.

'You may still see him again, Sasha. We have a long life ahead of us and Caleb is still very much part of the company. Father's anger will not last forever. We both may see him again.'

She wiped her tears from her eyes and stood up. She walked over to him and grabbed both his hands, a look of desperate intent on her face. 'Brenton, you will be the head of the company one day. Make this promise to me now. Whatever happens, whatever transpires in my life, if I am married and have children of my own and am happy in my life, promise me that we will see him again.'

He looked at his sister and knew that this was all he could do to help. So much could happen in the years to come and he thought it foolish to promise something like this. He was sure they would never see Caleb again, but this was not about him. He looked at his sister and saw in her eyes the hope which he could not destroy.

'I promise when I come to power, I will do everything I can to make that happen.'

A smile broke through her drained face, and she wrapped her arms around his neck to hug him tightly. It felt good to help her, to give her hope, even if they both knew that there was none.

'Come, Sasha.' He grabbed her by the hand. 'Let us go back to the warmth of the house.'

She nodded submissively, as he walked her out of the stables.

Chapter 16

The *Grey Cloud* had been trailing the Portuguese slave ship for a day and a half. It was common to see slaving and merchant ships sailing the same Atlantic routes and Jackson Bell had kept the *Grey Cloud* at a distance to avoid arousing any suspicion. Flying a flag of common slaving colours, the *Grey Cloud* looked as if it were en route to deliver its cargo to one of the many slaving ports in the Caribbean.

Jackson had had the lower decks filled with bags of sand to give the impression that he carried a full shipload of slaves. The *Grey Cloud* sat low in the water and any ship's captain peering through an eyeglass would not see her as a threat. Jackson would try everything possible to get the slaver to surrender without a fight. He wanted the ship in good sailing condition so it could join his cause. There would be a battle, but it would be against the *Retribution*, a much larger ship, and he would need every man available.

He ordered the crew to gradually dump the sandbags over the stern, and as the *Grey Cloud* became lighter, she became faster and easier to manoeuvre. He felt the ship's wheel free up in his hands as he ordered all sails unfurled to catch the morning wind. The cannons were at the ready, his men armed, and the *Grey* hit full tilt, ready to pursue her prey. Tacking to port, it only took a short time to cross the stern of the slaver.

They have not had enough time to prepare for this attack. They have a ship full of slaves weighing them down and will risk too much profit if they decide to fight. The captain will surely surrender when he finds out it is the Grey Cloud on her aft and who is at her helm.

A rush of adrenaline surged through Jackson as he spun the wheel and called for the yards to be tightened. The *Grey* heeled over and surged toward the slaver's starboard side. 'Adder!' he shouted from the quarterdeck. 'Raise the colours and set the hooks! All crew be ready in case she tries to run!'

'Aye, Captain!' Adder yelled back from the main deck.

Jackson watched his crew move into position as his trusted first mate relayed his orders. The men on the *Grey Cloud* had been trained to fight both on sea and land. It had been non-negotiable that any who sailed with her had to have fighting and sailing experience.

The false Portuguese flag was quickly lowered and replaced with that of the *Grey Cloud's*, dancing like the devil, high in the air. The flag was black with an image of a red hourglass in its middle – its message, simple and clear.

Your time has run out ... surrender or die.

Jackson arched his back, looked up to the sky and let out a shrill scream. His crew heard him and followed their captain. The *Grey Cloud* erupted with a chorus of bellows as if a demonic ship, sailed by the damned, had suddenly been unleashed from the sea.

The *Grey Cloud's* bow was approaching the starboard side of the slaver's stern.

'Slack off the sails, grapnels at the ready!' Jackson ordered. Adder repeated the order and the ship slowed dramatically.

'Master gunner at the ready,' the captain ordered. The gunners stood fast behind their cannons on the lower decks as sandbags tied to long ropes were flung over the rails of the *Grey Cloud*, dangling against her side to absorb the impact of the two ships.

'Away all grapnels!' The hooks with their lines attached thumped into the slaver's gunwales and were hauled in, securing the two vessels together. As Adder gave the order, Jackson saw a large, white flag roll over the edge of the slaver's stern.

You were nearly out of time, you bastards. You were nearly all dead. Now maybe only your captain will die because he was foolish enough to take so long to surrender.

The *Grey Cloud's* boarding party was assembled in its nominated sections. Some were ready to board, while others stood behind them with muskets to provide cover should the slaver try to defend himself.

Adder led the first wave onto the main deck of the commandeered vessel as Jackson made his way down from the wheel of the *Grey Cloud*. By the time he set foot on the slave ship, Adder and his men had cordoned the surrendered crew around the mainmast. Jackson immediately smelled the familiar stench of defecation and the rotting sickness of the slaves below deck. His eyes scoured his new ship from the bow to the stern and up the ratlines to the crow's nest.

At first glance, the ship appeared well looked after; meaning, at the very least, that this vessel was sailing with a competent quartermaster who ran the crew and the ship's operations proficiently. He looked over at the slaver's crew. He did not feel as though there were warriors looking back at him, but he could see a dozen strong, healthy young men.

'What is it you need from our ship, so we can pay it and be on our way?'

Jackson turned in the direction of the voice that had interrupted his inspection. The captain of the slaver was an older man, who looked to be a seasoned sailor. This would not have been the first time he'd had another ship disrupt his passage. He would know very well that he was not in a position to negotiate but would do what he could to save his men, his ship and his cargo.

'Do you own this ship, Captain?' Jackson replied.

'I do not. It is one of three that are owned by my employer in Lagos.'

Jackson saw his opportunity. These men were also slaves. Perhaps not like those on the lower decks, but they were far from being free men. He could provide their freedom.

'You ask me what I want, sir,' Jackson started again. 'What I want … is revolution!'

He saw that his words were confusing to the slaving captain, who would have assumed food, cargo or the ship itself to be a more likely demand.

'You work for a company to make other men rich.' Jackson now looked over the rest of the crew, addressing every man on the ship. 'You believe you are free and yet you do not choose how to live your lives. That is chosen for you by the men who employ you. I will give you the freedom to choose your own lives. If you join us in our revolution, there will be equal shares in riches, and every man who sails with us will choose his own fate. No longer will we sit back and allow the weak to rule us. No longer will we be denied our true destinies. If you are able to take because you are stronger, then that is exactly what you should do.'

The crew of the *Grey Cloud* let out a cheer and Jackson could see that the slaver's crew were now intrigued. He waited for the cheer to end before he turned back to the captain and continued. 'Our revolution begins now. We will gather those who are tired of being led by weaker men and take the New World for ourselves. We will at last create a world where the balance is true, where the strong rule the weak.'

Another cheer erupted from the deck of the slaver, this time from both crews. Jackson could see his army growing before him. It was time to answer the slaving captain's query.

'Hear me now. A great fortune has been hidden somewhere near the Brazilian borders. This is a fortune which will shape the New World and we who live in it.' He looked around to see men from both crews turning toward each other with excitement and curiosity.

'But we are not the only ones who know about its existence. There is a great merchant galleon which, as we speak, is sailing towards Rio to deliver the coordinates of this fortune to the Stevenson Transport Company.'

The ship erupted with cursing and yelling. Stevenson

Transport's wealth and monopoly over the trade routes was well-known. Many resented the power of the British companies, especially Stevenson Transport, as a result of their close ties to the British Navy.

'I will get down to the detail, then.' Jackson interrupted the cursing of the men. 'We need you and your ship to sail alongside the *Grey Cloud*. We are going to take down the *Retribution*. We are going to take possession of the coordinates and, if we must, kill every member of her crew to get them, and then we will sail to Brazil to find this fortune. Then, my friends, then we will build a new world for ourselves!'

As another great cheer arose from the decks, a single voice broke through in protest.

'Are you mad?' Jackson turned to the slaver captain, whose voice had silenced the cheering. 'The *Retribution* is the greatest merchant on the Atlantic, with many trained soldiers on board. Surely you do not expect us to agree to this?'

Jackson looked back at him and responded accordingly.

'A large beast can be taken down by a smaller pack. It can be sunk, and I will show you how. We will sail back to Rio and sell your slaves there. We will buy our provisions and our weapons. You will no longer have to carry slaves. From now on, we will grow our army by taking what we want, on both land and sea. Those who do not wish to join the revolution may go their separate ways when we reach port.'

He turned his back to the slaving captain, reached into his belt and drew a pistol. As he turned back around to face him, he cocked the hammer, aimed low and fired. A puff of white smoke flew out of the barrel as the shot hit the slaver captain in his stomach. The force of the impact sent him reeling back against the base of the mainmast. He held his stomach and groaned in pain. As he removed his hands, he looked down in disbelief as his white shirt quickly turned crimson.

There was not a sound but for the captain's groaning as Jackson tucked the pistol back into his belt. He walked slowly towards the dying man, unsheathing his large bone-handled knife.

'No, please.' The captain saw the knife and cried out, stumbling over the words as shock and fear now accompanied his pain. 'No, no, no,' he begged as Jackson knelt to meet him, face to face.

He gently caressed the captain's cheek with the blade, taunting him as he saw the fear in the dying man's eyes. He loved to look into the eyes of men who feared him, who knew that they were about to die by his hand. He looked directly at him and spoke loud enough so that each man on the ship could hear.

'You should not have surrendered. There is no room for cowards in the revolution. I will set you free now.'

The captain's eyes grew wide as he whimpered one last plea. He had barely spoken before the sound of choking replaced his muffled whimper and the knife ran deep across the front of his throat, opening his windpipe and letting a red waterfall flow freely down his chest. In a moment, the captain's feet stopped twitching, as he lay there motionless, his eyes open but vacant.

Jackson stood up and walked over to Adder, who looked pleased that at least someone had been killed. 'Split the crew between both ships. Cast a vote for a new captain but keep the quartermaster the same. We sail back to Rio in thirty minutes. We will sell off the slaves, resupply and sail to intercept the *Retribution*.'

As Jackson made his way back to the *Grey Cloud*, he heard Adder call for an assembly of both crews to decide the new captain of the slaver.

We are so close now.

He returned to the familiar deck of his ship and made his way to his quarters.

Chapter 17

Brightness flashed in and out, the silhouette of a swinging lantern rocked from side to side for a moment before there was darkness again, and Caleb heard faint and unfamiliar voices. He wondered if he were dead and if this was what the afterlife had in store for him, endlessly drifting in and out of consciousness, with strange voices urging him to wake when he knew he could not. Flashes of his parents entered his mind and they called to him to join them. He ran towards them but the faster he ran, the further they disappeared into the distance. Eventually, they faded completely. He screamed out to them.

Mother! Father! Don't leave me! Please don't leave!

He felt his face flush with blood as once again he saw the movement of the swinging light, now glowing brighter. He sensed himself rocking back and forth, and then he felt it.

The pain was nothing like he had experienced before, a combination of burning heat and stinging knives surged through his back and shoulders like rolling thunderbolts. He reeled, unable to scream. Only a muffled cry of disbelief left his lips. The sound of his scream was strangled by the pain in his body. It was pulled back into his throat, allowing only a choking, sputtering noise.

'Easy, boy,' he heard a voice say. It was a voice he thought familiar … one that he had heard in his recent dreams, calling him to waken. He could not see clearly through the tears in his eyes. 'You need to fight now. You need to fight the fever.'

'Am I dead? Where am I?' Caleb could hardly muster the

strength for the words before he felt himself fall back into darkness. As he drifted off, he thought he heard the voice again.

'You are on the *Retribution*, one of the finest merchant galleons on the high seas.'

Chapter 18

Captain Andrews was a simple man. He had lived a sailor's life in the British Royal Navy for six years before being approached by Jacob Stevenson himself to captain the *Retribution*. He enjoyed a life of structure, process, rules and discipline. These tenets had served him well and had made him a respected and loved captain to his crew, who believed him to be tough, intelligent and fair. At twenty-eight years of age and already approaching his sixth year as the *Retribution's* captain, he was considered extremely capable.

He stood proudly on the poop deck and looked down over his ship, observing the workings of the crew. The *Retribution* had been built seven years earlier and was used primarily for the transportation of cargo between England, Portugal, Spain and the Americas. Though it could hold and carry large shipments, it was also Jacob Stevenson's private transport vessel and, as such, was well armed and manned by crew members who had been trained to fight.

It was a four-masted galleon, with the mainmast spiking one hundred and twenty feet in the air. Above her, flying high, was the Union Jack, dancing superbly in the sunlight.

The square sail and rigging clung tightly to the yards as the morning breeze blew through the mizzen, main and foremast, pushing her fearlessly through the Atlantic swells. Her hull had been carvel built, allowing a smoother, faster ride through the water and, though she weighed a thousand tons, the *Retribution* glided through the ocean with impressive ease.

THE RETRIBUTION

He loved to sail and never took the good days for granted. So far, today was shaping up to be one of those. The breeze had been true and the sun shone brightly, giving him excellent visibility of the Atlantic swells as the great merchant ran with the wind.

They had been at sea for two days and had sustained an excellent pace. Andrews had chosen to divert the ship from the usual trade routes and sail further south, before turning her towards South America.

The *Retribution* was a great ship, which also made her a valuable target for privateers. If he could stay off the usual trade route, he would lower the risk of being identified and approached.

He walked to the starboard rails and down the stairs onto the quarterdeck, where men were cleaning the swivel guns. He walked over to the ship's wheel, currently manned by the ship's quartermaster: Benson, a man of similar age to him and an exceptional quartermaster. Andrews stopped next to the wheel and looked down, observing the working on the main deck.

'How does she feel, Benson?' he asked as he turned toward his quartermaster.

'She feels light and fast, Captain. The yards and sails on the mizzen, main and foremast have been hoisted, sir, and we have a strong breeze behind us. Would you like to take the wheel, sir?'

'Not yet, thank you, Benson. Enjoy the wind while you can. I will take over later. While we have the wind, hoist the jib and let us keep running with it to see if we can steal some time. I would like to make the South American coast in six weeks if we can manage.'

'Begging your pardon, Captain, the binnacle is showing us heading south-east and if she keeps running true, will we not end up too far below Brazil? We will have to start beating to windward up the coast if I'm not mistaken, sir.'

'You are quite right, Benson,' Andrews explained. 'I want us further south than usual to avoid company. In addition, I would like to inspect the southern coastline leading up to Brazil. With this breeze, we should not lose time and we may even arrive quicker than expected.'

'Aye, Captain,' Benson replied as he turned over to the main deck and yelled the order. 'Hoist the jib!'

The call was repeated along the main deck and up to the sailors on the forecastle. Andrews watched the men hoist the sail, running it along the bowsprit. The sail caught the wind immediately and the *Retribution* puffed out her chest and quickened her pace.

'I am going down to check on the boy. You have the ship, Benson.' Andrews turned and nodded at his quartermaster, who now had a look of contentment as he held the wheel with pride.

Andrews made his way to the starboard side of the ship once again and down the stairs to the main deck. Benson announced his captain's arrival to the main deck and a cheer rose in unison as the captain made his way around the great hatch, which was used as a passageway to load cargo into the ship's hull.

He walked aft through the door into the officers' cabins, where they had kept the boy's lodging, close to the surgeon. He entered the infirmary and looked over at Caleb, who lay on a bunk and had been positioned on his stomach since they had left port two days earlier.

He had whipped men before, young men. Although life on a ship and on the seas made men of boys in a matter of months, what lay before him was still a boy. He had been told by William Finch in London that the boy, once recovered, was to be treated well and to be given station on the ship.

'He is strong and able for his age,' Finch had told him. 'The boy is to be paid like any other crew member on the *Retribution*. Teach him seamanship and teach him how to fight.'

His wounds were deep for certain. Andrews had seen many wounds in his time and knew that the boy would carry visible scars for the rest of his life. The captain looked at his back and saw how the red, bruised cuts crossed over each other like wet bundles of straw that had been matted on the damp ground.

'The boy has broken the fever, Captain, and his wounds are healing well,' his surgeon said.

'Indeed,' Andrews replied. 'You have done a fine job on him. He has broken through the fever, yet he still sleeps?'

'I have been giving him a tonic to knock him out, sir. The pain would still be excruciating.'

Andrews looked down at the cuts covering Caleb's back. He had stitched them himself the afternoon of the whipping on the Stevenson Estate and was content with the job he had done. He turned to walk from the cabin.

'No more tonic,' he said as he passed the surgeon. 'He needs to be up on his feet as soon as possible. Call for me when he wakes.'

He left the room and headed towards the grand cabin. It was situated under the poop deck and was by far the largest cabin on the ship, spanning the whole width of the vessel. Large windows along the back and side walls invited the morning light into the room, illuminating the navigation maps and journals on the enormous table. Shelves filled with maps and books lined one wall. On the starboard side of the cabin was a small table and two chairs with a chessboard set up for play. A large duchess chest of drawers and mirror were situated aft. Next to them, a curtain partitioned the double bunk from the rest of the cabin. A quarter galley was built out on the starboard side of the ship as a personal balcony for the enjoyment of the afternoon breeze, a brandy and a smoke. On the opposite side, a similar galley provided a private head. In the middle of the cabin was a large rectangular table, oak built, with ten matching chairs for entertaining his officers or accompanying guests on special occasions.

It was a grand cabin to be sure and, though Andrews spent much of his time in there sifting through journals and inventory logs, he had never slept there.

This was Jacob Stevenson's cabin and was not to be occupied by anyone but him, regardless of whether he was on board for the voyage or not.

Andrews had his own cabin directly below the room he was standing in, on a deck shared with the other officers. It was far more modest, but he was a modest man.

He looked across the main table in the middle of the room towards the large painting that had been loaded onto the ship two days earlier. It had been the first item on board, with William Finch himself overseeing its safe arrival into the grand cabin.

'This is Stevenson's most prized painting, Andrews,' Finch had said. 'It is to be delivered to Simon Blake as a gesture of thanks for establishing our interests in South America. It is a thank you from the whole company. I want you to oversee the delivery of this painting to Blake personally. Is that understood?'

'Of course, sir,' Andrews had replied confidently, though he had not truly understood the fuss made over the gift. Over the years he had delivered far more valuable pieces of cargo for the company than a painting. Nevertheless, if it was important to the owner of the company, then he would see it done.

What was interesting was that the painting had been logged under the letter "X" on the inventory list. He looked over at the large box placed on the deck beside the painting and considered the possibility that something more valuable than the painting itself had been packed inside. Why else would there be such secrecy surrounding its delivery?

Not for me to worry about. I have my orders and they will be followed.

A knock on the cabin door interrupted his thoughts.

'Come in.'

The surgeon entered the cabin. 'Captain, sir.' He spoke calmly. 'The boy is awake.'

'Thank you. I will be down shortly.'

Chapter 19

A searing pain shot down his back as Caleb opened his eyes. He waited a brief moment while his vision cleared before he tried to make sense of his surroundings. He looked around at an unfamiliar room.

He tried hard to gather his thoughts but the pain in his back blocked out all rational thought, until it reminded him of exactly what had happened to him. He was certain he had died during the whipping but the agony in his muscles made him aware he had lived.

He inhaled sharply, noticing a difference in the smell and taste of the air from what he was used to. It smelt of salt and wet wood, lamp oil, canvas and hessian.

He tried to move but the pain crippled him as he collapsed back on the bunk.

'Easy now,' he heard a voice say. 'You need to go easy or you will tear the stitches.'

Caleb could not see to whom the voice belonged but nodded in obedience as he lay on the bunk.

'Try and drink some water, boy.' He heard the voice again. This time a hand holding a cup moved into his line of vision. He had not realised how thirsty he was until he saw the cup in front of him. He took the cup and drank quickly. The water had barely reached his throat before it came back up violently in a coughing, spluttering mess.

'What did I just tell you?' the voice said again. 'You need to go slow. Now try again.'

Caleb took a smaller sip, this time feeling the water flow down his throat and into his stomach. As it moistened his mouth, he felt the sensation of his tongue return, and the rawness in his throat ease.

He looked over to see who had given him the water. He was a tall, thin man, old, with grey hair tied back behind his head. His eyebrows were bushes of silver that curled up towards his tanned forehead and he had thick, grey sideburns covering each side of his face, shaven deliberately to show his bald chin.

'Come,' the man said. 'Let's get you sitting up.' As Caleb was assisted to a sitting position, he suddenly felt very ill. He fought off the urge to vomit and looked at the man standing in front of him.

'The captain stitched you up,' said the man, 'and, let me say, he did a fine job … saved your life, boy. You are lucky.'

Caleb could not believe his ears. Never in his whole life had he felt lucky. He certainly did not think this situation qualified. He looked around the small room and back at the man.

'Where am I?' As he spoke the words, he felt the whole room rock and move and the urge to throw up became too much. The man in front of him placed a bucket on Caleb's lap, knowing exactly what was about to happen. Caleb dropped his head and brought up the water he had just sipped.

'Seasickness is what that is.' It was not the man in front of him but a different voice this time. Caleb lifted his head to see a familiar figure walk into the room. He was much younger than the other man; also tall, tanned and well-built. He was the sailing captain he had seen alongside Jacob and his generals while he was chained in the estate's cellar.

'You need to eat but do not try to eat too much or you will waste it. Small bites until you get your sea legs. Ship's biscuits and water rations only, until you can calm your stomach. I will not have you throwing up beef or salted pork.'

Caleb's head started swimming again and the urge to throw up returned. He vomited in the bucket once more before he could speak again. This time he knew where he was.

'I am on the *Retribution*.'

'Indeed you are, Caleb. I am Captain Andrews and from now on you will address me as either Captain or sir. Is that understood?'

Caleb was surprised at the unwavering sense of authority in the voice of someone so young. It was calm yet resolute, soothing yet incontestable. He nodded as he looked up at the captain and agreed.

'Yes, sir.'

'Good,' Andrews replied. 'Now, try and eat something and hold down some water. I want you up and about on deck as soon as possible. You need fresh air and the breeze in your face. You are currently in the officers' quarters due to your condition and the need to be close to the surgeon.'

Captain Andrews motioned to the older man standing next to him and Caleb realised he was the surgeon who had been by his side when he first awoke.

'You are not an officer,' Andrews continued, 'and therefore must take lodging with the rest of the crew as soon as possible. Do we understand each other, Caleb?'

Caleb nodded again. 'Yes, Captain.'

'Excellent. If you continue with your present attitude, you will do a fine job on this ship.'

Caleb nodded again and took a bite into a biscuit he had been handed by the surgeon. It was plain and dense, but he welcomed the sensation of something in his stomach as it seemed to slightly diminish the sickness. He drank some water and felt better for it. He waited for a moment and was relieved that he had managed to hold it down.

'There you go, son,' the surgeon spoke up. 'Already taking control over it. They said you are a strong lad.'

'Come,' Captain Andrews interrupted. 'Stand on your feet, put on a shirt and let us make our way up to the main deck.'

The shirt was loose fitting, yet every time it caught against one of the stitches on his back, Caleb winced in pain. He stood and felt his legs buckle. As he did, the surgeon and Captain Andrews caught him before he fell.

He nodded at them both, signalling to them that he could stand as he felt the strength come back to his legs. He took another bite of the biscuit and a sip of water and followed Captain Andrews out of the cabin.

They walked into a narrow passage towards a closed door. Walking down the passageway, Caleb noticed plaques mounted on both sides as if he were walking through a trophy room. They reached the door at the end of the hall and, as the captain swung it open, the light burned into the back of Caleb's eyes.

He walked out, covering his face with one hand, trying to adjust to the brightness. His nostrils filled his lungs with salty air. He felt the warmth of the sun on his skin, and his ears were bombarded by the sound of busy movements and men singing loudly while they worked.

As his eyes adjusted to the light, he took his hand away from his face and looked around. He stood in amazement at what he saw. He had walked out into a different world.

He looked over the rails of the quarterdeck at the wooden beast before him. Dozens of men were scattered over the huge decks, working and singing in unison. Above him, he saw men climbing up and down roped webbing, reaching as high as the tallest trees in the estate's forests. He had never been this close to masts, sails and rigging and stared in wonder at the height of the poles and the broad, white sheets that seemed to cover the whole sky.

He walked to the railing and looked over the side of the ship. He had only ever imagined what the open ocean would look like, and it took his breath away. It was the most beautifully terrifying thing he had ever seen.

He no longer felt ill and the pain in his back eased a little as he looked out at the blue vastness of the sea stretching further than he could have ever imagined, finally ending at the line between the ocean and the sky.

'It is the horizon, Caleb.'

Caleb looked up at Andrews, who had walked over beside him. 'I never thought I would see something so beautiful, sir,' he replied.

'On that we can agree, son. I never tire of looking at it. Out there is where adventure and things not yet discovered wait for those who have the courage to follow their dreams.'

Caleb listened intently as he looked out over the ocean. He felt it instantly. This is why he had survived. This is why he had fought for his life. This would be his new world and it excited him greatly.

'Come.' Andrews motioned him over to meet a young man who was standing in the centre of the deck, holding the wheel of the ship.

'Benson.' The man at the wheel turned to face them.

'Aye, Captain.'

'Benson, this is Caleb. He will be joining the *Retribution's* crew.'

'Welcome aboard, Caleb. Have you sailed on many voyages before?'

'No, sir. This is the first ship I have been on.' Immediately he had finished his sentence, Caleb felt embarrassed. He could see all around him that the men worked hard and proficiently and had been sailing for many years. Benson must have picked up on the shame in his face and he gave him a wry smile.

'Well, you will be a seasoned sailor in no time. You are on the finest galleon to sail the seas,' Benson reassured him, and Caleb found himself smiling.

'Benson,' Andrews chimed in, 'Caleb has serious injuries on his back, which will take weeks to heal before he is fully fit for work. In the meantime, partner him with Bobby and allow him to follow and learn his duties. For the time being, he will work as a cabin boy and a swabbie. He will look after the stern decks and officers' quarters and be paid accordingly. He has a rucksack in the surgeon's room with personal belongings. I will take the wheel while you show him his new quarters.'

'Aye, Captain.' Benson nodded and, as he released the wheel, he walked to the edge of the deck and yelled to the rest of the ship.

'Captain has the wheel!' His voice was surprisingly loud, and Caleb realised that he had spent many years calling from that position.

He followed Benson as they picked up his rucksack and made their way down to the main deck. Sailors dipped their heads in acknowledgement as Benson passed among them. Caleb looked up as they made their way past the tallest mast on the ship.

The men above him swung on ropes from one side of the ship to the other, while one man was positioned in the crow's nest, higher than he had seen any man be before.

As they walked towards the bow of the ship, they entered a door leading them below decks. Darkness greeted them and they waited a moment for their eyes to adjust. Caleb took that moment to recall Captain Andrews' words, words he could not believe he had heard.

Pay him accordingly!

Caleb thought about those words and what they meant. Never in his life had he been paid for work and never had he possessed money of his own. The idea thrilled him and, as they made their way down to the gun deck below, he dared to imagine what he would buy first. Perhaps something to eat that he chose for himself or a shirt that had not been worn by anyone else. Given enough time, maybe he could buy his own horse and ride it along the beach and into the ocean.

He did not care what role he had to play on the ship. He assumed washing the decks and attending to the officers' needs would be the lowest paying, but he did not care as he realised it would allow him to work on the upper decks and look at the ocean, even if only for a short time each day.

As they walked toward the bow of the ship, they entered a

room filled with hammocks.

'Bobby!' Benson called out. A boy who looked about Caleb's age walked over to them. 'Bobby, this is Caleb. He is to be a swabbie on the poop and quarter and he is to tend to the officers' cabins. Show him a hammock and teach him his duties. This is Caleb's first time on a ship, so I will leave it to you to teach him our ways.'

'Yes, sir, Mr Benson.'

Bobby was a slight-bodied boy with black hair and narrow shoulders. Caleb assumed that the heaviest labour he had ever encountered was wielding a mop and bucket and carrying a dinner tray.

'Hello, Caleb. It's good to meet you.' The welcome was genuine and honest, and Caleb felt at ease instantly.

'It is good to meet you too, Bobby.'

Bobby nodded at him and raised his finger and pointed to a hammock. 'That one is yours. Throw your rucksack on and come with me. First, I will show you around the ship. There is a lot to learn, so let's get started. I will also show you how to do your duties.'

In spite of the terrible pain in his back, Caleb could not stop himself from smiling as his new life unfolded before him. He had found a home and it sailed across the Atlantic Ocean.

Chapter 20

Jackson Bell stood at the wheel on the quarterdeck of the *Grey Cloud*. The Scarlets had spent a week in Rio preparing the two ships for the battle ahead. The slaves had been sold at auction, with the profits used for upgrades to both vessels.

They were no longer to be used for slaving, but instead for war, and that included extra cannon shot, reinforced hulls, and weapons for the crew. He looked over the port side of the ship and watched the newly upgraded Spanish slaver sail proudly alongside the *Grey*.

Adder had been voted in as the new captain of the Spaniard, which he had aptly named *The Grey Revolt*.

The crew of the *Grey Cloud* had been divided and mixed with the slavers so that each ship now had an equal mix of Scarlets to train and watch over the new recruits.

They had been sailing for two weeks along the most common of the trade routes used to transport goods from London to Brazil. They had crossed paths with three ships so far, but none was the target. They had agreed that trying to take the *Retribution* intact would be too difficult and had decided that she needed to be wounded badly and eventually sunk if they were to taste victory.

Surely with me at the helm, the Retribution would become the greatest, most fearsome ship to sail the Atlantic.

But he knew it could not be.

Jackson smiled to himself as he imagined the look on Stevenson's face when he was told that his prized ship now lay on the bottom of the ocean.

He and Adder had agreed that the best chance they had was to fly under false flags as British merchant galleons and let the *Retribution* sail between them as an ally. When she passed through, they would inspect her to see if she had encountered any troubles on her voyage that could be used against her. A sail, or even masts, could be weakened by the unmerciful squalls on the Atlantic.

If they were extremely lucky, the *Retribution* would signal for them to stop and perhaps trade for fresh water or food supplies. The *Retribution* carried many on board, and if their food rations had gone bad, a fellow merchant ship coming across her path would be a welcome sight.

One of the ships could then come alongside her and take the crew by surprise in hand-to-hand combat without having to fire a shot, while the other ship could advance and grapple onto her from the other side.

Jackson thought that the best-case scenario but knew they would have to devise a strategy for a different, much more likely, sequence of events. They would let the *Retribution* sail through and investigate her as she passed unawares.

Once through, they would turn about and take out her rudder, leaving her helpless in the ocean. The *Grey* and the *Revolt* would then be able to circle her, firing at her stern and bow, from where she could not properly retaliate. They would fire low, hoping to spill the ocean into her lower decks until she floundered hopelessly and her broadside cannons could no longer be used. Then they would latch onto her as a pack of lions latched onto its prey.

Three more days passed, and another three after that, with no sighting of the *Retribution*. They had seen eight ships pass through with British flags, and each time he let a ship pass, his frustration grew.

By the end of the fourth week, Jackson's frustration had turned to panic as he realised that they had missed her. The *Retribution* had detoured from the usual trade route and had more than likely passed by, sailing further north towards the United Colonies or sailing south along the African Coast and below them, both dangerous routes as it would take longer to reach Rio. Food and water would run low towards the end of the journey. But the *Retribution* was carrying with it a great secret, and so the captain must have felt it worth the risk.

He sat in his cabin looking at his coordinates. The *Retribution* was beyond them. He hammered his fists on the table, screwing up the maps and screaming in anger. He ran out to the quarterdeck.

'Turn about! Signal to the *Revolt*! We sail back to Rio! Make quick speed! The *Retribution* is beyond us. We will need to take the prize on land.'

As Jackson went back into his cabin, he thought about the difficulties the new plan would create. His main target now was no longer the *Retribution*, but Simon Blake. The *Retribution* would reach the port of Rio before them, and Blake would have the coordinates in his grasp.

Jackson spat at the thought of it.

I should have killed you when I had the chance, Blake. But you will be dead soon enough. I will use my knife to carve the truth out of you.

He gripped the edge of the table as he felt the ship heel leeward until she found her balance again and began running with the wind towards Rio.

Chapter 21

Two months at sea had passed since Caleb had first woken up on the *Retribution*. They had sighted land that morning and had begun sailing north toward the Port of Rio. He stood with the other men on the main deck and leaned over the portside gunwale, taking in the new world around him.

His time on the *Retribution* had been a crash course in seamanship. The wounds on his back had healed well and he was now able to move freely and without pain. By the third week, he had regained his strength and was able to perform his duties with ease and proficiency. He had found working on the *Retribution* far less demanding than working on the estate.

Every day he would wake early and set the table in the officers' quarters. He would deliver their meals, then head up to the decks to start scrubbing. First, he would start with the poop deck and then down a level to the quarterdeck. He would scrub for an hour, by which time it was eight o'clock and the ship had become a hive of activity.

Then he would clear the officers' tables and take the crockery down to the galley to be washed. Afterwards, he would return to his bucket of soapy water and scrub down the main deck, beginning at the stern and making his way to the bow, meeting Bobby approximately halfway. It was then time for him to eat quickly before setting up the officers' cabin for lunch.

After lunch, he learnt how to manage sails, tie knots and work the rigging. He also spent an hour each day practising with a sword, mandatory for everyone on the *Retribution*. He had practised many times on the estate against Brenton Stevenson and surprised many on the ship with his proficiency. Unlike his duels with Brenton, here on the ship he was permitted to win a fair contest against other sailors without fear of revenge from someone who could not bear to be defeated by an opponent of such low social status.

Afterwards, he was able to have an hour free to himself, and he would usually spend this time down in the crew's quarters with Bobby, playing checkers, learning to read and write and talking about what they would buy with their earnings when they landed in Brazil.

Then, it was back to the other end of the ship to set up for dinner and wait on the officers, who would spend their nights singing, drinking and telling old stories of battles and adventure.

Caleb would stand at the back of the dining room and listen intently without saying a word, replaying the songs in his head as he cleared the table. Then he would make his way back to his quarters to eat his evening meal.

The food consisted of biscuits and water for lunch and a stew, fish or salted pork for evening meals. He did not mind the food, though he was used to having more vegetables and greens to eat than what was available on the *Retribution*.

At night, sailors would tell stories of the Atlantic and of tyrants and sea monsters, mermaids and treasure ships that had gone missing, their cargoes never to be seen again. They would tell stories of the New World and its cheap land, affordable even for a common sailor. He would lie in his hammock and listen to the stories and allow himself to believe that he would one day make enough money to own a horse or farm.

When the last candle had been blown out and darkness overtook the ship, he would lie in his hammock with his eyes still open, taking a moment for himself as the ship rocked him back and forth and eventually to sleep. In those moments, he often thought about his parents and what they would think of him now. He thought about the estate and the horses he used to tend. He thought about the Stevensons. He thought about Sasha, the night in the stables and the fateful moment by the waterfall when his life had changed so dramatically.

He thought about how they had stood on the stairs and watched him while he was being whipped. The pain in his back had disappeared but his anger for the Stevensons remained. He had buried his love for Sasha, knowing that they would not cross paths again.

She would complete finishing school in London and be married off to a wealthy suitor. She would live a life of luxury and would forget he had ever existed. Caleb's jaw clenched in anger whenever he thought about her, as he both loved and hated her.

During his afternoon break on a hot day nearing the end of the voyage, when he and Bobby were looking excitedly towards Rio's approaching harbour entrance, Quartermaster Benson strolled along the deck inspecting its cleanliness. 'Caleb, you are needed in the main cabin. Go and tend to the captain at once.'

'Aye, sir, Mr Benson,' Caleb replied. He walked up to the quarterdeck, through the corridor to the grand cabin. He had been in there before to serve the captain and officers who used it on special occasions. It had been Captain Andrews' birthday and extra rations of ale and meat had been given to the crew, while the officers celebrated in the extravagant room built for Stevenson himself. He should not have been surprised that Stevenson's lodgings were so grand. He knocked on the door and waited for permission to enter.

'Come in.'

Caleb opened the door and walked into the lavish cabin. Captain Andrews stood behind the large desk with his back to him, looking out through the open windows of the stern.

'You wanted to see me, sir?'

'Yes,' Andrews replied as he turned to face Caleb. 'Come in, son. How have you found your first voyage, Caleb?'

'Very well, thank you, Captain.'

'Good then. Benson and the other officers tell me that you

are fitting in well, that you are working hard and that you are also very capable when practising the sword. You are fourteen, yes?'

'Yes, sir. Fourteen-and-a-half, Captain.'

'When I was your age, I also scrubbed decks and tended the officers' tables.'

Caleb nodded politely, still unsure why he had been summoned. There would not be another meal on the ship before they reached port so there was no need for him to set tables. He was unsure how to respond and, thankfully, the captain spoke again before a reply was needed.

'I saw your talent with the horses on the Stevenson estate. I saw you with Stevenson's daughter by the waterfall. I saw you whipped on the hill. You have qualities which few men dare to unleash, Caleb. You are strong, intelligent, calm and fearless. You took your punishment like a man, where most men would have fallen apart.'

Caleb bowed his head slightly in recognition though he did not wish to hear such things. He had rarely been paid a compliment in his whole life and was embarrassed by Andrews' words.

'Caleb, when we disembark, you will accompany me when I visit Simon Blake. I would like you to start taking on more responsibility on this ship, perhaps one day to become an officer yourself.'

Caleb could not believe his ears. He had believed he would scrub the decks for the rest of his life and was happy to do so – to be an officer on a ship was beyond his dreams.

'Thank you, sir. I am glad you are happy with my duties thus far, and I would enjoy taking on more responsibility.'

'Very good, then,' Andrews replied as he walked over towards the starboard side private balcony and lit a pipe. 'Wait for Mr Benson and me at the end of the jetty. Now gather what you need for the next few days.' With that, he walked out to the balcony and out of sight.

As Caleb made his way back to the main deck, he heard the anchor chain roll out from the bow. The *Retribution* had made port. He walked out to the quarterdeck to see Guanabara Bay stretching out before him. The harbour was busy with ships being loaded and unloaded all along the jetties.

Benson sat at a table next to the gangplank, which had been lowered to provide access to the jetty below. The men lined up without direction. There was a sense of excitement on the ship. He walked to the end of the line, where he saw Bobby, and decided he would be the best person to ask what was happening.

'What is this all this about, then?'

'We are lining up to get paid. The ship carries enough money to pay the crew whenever we dock. Then the cargo is unloaded or loaded, and we sail back to London or to somewhere else. We get paid again on our return to London. That's how it works.'

Caleb lined up with the others, excited and eager. He had no idea how much money he would receive. Very little, he assumed, but that was more than he had ever been given before.

'Come, Caleb.' Bobby grabbed his arm. 'The others will spend all their earnings on whores and ale. My advice to you is to save two of your shillings and spend the rest. That way, after a while you will have enough to buy that horse you want, perhaps even some land here in the New World. It will take many years, but eventually you could do it.'

'That sounds good to me.' And it did. Caleb would save and eventually buy a horse and ride up and down the beaches as a free man.

When he got to the front of the line, he saw a large logbook with sailors' names, their duties, years on the ship, the name of the port, the date and the amount to be paid. Benson looked up at him and then again at the book. He looked back up at him, puzzled.

'Caleb, I just realised we do not have your surname here. What is it, boy?'

'Ferry, sir. My name is Caleb Ferry.'

'Very good. Thank you, Mr Ferry. You are to be paid four shillings for your eight weeks of work on the *Retribution*. Don't spend it all at once.'

The men in the line behind him roared with laughter. Clearly, it was no fortune.

'Thank you, sir,' Caleb smiled, undeterred. He turned to Bobby, who was looking at him and rubbing his thumb and forefinger together in front of his face. Caleb understood the meaning of the gesture immediately and turned back to Benson.

'Mr Benson, sir. Can I save two shillings please?'

Benson looked up at him. He then took back two shillings and placed them back in the chest.

'Noted that Mr Caleb Ferry now has a line of credit to the amount of two shillings.'

Another roar of laughter erupted throughout the *Retribution's* decks. Benson looked back up at Caleb and smiled.

'Smart, Caleb. Very smart.'

Caleb smiled as he walked down the plank and onto the jetty, where he waited for Bobby to join him. They looked down the length of the crowded wharf where sailors and dock workers were busy unloading the *Retribution's* cargo. At the end of the jetty was a large, white building – Caleb counted it to be three storeys high – with a sign on the second storey wall that stretched the width of the building. He asked Bobby to read it out to him and, upon hearing the words, couldn't help but sigh.

'*STEVENSON TRANSPORT'* was written in large, bold letters, defacing what seemed to be otherwise a beautiful building that looked over the harbour of Rio.

'Come on, Caleb.' Bobby said excitedly. 'We have money in our pockets and an exotic land under our feet. Let's go see the markets. Apparently, there is a festival happening at the moment.'

'Bobby, I have been asked by the captain to go with him to see a Simon Blake. He has not let me know why.'

'To see Simon Blake? Well, there you go, hey.'

Caleb sensed a little disappointment in Bobby's voice. He was also disappointed that he could not go exploring with his friend. He was desperate to see this new world.

'I will not be long and then will come find you.'

Bobby smiled at him. 'The inn where we stay is a street down from The Monkey and Rat tavern. I will get us a room and leave your name at the door. I will be at the markets so look for me there.'

With that, Bobby walked along the wharf and disappeared into the crowd. As he did, Captain Andrews appeared next to Caleb, with Benson beside him.

'Come.' Captain Andrews pointed over at men pushing carts carrying a load from the *Retribution*. 'This section goes to Simon Blake's office.' He walked after the cart, with Caleb and Benson following. As they made their way towards the building, they walked past men heaving large ropes attached to pulleys that lifted the huge cargo nets from the hull of the *Retribution* and onto the carts lined up on the wharf.

Once loaded, the carts were pulled by horses towards the Stevenson building, where they veered right and disappeared through a large passageway leading to a warehouse on the eastern side. Caleb had not realised until they were further down the wharf that the enormous warehouse next door was attached to the Transport Building, the structures combining to form one very impressive establishment. He imagined all the materials that had been unloaded, over the years, onto this very wharf and into the warehouse in front of him – materials used to construct a new world to help feed the old one.

When they arrived at the side of the Stevenson Transport Building, Caleb assumed they would veer right with the rest of the carts but, instead, Captain Andrews stopped them and instructed two men to pick up a large, square item covered in hessian. He then motioned the men to go left, as he led the way along a paved platform and down the western side of the building.

Caleb noticed two large stone pillars ahead of them. On his left was the port square, consumed with the activity and excitement of the markets. He could not wait to be done with his duties, meet up with Bobby and join the festivities.

When they reached the pillars, they turned towards a pair of large double doors, which Caleb now saw acted as the main entrance to the building and was where customers, clients and people with enquiries would enter. They walked into a large foyer, decorated with fresh flowers positioned at the bottom of a large staircase. The interior, with marble flooring and more stone pillars, was extravagant and built to show off the Stevenson wealth and reputation.

At the edge of the stairs, stood a man of middle age, about forty years old Caleb guessed, though he was still strong and wiry. He looked eager to meet them as Captain Andrews walked up to him and extended his hand in welcome. The man met Andrews' hand with his own.

'Welcome back to Brazil, Andrews. And to all of you, welcome.'

Andrews responded accordingly as he shook the man's hand. 'It is good to see you again, Simon.'

Chapter 22

Caleb followed Simon Blake, Captain Andrews and the *Retribution's* quartermaster, Benson, up the large staircase to the second floor of the Stevenson Transport Building. The second floor was a huge open space with coffee tables, leather sofas, a large desk and a bar. Caleb imagined it would be similar to what a brandy room on a rich estate would look like.

There were large windows on all sides of the building allowing the natural light to brighten the space. Caleb realised that from this room one could see the port square towards the Government Fort and the lush gardens beyond and, with a turn to the left, could then look out to the harbour and see the ships approaching and departing, as well as the activity on the wharfs. Another turn to the left would afford a view inside the warehouse next door, where one could observe the loading bay and the workings inside the huge storage shed. This was a war room, where Simon Blake could run the Stevenson Transport operations, whilst at the same time being able to keep watch over the world outside.

Two of the sailors from the *Retribution* walked up the stairs behind them. They had taken the item that was wrapped in hessian from the cart and carried it up to the second floor. Both men looked at Simon for further instructions.

'Leave it against the wall, thank you,' Simon ordered. As the men nodded, Captain Andrews chimed in.

'Actually, Simon, Jacob told me personally that we are to hang it for you right away.'

'I see.' Simon looked confused. 'Very well then, over on the back wall you will find a heavy nail that should suffice.'

Andrews motioned to the men who unwrapped the package. It was a large painting of a ship, sailing in a ferocious storm. The two men took no time at all to hang the painting.

As they all moved to the other side of the second floor to look, Caleb could see that it had been painted to show the port side of the ship, as if it were tacking and sailing out of the painting itself. It was a grand painting, Caleb thought, and then realised that he was staring at a painting of the *Retribution* herself.

'I didn't see this on the log, Andrews,' said Simon. 'What is the story with this?'

Andrews stood next to Simon as they both stared at the impressive painting.

'Actually, it is on the log, Simon. This is Jacob's favourite painting, which has hung above the fireplace in his office on the Stevenson Estate for many years. I believe that he wanted to surprise you with it and therefore did not describe it in the logbooks. He ordered the painting to be marked only as "X".'

Caleb saw that Andrews' disclosure had sparked an immediate interest. As Simon turned quickly to the captain, his words were now direct and abrupt.

'This is the item marked as "X"?'

'Yes, Simon,' Andrews replied.

'Are you absolutely sure, Captain?' Simon questioned again.

'Yes, Mr Blake.' Andrews was now the one who seemed confused. 'Jacob brought me into his office before we set sail and told me that this painting was to be a great gift to his general manager of South American operations and that it was to be marked only as "X" so that it was kept as a surprise. He instructed me to personally see it loaded onto the *Retribution* and kept within the grand cabin. I was then to oversee the delivery to you personally and have it hung on your wall. He was very specific, Simon. He told me to keep it secret and to keep it safe. Is everything all right?'

Blake looked back at the painting and took a deep breath.

'Yes, Captain, forgive me. It is just that I was not expecting such a grand gift as this. Please let Jacob know that I am as surprised as I am grateful. I shall write a letter thanking him and you shall deliver it to him personally.'

'It would be my pleasure, sir,' Andrews replied as he turned to face Simon. 'Sir, I would like to introduce you to my quartermaster, Benson.'

'Pleasure, sir,' Benson said as he leant in and shook Simon's hand.

'And,' the Captain continued as he turned towards Caleb, 'this is Caleb. Caleb used to work on the Stevenson estate and has recently joined the crew on the *Retribution*.'

Caleb leant forward and shook Simon's hand. 'Pleased to meet you, Mr Blake, sir.'

Simon's hands were rough and strong.

This is not a man who has lived his life in this office. This is a man who is accustomed to doing things himself.

'Caleb has quite a talent with horses,' Andrews continued. 'Stevenson himself praised the boy's gift and he alone was charged with the care of the prized stallions and mares on Jacob's estate.'

As Andrews spoke, Caleb wondered if this was why he had been asked to attend the meeting. If so, he was relieved that this was to be his role, and that he would be able to work with horses again. He had been dreading the possibility of being told he was to be handed over to Simon to work in the warehouse. He found Rio fantastically exciting and would not have been too opposed to the idea if he had not been so deeply affected by the ocean.

He loved being part of the *Retribution*, and wanted more than anything to stay with the crew and with his good friend, Bobby.

'Is that so?' Simon looked over at Caleb. 'It just so happens I may be in need of a rider in the next few days. Though, if you are as talented as Andrews says, I am not sure why Stevenson would send you to work on the *Retribution* and not keep you on the estate.'

Caleb looked at the captain and then to the floor in

embarrassment. He felt the blood rush to his face. An awkward silence fell over the room and it seemed to go on for an age. Andrews sensed the tension and took it upon himself to break it.

'Mr Blake, sir, we will be in port for a week. We will be staying at the inn near The Monkey and Rat should you need anything.'

'Thank you, gentlemen,' Simon replied. 'Please dine with me this evening. There are festivities happening in Rio over the coming days. You have arrived at a good time to see this growing, evolving city come to life. I have important guests coming and would be obliged if all three of you would join me.'

Caleb looked up at Simon in surprise. Firstly, he had never been called a gentleman before, nor had someone of Simon Blake's station ever thanked him for anything. He certainly had never been invited as a guest to a dinner of importance. He was sure that Simon did not mean him.

Simon nodded at Caleb, noticing the surprise on his face. 'Yes, you as well, son. I would like to hear about the Stevenson estate and how it has grown its esteemed reputation. I have not been there for many years.'

Caleb nodded back. 'It would be my pleasure, sir.'

With that, Benson and Caleb turned and left Simon with Captain Andrews. Caleb had seen straight away why Simon was well-known and respected within the company. He was a strong man who stood tall and proud. When he spoke, his tone was calm and sure.

Kind, yet strong.

As they walked out of the Stevenson Transport building and into the town square, Benson's voice sounded behind him.

'Caleb, take this.' He handed Caleb a brown leather coin purse.

'Sir?' It was all Caleb could say in his bewilderment.

'If you are coming to dinner, you will need to buy some new clothes, son. You will need a jacket and shoes also. We will see you at the Stevenson Transport building at six. Do not be late.'

With that, Benson walked off to the right of the markets

towards the inn.

Caleb looked around at the town square in front of him. He was finally able to take in his surroundings. He had been on an adventure – that was for sure. He had sailed across the Atlantic and set foot in the New World.

The markets ahead of him were busy and thriving. Musicians played next to the stalls, entertaining the passers-by, who would place a coin in a hat on the ground if the tune pleased them. The square was filled with tents and stalls, some selling clothing, some food.

He looked around and saw bakers and butchers, sugar farmers and fruit growers, tobacco stalls and pens with livestock, leather and spice stalls. Blacksmiths were sweating over their forges. Jewellers and miners were trading precious metals, while actors performed a play on a stage. Caleb looked around in wonder. He had never seen anywhere so alive, so vibrant and exciting. The different aromas of the food stalls filled his nostrils and made his mouth water.

As he headed in the direction that the scent of food was coming from, he saw a familiar arm waving in front of him. Bobby had already had the same idea and was eating a type of meat that had been skewered onto a wooden stick. Caleb walked up to the stall to meet him.

Bobby said nothing, only making noises of appreciation and pointing to a stall as he devoured the meat. He nodded, motioning to Caleb to go buy his own.

Caleb understood the message and quickly ordered the same. He paid the stall keeper a halfpenny and was handed one of the wooden sticks off the grill.

The food was hot and steaming. With the first bite, Caleb inspected the meat. It was lamb cooked over hot coals, cut up and skewered with capsicum and onion. The meat had been basted in a mint sauce and then seasoned with spices and was the most wonderful thing he had ever eaten in his life. His tastebuds danced in delight as he chewed the tender meat, and the two boys looked at each other and laughed as they ate.

'Well,' Bobby said as he finished his last mouthful, 'that won't be the last time I eat one of those.'

Caleb did not reply but nodded and smiled as he took another bite.

'Here,' Bobby continued, 'drink this to wash it down.' He held out a large mug to Caleb. 'Tell me what happened with Simon Blake and Captain Andrews. They say Simon was a secret spy for the Royal Family. They say he is like a ghost, that he can disappear at a moment's notice without a trace, and that he has killed many men. Did you speak with him?'

Caleb enjoyed the last mouthful of his meal and swallowed hard, taking the cup from Bobby and drinking. He was expecting clean water but again was surprised by the taste. It was bitter and cold. He felt the back of his throat tingle as it washed through his mouth.

'What is this?' he asked as he looked up at Bobby to see him smiling.

'That, young Caleb, is a cup of ale.' He stood back with a cheeky yet satisfied expression, as though he had just made a great discovery.

'Amazing,' Caleb replied. 'And... Wait a second. What do you mean "young Caleb"? Aren't we the same age?'

Bobby shrugged his shoulders and again both boys began to laugh, as the markets continued to bustle around them.

'Well, what was Blake like, Caleb? What did he want?'

'He invited me to dinner tonight with the captain and some of his guests.'

Bobby looked back at him, stunned. He grabbed the cup back off Caleb and looked down into its contents. 'It is true what they say about ale, then. I have only had a couple of sips and already I am hearing things.'

'He wants me to tell him about the Stevenson Estate. He may need help with some of his horses and thinks I may be of use. But I need to buy some clothes for dinner. I was given the money to buy a new shirt, jacket and some shoes.'

'Well then, we had better sort you out with the tailor.' Bobby laughed again, his head leaning back in disbelief.

They made their way through the markets, searching for one of the clothing stalls. They were masters of their own lives and could do as they pleased. They had money in their pockets and fresh air in their lungs as the New World surrounded and consumed them.

How amazing to be paid a wage and buy what I want.

Yet, in that moment, for some reason, he thought of Sasha. He understood now that he would never have been able to buy her the things she wanted. Yes, he could pay for a meal from a market stall, but he had never, till now, contemplated how rich he would have to be to afford the life she was born to, used to. He would never be a rich man and, therefore, would never have been able to keep her happy.

It was only ever a dream.

Chapter 23

Simon Blake stood facing the back wall in his office and looked up at the painting of the *Retribution*. It had been marked as an "X" on the logbooks for a purpose. Not as a surprise gift for Simon, like the young captain standing next to him had been led to believe, but because it was in some way connected to the message Jacob Stevenson had sent to him eight weeks earlier. He pulled his gaze away from the painting before the captain, standing beside him, became suspicious. The painting was a message from Jacob, and he did not want to draw more attention to it than necessary.

He sat at a leather-bound sofa in the middle of the room and poured a glass of brandy from a decanter on the coffee table in front of him. He nodded at Captain Andrews to take a seat on the opposite couch.

'So, Andrews. Come across any trouble on the voyage?'

'No trouble this voyage. We sailed south down the African Coast and took the southern Atlantic route. We sighted land six hours sail south of Rio and headed north from there. I felt it was a safer option to take a little longer and travel a little further to avoid any issues. Stevenson was adamant that this voyage had to go like clockwork.'

'Come. Let me pour you a drink.' Simon passed over a brandy and waited for the captain to take a sip before he continued. 'I fear it is becoming harder to avoid the ever-present danger in the New World, Andrews. Every week new ships enter the port to sell off the slaves stolen from their homelands. They are treated worse than beasts, you know. Have you seen what is happening lately, Andrews, to these people? Is it not bad enough that they are ripped from their land and families and then dragged across the Atlantic in a wooden hotbox, just to be sold to work lands not their own? No, it has become worse than that. The ships are only the start of their troubles. Some are used for the plantations, some for the roads and now some for sport.'

'Sport?' Andrews gazed across the coffee table at Simon, confused.

'Yes, wealthy prospectors are paying very well to hunt the African man. They are being freed only to be tracked and gunned down, Andrews.'

Simon could see that the news angered the young captain.

'And what does the British Government have to say about this atrocious behaviour? Surely if word of this reached London, there would be cause for action.'

'Cause for action, ha!' Simon huffed as he took another sip of brandy. 'They have no real power here. Not any that is enforced. Not with the Portuguese, the French, the Spanish and now the Yankees from the north. We have no more power over this land than we do over the Atlantic. Not until a law is passed and signed by all countries will we see change.'

'And who facilitates these hunts? Who is accountable for this?'

'Men who find wealth in the worst type of human suffering.' Simon reached over to refill both glasses.

'No doubt Jackson Bell would be involved somehow,' Andrews mused.

'Bell and his crew are worse still,' Simon went on. 'He and his Scarlets do it, but not for the money. Jackson Bell and his crew of evil bastards hunt and kill because they can, because they want to show the world that they cannot be governed. Bell has lost his way. He has sunk too deeply into hell and is unable to return. I doubt he would even if he could.'

Both men sat there in silence and stared out towards the Atlantic, the *Retribution* now standing tall in the fading sun.

Andrews spoke next, happy to change the subject.

'Something else of interest came on board with us this trip, an addition to the crew. The boy you met earlier – Caleb, the fourteen-year-old from the Stevenson estate. He has no family, and he has been whipped badly as per Jacob's orders. He was lucky to survive the punishment. I have seen many grown men who would not have fought through such a fever.'

'What did he do to deserve that?' Simon asked.

'He was found kissing Sasha, Jacob's daughter of the same age.' As he spoke, Andrews raised his eyebrows as if telling the story still surprised him.

'Can he sail?' Simon smiled, seemingly amused with what he had just heard.

'Not yet, but he is strong and a quick learner.'

'Can he fight?'

'He has skill with a sword and has plenty of courage and fight in him. He has balls, I'll give him that. The rest we can teach.'

'He has balls all right,' Simon exclaimed. 'Mucking around with the daughter of Jacob Stevenson – huge balls.'

They both began to laugh at the remark. Simon finished his brandy and stood up.

'Well, Captain, I will see you tonight for dinner. For now, I will need to oversee the logbooks of the *Retribution's* cargo. We will have guests tonight who have claim over the latest shipment, and I will need to see that their deliveries are in order.'

With a nod, Andrews stood up and walked out of the room. As soon as he was out of sight, Simon moved to the windows facing the town square and closed the blinds. He knew the height of the second floor would not allow anyone outside to see in, but he would not take the chance.

He pulled the note out from the inside breast pocket of his jacket and read the message for the hundredth time.

Blake, my most trusted.
I am sending you the key. We must keep it hidden from them.

THE RETRIBUTION

The answer is in the borders of the sea.
Keep it safe, my friend. Our world depends on keeping it hidden.
Keep it safe.
Jacob

Simon looked around and listened intently. He could hear the noises of the markets and the movements inside the warehouse downstairs. He was comfortable that he was alone and would not be disturbed for at least a while.

He had figured out the meaning of the message as soon as Andrews had told him that the painting of the *Retribution* was the item marked "X". He had kept his excitement contained, acting as he normally would, in order not to raise suspicion, but now that he was finally alone, he could not control his curiosity any longer. He walked over to the wall and inspected the painting.

He stared down at the message and looked back at the painting.

The answer is in the borders of the sea.

He assessed the swirls of blue, white and green, which made up the waves crashing around the vessel. He searched for letters, for a symbol, for anything that would stand out to someone who knew to look closely. Nothing.

He looked back at the message and then it came to him. The painting's frame was the border of the sea. He removed the painting from the wall and leant it against the coffee table, turning it around, looking for engravings or a message strapped to the back of the frame. Nothing.

He ran his finger along the edges of the wood and suddenly realised that the frame had been made from two pieces of wood that had been fixed together. He hurried to his desk and took out a knife from the top drawer. He looked around again to ensure that he was alone.

He hurried back to the painting and wedged the blade in between the bonded wood, forcing the steel deeper into the groove as the two pieces began to separate. He carefully repeated the process along the frame until it sprang apart. As he looked at both pieces, he saw the deception. The painting had been originally attached to the front frame, with a second frame only recently added over the first. Letters had been carved in tiny script into the top horizontal piece of the second frame. Simon quickly rehung the painting. He broke off the top piece of wood making up the second frame and went over to his desk where there was better light to inspect the writing.

As he sat down, he felt his heart pounding in his chest. He took a deep breath before inspecting the letters carefully. The message had been cut intricately into the wood by Stevenson himself. As Blake read the words, he felt a rush of adrenalin. He had thought this was a legend … a bedtime story.

Simon – Three of the Tierra Firme Fleet were not lost in the great storm. Mutiny against the crown. Ride north until you reach the great river - then turn west.

In the Brazilian mountains north of Rio. A waterfall hides the entrance.

Keep it hidden.

Keep it safe.

Simon sat back in his chair, trying to comprehend the gravity of the new information. The stories of the great Spanish Treasure Fleet were well-known around the world. Twelve ships named the Tierra Firme Fleet set out from the New World en route to Seville carrying unimaginable wealth, enough to pay the extensive Spanish debt accumulated as a result of the wars against the Ottoman Empire. The fleet had been all but destroyed by a great storm and the ships had sunk to the bottom of the Atlantic, along with the great treasure they carried. However, this message indicated otherwise and told of three ships in the fleet that did not sink. Their crews, in fact, had committed treason against the Spanish crown.

Simon tried to play out the scenario in his mind. Rio was a long way south of the Caribbean Islands and in a completely different direction to the fleet's intended destination of Seville.

The surviving rogue ships sailed south to try to outrun the storm. Or maybe they were separated from the fleet and pursued by rogue vessels. Perhaps both. They stayed close to the coastline but were battered by the storm and eventually had to make land to carry out repairs. Three ships lying helpless in the shallows, filled to the brim with Spanish bullion and Aztec gold, would not have gone unnoticed for long, and with the rest of the fleet destroyed, it would have been safe to assume that the next vessel to cross their paths would not be an ally.

Simon sat back and smiled to himself. There was a great river two days ride north of Rio, which flowed out to the sea.

They did not come ashore to mend the ships. They had just committed treason. They came ashore to scout for a place to hide. They found it in the mountains behind a waterfall. They went there and hid before anyone realised that the ships had not been sunk in the storm.

Suddenly, it dawned on him that he was now in danger. He did not know how Stevenson had come across this information, but it made sense to Simon that Stevenson would not have been the only one to have known, and a secret such as this would not stay quiet for long.

He thought about the message. He imagined Jacob himself carefully carving into the wood in his office late at night and fixing a new frame to the painting. He had taken such care to ensure the message was clear and undeniable.

A huge weight had been put on Simon's shoulders. He understood the importance of keeping this secret safe. The South and North Americas were wild, and if this secret was revealed, it would create panic and chaos.

The rich and powerful from all over the world would set sail for Brazil to take claim. Blood would flow through the streets as armies, governments and bandits all fought for the prize. Spain would try to claim it. The British, French and Dutch would try to commandeer it, and everyone else would try to steal it. It would create war, and whoever was victorious would establish themselves as a power in the New World.

He knew the only way to truly ensure the fortune be kept secret would be to find it first and either protect it or move it, so that if anyone other than Stevenson had been given the coordinates, the new location would keep it safe.

He would need help for this, and immediately thought of his men in the Royal Couriers. They were fierce and loyal, disciplined and moral men, who could move about unnoticed in plain sight and defend themselves if need be. Many had sailed over to Brazil with him and now worked unofficially in the Stevenson Transport Company. They were Simon's eyes and ears in Brazil. These were the exact men needed to safeguard such an important secret.

Chapter 24

Caleb took his seat at the dinner table, trying his best not to look out of place. He had bought a dark green second-hand coat and second-hand boots, which were slightly too big for him. He was content with his new outfit, and though he knew he still looked poor compared with the rest at the dinner party, he was pleased not to have to sit there in his usual rags.

There were twelve guests and, though he could not remember all their names, he could recall their introductions. On his right was Benson, the quartermaster of the *Retribution*. Next to him sat a man named Lupe, with his wife, whose name he had forgotten.

Lupe was Spanish-born and had started working for the Stevenson Transport Company as a translator eleven years earlier. He had worked his way up to being second-in-charge of South American Operations and Simon Blake's right hand. On the opposite side of the table sat three local plantation owners, two of whom farmed tobacco and one, sugar. Their wives wore expensive dresses and extravagant jewellery to showcase their wealth.

Simon had changed into a red velvet dinner jacket and sat at one end of the table, next to a man named Thomas, who had not said much over the course of the night except, Caleb noticed, when he occasionally spoke to Simon, quietly, so no one else around the table could hear.

The table itself was beautifully decorated and the feast in front of them was unlike anything Caleb had ever seen. There was peacock and honey-glazed ham, sweetbreads and creamy potato mash, garden salads and roasted carrot, pumpkin and spinach. Caleb made a conscious effort not to chew with his mouth open or eat too fast and copied the actions of those around him, who were far more accustomed to such evenings.

The conversation turned to politics when one of the plantation owners opposite him brought up the topic of raiding parties along the east coast of South America.

'Simon,' the plantation owner started. 'Raiding parties have intercepted three of my transport caravans this month alone. They robbed my staff and stole as much tobacco leaf as their horses could carry.'

'The same happened to two of my transports,' added one of the other men. 'Who is policing these lands? The Portuguese? The British? It is getting more and more dangerous in these parts, and something must be done.'

As each person at the table turned their gaze towards Simon, Caleb again saw how revered and respected the man sitting at the head of the table was in this part of the world. He looked at him in awe while the room fell silent, all waiting for his response.

Simon looked at the plantation owners and then up towards the back wall. Caleb followed Simon's gaze and saw that he was looking at the new painting of the *Retribution*, now hanging, superior and proud, in the candlelit room. He looked back at Simon and saw that he had not removed his gaze, as if it were only he and the painting in the room and no one else. Suddenly, Simon's gaze shifted from the painting and fixed on something else in the room. A rush of blood filled Caleb's face as he sat there in his new green jacket, unsure of how to respond. Simon was looking at him.

He stared at Caleb for a long time before he spoke.

'The British government will protect its assets in foreign lands and that includes Stevenson Transport. Beyond that, is not mine to decide.' As he spoke, he looked back towards the painting on the wall.

'However,' he continued, 'Stevenson Transport garrisons

around seventy British soldiers, who are stationed here to protect the Crown's interests along with all British nationals living in Brazil. I will be happy to scout some of these transport roads and report back to the British correspondents.'

'Well, I knew we could count on you, Simon,' the sugar plantation owner said.

'Hear, hear,' the other owners called as they raised their glasses in salute. Caleb followed suit, and everyone held their glasses high for a toast to what had seemed like a very passable solution according to everyone at the table. As Simon met everyone's glasses with his own, he stood and looked around the table.

'All our interests are intertwined. The company needs to maintain supply chains to the plantations and the plantations need safety to continue to purchase supplies. Captain Andrews and his present crew need to be able to keep delivering these shipments and so, you see, the safety of your transports is as important to me as it is to you.'

Simon's words seemed to please everyone greatly. However, Caleb sensed that there was something more important on his mind than the transport raids. He watched as Simon looked up at the painting again and then back down to the table before continuing his address.

'I will take with me a small caravan made up of a few well-trained men and scout these areas. There is no time to waste. I will be leaving tomorrow. Captain Andrews!'

'Yes, sir.'

'I will be needing young Caleb to accompany us so that he may tend to our horses.'

He once again locked eyes with Caleb. This time, his gaze was filled with purpose and determination. Caleb sensed everyone's eyes turn towards him and suddenly felt uncomfortable with the fact that he was now the centre of attention.

'That will be fine, Simon,' Andrews agreed.

'Excellent.' Simon sat back down in his chair and looked to the man on his left. 'Thomas here will show Caleb to the stables and get him ready for the expedition. Lupe will look after company operations until I return. I suspect we will be a week at least if we are to cover the needed trade routes up the coast and through the plantations.'

'Yes, sir,' replied Andrews. 'We will wait until you return. It will give the men some much needed rest, which I am sure will do them good. Would you like me to accompany you?'

'Thank you for the offer, Captain, but you stay here and watch over your men. I could, however, use someone who is willing to cook and help Caleb with the horses.'

Caleb suddenly realised an opportunity and spoke without hesitation.

'Bobby will come with us.'

The table fell silent and once again heads turned towards him. Caleb realised that his opinion was not needed, and that his captain was looking over at him with frustration and annoyance.

'Excuse me, Simon,' the captain said, still looking at Caleb. 'Bobby is our other swabbie, around the same age as Caleb. I know he can ride and is also a decent cook. The two boys work well together on the *Retribution* so, if it pleases you, they can both accompany you on your journey.'

Simon nodded at the captain and looked over to Caleb. 'Caleb and the other boy will meet with Thomas at the stables next to the warehouse tomorrow before the sun rises. We will set off at dawn.'

Chapter 25

Caleb and Bobby woke around four o'clock the next morning. Brimming with excitement for the adventure ahead, they quickly gathered their rucksacks and headed out of the inn towards the Stevenson Transport building. They made their way across the port square, now open, spacious and quiet compared to only hours earlier when it was filled with the sounds and sights of the markets.

The night was lit by an almost full moon hanging low in the sky, preparing to disappear and hand the duties of the morning over to the rising sun. As they made their way around the back of the building, they could see light coming from inside the stables. They approached the door and knocked lightly. Almost immediately, the door swung open and a familiar figure stood in front of them.

'Come in then, boys,' Thomas motioned as Caleb and Bobby made their way inside to see Simon Blake packing his horse. He turned around to greet them.

'So, this is Bobby, I assume?'

'Yes, sir,' Caleb stated. 'Bobby, this is Simon Blake.'

Bobby nodded eagerly. 'It is a pleasure to meet you, Mr Blake. Your many adventures and exploits are well-known to me and the other sailors on the *Retribution* and I would like to say thank you for allowing me to join you on this important assignment.'

Simon laughed when he saw Caleb roll his eyes. 'Good to meet you also, Bobby. You are to assist Caleb with the horses and also cook our meals. Are you able to do this, son?'

'Yes, sir,' Bobby replied confidently.

As Caleb looked around, he noticed that it was only the four of them in the stables. He found it odd that they would need both him and Bobby for a party of only four. Simon seemed to notice his curiosity and spoke again.

'I sent off two of my men in advance. They will be gathering others and meeting us further up the road. We will be riding north. Many raiding parties are making their way south on land. They will have a ship trailing them along the coast, and will anchor at specific locations. Once they raid, they head to the coastline to load up the ship before finally sailing to an outpost to trade or sell their stolen cargo. We will be riding hard and trekking through jungle, so you will need more suitable attire than what you are wearing. You will need to keep dry from the rain and have proper footwear for the jungle floor.'

Caleb could see that Simon carried two swords and a pistol on his person, with two long rifles packed on his horse. A machete and another pistol were strapped to the front of his saddle. Caleb assumed that Thomas was packed with a similar arrangement, and he realised that this expedition was not without danger.

He suddenly felt guilty that he had brought his good friend into such peril, but as he looked over at him, he saw that Bobby was grinning from ear to ear. Bobby had grown up on stories of the Royal Couriers and Simon Blake, and now he was standing in the presence of the legend himself, about to embark on an important assignment – it would be a story he would be able to retell on the *Retribution* for years to come. Caleb felt his guilt wash away and be replaced by the thrill of what was happening around him.

'Come with me,' Thomas said quietly as he walked through the stables. The two boys followed him into the storage room, which also served as an armoury. Inside, there was riding equipment, weaponry and everything needed to pack a horse and live in a mobile camp.

'You will need proper equipment for the next week,' Thomas

began. 'Take what you need. I would recommend a spare set of clothes to keep dry, leather boots, one of these riding cloaks and a hat. The climate here is tropical but wearing a coat to keep the rain out can be the difference between living and dying in these parts. Consider it payment for the week's work.'

'Thank you, sir,' Bobby exclaimed. 'Do you mind my asking, Mr Thomas, sir, were you also part of the Royal Couriers with Mr Blake?'

'I was,' Thomas replied. 'Simon was my captain. Many of us live here in South America now. We are still sought after by some in Europe for the information we once carried. It is ironic that we are actually safer in these wild lands than back in our own country. So, in saying that, the next things to pack are a sword, a pistol and a rifle each. This is not up for discussion. Lastly, you will have two packhorses to load. I suggest a shovel, tenting equipment and, of course, what you will need for cooking. We leave in twenty minutes. Make haste and have your horses packed ready to go.'

Thomas left the room and the boys began to work. First, they changed into new clothes and packed a spare set of pants and shirt into their saddle packs. They each picked out a pair of leather boots, which covered their legs from just below the knee, a wide-brimmed hat and one of the long, oiled coats to protect them from the rain. Next, they armed themselves with a sword, rifle, pistol, shot and gunpowder. Caleb also took a machete, rope and a large knife. They each picked up a rolled sleeping mat and blanket and packed their horses with their new gear.

Once their mounts were ready to ride, they worked quickly, sorting out the packhorses. Pots and cutlery were packed, followed by shovels, hammers, winches and rope, fire torches, camp mats and mosquito nets. Next, they went to the pantry and loaded baskets with vegetables, seasoning and flour, sugar and spices and salted meats. Finally, they packed tobacco and bottles of brandy.

Caleb mounted his horse. It was a young stallion and he

had been able to tell, just by looking, that the horse had been broken-in well and that he was fast, strong and accustomed to being handled. As he kicked his heels, he assessed the stallion's gait. Each step was well-balanced and surefooted as they passed through the door of the stable and out into dim light. Thomas rode in the front of the line, with Simon behind him. Caleb rode next with one of the packhorses, and Bobby, with the other packhorse, rode last.

They travelled down the main street through the city, before turning right and heading north. Thomas set the pace and the group sped to a gallop as soon as they had reached the service road.

They were the only ones on the road, and Caleb guessed that the time would have been just before five o'clock in the morning. The moon had dropped out of sight, the morning light began to show them the coast road in front, and they were able to keep a steady pace for the next two hours.

Caleb was impressed with the way his horse kept his form and rhythm at the pace they were riding. He was also impressed that Bobby had kept pace and was clearly a very competent rider.

They had taken the service roads, which had been built to stretch all the way up the coast, passing through small villages and the slave ports dotted along the ocean highway.

It was an overcast morning with storm clouds looming behind them. Caleb was happy that he had been given his new clothing and boots to keep him dry when it rained. As they galloped onwards, they rode through another village, passing locals who were attending to their morning chores.

On the road ahead, near the end of the village, Caleb saw six men on horseback. They were lined up, three on each side of the road, and he suddenly felt nervous. Were these the raiders he had been told of? As his party rode closer, he noticed the men were dressed in a similar fashion to him, and he realised that they were the remainder of Simon Blake's scouting party and surely were all ex-Royal Couriers like Thomas and Simon.

They did not slow down to make introductions but, instead, charged through the gauntlet, the strangers kicking their horses and riding up behind to join the column. Their small party of four had now become ten, and almost as soon as they joined the ride, Thomas pulled his horse left, down a less-trodden path, leading them off the main road, heading west and into the hinterland.

They rode on a narrow track, only wide enough for single file, for what seemed like half a day. The jungle closed in around them, and each time it appeared that they had reached a clearing, it would close in on them again. However, Thomas rode as if he had been there before, as if he knew where he was leading the party.

Caleb had the feeling that he and Bobby were the only riders who had not yet ridden these trails. The tracks were so well hidden from the service roads yet led them in the same direction, and Caleb wondered if they had been purposely created by Simon and his men to enable them to travel quickly and undetected parallel to the highway. He felt as if he could close his eyes and release the reins and his horse would know exactly where to take him, though he did not dare miss seeing a moment of the expedition. He felt alive and he was going to soak up every bit of excitement the day would bring.

They had ridden for most of the day before Thomas eventually slowed the party to a walk. They came to a small clearing and stopped. Caleb had never ridden for so long before, and he welcomed the chance to stretch his aching legs. He looked around the clearing to see a fire pit and wooden benches and heard the sound of running water close by. This was a purpose-built camp and a designated checkpoint for the Couriers. He led the horses to the stream, two at a time, while Bobby built a fire and started preparing a stew.

South America was certainly a beautiful place. Caleb had been impressed by the sweeping jungles through which they had ridden earlier that morning – lush, green and thick. It was an ideal place to hide and prey on those travelling along the transport roads. A raiding party could appear from anywhere and ambush unarmed transport caravans, take all they could carry, and disappear back into the jungle.

Dusk had overtaken the day by the time Caleb finished tending to the horses. He sat at one of the benches around the fire, and Bobby handed him a bowl of stew. It was a fine tasting meal and welcome to an empty stomach. The others obviously agreed as they praised Bobby, some of the men licking their plates clean as a sign of appreciation.

That night they set camp beneath the stars. Thomas sat at the fire and took first watch with Caleb and Bobby. He told them of the days when he had been a Royal Courier and the many missions with which he had been charged. The two boys hung on every word and Caleb imagined himself as a secret rider who was entrusted with crucial documents. As Thomas finished his stories, silence fell over the three of them and the noises and sounds of the jungle filled the air around them.

Caleb knew he was in a dangerous part of the world, yet he was surprised at how calm he felt. He was not afraid and felt strangely at ease in the wild. Two men relieved them of their watch. Caleb and Bobby rolled out their sleeping mats and looked up at the stars before drifting off into a deep sleep.

Chapter 26

Caleb felt a strong arm shake him awake.

'Shhh. Do not make a sound,' the voice whispered. It was Thomas who had woken him. Caleb quickly familiarised himself with his surroundings. It was still dark, yet he could see the silhouettes of the other men moving quietly around the camp.

'Get your things together, Caleb. Stay silent and do it quickly.'

Caleb jumped to attention, rolled up his sleeping mat and repacked his horse. He looked over to Bobby, who had also been woken and given the same instructions. He looked around to see the other men checking their weapons and unsheathing their swords with focus and intent. He realised that he had not been woken to help make the camp breakfast.

Simon walked over to him and motioned to Bobby to join him. He was heavily armed, with all his weapons now on his person. His two long rifles, which had been strapped to his saddle, were now slung over his shoulders.

'Mr Blake, sir, is everything all right?' Bobby whispered nervously as he looked up at Simon.

'Everything will be fine, boys,' Simon said in a quiet and calm voice. 'But you must do exactly as I say, now. Do you understand?'

Both boys nodded in agreement.

'There is a camp about twenty minutes trek north of us. It is a large party of around twenty men. They are raiders.' The words echoed through Caleb's ears and he felt the scars across his back start to tingle.

'We cannot go around them,' Simon continued.

'And nor should we,' Thomas said quietly as he made his way over to them. Caleb and Bobby looked back at Simon as he smiled sympathetically and nodded in agreement.

'Sometimes you have to go through and not around, boys. Sometimes it is up to you to do what is needed.' As Simon spoke, he looked up at the sky, which had started to show the beginnings of dawn.

'Boys,' he continued, 'the horses are too noisy to take with us. I need you both to walk with us and carry extra rifles, but you must stay silent. Concentrate on each step. Listen to the bottom of your feet as if each step was a story told. If you feel as though the ground is going to give or a stick will crack underneath your foot, raise it back up and balance on your other leg. Choose another place to step and start again. This is how you stay silent, by becoming aware of your surroundings and staying focused.'

Both boys nodded silently again as Simon continued. 'Thomas will signal to you when we are close. When he does, you crouch down and do not move. You will be able to see what happens, but you will not participate. Is that understood?'

'Yes, sir.' Bobby answered first, with Caleb repeating the same words straight after.

'If we go down, if we are killed, you are to run back here and ride straight to Captain Andrews. You do not stop until you reach him. You tell him that I have fallen and that he must get this message to Jacob Stevenson as a matter of urgency. You tell him that I have fallen in my search. He will know what that means. Is that understood?'

Both boys nodded yet again. 'Yes, sir, Mr Blake,' they added to show him they were clear.

'Good,' Simon said as he looked up at the sky for the second time. 'Grab your gear and stay close to Thomas. It is time to go.'

Caleb took the sword and musket from his saddle. He then grabbed his long rifle and strapped it over his shoulder. He took his bag of shot and gunpowder and placed them in the pouch attached to his sword belt. He noticed that the other men were not wearing their long coats and so he also left his rolled up on his saddle.

Smart, he thought. The coat could brush up against leaves or shrubs and create noise. It was also lighter and easier to move without it and, if needed, he had better access to his sword without the risk of it getting caught. He collected three extra rifles and slung them over his shoulders.

This time it was Simon who led the party, with Thomas, Caleb and Bobby taking up the rear. As they left, Caleb tried to do what Simon had told them: concentrate on each step as if it were its own story, make no sound by feeling the ground underneath and take each step lightly before applying pressure.

They had moved off the path and into the jungle, which gave them complete cover. The ground, however, was hard to navigate. His footfall was uneven at first and, though he tried to stay quiet, he felt like the stork birds that used to congregate around the lakes on the Stevenson estate. They had never really looked as if they knew where to step, Caleb thought, and he felt as though he would have looked very much like one at that moment. He watched Thomas, who outweighed him, walk across the jungle floor effortlessly and soundlessly. Then he saw Bobby, another stork bird in the party.

After about ten minutes, Caleb saw Simon raise his left hand and point with his right. As he did, the men in the middle of the party broke single file and fanned out into the jungle, leaving a space between each man.

They were at the raiders' camp. Simon raised his hand and they all crouched down on one knee. They were still in the deep cover of the jungle, but the first light of the dawn now made it easy to see what was ahead of them in the clearing. Thomas turned back to him and Bobby and gave them the signal to stay hidden. He darted up to Simon without making a noise.

Caleb looked through the thick leaves and into the camp,

which was far more established than the one they had made that night. There were erect tents and a number of smouldering fires.

Caleb could smell a large pot of stew, which had been left to warm for the morning breakfast and, as its aroma wafted through the jungle, he realised that Simon had led them east off the path so that they were now downwind from the camp and undetectable to those ahead of them. He counted twelve men sleeping on the ground near the fire and six large tents throughout the camp.

Ahead of him, Simon signalled again, and instantly the men on his left and right started to creep off and surround the camp. Only a minute had passed before Caleb saw three men come out of their tents and head towards the largest of the fires, which was keeping the stew warm. The men had their backs to them as they sat down on a large log.

No! We are too late.

Just when Caleb thought that the Couriers had lost the element of surprise, Simon stood up and darted out of the jungle and into the clearing. Thomas followed suit and the two men ran quickly and quietly, passing the tent from which the raiders had emerged.

The three outlaws, with their backs turned, had not heard them approach and yawned and stretched in the early morning light. Before they knew what was about to happen to them, both Simon and Thomas pulled knives from their belts and fell upon them.

Simon took the two on the right with ease. He cut the throat of the man in the middle, swiftly running his arm from left to right. His arm moved past the man's throat and out to the right, towards the other sitting next to him. He flipped the knife in his hand, allowing the blade to shift and now become a spear, pointing from the back of his hand as it plunged into the throat of the second man. As the second man's head dropped, Caleb saw the third man drop at the same time as Thomas lifted his knife backwards and into the air. All three fell to the ground with barely a sound.

Caleb's gaze moved to the left of the camp, where another of their party had now sprinted out of the jungle to join the fight. Another ran from the other side of the camp and two more from the northern perimeter. They had surrounded the raiders and were now on a rampage. Swords were drawn, and raiders were falling, two and three at a time. The noise woke the others, who scrambled desperately for their weapons.

There was no longer any need for stealth. Simon and his men reached for their muskets and aimed at their prey. The morning air was suddenly filled with the sound of gunfire and screams as shots tore into flesh. While the raiders scrambled to resist, the Royal Couriers worked their way through the camp with unmerciful precision.

Within moments, it was silent again. Out of the smoke, Caleb saw Simon and Thomas walking towards where he and Bobby were crouching. The remaining Couriers walked around checking the camp. As he and Bobby stood up and made their way into the clearing, they heard a yell.

'Straggler to the east!' one of the Couriers called out as he pointed to a man riding out of the camp towards the coast.

'Take him!' yelled Simon.

'I'm unloaded,' yelled the pointing Courier.

'Somebody take him down. He cannot make the coast,' Simon ordered.

'I am out,' another yelled.

'As am I,' called another.

The rider galloped down a track that led south-east toward the coast. The men had fired their long rifles and a few tried firing with their muskets, but none came close to the target. They had no horses with them to make chase and, as the rider made his way through the clearing past Caleb and Bobby, Caleb saw his chance to help.

He raised his rifle, keeping the barrel sight aimed in front of the moving rider. He thought back to when he had shot pheasants on the estate for the Stevensons and their guests. But this was not a bird, this was a man, and he had never shot a man before. He did not know if this man deserved to die, but, in that moment, Simon was his commander and had ordered that the man be stopped. He, Caleb, was the only one with a chance of making that happen.

He judged the rider's distance. He sighted his rifle carefully and breathed out slowly. He waited calmly until, with a clear line of sight, he squeezed gently on the trigger.

The rider fell from his horse and hit the ground with a thud, rolling for a moment until coming to a complete stop. He lay there, motionless, and Caleb knew that he was dead. He had aimed for the rider's head and he had hit his target.

'Caleb,' Bobby whispered, 'you killed him.'

He turned to Bobby and saw the look on his face. It was not one of excitement, nor of disappointment, but one of disbelief. Caleb looked up to see the rest of the men staring back at him. He threw his rifle over his shoulder and walked past Bobby.

'He was getting away,' he uttered as he walked ahead of his friend and into the clearing. As he approached Simon and Thomas, he prepared himself for harsh words.

'Remember when I told you that you were not to get involved, no matter what?' Simon said as Caleb stopped in front of him. 'I don't like being disobeyed, but I am glad you did.' With that, Simon turned around and headed back towards the camp with the others.

Thomas laughed as he followed. 'The boy is a crack shot. Who would have thought?'

He laughed again.

Caleb followed them into the camp, relieved that Simon was not going to punish him. He did not know yet how he felt about what he had just done. He could not stop replaying the image of the rider falling off his horse and lying motionless on the jungle floor with his bullet in his head.

As he and Bobby walked further into the camp, they came

across a gruesome sight. A black slave girl was tied to a tree, naked and beaten badly. Beside her, another slave, a man, had been decapitated. The poor girl had been tied next to the bloodied body of a companion for what looked like days.

One of the men took out his knife and cut through the rope that bound her hands. She winced in pain as her arms were freed. 'The bastards have broken her ribs,' the man who cut her loose grunted angrily as he wrapped a blanket around her. He looked over at the decapitated male next to her. 'God knows, she would have met the same fate as soon as they had finished having their fun with her.'

Caleb looked at the young woman who had now curled into a ball, terrified, and wrapped in the blanket. He walked over to the fire and counted five bodies lying dead on the ground. He filled a bowl of warm stew and walked back towards her. He knelt down near her, but not so close as to frighten her any more than she already was.

He held the bowl out towards her and gave a foolish smile. She looked at him a moment, then at the other men around her and curled herself up tighter inside the blanket, covering her face.

'Leave it on the ground next to her, Caleb,' Thomas said quietly. 'Go and find her something to wear. She will eat when we leave her alone.'

'I will take care of the clothing,' Bobby announced and walked into one of the tents.

Caleb turned away from the woman and looked over the camp. At least twenty men had been killed and yet all of their party had survived, and without injury it seemed. They had held the advantage of surprise, it was true, but it was evident that the Royal Couriers were warriors in their own right.

'Caleb.' He turned to the voice of Simon Blake. 'That was the first man you have killed?'

Caleb never thought he would be asked such a question, as it finally dawned on him what he had just done.

'Yes, sir, Mr Blake. I am sorry that I disobeyed your orders, but I just thought I could be of help, sir.'

'Indeed, you did help and I feel at a price that you can bear better than most. It is no small thing to kill a man.'

Caleb looked back at the young woman who no doubt had been brutalised by the very man he had shot. He had no guilt in his mind and was happy such a monster was now dead.

'Yes, sir. I have already made my peace with it.'

Simon looked at the rest of the men and then back at Caleb a moment, as if he were looking at something he was contemplating buying from a store.

'All right, boy,' he finally continued. 'Go with Thomas and the others and fetch the horses and the rest of the gear back at camp. Be quick. We do not want to hang around here any longer than we need to.'

Caleb nodded and followed Thomas and three of the other men. He moved off along the path towards the camp they had left silently, earlier that morning. As he ran with his rifle around his shoulder and his sword on his hip, he felt more alive than he had ever felt before.

He could not feel the air in his lungs as he did not need air to run. He moved quickly and silently, as the other men did. He had found his rhythm and moved through the jungle with silence and ease. He was alert and more aware of his surroundings than he had ever thought possible.

I am no longer a boy. If only Jacob Stevenson could see me now.

Chapter 27

The Couriers had not come across another raiding party for two days. They had passed camps that had been used only days before, but the occupants had left well before Simon's men had arrived. Each time a new camp was discovered, Caleb's excitement rose and his senses heightened. He had crossed a line only days earlier when he had killed his first man. It had changed him in a way he had not expected.

He had been unusually calm when faced with the violence and the pressure of marksmanship at a time of desperate need. He had relished it. He caught himself smiling as he remembered every moment of the shot.

'What is so amusing, Caleb?' Bobby repeatedly asked.

'Nothing,' Celeb eventually replied, hiding the truth. 'I just never thought I would be on such a great adventure.'

Bobby smiled back in agreement and immediately sat upright in his saddle with one hand on his hip and his chin raised high in the air as if he were the King of England himself riding through the jungle, causing them both to laugh quietly as they rode along.

It was mid-afternoon on the third day when they came across a large river and turned west into the mountains. The terrain was rugged and uneven, with ravines and mountains on either side of the horse trail, and there were no longer signs of farming or civilization. They were in lost country, which was as hidden as it was vast. They descended to a clearing beside a stream and Simon halted the party. He gave the order to make camp, and Bobby and Caleb went about their usual work, making a fire and tending to the horses.

The sight of storm clouds above the mountains gave them reason to build a shelter out of tree branches and dried-out reeds from the river. They ate a watery potato stew with dried salted beef and got ready for the afternoon ride.

'No horses,' Simon ordered. 'Where we are going, they will slow us down. A few of you will stay here at the camp and await our return. Bobby, make sure the fire stays burning.'

Bobby nodded, looking relieved that he did not have to trek into the mountains surrounding them.

'Yes, Mr Blake, sir.'

Two of the Couriers stayed at the camp with Bobby, while the others continued on foot along the river and into the mountains. They moved through the jungle, creating their own path and always keeping the sound of water close by. They trekked for hours until the light quickly faded in the shadows of the peaks. They made a fire and slept on the ground, with the jungle noises all around.

At first light, they set off again. After two hours of trekking, they heard it – the sound of distant thunder, endless and constant. Simon quickened the pace as they climbed further into a gorge. The walls of the jungle were now replaced with large boulders and cliff faces as they made their way through a narrow, rocky passageway.

It wound and turned, and was only wide enough for two men to walk beside each other. Simon felt uneasy.

A perfect place for an ambush. If there were men on the cliffs above us, we would be slaughtered in seconds, without any chance of defence.

The climbing path levelled out as it came to another small clearing, and as they walked into the open space, they were met with a magnificent sight.

Ahead of them was a great mountain with a lush valley at its base. The thunderous noise was a huge waterfall, which tumbled out of the side of the cliff face into a crystal blue lagoon below them.

Mist rose, filling the void and giving view to rainbow-coloured flickers of light, which danced along the face of the cliff. They stood there and stared in awe. No man could ever build a place as mysterious and beautiful as this, Simon thought. Ethereal and hidden and, if he was right about what was behind the wall of water, the most dangerous place in the world – a sacred Garden of Eden, which would cause men to slaughter each other in the thousands should its secret be discovered. Simon stood there a moment and calculated the odds of this being the place he was looking for. Could this be where the treasure had been hidden?

It was a long way south from the trade winds of the Caribbean. There were many waterfalls in Brazil and many mountains to search further north, so why would they have come this far south? Simon tested the theory in his head. They were outrunning a storm, he speculated, and the ships would have been damaged. The bounty hunters would have forced them to continue sailing south. They tried to sail close to Rio, a safe port where they could have repaired the ships, but did not make it that far. They came across the mouth of a river and scouted for a place until they found this, hidden and easily defended with its narrow passages and its high cliffs. The river would have allowed them to raft the bullion almost the entire way to the waterfall.

This has to be it.

Simon gestured for the small party to continue. They made their way down a track and, as they did, he got the feeling that it had not been carved out by animals. It had more purpose and direction. It was leading them towards the waterfall.

Men had created this path.

His heart rate quickened.

At the edge of the waterfall, while the others stood fast, Simon and Thomas lit fire sticks and continued down the path that would lead them behind it.

Caleb watched the glow of the fire sticks moving behind the wall of water until the two men disappeared into the darkness.

It was damp and cool behind the waterfall. Simon turned back to Thomas and they both drew their muskets. There was a past there, and Simon could feel it. Other men had been there before, and he prayed it had been the Spanish defectors.

The narrow path led them into a small cavern in the mountain. There were no more paths and Simon's heart sank when he saw that they had met a dead end. He was so sure that this had been it. How could it not be? It made sense that this was the location. He looked over at Thomas, who returned the look of disappointment with his own.

'There are many waterfalls, Simon. Would they have sailed this far south to begin with?'

'They would if they were trying to hide it close enough to Rio. The message from Jacob was clear. They had to have come this far south.'

Thomas nodded as he heard the words. It did make sense, and the message Simon had been sent would back the theory.

'There is nothing here, Simon. There may be another way on the other side of the mountain.'

Simon stared at the back wall of the cave, ignoring what he had just heard. The sound of the water crashing into the lagoon below them brought back the words in Stevenson's message.

In the Brazilian mountains north of Rio, a waterfall hides the entrance. Keep it hidden. Keep it safe.

He moved towards the back of the cave. As he got closer, he held up his light against the wall and realised that a section of it had a distinctive appearance. It was a lighter shade and had a different texture from the rest of the cave. This wall did not belong there. It had been built by someone to hide what was behind. He ran his hand along the wall as he traced over it. As he came to the edge, he could see that it was protruding from the original cave wall.

Between the handmade barrier and the natural back wall was a space. He had not seen it when they had first entered the cave. From their angle, it had appeared to be a single flat wall rather than two walls with a space between them. Simon looked back at Thomas, who nodded eagerly. They moved through the space and into a narrow tunnel. Simon raised his light once again and stopped, looking straight ahead. He stood like a statue, motionless and stiff.

Thomas entered the tunnel and saw it as well. The men stood by each other without saying a word, their gaze fixed on what was at the end of the tunnel.

Their lights showed the passageway about ten feet ahead, and at the end of it was a large wooden door. When they opened the door, they expected to see chests of gold and silver, but what they discovered turned out to be much more than that.

Afterwards, when he had returned to Rio, he was besieged by visions of what he and Thomas had seen when they had opened that door. He had been able to think of little else. The world had now changed and had become far more dangerous and susceptible to corruption.

Chapter 28

It was two days since the Couriers had made their way back into Rio, and the *Retribution* had left Rio for London that morning. Caleb knelt on the quarterdeck, scrubbing intently, excited to be sailing the seas once again. The day was humid and overcast and there had been several showers already that morning.

He looked back at the tall peaks of the Brazilian mountains and imagined the raiders lying dead in the mud somewhere in the distance, picked apart by crows. He derived a sense of pride from knowing that he had played his part in leaving the land a little safer. He was ready to start another adventure, to learn his seamanship on the Atlantic. His wounds were healed, and he could now work at full pace to earn his living.

The ship was a hive of activity and excitement. The decks were full of sailors, cheerfully singing after their layover in Rio. Their bellies and beds had been filled to the brim and they were all ready to refill their pockets.

It was only an hour after they had left the bay when they heard the call from the crow's nest.

'Ship ahoy, port side!'

'Not a surprise to see ships coming in this close to port,' Bobby said as Caleb walked down to join him on the main deck. 'But we all have a look to see what colours they are flying. Rio is becoming one of the busiest harbours in the world and is attracting ships from all countries. It is a rule Captain Andrews has on the *Retribution*.'

'Two ships passing, port and starboard!' The call came from the crow's nest again. Suddenly, Caleb felt the mood on the *Retribution* change as Captain Andrews called out the next orders.

'All men to their stations and make ready!' The actions on the deck changed from cleaning and singing to a war footing as men prepared the *Retribution* for battle.

Caleb followed the drill, emptied his soapy buckets down the scuppers and made his way to his quarters. He and Bobby unrolled their new rucksacks and armed themselves in the same way as they had when there were riding with the Couriers only days before. They made their way back to the main deck, where they joined the rest of the crew and waited in anticipation. As the two ships came closer, they heard the call from the crow's nest again.

'White flags, Captain. Both ships flying white flags for a peaceful pass.'

Sighs of relief could be heard as the crew watched the two ships on either side of their flanks begin to pass. Caleb watched as the first ship came along the *Retribution's* port side, relaxing when he saw the small crew wave towards them in recognition. He heard them singing cheerfully as they worked on the ratlines and rigging.

Over on the starboard side, he saw that the second ship was doing the same. Crew members from each ship exchanged pleasantries and the two smaller vessels cruised past the *Retribution*.

'Starboard ship turning about, Captain! She's raised another flag.'

There was a pause from the nest as the *Retribution* fell silent.

'Are her guns out?' Captain Andrews yelled up. There was no reply from the nest.

'Answer me, damn you!' Andrews yelled up at them.

'They have raised another flag, sir.' There was another pause from the man in the nest. His next words were filled with fear and terror. 'It is the flag of the *Grey Cloud*. It is Jackson Bell!'

Captain Andrews handed over the wheel to Benson and ran up to the poop. As he ran, they heard it. The sound of screaming animals from the ship that had manoeuvred behind them. The screaming sent shivers down Caleb's spine, but instead of his muscles seizing and feeling like he wanted to hide, he felt alert and his senses heighten. He looked over at Bobby, who had a look of horror and shock on his face.

'We'll stick together, no matter what, and watch each other's back. All right, Bobby?' Bobby nodded blankly, and Caleb could tell that his friend was not at all ready for battle.

Captain Andrews had not quite made it to the poop deck when the *Grey Cloud* fired into the stern of the *Retribution*. A shockwave passed through the hull below them and the crew staggered to find something to hold onto.

'Hard to starboard!' Andrews yelled. Benson echoed the order but it was too late. The *Retribution's* rudder had been dismantled and they lay helpless in the water with no way to steer the ship, floating aimlessly like a wounded whale being circled by two hungry sharks.

Another thunderous roar of cannon fire erupted from the second ship, which had positioned itself on an angle, with its guns pointed at the corner of the *Retribution's* stern. Again, the thud of the impact rocked the ship, and this time they could feel the balls rocket through the decks below them. Screams came from below the main deck of the *Retribution*, as men were cut in half by shot and splintered beams.

'Fire the bow cannons. All arms to the poop!' yelled Andrews. The crew of the *Retribution* ran up the stairs to the top of the bow and began to fire their rifles.

Another billow of smoke burst from the *Grey Cloud* and the shot crashed into the back windows of the main cabin, tearing its way through the officers' quarters and out onto the quarterdeck. The damage was severe, yet the *Retribution* was mighty and still stood proud.

THE RETRIBUTION

The *Grey* manoeuvred closer to the bow of the *Retribution*, now within range of the rifles. Its stern slid up along the *Retribution's* port side and grappling hooks flew over the gunwales and clawed their way into the timber of the sides of the poop and quarterdecks. Caleb could hear the harrowing war cries being chanted from the circling ships.

'Cut the lines!' Benson ordered, but the cover fire from the *Grey Cloud* was fierce and shot down those who tried to set the *Retribution* free. The *Retribution* and the *Grey Cloud* were now grappled together as the third ship circled around the *Retribution's* starboard side and fired her large cannon towards the main deck. A whistling noise flew past Caleb's ears as the balls hit the mainmast. Large splinters of wood flew into the overcast sky as the base of the mainmast was shattered, killing many of the crew. Black smoke billowed out from the hull of the *Retribution,* and the smell of burning rope and oil filled Caleb's lungs.

'Ready arms and draw swords, men!' Andrews called the order as he lined the crew into their stations. 'Cut them down as they jump the gunwales and send these bastards to the deep.'

A cheer from the crew of the *Retribution* rose through the smoke, and the sound of swords being released from their sheaths echoed across the decks.

Another round of cannon fire hit the *Retribution's* starboard flank and smashed into her hull. The ship rocked violently and sent the crew rolling along the decks. All of a sudden, men from the attached *Grey Cloud* spilled over the portside rails.

Caleb saw the first of them. He was a large, shirtless man with scars that covered his face and shoulders. He screamed as his feet hit the main deck. A wave of Scarlets followed the first warrior as they collided with the *Retribution's* crew. Caleb ran with Bobby towards the forecastle as the sound of swords clashing and men dying filled the ship. The second ship hooked itself onto the starboard side of Stevenson's flagship and the *Retribution* was now surrounded. Attackers spilled onto her decks from either side as the attack came from both flanks.

'We are done for, Caleb!' Bobby cried. 'There are so many of them and so many of ours have been killed by their cannons. They are going to kill us all!'

Caleb saw the horror on his friend's face. Bobby was a sailor and not a soldier. He was never intended for this.

'Let's move to the forecastle deck and use those barrels as cover. I will fire, and you reload. All right, Bobby?' There was no response as Bobby sat frozen, watching his crew die on the deck of the greatest merchant vessel afloat.

'Bobby, damn it! Listen or we will die! Can you reload fast enough for me to fire?' This time, Caleb received a nod and they made their way up to the foremast.

'I will shoot, and you reload… Make it quick!' They had three rifles with them. Caleb crouched behind the barrels at the foremast and monitored the battle happening in front of him. There were so many choices. He aimed at the attackers closest to them, who were fighting on the main deck. He fired and hit his target – a shot to the side of the temple. A red mist sprayed out from the other side of the Scarlet's head and white bone fragments followed as the man hit the deck, freeing his opponent to now help a *Luchen* companion.

Bobby held up the second rifle and took hold of Caleb's, busily reloading the long barrel. Caleb aimed and fired again. Another headshot. Then he was handed the third rifle and hit yet another man point-blank in the head.

Five, seven, ten men went down before they were noticed. Three men charged their way up the stairs to the forecastle. Caleb stood and fired his rifle at the first man. The bullet hit him in the chest and forced him back into the other two. Caleb unsheathed his sword and used the first man as a shield as he felt his blade crunch through the breastplate of the second attacker. All three fell back down the stairs onto the main deck. Caleb dropped his bloodstained cutlass and picked up one of the loaded rifles, which he used to dispatch the third attacker.

He looked around at the battle in front of him. They were losing the ship. So many of the *Retribution's* crew were falling to the deck as they held their pierced stomachs and screamed in pain, gasping their final breaths as they were killed where they lay.

Benson, the quartermaster, knelt on the quarterdeck against the ship's wheel, trying in vain to pull out the sword that had been lodged in his stomach. The shirtless, scarred warrior crouched behind him and ran a knife across his throat and Benson fell to the floor in a bleeding lump.

Andrews fought with five other soldiers on the poop, holding fast and slaying those who made their way up the stairs. Caleb looked around, not knowing where to fight. He felt helpless and wanted desperately to get to his captain, but he could not leave Bobby, who was still crouched behind the barrels at the base of the foremast.

The fight on the main deck was all but lost when a man climbed over the rails of the *Retribution*. A cheer went up amongst the attackers as the huge man drew his sword. He held it up, pointing towards Captain Andrews and screamed up at the sky. Caleb stood frozen on the foredeck, hopeless, as the fight quietened and the attackers halted and stood fast for a moment.

'The *Retribution* is done for, Andrews!' the large man called out, still pointing his sword at Caleb's captain. 'You have the power to save what remains of your men. What say you?'

Andrews stood proud, his face, sword and shirt soaked dark red with the blood of weaker men.

'You will let them live, Bell?'

Caleb looked away from his captain and stared down at the man who had turned out to be Jackson Bell, the tyrant of so many stories he had heard the sailors of the *Retribution* tell at night. The warlord of the Scarlets was on board the *Retribution* and he looked as fierce and as violent as Caleb had imagined he would.

'I am a fair man, Andrews. I will give you that power.' The

155

ship was silent but for the gushing of water flowing into her hull. The *Retribution* was sinking beneath them. 'I will give you the chance to save your men, but if you refuse me, I will cut the life out of all you dogs and boil your livers for my lunch.'

Andrews looked around at the men he had left. Two dozen at the most, Caleb thought.

'What is it you want, Bell?'

'I want a word for a start, Captain.' He looked around the slowly sinking *Luchen*. 'Take what you can. Strip the main cabin and load up the *Grey*. Take them to the brig.'

They were rounded up and loaded onto the *Grey Cloud*. They were taken below to the bottom deck and crowded into iron cages. Caleb counted seventeen of them in total who were now the prisoners of Jackson Bell.

Chapter 29

Jackson Bell stood on the main deck of the *Grey Cloud*, smiling at the slowly sinking *Luchen*. Adder had reported thirty-eight dead amongst the crew of the *Grey Cloud* and his ship, the *Revolt*. It was a hefty price to pay to lose so many loyal men, but Jackson was as resolute and defiant as ever.

He had taken down the ship that could not be defeated and was about to blow her out of the water forever. He looked over at Andrews who stood there, bloodied and defeated. He had counted seventeen prisoners, including the captain, now under his control. He knew, however, he would have to cut that number down severely before the rest would completely surrender. The crew of the *Retribution* was loyal and courageous, and they would have to be broken before they became loyal to the *Grey*.

'Fire!' he commanded, and the belly of the *Grey Cloud* erupted with a burst of white smoke. The cannon balls hit hard into the port side of the sinking *Luchen*, opening her up and letting the Atlantic pour in and flood her hull. The great ship listed and creaked as her middle deck gave way to the weight of the water and began to split. The bow disappeared under the water and her heavy rear end dragged the rest of her down.

As the parted waters swirled back above the sunken ship, Jackson looked over at Andrews and basked in the despair in his eyes. The sinking of the *Retribution* was more than that of wood and iron. It was a message to Jacob Stevenson and the rest of the aristocratic devils that his revolution had begun, that the

Atlantic was ripe for the taking and those who sailed on it would no longer be controlled.

'Bring him into my quarters,' he ordered. Adder shoved Andrews forward with a violent push, knocking the captain face down on the deck. With his hands bound, he was unable to break his fall and blood began to stream down his cheek and from his mouth. The men around him laughed and spat as Adder dragged him away and roughly sat him in front of the captain's desk in the main cabin. It was as Andrews had imagined: dark, rugged, crude and uncared for.

A fitting kennel for a bloodhound.

Jackson sat at the table, with his back towards the stern windows. The light shone from behind him, masking the details of his features and showing only the silhouette of his large frame. The demon shadow spoke.

'You asked me what I want.' His voice was calm, yet had an eerie presence of desire. 'I want to be free, Andrews. I want to be free of the shackles you and your masters have chained us with for too long.'

Andrews looked at the shadow with defiance, as he knew in his heart that he would not live through the day. There was no longer any reason for fear, nor hope of survival.

'From what I hear, you do as you please, Jackson. Is that not freedom?'

'Not if you are outlawed for it. Not if you are unable to walk the streets of London without being sent to the gallows. What freedom is there in that?'

'You have made your choices. You knew it could only lead to this. You chose to ignore the laws that keep the world in order.'

'And whose order is that?' The shadow's voice was now sharp and violent. 'You speak of a world that has treated me as a dog. What is a soldier's life but for fighting to enrich the selfish cowards who are too pathetic to fight for themselves? At least I fight for my own station in this life. I fight for those who have been crushed so far underneath the boots of the wealthy. I will be their saviour, and show them a world in which they can feel like real men.'

Andrews chuckled as he choked on the blood streaming down his throat.

'You believe you fight for the weak? Interesting point of view, Bell, coming from a slaver.'

'Mockery will not serve you well in your position,' the shadow snorted.

'You only fight for yourself, Jackson. You are as greedy as you are foul … and your end is coming soon.'

Tension rose in the cabin. Adder clenched his axe tightly, his knuckles turning white. One quick swing and he could split the captain's head like a melon.

Jackson leant forward out of the shadow and Andrews could see clearly the mauled face staring back at him.

'Not as soon as you, Andrews. Of that, I am certain. What do you know of the lost Tierra Firme Fleet? I know you delivered the coordinates to Simon Blake on your last voyage.'

Andrews answered with a bloodied smile, 'You have finally lost your mind, Jackson. You have created a ghost story to feed the weak minds of your foolish crusade. You are a slaver of the worst kind, a trade soon to be outlawed, and then you will have nowhere left to turn. I may not see the sun rise again but I'll die happy, knowing you will not be far behind. That also goes for your monster behind me.'

Adder stepped forward and lifted his axe, only to be stopped by a look from his captain.

'Either you tell me, or I continue to Rio and cut it out of Blake. You can save yourself a painful death. What say you?'

Silence fell over the cabin again. Jackson leant back into the light once again, becoming the shadow, waiting for a response from the *Retribution's* captain, which did not come.

'Very well, Andrews,' the shadow spoke quietly now, as he turned to Adder. 'Keelhaul the *Retribution's* crew and let the brave captain watch his men die slowly. Maybe that will loosen his tongue.'

Adder smiled and dragged Andrews back out to the deck. He tied him to the base of the mainmast and wiped the blood from his eyes.

'I want you to be able to see clearly, Andrews,' Jackson whispered in his ear. 'And if you look away, even just for a moment, I will flay your men in front of you and force their intestines down your throat. You can save them. Tell me what you delivered to Blake. Tell me about the Tierra Firme Fleet.'

'I cannot tell you what I do not know, Bell. Keelhaul me and let the others work on your ships. They are skilled sailors and will serve you well. Let them live, I beg you.'

Jackson Bell moved around to whisper in Andrews' other ear.

'The New World does not have room for beggars.' His face stayed intimately close but his next words were louder, intended for both crews of the *Grey* and *Revolt* to hear.

'Bring them up in a line and we'll see how many men it takes to loosen the captain's tongue.'

Andrews dropped his head as his men were lined up on the deck in front of him and members of the Scarlets fixed a long rope underneath the *Grey Cloud*. Andrews imagined the bottom of the ship and the thousands of razor-sharp barnacles that were about to tear his crew to shreds, one by one.

'It was a painting,' his voice was weak and desperate. He could feel the blood drip from his body, and he knew he would soon be dead. All he could do was save his men from an excruciating death. He raised his head and looked up to meet Jackson, who raised his hand, shushing the eager crowd.

'Stevenson told me to deliver a great gift, marked "X" on the *Retribution's* register. I was to deliver it to Blake personally. It was just a painting, Jackson – a painting of the *Retribution*.'

Jackson walked back over to the dying captain.

'And what else?' he asked with urgency. 'A note? A message? What else?'

'All I saw was the painting. I swear it. There was no message of a hidden treasure, Jackson. It is a fable. It is on the bottom of the Atlantic, lost in the storm. Give up this foolish fantasy and spare these men. They have no reason to die today.'

Jackson stared blankly back at Andrews. Caleb could hear the nervous breathing of the man who had been lined up next to him. Jackson turned slowly to the line-up of terrified prisoners.

'Him.' He pointed to the first man as he said it. The crowd cheered as one of the *Retribution's* survivors was tied to the rope, screaming for mercy as his feet and hands were bound. Andrews yelled in desperate protest as his crew member was lowered into the water. He screamed until, fully submerged, his screams could no longer be heard.

It felt like an age as the rope was pulled up over the starboard gunwale, held tight against the port side and allowed to trail under the *Grey Cloud*.

'First one coming up!' a Scarlet on the starboard side called. Caleb froze as he looked over at his captain, tied helplessly against the mainmast, the ropes around his chest stained red from his own blood.

As the *Retribution's* sailor was pulled over the rails, Jackson Bell's men cheered. The sight was horrific. What had been submerged as a man had been turned into something else.

There were no more screams coming from what now looked more like dog meat than human. He lay in a shredded lump on the deck. The hundreds of deep lacerations that covered his flayed skin fountained out his blood as his body convulsed, and then lay still. Caleb felt the scars on his back tingle. He looked over at the other men in the line-up and saw a shameful puddle build at the base of a set of feet. He looked up at the owner and realised immediately who it was. Adder had also spotted the yellow pool and pointed, yelling to the rest of the ship.

'Look … this one has pissed himself!'

The ship erupted, cheering and chanting vile names. Bobby started whimpering as the wet patch soaked into his britches.

'Him next,' yelled a Scarlet.

'Yes, keelhaul the little coward,' another chimed in, pushing Bobby in the back and sending him crashing onto the deck.

'Look, he can't even stand up, the little girl,' another sailor cried out as the crew jeered and laughed once more.

Caleb felt like vomiting and watched helplessly as they tied his only friend to the ropes. Bobby was crying loudly now, pleading for his life, and a surge of rage ran through Caleb's body. He would rather be shot or run-through than dragged under the ship to die, and he knew that a quick death was also better for his good friend.

He broke from the line and darted over the main deck towards one of the men tying the rope around Bobby's feet. He pulled out a knife lodged in the sailor's boot and stabbed it into his side, guiding the blade through the Scarlet's ribcage.

The sailor let out a horrified scream, turning in shock to see Caleb crouched in front of him. Caleb did not wait before plunging the knife up under the sailor's armpit. The crowd stood in silence, stunned, as the Scarlet choked on his own blood.

Caleb prepared himself for the inevitable sound of the musket and the feel of the shot entering his body. He took his last moment to smile at the Scarlet, who began to lose his footing and fall to the floor. Around him, men drew their swords and pointed them at him. Caleb looked down at the dying man and began to laugh.

'Now, whose legs have failed him?' he sang out loudly, so all could hear. He felt the barrel end of a musket touch his temple and closed his eyes. In that instant, he thought it strange that Sasha Stevenson entered his mind.

'Wait!' The call was deep and controlled. Caleb opened his eyes to see disappointed sailors back away from him as if a pack of wolves had just been denied their freshly killed carcass. Jackson Bell entered the circle and stared at Caleb a moment, looking him up and down.

'Keep this one alive. He has fight in him.' Murmurs of discontent could be heard throughout the ship. Caleb looked up at the fierce man in front of him.

'I will not fight for you. I am loyal to the *Retribution* and to my captain.' Caleb was surprised that his own voice showed no fear, but instead was calm and direct. His eyes did not move from Jackson's gaze. He was not afraid of him. On the contrary, the man's presence brought out a strength in Caleb, fuelled by a hatred that he had unknowingly stored inside himself, ready to be released when necessary.

Jackson moved closer to him and tipped his head toward the mainmast behind Caleb's left shoulder.

'Your captain is dead, boy.'

Caleb did not want to look behind him, but forced his head towards the mainmast of the *Grey* to see the lifeless body of Captain Andrews. Blood continued to drip from the long strands of hair that dangled in front of his bowed head, pooling at his dead feet.

'Look at me, boy,' Jackson called his attention. 'You have fight in you and skill to match, which is rare in someone so young. Adder will be your captain now.' Jackson pointed to the large bald-headed man who had first brought the crews' attention to Bobby's accident.

'He is a great warrior and will help you to hone your skills to be a soldier of the revolution.'

Caleb weighed up his choices. Deny Jackson and be keelhauled with the rest of his crew or sell his soul and make a pact with the devil to save his own skin.

He wished the last three months had never happened. He wished he was back on the Stevenson estate working on the holding pen with the other men. He had longed for a better life but the one that had been laid out before him was as cruel and unfair as the lifeless existence from which he had been ripped away.

Is there such a thing as a life in which someone could feel free?

His thoughts were interrupted by a loud crack, which was followed by a whistling sound. The cannon shot crashed into the water only yards from the sterns of the two vessels.

'Ship ahoy!' The call came from the crow's nest of the *Grey Cloud*. With both the crews immersed in the violent spectacle on the main deck, the approaching ship had not been noticed until it was nearly upon them.

'She's a Man O' War, Captain. Flying the Union Jack!'

Immediately the attention of the crews switched to the warship, which was storming up on them.

'Cut the lines!' Jackson yelled. 'Take this one onto the *Revolt*!' he ordered, pointing at Caleb. 'Shoot the rest of them and throw them over the side!'

Caleb froze as he saw rifles raised to fire at the *Retribution's* remaining crew members. Bobby, who had been forced back in line with the others, looked over at him, horrified, tears streaming down his face. Time slowed to almost a stop and Caleb could see in slow motion everything happening around him.

Men cut through the lines locking the three ships together, while others on both *Greys* worked frantically to make all sail in an attempt to outrun the approaching warship. Others made their way to the lower decks to prepare the heavy guns. Caleb felt the powerful arms of Adder wrap around him and force him over the rails of the *Grey Cloud* and onto the deck of the *Revolt*.

'Bobby,' he called out in desperation, as he lost sight of the *Grey's* main deck.

'Cal–' Bobby's reply had been cut off by the sound of the rifles.

'Bobby! Bobby!' Caleb screamed. The grip on his arms tightened, almost breaking the bones between his wrists and elbows.

'You want to see your friend, boy?' Adder spun him around towards the *Grey Cloud*, which had now been cut free from the *Revolt* and had started slowly making its way back towards Rio.

Caleb looked in horror as the bodies of the *Retribution's* crew were thrown over the sides, into the sea below. As Caleb stood helpless, he watched them drop, one by one, until, finally, he saw

Bobby's body lifted into the air. The bullet had hit him in the left eye and had travelled through his head, fracturing the back of his skull. His light frame was tossed over the gunwales and hung motionless in the air for a moment before it followed the others into the sea.

Caleb screamed as Bobby crashed into the Atlantic. He felt himself being jerked violently around to face the gruesome sight of Adder.

'Sympathy is for the weak, you little shit. No one cries like a woman on my ship. Shut your mouth and start helping or you can join the coward who pissed his pants.'

Adder grabbed Caleb by his hair and slammed his head into the side of the ship. The back of his head smacked hard against the wood and his vision blurred as he listened to Adder yelling orders at the *Revolt's* crew.

'Hoist the sails and man the guns!'

But it was too late to outrun the approaching warship. The *Grey Cloud* was now away, safely on its way back to Rio, abandoning the *Grey Revolt*, which was only just slowly starting to move. She had not made it far before the Man O' War had thrown her grappling hooks over the gunwales and reined her in.

Caleb leant against the side of the ship and watched, dazed, as men jumped over him, and started to attack the crew of the *Grey Revolt*. Adder fought furiously, landing blow after blow, cutting through the invaders like a cornered animal fighting for its life.

'Adder, you swine!' The call came from a strong-looking man who had made his way onto the *Revolt*. His beard was thick and dark and his jet black hair turned to grey towards the sideburns.

A Scarlet attacked to his right, but he parried easily and ran his sword through the man's stomach. Another attacked from the left and he ducked under the swinging blade and cut his sword across the other's belly, letting him fall onto the deck.

Men were fighting and dying all over the *Revolt* and, for the second time that day, Caleb did not know where to turn. He wanted to join the men of the warship and kill Adder, but knew if he picked up a sword that he would be mistaken as an enemy and a slaver.

The stocky man with the heavyset beard made his way to Adder and the two men circled each other as the battle around them continued. Adder lunged and they clashed swords, again and again, until Adder landed a blow that knocked the stocky man onto his back, his sword flying out of his hand.

Adder strode over to him and began to raise his sword. A boy not older than Caleb moved in and tried to help the bearded man to his feet but they both fell back, slipping on the blood-soaked deck.

'Two ship builders for the price of one, hey?' Adder laughed as his sword hovered above the two helpless figures below him.

Caleb saw his chance. While Adder's attention was fixed on the man and boy lying on the deck, he darted past two men fighting and picked up a sword from a dead man's hand. He moved quickly, concentrating on each step as he had done in the jungle with the Royal Couriers.

His balance was steady and his speed swift. As Adder's blade descended on the men, Caleb slid underneath, crouching over them, holding the blade of his sword above his head with two hands. The force of Adder's blow sent a shock wave through Caleb's arms, nearly knocking the sword from his grasp. Nearly, but not quite.

He stood up and lunged at Adder, his sword piercing the slaver's thigh. Adder winced and backed away, only to regain his balance. They clashed swords, Caleb being careful not to lose control, to concentrate. He could not match his opponent's power and strength but he had speed as an advantage.

He ducked and swung, pivoted and swung again. Adder evaded all of Caleb's attempts. He moved freely for a wounded man. Caleb feigned a move to his left and quickly changed his direction and attacked from his right. Adder's sword hand had not followed quickly enough, and Caleb had his opening. He sliced his sword across Adder's side, just scraping over his face.

A large cut opened across his nose and cheek and he winced in pain, dropping his sword. Caleb lunged again, but this time Adder was ready for the shift in direction and let his fist fly, connecting with brutal force against the side of Caleb's head.

Caleb fell backwards, once again hitting the back of his head on the hardwood of the *Revolt's* deck. The world went silent and his vision began to blur. He saw Adder fall to his knees, with men pointing rifles at him. He saw the face of the bearded warrior and the younger boy standing over him.

Before he lost consciousness, he felt rough hands lifting him up. He felt the blood trickle down the back of his neck and, seconds later, the world went dark.

Chapter 30

Simon Blake stared in disbelief as he stood on the roof of the Stevenson Transport building. He often went up there to look through his telescope to view the ships that were sailing in and out of the Port of Rio from far and wide.

He had gone up to the roof to farewell the *Retribution* on its way back to London and had witnessed the battle take place from a position of helplessness. There was no British Navy vessel in port to call on and no other ship that could have made it to the *Retribution's* aid in time. He stood there and watched in shock and horror as the great merchant flagship had been blown out of the water by the two smaller ships.

It was an hour later when he saw a third ship move up behind and engage them.

'Simon,' Thomas's voice was gravely quiet. He was standing next to him and had seen the battle unfold. 'Simon, what are we to do?'

Simon did not reply. His grief was too fresh to think of the next move. He thought of his friend, Andrews, the first mate, Benson, and the two young boys, Caleb and Bobby, who had now perished. The crew of the *Retribution* counted over one hundred men, all company staff who had now been killed in the battle.

To take the great merchant ship down had been the one intention of the two flanking ships. They had succeeded but, whilst gloating over victory, they had allowed a third ship to approach close enough for an attack.

'We wait to see who the attackers are.' He had to know. The two ships had separated and one was making its way to the port under full sail. The other ship had not had enough time and had been engaged by the third vessel.

'It was a calculated attack, Simon,' Thomas continued. 'They were hunting the *Retribution* and gave her no quarter.'

'We wait until we know,' Simon ordered.

It took only twenty minutes before the approaching ship was recognisable. The colours of the flag were undeniable. It was the *Grey Cloud*, and it was heading into port with one target in mind. Him.

'Bell,' Thomas whispered. 'He is coming for you, Simon. He knows, he knows about the waterfall. He knows about the—'

'He knows nothing!' Simon interrupted. 'Calm yourself, Thomas. The information was sent in pieces on different voyages. Even if he was made to tell Jackson what he knew, Andrews did not have all the information. He did not have the first message and would have no idea where to look for the second.'

'So, what do we do, sir?'

The *Grey Cloud* was approaching the harbour. It would dock within the hour and Simon knew that its crew and captain were heading for one place – the building in which he was standing. He raised his telescope to the horizon. The second ship that had attacked the *Retribution* had been sunk and the Man O' War was now in pursuit of the *Grey Cloud*.

Would Jackson stay and fight the Man O' War? It was too much of a risk. Jackson and his crew had an hour's head start on her, and Simon's defences would not be able to hold back the Scarlets long enough for the pursuing ship to come to his aid. He knew what had to be done. In his heart, he had known over the last weeks that this decision would be forced upon him, one way or another.

'Assemble the Couriers and ride ahead.'

'Simon, if you stay and he catches you—'

'He will not,' Simon interrupted Thomas, again. 'I need to

give instructions to Lupe and will meet you at the crossroad. We no longer work for Stevenson Transport. We have a much more important task ahead of us now. We must keep it secret, Thomas … We must keep it safe. We go into exile until it is safe to return.'

With that, Thomas nodded and left. Simon walked down the stairs to his office and called for his horse to be readied. At his desk, he hastily wrote a declaration naming Lupe, his second-in-charge, the new General Manager of Stevenson Transport, South American Operations. He signed his name and made his mark with a wax candle and stamp.

Simon called a clerk and ordered him to take the sealed note to the Government Fort immediately and to have it handed to the Portuguese authority. He gathered a few small possessions: a journal, ink and pens, and maps of the Brazilian country terrain. He looked up at the large painting hanging on the wall at the other end of the room one last time. He left everything else.

He made his way to the ground floor, greeting the workers as usual so as not to cause alarm, and he headed to the stables. He quickly inspected his horse to see that it had been prepared according to his instructions – two rifles, machete, saddle bags filled with light provisions and a sleeping mat with blanket. He went into the armoury and dressed himself as he had done a hundred times before – large coat, long sword, short sword, assorted knives and a musket. He walked outside and mounted his horse.

'Close the warehouse and lock the building down. Tell all workers to make their way home and stay there until they hear from Lupe. He is now in charge.' He spurred his horse's flanks and rode at speed through the streets, making the main transport road and turning north.

He galloped hard until he reached the top of the escarpment. Reining in his horse, he looked down over the Port of Rio. The *Grey Cloud* was coming into port at alarming speed.

Jackson Bell has not got what he wanted from Andrews and is desperate to get to me now.

Only he and Stevenson had the answers Jackson needed, and Simon was certain that Jackson would not risk setting foot on English soil, where he was a wanted outlaw. It was now up to Simon alone to keep it secret, to keep it safe. The Royal Couriers had been assembled for another great task and he, their captain, would see it done.

The Man O' War was entering the mouth of the harbour in pursuit of the *Grey Cloud.*

Good. Jackson and his crew will have to disperse and run or, even better, fight and be killed. The warehouse should be safe.

He looked over Rio and prayed they would be so lucky. He spurred his horse again, and it reared up on its hind legs, leaping into a gallop.

Into hiding then, until it is safe for me to return.

Chapter 31

Regan Deery cursed the sudden lack of wind as he stood looking at the flattened sails above his head. Fortune had been on their side, until now. They had advanced on two slave ships tied together and were unnoticed almost until their guns had been in range. His mouth watered when he saw that Adder was on the ship they had cornered. It meant only one thing. The second ship, which had sailed to safety, was the *Grey Cloud,* and on it would be Jackson Bell himself.

Regan had no love for the slaving trade and had made it his personal crusade to take down any slaving vessel he came across. His crew had been hand-picked and were as fierce as they were loyal to the cause.

Men from England, Europe and Africa made up his crew and they sailed for one reason: to take down as many slave ships as they could find.

Regan looked over the powerful Man O' War named the *Charlotte Arms* after his late wife, who had died during the birth of his only son, Luke. He missed her greatly, but he loved his son and was proud of the man he was growing up to be. The crew had nicknamed her *Ol' Charlie,* which he had welcomed.

Regan was an Englishman whose family had long been in the ship-building business and who had become extremely wealthy through naval and merchant contracts. While his shipping yards were in Liverpool, he spent most of his time in Africa and on the Atlantic, only visiting England for short visits every few months to oversee the progress of the business. The Deery Shipping

Company built, repaired and maintained great warships for the British Navy and large merchant vessels for numerous large enterprises. With Britain boasting the largest navy on the oceans, and the New World creating the need for more merchant vessels, business was better than good, and it made him a very rich man.

But it was the excitement of battle that fuelled his heart and gave him purpose. Stories of his warring against the slave trade had made their way back to London and even into books that were sold as heroic tales.

'Father, is it really the *Grey Cloud*?'

Regan looked over at the ship, which had now made port.

'I believe it is, Luke.'

'Jackson Bell?'

Regan kept his eyes on the docks, ignoring the excitement in his son's voice. 'Yes, but we're too late. They have made port and Rio still offers *assiento* – protection for slavers in their ports. We lost the wind and are now helpless to do anything. Damn you, Bell, you snake,' he cursed at the sails above.

'What will we do with Adder and his crew, Father? He is one of the worst slavers on the Atlantic. We should cut their throats and throw them overboard and be done with it.'

'We are too close to port now, Luke. We can't be seen throwing dead men over our gunwales. There'll be too many eyes on us, and we can't cross that line. We do that, and we risk the business. No, we will need to hand them over to the authorities.'

A look of disappointment crossed Luke's face, though he knew his father was right. They had had their chance to kill Adder in a fair fight on the open sea and he had seen his father charge at him, but Adder had been too strong even for the experienced fighter he knew his father to be. They would have both fallen under Adder's sword if it had not been for the young slaver who had saved them.

The boy had been on Luke's mind ever since they had sunk Adder's slaver and taken their prisoners aboard *Ol' Charlie*.

'Father.' His tone was quieter now. 'Earlier during the fight,

Adder had us for dead and that slaver boy came to our aid. We owe him our lives.'

'Aye, that we do, Son. That we do…' His voice trailed off as he pondered the situation. There was no doubt that he would not be standing on his quarterdeck alive next to his son if the boy had not intervened.

'Where is the little slaver now?'

'In the infirmary, Father. Adder knocked him unconscious and he was taken down to lie on a bunk.'

'I see. Well, we best go and talk to this boy. For whatever reason he did what he did, he owes us an explanation now. He stays on *Ol' Charlie*. First, we hand over Adder and the others to the Rio authorities. Then we question this little slaver.'

Chapter 32

Jackson Bell stood on the quarterdeck of the *Grey Cloud*. They had been anchored in the southern section of the harbour and had watched the Man O' War trail in behind them and dock at the northern side. He had heard of the Deerys and knew that they were not to be messed with. He was safe as long as he remained on the *Grey Cloud*. He had watched in fury as Regan Deery and his men led Adder and what remained of the *Grey Revolt's* crew to the barracks next to the Government Fort in the town square.

He would not let his greatest and most loyal soldier hang. Adder's destiny was to die fighting with glory, not hanging like a common thief. He looked past the Man O' War to see the Stevenson building, dark, closed and empty. Blake was gone and a man like that would stay gone. Despair and anger flooded his mind.

So, it is lost then. I have failed.

His jaw clenched hard and his knuckles turned white as he balled his hands into fists. Blake had run like a coward to keep safe what did not belong to him or Stevenson.

The thought of Jacob Stevenson having won was almost enough to drive his anger to insanity. It was futile to attempt to find information about Blake's whereabouts. As much as he hated Blake, he knew that he and his band of Couriers were now hidden from the world and would stay hidden for as long as they needed to. The only thing he could do now was draw his enemies to him.

Freeing Adder and the rest of his men would be an easy task. Jasper Cole would allow him safe passage into the barracks. He would go in with a select few and cut the soldiers to pieces while they slept.

After tonight, he would also have to go into hiding, at least until calm had resumed across the land. South, perhaps, where he could rebuild. He would steal horses from the stables and ride south from Rio along the coastline, where Portuguese rule and the British Empire had no presence. The *Grey Cloud* would stay in port until the Deerys had left and then would sail south to meet him.

He would be patient and wait until the time to strike presented itself once more. The Treasure Fleet was real. Why else would Blake have run so quickly? It was real, and it was out there to be taken. Jacob Stevenson would hear the news that his most trusted general had disappeared and would also know that Blake had received the coordinates.

Yes, he would build an army of free men and wait for Stevenson to sail to Rio. He could be patient. He would build his own fleet of slaving ships the way he had taken the *Revolt* and dominate the trade across the Atlantic, cutting down anyone who stood in his way. He would sail in a convoy of three ships at all times to ensure the safety of the *Grey Cloud*.

I will have my revolution. The Stevensons, the Deerys, Blake and the whole British Navy will not keep me from it.

He stood alone in the fading light and bottled his hatred. He had suffered a setback but revelled in the knowledge that the Tierra Firme Fleet treasure was real and was hidden somewhere in Brazil. He would never give up his search for it.

As the fading sun set over the peaks of the western mountains, Jackson gathered his men, armed himself and jumped in the longboat. He sat quietly while the oars made rhythmic ripples in the dark water.

He had an insatiable thirst to kill a man, and very soon there would be many soldiers to satisfy his need. He turned his head slightly to his men behind him and whispered eerily.

'We separate their heads from their bodies and open their bellies, all of them. Then we free our men and ride south.'

After tonight, and in time, his name would become rumour. He would be lost and forgotten by the British and Portuguese governments, and he would wait for his time to return with a much greater force.

As soon as he had finished speaking, he turned back towards Rio, already feeling better about the night ahead.

Chapter 33

Caleb lay in a bunk with his head bandaged. He had heard the surgeon and the men who were guarding his room refer to him as a slaver. He remembered the events of the day and felt a rush of nausea. He closed his eyes and could see Adder and Jackson Bell leaping over the rails of the *Retribution* with fury and hatred in their eyes. He could hear the screaming of men dying around him, and see the shredded skin of the keelhauling, the lifeless body of his captain strung to the mast and, worst of all, Bobby's dead body falling through the air into the Atlantic.

Tears rolled down his face as despair overwhelmed him. He had tried to avenge his friend by killing Adder but he had been too weak. He had failed his friend and would now be hanged as a slaver.

He tried to imagine what it would be like to die from hanging. He had been told by other men on the Stevenson Estate that it was a ghastly spectacle to see a man hang. He would flap around like a dying fish at the end of a rod, hopelessly trying to free himself from the rope around his neck.

Some even soiled their breeches, he remembered one of the men saying. It had been three months since he had left the estate, yet it felt like a lifetime. So much had happened and so much of it he wished he could change. He heard footsteps coming down the passageway and he wiped the tears from his face. He was about to be taken off to be hanged, yet he would not give them the satisfaction of seeing him break.

The door swung open and three men walked into the cabin.

On closer inspection, Caleb realised that it was two men and a boy around the same age as himself. He recognised them all instantly.

The first to enter was the surgeon who had bandaged his head. Following him were the man and the boy who had been Adder's targets on the *Revolt*. They were both shorter than he was but had broad, rounded shoulders, which bulged uncomfortably through their jackets. Their necks were as thick as a man's thigh and their legs were like short logs, holding up their triangular torsos. Immediately he noticed the resemblance. The younger boy had not just gone to his captain's aid against Adder, he had gone to his father's aid.

'You're awake,' the captain spoke first. 'Good. We have questions for you. My name is Regan Deery, and this is my son, Luke. Next to me is our resident surgeon, whose name does not really matter at this moment.'

Caleb sat up on the bunk, and both Regan and Luke placed their hands on their sword handles. *Get it over with*, he thought. Better to die by the sword than at the end of a rope.

'You stopped Adder from killing us. Why?' It was now the young Luke who posed the question. 'Why go against your captain to save us? After all, it was we who attacked you, slaver.'

'I am no slaver. But I have been a slave my whole life to men with power. I have cause to see Jackson Bell and Adder dead just as much as you.'

Suddenly, the mood in the room changed and the three men looked at each other.

'You sail on a slaving ship, yet given the chance, you attack your own crew!' Regan said to the strong, young man sitting silent on the bunk in front of him. He did not have the usual cruel and ugly demeanour of a slaver, but he could see that there was a fire burning within. Many young men were grabbed as boys and made to work on slaving ships against their will. Perhaps this boy had seen his chance to free himself of the trade by taking arms against his own crew.

'What is your name, boy?' Regan asked. Caleb thought about the question and realised that he hated his name. What had life given 'Caleb' but pain and heartache? Caleb was a poor worker with no chance of becoming free. He found it nearly impossible to utter the name.

'My father asked you a question and, if I were you, I would answer. It is the only way you will avoid the gallows.'

Caleb looked up at the boy. He was proud and tough but at the same time educated and refined. He immediately respected him. Caleb looked back down at the floor, still unable to find his words. Death was better than being Caleb. Perhaps the gallows were his only chance of release.

'You do have a name, don't you?' the boy asked again, this time with a less patient tone.

Suddenly, it dawned on Caleb that the men standing in front of him had not once mentioned the *Retribution's* battle with the Scarlets. They had turned up afterwards to see the *Grey Cloud* and *Revolt* tied to each other, and for now were completely ignorant that Stevenson's great merchant flagship was sitting on the bottom of the sea floor below them.

As far as everyone was concerned, Caleb would be pronounced dead with the rest of the *Retribution's* crew, and what stood in front of them now was a bedraggled slaver who had turned on his own kind.

It was a risk to lie, he realised. But a risk he was willing to take.

'Ben. My name is Ben.' It was the first name that had come into his mind.

It was the name of the packhorse he used to ride when accompanying Brenton and Sasha Stevenson on their estate rides. It was seen as an inferior animal compared to theirs, bred for hard work and little thanks.

A fitting name.

'Just Ben or do you have a last name that accompanies it?' Regan asked.

Caleb looked them in the eye and lied for his freedom.

'My parents died when I was very young,' he began. 'I do not remember them. All the memory I have about myself is being moved from ship to ship. I have no love for slaving and would welcome a fight against any slaver. I know I am fourteen years old and I have only ever been called Ben.'

Regan looked at his son and back at Caleb.

'We find ourselves indebted to you, Ben. We would both be meat for the crows if you had not shown up. So, I am going to save you from the gallows and let you join our crew. You say you want to fight slavers?'

Caleb breathed deeply. His lie had worked, and he was now safe from a hanging. He thought of Bobby and how he wanted more than anything to see Jackson Bell and Adder dead. He would become Ben and leave the name Caleb at the bottom of the Atlantic with the rest of the dead.

'Yes, Mr Deery, sir.' Ben stood, declaring his loyalty to his new captain. Luke turned towards his father and nodded in appreciation. The room was silent.

After a pause, Regan replied. 'You are on the right ship, then.'

Part Two–Coming of Age

1748

Chapter 34

Sasha had scarcely noticed her little sister talking as her mind wandered with the sounds of the markets around her. It was springtime in London, her favourite time of the year. Her twenty-first birthday had just passed, and she had truly reached womanhood.

'Did you hear me, Sasha?' Penny asked as she nudged her older sister. 'Father says he has exciting news for us at dinner tonight.'

Sasha tossed her head and rolled her sky-blue eyes.

'It is probably an announcement of a new ship or a prize stallion. Really, Penny, how interesting could it be?'

She walked through the crowd towards a flower stall. Wealthy suitors of high-society London tipped their hats and offered assistance as she made her way past them.

'May I accompany you, Miss Sasha?' one man asked.

'Miss Sasha, will you and your sister be attending my family's ball next week?' another called out.

She had become accustomed to this sort of attention from the young London gentlemen. Though she remained unmarried, there had been many suitors. She was a beautiful woman or, at least, this is what she had been led to believe. She also knew that it was her outspokenness that had earned her a reputation for being wild and untamed. She was seen as a conquest to pursue.

Of course, the fact that she was a Stevenson made her even more attractive. A marriage to the eldest daughter of one of the wealthiest merchants in England was an exciting proposition for affluent and ambitious families from all over Britain and the New Worlds.

Yet, in spite of this, she was determined to marry for more than her father's wishes of money and title. She wanted conversation, passion, adventure, trust and love.

She had become politically vocal when it came to slavery on the Atlantic and the need for it to be abolished. She had developed these strong opinions seven years earlier when her father had read her a letter that told of slavers taking down the *Retribution*, leaving none of the crew alive. A copy of the *Retribution's* register had been obtained from the port of Rio and the names of the crew who sailed on that voyage were listed in this letter. It began with the captain and first mate and went on and on down the ranks. Then her father looked at her and stopped. Caleb's name had been listed with those who had been killed in the battle.

Sasha could remember her world turning upside down. She would never see him again. She would never be able to tell him that she still loved him, that she was sorry for what had happened.

Seven years had passed.

She had told herself that it had been a young, foolish love and, yet, it had been the measure of every romantic encounter since. All had fallen short and time was no longer on her side, for she knew that she would have to marry soon, or she would be too old for one of the younger suitors and might have to settle for being the second wife of someone far older. She knew her father would choose for her before it would come to that, and she could not decide which would be worse.

'Pick your favourite flower, and it will be my pleasure to buy them all for you.' It was a familiar and welcome voice, and she turned to see her older brother and his friends.

'You have known me all my life,' Sasha replied playfully. 'Shouldn't you already know my favourite flower, Brother?'

Brenton was with two colleagues, Harrold Stock and Edward

Barrington. Both men were from wealthy families and the three had been friends since they started university. Now, all were rich men, ready to take their places in their respective family enterprises.

Brenton himself was twenty-three and already a graduate and the chief financial controller in the Transport Company. This position required him to accompany his father to meetings and on business trips at any time and to be a part of the decisions that determined the company's future. It made him second-in-charge of all operations. The Stock family business was in cotton and the Barrington's, sugar. Their families had plantations in both North and South America and used Stevenson shipping to transport their goods to be sold throughout Britain and Europe.

'I believe daisies would be your favourite, Miss Sasha.'

'And what makes you think that, Mr Barrington?' she replied, playing along.

'No, not daisies,' interrupted Harrold Stock. 'A pink tulip to complement your famous blue eyes.'

'Infamous is more like it,' Brenton interrupted, and Sasha hit him lightly across his arm, pouting as she did.

'Unfortunately, neither of you are right. I am a classic red rose admirer and, like the bloom, just as beautiful, prickly and dangerous.'

Both Harrold and Edward swallowed hard as they heard the playful seduction in her voice. Sasha was a true beauty, with a stunning figure, warm skin, red lips, piercing blue eyes and dark hair, which flowed wildly over her shoulders and down the centre of her back.

Harrold and Edward had been infatuated with Sasha for years, but both had been unsuccessful with their advances, though not from lack of trying nor pressure from their families.

Penny walked over to the group in her usual playful manner. She had also become a beautiful woman, though with different features from her older sister. She was shorter and had blonde curls. Penny had also inherited the sky-blue eyes, but hers did not blaze so fiercely and with such passion as Sasha's.

Penny had become a true lady of London society and wanted a life of luxury: high teas, turns around the grounds, balls in the evening and gossip at all times in between. She could not wait to marry a wealthy suitor with an excellent reputation and hold social gatherings in her own apartment in London, or in the lavish gardens of her country estate.

'What do you think father has to tell us, Brenton? It sounds like something important. I hear the Barringtons and Stocks will be joining us tonight as well.'

Brenton looked at Penny, amused. 'There's not much that you don't hear, is there, Penny?'

She smiled back at him, making sure that Edward and Harrold were watching.

'That being said,' Brenton continued, 'we should be leaving for home. I will see you chaps for dinner then.'

Both Penny and Sasha followed their older brother aboard the coach. It bumped over the streets as it wended its way to West London, where the apartments of rich merchants and wealthy landowners mingled with those of the aristocracy of Kensington Gardens.

Later that night, the guests began arriving at the Stevenson house. The Stocks arrived first, and the Barringtons soon after. William Finch and Wendell Prince were next and, finally, an assortment of parliamentary officials completed the gathering.

Annette and Jacob Stevenson entertained their guests in the large sitting room on the first floor before the butler announced dinner. Once in the dining room, Jacob Stevenson stood at the head of the large oak table and addressed his guests.

'Thank you for coming this evening. Tonight, I have news I would like to share with you all. Over the last seven years, I have had William and Wendell monitor the development of the company's South American assets. Rio de Janeiro has become the commercial capital of Brazil and now offers nearly every service that one would find here in London. I look over to see the Barringtons and the Stocks and know that they, along with us, have vested interests in Brazil. However, we have not been there in over a decade. We have not seen what it has become.'

Sasha's heartbeat quickened as she listened. Was her father about to announce a voyage? Would she be able to sail the Atlantic and see the exotic lands of South America, which she had heard so much about? She listened intently as her father continued.

'I am also aware that my daughters are now at an age that they need to marry. Annette and I have spoken about this at length.'

Suddenly, Sasha's racing heart began to slow. It was a moment she had known would come eventually, but she was dreading hearing the next words from her father.

'I have contacted an old friend and business acquaintance while he has been in London. I think you will all have heard of Regan Deery.'

The looks on the faces of the dinner guests were mixed. Brenton, Edward and Harrold revered the Deery name and had grown up, like all the other young men in London, reading about Regan's African exploits and vicious battles against slaving ships.

The older generation at the table had a more reserved response as there were also opinions in London society that Regan Deery and his men used violent militia tactics against slave ships, rarely leaving any men alive to tell tales, which, in their opinion, crossed the line of British decency. After all, it was still legal to transport, sell and own slaves, even though most people in London now opposed the trade. There were still those who profited greatly from it, and there were even those sitting at that very table who used slave labour on their South American plantations.

Sasha herself had read the stories of the Deerys' exploits along the West African coast.

'As I was saying,' Jacob hushed the noise at the table, 'despite your opinion of Deery and his so-called escapades, he is head of a prominent, long-established family who are major ship builders. Regan himself was here only two days ago to sign a six-year extension to his contract with the Royal Navy.

'Now, I have brought you all here for two reasons. The first is that it has been too long since I have seen our South American operations first-hand. Over the last ten years, Rio has become a thriving commercial hub, attracting business and enterprise from all over the world. What was a dangerous and unlawful place has been governed well by Portuguese rule and our British presence has grown along with it.

'I have decided to meet Regan Deery in Rio three months from now. What's more, I suggest that all at this table accompany me on this voyage.'

All the guests began talking at once.

'What a fantastic idea!' old man Barrington cried out. 'It will be good for our sons to see the plantations and the ways of the New World.'

'Here, here!' chorused old man Stock. 'We shall make it a grand old voyage.'

'Not just our sons,' Jacob's voice was loud and again warranted silence at the table. Sasha could barely keep herself still in her chair. Was he about to let her sister and her accompany them?

'I am also taking my wife and daughters on this voyage with me.'

'Father, thank you, thank you.' Sasha leapt out of her chair and ran to hug him. As she did, she could not recall the last time she had sought to embrace him. He hugged her tightly and allowed Penny to join in.

'Ah, girls, it warms my heart to see you so happy. But the news is not yet over.'

'I am not sure I can take any more excitement tonight, dear husband.' Annette looked around the table and everyone joined in the laughter.

'Please, girls,' Jacob continued, 'take your seats. I am yet to announce the final reason for our taking the voyage. In three months, we will meet up with the Deerys in Rio. Regan Deery has announced that it is time for his son, Luke, to take a wife.'

Sasha's soaring heart plummeted as her father continued.

'Both Regan and I have agreed that either Sasha or Penny will be a fine match for Luke Deery, and a marriage will signify a welcome union between our two great families.'

Both girls sat still in their chairs, stunned by the news. Sasha was wild with anger, yet Penny was quite the opposite.

'So, is this Luke Deery handsome?'

Again, there was laughing, this time at Penny's cheek. From all, that is, but one.

'And what if we do not find Mr Deery agreeable, Father?' It was posed as a simple question, but Jacob knew his daughter well and realised it was more of a challenge.

'Sasha, you have had your chance to marry and yet have denied many suitors, and they have come and gone. Should the Deery boy choose you, you will marry him, and you will find him agreeable. I will not be questioned on this. That is the end of it. Understood?'

An uncomfortable silence hung over the table as Jacob grew impatient with the lack of response from his daughter. Old man Barrington decided to change the subject before rage overtook his host and ruined what had turned out to be an excellent evening thus far.

'I have been told he has two sons of similar age.'

'Yes, Father,' Edward Barrington interrupted, 'but one is adopted and has taken on the Deery name. I believe he is called Ben Deery.'

'Yes, Ben Deery is his name,' Harrold Stock chimed into the conversation excitedly.

'Rumour has it that this Ben Deery was found on another ship and was taken in by Regan and treated as his own son. There are stories about him that are too violent for this table but apparently he is a great sailor who has taken down dozens of slaving ships on the open seas.'

'I would certainly like to see Rio and meet these Deerys,' old man Barrington announced cheerfully, keeping the conversation away from marriage.

'And I should like to hear more about this Omiran fellow we all keep hearing stories about. It seems in every tavern from London to Liverpool there are tales being told about a hunter who frees slaves and chaperones them to safe havens. I believe he sails with Deery's fleet?'

'Frees slaves?' Penny asked, enthralled by the evening's discussion. It was her older brother's turn to answer.

'Apparently, there is a man with no past, a wild savage man who sails with the Deerys. He is known as Omiran, a name given to him by African warrior tribes and blessed by a witch doctor. He cannot die they say.'

'That is quite enough, Brenton.' His mother's words were serious. 'Leave that sort of foolish conversation for the stables, and spare everyone from these ghost stories you boys enjoy telling so much. Come, I believe I will retire to the living room. Penny, would you be so kind as to play for us?'

As the guests moved into the living room and took their seats around the piano, servants cleared the table. Sasha's mind wandered in amazement. She did not want to marry a man she had never met but at the same time could not wait for the journey ahead. To sail on the Atlantic and see the New World was something she had dreamed of since she was a small girl.

It seemed, however, that there would be a price to pay. The Deerys sounded like honourable men who sought righteousness and adventure, two qualities that she would find attractive in a partner. But how could she make up her mind until she looked into someone's eyes and felt passion, longing, desire and love? She had to feel as if she were flying or she knew she would never be truly happy. She knew that as a woman she should be thankful for an agreeable marriage, but her life was too valuable to abandon love.

Later that night, as she lay in her bed, Penny entered her room and started to chatter insistently, clearly showing that sleep was not on her mind.

'How exciting,' she exclaimed.

'Exciting?' Sasha shot back. 'Do you not feel violated that father has made up his mind about whom we will marry?'

'Sasha, you think too much about such things. We are going on an adventure and, besides, what makes you so sure that Luke Deery will pick you? He may fancy the fairer type and choose me.'

Her sister's words did not come across confidently to Sasha, but in that moment, she realised that this was true. The decision had not been made, and Penny was a beautiful girl who would make a very agreeable partner.

And her sister was correct. They were more fortunate than most and were about to take a great voyage to an exotic new world.

Be thankful, Sasha. Be thankful for what you have.

'You are right, and I am sorry if I have ruined the fun. I am excited and cannot wait to go on our adventure.'

The next morning, Sasha awoke to the sounds of a beautiful spring day and she felt exhilarated. It would still be weeks until they set sail for Brazil but the news she had received the night before had filled a void, and she brimmed with excitement in anticipation of what was to come.

Chapter 35

Ben looked down at the campfires burning below the ridge. It was a dark night with only a sliver of moon, and this served his purpose well.

Much easier to stay hidden in the darkness. We can get all the way down to the camp before anyone sees us.

He looked up at the stars, which seemed to be working against the accommodating moon. They lit up the African sky above the Dahomey Kingdom, blazing in unison and threatening to spoil his attack.

He glanced to his right where Luke and five of the Deery Company were crouched, ready for his signal to advance. On his left, he saw the three African natives, warriors from the Imbangala region of Angola, fierce in nature and loyal to anyone who paid for their mercenary work.

Ben had employed them two years ago and had seen countless returns on his investment through their bravery, local knowledge and skill with modern weapons. They had been his scholars as much as they had been his employees, and even Luke had grown to trust these men with his life.

The leader of the three natives was known as Musungo, with Ben calling the other two by the common term of Gonzo. Musungo was a great warrior who used a hatchet and club as his weapons of choice. These men were well-versed in European ways because of Portuguese colonisation, yet had no love for its politics or ambitions. This made them invaluable to Ben, who drew upon their local knowledge as well as their Western understanding. He paid them well, though he knew after two years that they would follow him, regardless. It was adventure and battle that they longed for, and Ben's campaigns delivered an abundance of both.

The 'Company', as Luke Deery had named it, had formed as a small group of ten men, who would embark on guerrilla missions across Western and Central Africa. It was separated from the Deery name so as not to cause backlash to the family business, which funded their cause.

It had been seven years since he had met the Deerys, and Regan and Luke had treated him as their own. He had saved their lives and, in return, Regan had given him his. Ben's skill with the sword and rifle had earned him respect amongst the crew, and in times of battle he had shown fury, courage and valour. When Regan handed him the adoption papers in Portugal, he was overcome with emotion. Luke had laughed and joked with him.

'Well, are you going to sign it, Brother?' he had asked.

'Ben,' Regan began, 'Luke is the heir to the company and we have spoken about this in detail. You are like a son to me now and a brother to him.' He pointed over to Luke, who had nodded, not able to keep the grin off his face.

'A man needs a surname, especially one as big as you. If you go on just referring to yourself as Ben, people will think you are simple in the head. It would be our honour for you to join us as kin and take on our name.'

Ben remembered his throat clenching, and having to fight back tears so as not to look pathetic.

It had been years since he had thought of his old name and his old life. As Caleb, he had had nothing and could gain nothing. Ben would now be a Deery, an adopted son. The name carried with it stature and power.

'I would be honoured, sir,' he had exclaimed as he signed his name on the papers.

'Then, Ben, call me Father.'

The adoption papers came with a contract agreement

providing him with a ten percent share in the Deery Shipping Company – to be elevated to twenty, with Luke owning eighty percent, should something happen to Regan.

'Now, don't you cheeky bastards get any ideas about running me through just yet.'

They had all laughed as they made their way to one of the ale houses to celebrate. They smoked fine cigars and drank expensive brandy and Regan, who had drunk twice as many, announced to every person entering the establishment that he was celebrating with his two sons.

Later that night, after Regan had fallen off his chair one too many times and had to be carried to his room, Ben had asked Luke his thoughts on the matter.

'How do you feel about this? I mean, really. This is not something to be taken lightly and I would understand resentment. I will tear the papers up now and be done with it if it meant we would not go on as we are, Luke.'

His new brother looked at him and smiled.

'I want you involved in the company, Ben. Ten percent has made you a wealthy man now, and when I take over from our father, I will need people I can trust. I trust you more than any other and want you to have equity to back it up. My father loves you like a son and I love you as a brother. It was his idea to adopt, but it was mine to give you a share of the company.'

It had been three years since he had signed the papers and his share had made him wealthy indeed. Not as rich as Luke or Regan, but still beyond anything he had ever imagined. Regan had gifted him with a Man O' War named the *Gabriel*, which he now captained alongside the flagship, *Ol' Charlie*.

He hand-picked his crew, with each man needing to show two attributes above anything else – courage and loyalty. The *Gabriel* had built herself a reputation for exploration and adventure, attracting constant requests from men to sail with her at each port she docked.

On the ridge, he heard the quiet whisper from Musungo.

'Omiran. Look out there. It is time to move in.'

The Africans had named him Omiran due to his size. The word meant 'giant' in the native tongue. He had grown tall, with hard muscle protecting his towering frame. He was strong yet surprisingly agile, attributes he had used in many bar fights and battles over the years.

Though he did not care much for the name, it had stuck as soon as his brother, Luke, had been told its meaning and began calling him Omiran in playful banter. However, over time, he had found it useful as a mask to disguise the Deery name. Ben Deery was a gentleman – Omiran was anything but.

He nodded towards Musungo and turned to his right to signal to Luke and the others. There was no need for talk or planning from that moment. They had made a profession out of taking down raiding parties and operating effectively in complete silence. It was the key to their success.

They made their way down the escarpment, with Ben occasionally raising his hand, halting the party so he could be sure the wind had not changed and taken their scent ahead of them.

As they crept nearer to the camp, they broke off into three groups, fanning out to surround the slavers. The three Africans made for the left of the camp and Luke and his five circled to the right.

No matter how many times the Company moved in this way, it always brought back the memory of the first time he had seen it done, years ago with Simon Blake and his Couriers. It reminded him of the first time he had killed a man, standing there surprisingly calm, as he had tracked and shot dead his target. He had killed many men since then, in many ways, on both sea and land, and tonight he would gladly add a few more to his tally.

He took the centre path, moving low, using the wagons for cover. The sound of chattering and sporadic laughter coming from around one of the fires could be heard clearly. They had counted twenty slavers from the ridge. Almost too easy with their ten, who had experience, purpose and surprise on their side.

He pulled the long, bone-handled knife from his belt and the pistol from his hip. He darted around the wagon, moving surprisingly quickly for his size. His legs felt strong and surefooted.

As he neared the fire, he could see out of the corner of his eye the other men sprinting into the camp ahead of him. There were four slavers sitting around the fire, and as one saw him bounding towards them, he jumped to his feet in surprise and shock at the sight of Ben's huge frame emerging from the darkness with his pistol raised.

The shot hit him between the eyes and sent him flying backwards over the log on which he had been sitting. A scramble for weapons began around the fire as Ben drew another pistol from his belt, shooting the second man on his right.

He did not stop running as his knife sliced into the third slaver's jugular, blood spurting across both their faces. Enough time had passed for the fourth man to find his rifle and he raised it towards Ben.

He shielded himself with the dying man as he released his knife with fierce precision. The blade made a thud as it pierced the man's chest. Desperately, the slaver pulled the trigger of his rifle but the shot hit the ground at his feet and he dropped. Ben picked up a loaded rifle from the other side of the fire and walked over to him, reclaiming his knife before shooting the dying man in the head. He looked over to see how the rest of his men were faring and was not surprised to see them all walking towards him unharmed.

'We've been waiting for you to finish, young son,' Luke mocked as he cleaned the blood from his blade. The Imbangalas dragged their kills behind them to prove their worth, as always. Sometimes Ben thought they were dragging them up to him to ask permission to eat their kills, just as a dog would bound up with a bone. Ben knew it was their custom but, even though he had no love for slavers, he would not allow cannibalism in his presence. The thought of it made his stomach turn.

'Well, it is easier when you only have two to take out and not four,' he justified.

'Hey, you were the one who planned it. You were the one who had to go down the centre as usual,' Luke replied with his usual brotherly banter.

'Omiran, we see maybe thirty slaves chained to big wagons.'

'Well, there you have it, Omiran,' Luke looked back at him. 'Twenty dead slavers and thirty freed slaves. I would call that a successful night, wouldn't you, Giant of Africa?'

'I would,' Ben replied, ignoring the baiting tone in his brother's voice and the chuckling among the Company.

They unchained the natives and fed them from the stores in the camp's wagons. They loaded the dead into one of the larger wagons and set it alight, the flames leaping into the hot African night.

They camped there for the remainder of the night, as the slave camp was well-stocked with wine, brandy and salted meats. They feasted from the raiders' pantry and talked into the night. The Imbangala stood watch around the camp and even though they were invited to the festivities, they always declined politely and kept watch.

'Ben, how long do we do this?' Luke asked as they ate around the fire.

'I am not sure what you mean, Brother.' Ben looked at him, perplexed.

'I mean how long do we keep fighting this fight?'

Ben's confused look remained the same.

'Luke, we are Deerys and our father has fought this fight for those who cannot fight for themselves.'

'Ah, yes, that's right,' Luke replied. 'But when do we stop to live our own lives? If you think about it, we live a similar life to those slavers whose ashes lie on the ground over there. We sail the same seas, we work in the same industry, except that we are on different sides. They kill to enslave, and we kill to set free. All I'm saying is that there is a whole other life we could live, one which my father buried along with my mother, God rest her soul.'

From across the fire, Ben sensed the mood change in Luke's face.

'My father calls this his crusade against evil, but I know what it really is. It is a crusade to bury his own guilt. The guilt a man feels when someone else dies in his stead. My father had as much to do with making me as my mother did. Yes, she carried me and bore me, but the conception took mutual effort. When she died giving birth to me, my father did not blame me; I know that for sure. But he is a man and so someone had to be blamed. So, he blamed himself.'

Ben pulled back his long hair from his eyes and scratched at his beard, which had grown down to his chest. Feeling as though he should say something, he leaned forward but was cut off as Luke continued.

'I have lived a life of great adventure, becoming a man at a young age and having a friend as a father. I cannot be anything but grateful, Brother, but I wonder often, if my mother had lived, would Regan have gone back to the seas and lived this life?'

Luke sighed as he stared deep into the fire. 'Ben, our father has sent me news. A courier in Porto-Novo met me with a letter before we set off three days ago.'

'What is it? What has happened? Is he all right?' Ben was all attention now.

'Yes, yes, sit down for God's sake, sit down. Yes, Brother, he is fine. He has decided that I should take a wife. He says that he has someone in mind. I wanted to tell you on the way but thought we should get through tonight first and then talk about it when we had nothing else pressing. I hope you don't mind me keeping it from you.'

'Of course not, Luke. Well, marriage, hey! That is interesting indeed.' Ben took a sip of his brandy and drew hard on his cheroot, letting the smoke drift from his nostrils. 'Very, very interesting.' There was a pause in the conversation.

'I want to get married, Ben. The whorehouses and gentlemen's clubs are all well and good, but they are fleeting and leave a man with a strange feeling of emptiness.'

Ben chuckled through the smoke.

'You find that funny?' Luke said in protest.

'Well,' Ben replied, 'isn't that the sole purpose of the courtesan: to leave you slightly emptier than when you arrived? I would be reluctant to pay them otherwise.'

The heads of the slaves and the other men turned in curiosity as the two brothers rolled around in a fit of laughter.

'Ah, you do know how to make me laugh, Brother,' Luke coughed on his cigar as he tried to spit out the words.

'Seriously, though, Ben. What about you? We are men of age now. A wife and sons of our own would be worth thinking about. I want to be able to stay in one place long enough to see something grow.'

Ben contemplated Luke's question. He had dismissed such thoughts years ago and had made peace with the life he had now forged. He was someone in this world. He was a captain of a great ship; he had control, resources and his home was the *Gabriel*, which lay anchored in Port Alto, waiting for him to return to her. Apart from Regan, Luke and the crew of his ship, he concerned himself only with things that could be bought and promptly left behind. A hot meal, a suite in the many ports around the world, the feel of a woman, the companionship of momentary friendships at the card tables, the pleasure of expensive whisky and cigar smoke burning his throat. What else did he need?

He was finally free. Something he thought had been lost until he landed on *Ol' Charlie*. He had been handed his freedom and he would happily die before he handed it back.

'I am not sure about marriage,' Ben finally answered. 'To be honest, I have not given it much thought, what with how we currently live. It is not exactly compatible with marriage.'

'Exactly, Ben. This life is not a family man's life; that is for sure.'

'So, who is this future wife of yours and where does she hail from?'

'The letter did not say, though I think it would be safe to assume she would hail from London. Maybe that is where you are from also, Ben. You have never told us where your home is.'

Ben hated the question as he had hated lying to his father and brother over the years, but answered with the same response as always.

'I have told you before. I have no memory of a home. Only a life on the seas from ship to ship, until I ended up with you.'

Luke nodded and stared through the fire towards him. 'Ben Deery, Omiran, the great warrior giant with no memory of peace and a lifetime of battle. No wonder stories which carry your name are becoming legendary.'

'Stop, Brother,' Ben retorted, frustrated by Luke's mocking praise. 'You know me better than anyone.'

'Yes, I think that I do, at least as much as anyone can. You should marry and have children, so you have a legacy to leave behind. Be it sorcery, skill or dumb luck, or maybe a combination of all three, even you can't keep cheating death forever. I am coming to believe that no living man can kill you, but time is an enemy no man can defeat – not even you, Ben.'

'Come, we need to sleep. We are up before dawn tomorrow,' Ben replied, tired of the conversation that now centred on him, and they retired under the starlit African sky.

In the light of dawn, they assessed what could be salvaged from the camp. Three large wagons were loaded up with provisions and, with a procession of thirty freed and cheerful natives marching behind them, they set off towards the southern coast of Benin, towards the floating village of Ganvie.

Ganvie sat on the northern edge of Lake Nokoué and had

been established as a haven for freed slaves. The Dahomey war tribes, who were supplying the Portuguese raiders with local slaves, would not fight on water, and so the floating village served as a perfect hide for those escaping the slave ships.

It took them two days to reach the Nokoué. They gave the natives the stock in the wagons, previously owned by the slavers. It took an hour before they were allowed to leave because of the overwhelming thanks and praise from the inhabitants of Ganvie, many of whom had previously been saved by the Company.

They kept the horses and rode further south towards the large town of Cotonou, where the *Gabriel* was anchored with *Ol' Charlie*.

Ben booked a room at the biggest hotel in town. He welcomed the feel of a warm bath and smooth whiskey. He had one of the Gonzos go to the port and have a fresh set of clothes brought from his ship to his room.

Clean and fresh, he shaved the hair around his neck, combing his full blond beard and tying his hair back out of his eyes. He put on a clean shirt and vest and tucked his bone-handled knife inside his large leather boot before making his way downstairs to the tavern below, where Luke and Regan were sitting at a table, already halfway through their first brandies.

'Ah, come on over, Son,' Regan called as he saw him walk into the bar. 'Come. We have things to celebrate.' Regan motioned for another bottle and glass as Ben took a seat at the table.

'My biological son has agreed to marry, and it pleases me greatly.'

'Yes, I heard,' Ben replied as he lifted the brandy to his mouth. 'I think it is a fine idea.'

'Ah, it is that, indeed,' Regan went on. 'We set sail for Brazil. We are Rio-bound.'

'Delighted to hear it,' Ben replied again. 'I do enjoy Rio.' Over the last seven years he had grown comfortable with the exciting bustle of Rio de Janeiro and had put to rest the tragedies of his first visit all those years ago. It was a different place now, with proper governance and order. It had become a great city of trade, which attracted people from all over the world, mixing cultures, beliefs and ideas. It was an exciting place to be, an up-and-coming city.

'So,' Ben continued, lifting his brandy glass, 'is your new wife a young baroness from Brazil, Jack?'

'Heavens no, Ben,' Regan burst in before Luke had time to answer 'No. Stevenson has decided to take the voyage to Rio with his family. And about time, too. I can't remember the last time he took time to see his businesses in that part of the world.'

The glass in Ben's hand stopped an inch from his mouth and stayed there suspended as he tried to comprehend what he was certain he had just heard. The hairs on the back of his neck stood up and the blood in his cheeks grew hot.

'Who?' The word was quiet and almost unbearable for him to say through the gravely lump that rolled down his throat.

'Jacob Stevenson, Ben. Surely you know of Stevenson Transport. Jacob is an old acquaintance of mine. We knew each other when I was a Royal Navy captain and Jacob had just expanded his transport business by hiring our ship-building services. A long time ago that was now, but he has two very beautiful daughters who have come of age, and it has been decided that this marriage will not only be fruitful and good for Luke, but will also bring our two wealthy families together for a common purpose. Stevenson Transport is the largest transport business on the Atlantic and no doubt this union will see us take over the building contract to supply their expanding fleet. Not only will it secure a beautiful wife for you, Luke, but it will bring sustainable wealth to the business. I couldn't have thought of a better match if I tried.'

The shock had knocked Ben into a haze. He had not heard the name Stevenson in a long time. Here and there as a company name, but not so close to his own life. He had never imagined that name would enter his circle again. Immediately he thought of Sasha.

'You say daughters. Which one will you marry?' He realised as he said the words that he felt ill.

What if it is Sasha? What will I do?

'I am not sure,' Regan went on. 'He only has two daughters: Sasha, the older, and Penny, the younger. Both very nice to look at, I am told, but one is more of a pain in the arse than the other. The older one, I hear, says whatever enters her head, which can lead her into trouble. She has strong opinions against the slave trade. Actually, she would probably be a good match for you, Ben, hey?' Regan and Luke both started laughing as Ben continued to try to hide the shock on his face.

He let out a 'huh', which did nothing to conceal the irony of the situation as he drank his brandy and filled another glass to the brim. He drank that down in one mouthful and placed the empty glass on the table.

'So, when do we leave for Rio?' Luke spoke up.

'We sail the day after next,' Regan answered. 'I believe the Stevenson entourage is already on its way. Six ships in total, I hear. Four Man O' Wars filled with British soldiers surround Jacob's new flag ship, the *Mary*, and a scout ship to lead them. An armed fortress on the Atlantic to carry them over. What a sight they will be coming into port. If the wind is with us, we may just get there before them to watch the spectacle ourselves.'

Ben sat there motionless, his head spinning; not from brandy but from past horrors he thought were behind him.

'I will take my leave, then. I need to let my crew know we sail the day after tomorrow.'

'What, so soon?' Luke protested. 'Why not stay a while?'

'I am tired. I will take my leave. Good night and congratulations, Brother. It will be a momentous affair; of that I am certain.'

Ben stood and faced the table. 'Do you remember our conversation last night, Luke?'

Luke nodded as Ben continued.

'Love only needs a moment to change our world.'

MIKE WARDLE

He turned and left the room.

Chapter 36

Sasha shut her eyes, letting the salty afternoon wind blow through her hair. She felt the rocking in her legs as the great ship cut through the Atlantic swells. The sound of the waves breaking against the bow hissed around her head, and she welcomed the smell and taste of the ocean spray.

For four weeks she had been a passenger on the *Mary*, her father's newest flagship. He had spared no expense building her and the result was a magnificent floating giant. It took what seemed like a small army of men to sail her safely, and she had ample room, storage and resources for all her guests and crew. Rumours had spread around London over the course of the three years it took to build her that the *Mary* cost Jacob Stevenson over sixty thousand pounds and a forest of oak trees.

The *Mary* was a statement just as much as she was a luxury, Sasha thought. Her father had lost the *Retribution* to an attack years earlier and, with it, his lead captain. Sasha had also lost much in that battle, with confirmation of Caleb's name being on the ship's register, along with the sickening news that none of the crew had been spared. The *Mary* was built bigger, faster and stronger than the *Retribution*, and a flotilla of warships created an armed perimeter around her everywhere she sailed.

As the wind blew into her face, Sasha opened her eyes and surveyed the deep blue expanse of water in front of her. The excitement of the voyage had been overshadowed by seasickness in the first two weeks, but her stomach had become accustomed to the rocking of the ship and she had been able to take meals without fear of sending them back over the side.

Sasha and her sister had opposite reactions after being told by their father months ago that one of them was to be married to a man they had never met. Sasha was still furious at the idea and refused to comply with her parents' wishes. She had tried to avoid her father's conversations over the past months in the hope that he would naturally turn his attention towards her little sister, who seemed to be more excited with the prospect of marriage than of anything else.

Night fell over the Atlantic and the stars appeared to fill the sky. Sasha made her way down to the *Mary's* large cabin, large enough for all her father's esteemed guests to sit in and dine at leisure. It was a ballroom in its own right, with extravagant furnishings, and large windows, which spread the width of the stern and around to the side of the ship, allowing the stars and the moon to take part in the nightly festivities.

Two long tables were situated parallel to each other pointing stern to bow and at their heads, situated just in front of the large windows, was a narrow, main table that ran nearly the width of the stern.

Jacob and Annette Stevenson would sit at this table, rotating their guests each night to dine near them. Sasha sat next to Penny and Brenton on one of the longer tables. She sat opposite the captain of the *Mary*, John Straw, and his first mate, Peter Masson. Next to them were the Barringtons and Stocks and beside her, on the other side from Penny, sat Paula and Charlotte Sheffield with their parents.

The Sheffield twins were Penny's age and their family had investment interests in South American sugar plantations. They were among the very wealthy London families who had taken advantage of the free trip to the New World on the grandest vessel on the Atlantic.

'So, tell me,' John Straw started as he cut through the spatchcock on his plate. 'How are you fine young ladies enjoying the voyage so far?' He sat up proudly as he addressed the opposite side of the table, expecting a chorus of thrilled and jubilant responses, as only a captain of a mighty ship could.

'I am finding that I can hardly contain myself with excitement,' Charlotte answered without hesitation, quickly beating her twin sister into the conversation. The table waited for Paula to speak next as, invariably, an instant after one sister spoke, the other would follow, often completing her sister's sentence.

'And we have to commend you, sir, on the safe journey so far,' Paula completed her sister's compliment, exactly as expected.

'Well, we have to be thankful for the *Mary*. Mr Stevenson has certainly spared no expense on her and I would put a wager on it that there is no finer ship on the Atlantic, possibly in the world. The Spanish Royal Family would indeed be envious of such a vessel,' John Straw replied, content with the positive response.

'And you, Miss Penny and Miss Sasha?' Peter, the first mate, entered the conversation. 'You must be quite proud to have such a magnificent ship sailing under your family's name.'

'Indeed, we are, sir,' Penny replied politely, 'and I must also agree with Charlotte and Paula when I say that such a ship requires a most skilled and experienced crew to guide her, and what we have seen thus far confirms that.'

'You are very kind, Miss Penny. We will endeavour to maintain such standards for the remainder of the journey.'

'And how much longer is the journey to Rio, Mr Straw?' Sasha asked.

'Well, we have been sailing at a leisurely pace thus far, so that all guests on board may get accustomed to the sea. I believe, however, Mr Stevenson will want to stretch her sea legs soon and we will quicken our run from here, weather permitting. I would estimate, if the winds stay with us, that we will see the Port of Rio in just under two weeks.'

'Ah, that is fantastic news,' Sasha continued. 'I am desperate to finally see Rio. I hear it is different from London in almost every way.'

'It is that, Miss Stevenson. It has become a thriving port and capital now. It is exotic and tropical with that ever-present hint of uncertainty that comes with the New World.'

Sasha welcomed the description and willed for strong winds to hasten the journey. She had dreamt about seeing the New World many times over the years, and to be so close now was so exciting.

'I hope it is not too dangerous,' Penny exclaimed. 'I have heard that there are unsavoury folk and men of ill reputation who dwell in Rio.'

Captain Straw smiled at the four girls in front of him. 'Please, do not concern yourselves in the slightest with your safety, ladies. There are four Man O' War ships full of British soldiers who will accompany us on land and you will all be staying at the British Consulate inside the Government Fort, which is impenetrable and boasts large, beautiful grounds within its high stone walls. You will all be quite safe there, I assure you.'

'In addition to that,' Peter Masson took the lead from his captain, 'the Deerys and their two ships will also be in port. There will be more than enough able-bodied men to ensure your safety, ladies.'

'Ah, yes, the Deerys,' Paula Sheffield re-entered the conversation. 'They say that they are great warriors, heroes even. They are the topic of conversation in every tearoom in London now. Is it true that they make it their business to track and war with the slavers…?'

'…and that then they take the slaves back to their homes in Africa?' Charlotte finished her sister's sentence on cue.

'You must not believe everything you hear in the gossip circles of the London Court, ladies,' Captain Straw answered. 'The Deerys are shipbuilders, and fine shipbuilders at that. Who do you think built the ship you are on right now?'

There was an exclamation of surprise from the twins as Straw continued.

'Remember that slaving, even though it is considered an unfortunate business, is still legal, and if the Deerys were to attack slaving ships without just cause, it would be considered to be against the law.'

'Without just cause?' Sasha spoke with animation in her voice. 'What could be more just than to free those who have had that very freedom stripped from them without consent?'

'Please, Miss Sasha,' John Straw quickly moved to explain himself before the notoriously defiant temper of Sasha Stevenson spoiled the evening. 'Please understand that I do not mean to disagree, and I, too, would see slaving abolished from the world because it is a ghastly business indeed. I am just making the point that, as we stand now, by law it is considered a crime to attack a ship unprovoked and outside the parameters of war, regardless of its cargo and, from what I understand, the Deerys are by no means a family who would act outside the law.'

'Of course, sir.' Sasha concluded the conversation as the waiters made their way around the cabin to clear the main course plates and refill glasses of wine.

'And,' Straw continued, 'the marriage which is to occur will certainly put both families in excellent positions for the future.'

'Have you met the Deerys, Mr Straw?' Penny's enthusiasm in the conversation had just heightened.

'I have had the pleasure indeed, miss. On a number of occasions our paths have crossed.'

'And tell us, what are they like, sir? Have you met Luke Deery? What is he like as a man?'

'I have met all three, miss. Regan Deery is an accomplished and educated man and has brought up his sons accordingly. Luke is a fine and honourable young man who will inherit the wealth of the family. He would be a very suitable match for any respectable young lady.'

'And the other son?' Charlotte asked, and there was the usual echo as Paula continued on behalf of her sister.

'Yes, the other son, Ben. Pray tell, what is the story behind his adoption?'

'Well,' Straw began, 'I do admit that it is an unusual set of circumstances. Ben Deery is loved by Regan as a son and, as such, was legally adopted three years ago on his eighteenth birthday. There was, I admit, consternation among London society, but I believe that has all calmed down now as all tantalising news tends to do in time.'

Sasha looked over at her sister and then back towards the captain. 'Sorry, Mr Straw, what do you mean by consternation?'

'Oh, nothing at all, miss. I should not have said anything about it. Too much of the old sherry for dinner, perhaps.'

'Please, sir,' Sasha insisted, 'at the very least, if either I or my sister is to marry into a family not of our own choosing, we should be given an insight into the nature of that family.'

The captain smiled sympathetically from across the table as he twirled the stem of his wine glass.

'Well, then, not that it is any business of mine, but the adopted son, Ben, was not of high-born status. In fact, from all reports, it seems that the boy was a young slaver.'

Sasha's anger began to rise.

'A slaver!' The words were intentionally loud enough for her father to hear from the end table as she looked towards him. She waited until she had both her parents' attention before continuing.

'So, we are to be married into a family who adopts slavers? Is that the respectable union we might expect for our futures?'

As she finished her words, she realised that the cabin had now fallen silent and all attention was on her. Even the waiters paused in their duties and stood uncomfortably at attention while the creaking of timber as the ship hit the ocean swells and rocked back and forth was the only sound to break the unbearable silence.

She looked over to the main table to see her father glaring back at her with seething irritation in his eyes.

Annette Stevenson quickly took charge and raised her glass high towards the other tables in the cabin. 'I do not believe that I have had the pleasure of welcoming you all on our voyage, though we are now halfway across the Atlantic. I must give praise to the *Mary*, her prestigious captain and her wonderful crew.'

'Hear! Hear!' cheered the guests, and the noise of enthusiastic conversation filled the room, ending the awkwardness that had occupied it for what felt like an age. Sasha looked back over at her father, who was still looking in her direction. A momentary look of disappointment in her actions filled his eyes before he raised his glass and smiled at her. She felt relieved that she had not provoked the situation any further, but no amount of wine could wash the foul taste from her mouth.

Above all else, this was against everything she held dear. She would fight against marrying a man she did not love, she would fight against being used as a bargaining tool for her father, and, above all else, she could never marry into a family that had slaving ties – she would never!

Chapter 37

'When will you marry?' Ben asked as he held the wheel of *Ol' Charlie*.

'Not for a while,' Luke replied. 'Perhaps a year. I need to meet them both and decide first. I believe we will marry back in London.' He looked over at Ben and smiled. 'Yes, you will have to set foot in London society, Ben, and I know the thought pains you that, briefly, you will be stolen from the hunting, the heat, the dust and the thorns of Africa.'

'First, he will have to make sure you reach the altar alive,' a voice wafted up the stairs as Regan made his way onto the quarterdeck.

'Captain at the helm!' Luke shouted over the decks and heard it echoed by sailors across the ship.

'You never know, Ben,' Regan continued as Ben let him take control of the ship's wheel. 'Once Luke chooses a Stevenson girl, you may be given the other's hand in marriage. Apparently, our actions over the last few years have not gone unnoticed, and stories of the *Gabriel* and her crew have begun to filter through the streets of Spain, France and England. It seems you are a well-known man in your own right now, and it will be no surprise that families will consider you as a suitable choice for their daughters' hands. What with you now having financial stakes in the shipping company, you will provide a wealthy life for a bride and her family.'

'Yet, I wonder how I will be received?' Ben stated, not really wanting a reply.

'Well, some think you are a hunter, some think you are a slaver, and some think you are a criminal. It is all a matter of who you are talking to at the time. Nevertheless, they know your name.'

'You mock me, Father. I mean, how will I be received as an adopted son?'

'Oh, I do apologise. I mistook the meaning of your question, dear boy.'

Ben looked over at Luke, who was chuckling to himself. Ben had spent the last five weeks battling his tangled emotions since he had heard the news that Sasha and Penny Stevenson were the choices for his brother's marriage.

He had buried his love for the Stevenson family many years ago and had replaced it with hate and resentment, which were still very much present within him.

He was happy with his own life. He was young and rich and had lived a life of great adventure since meeting the Deerys. He would do nothing to put that in jeopardy. He was happy for his brother and was sure that he could keep his emotions in check, even if Sasha was the chosen of the two. But he was less certain that he could keep his true identity secret once face to face with the Stevensons. He had changed from boyhood to manhood over the last seven years and was not in any way the unfortunate child who had been whipped on the Stevenson estate, even though the scars on his back remained clearly visible. He hoped that they were the only evidence connecting him to his past life and that a shirt and jacket would conceal his secret.

He knew it was possible that his brother might choose to marry Sasha; though, over the years, Luke had shown a tendency to prefer blonde-haired women. Despite his disdain for the Stevenson family, he secretly hoped that little blonde Penny Stevenson had grown to become a fine young woman who would catch his brother's eye.

'Ship ahoy!' The signal was coming from the crow's nest of the *Gabriel,* which sailed beside them and was currently in the charge of Ben's first mate. Ben often moved from ship to ship and dined with his father and brother. This gave them the chance to let each crew mingle and mix with the other or separate any disputes on the rare occasion there might be trouble amongst the men.

'Captain! We have a ship port side heading south in front of us.' This time the call came from *Ol' Charlie's* nest.

Ben grabbed an eyeglass and bounded down the stairs, onto the main deck and up to the forecastle. He opened the eyeglass to its full length and scoured the horizon from the bow. He could hear the ship's crew sharpening their swords around him and it was like music to his ears.

Hopefully, it was a slaver on its way to Brazil. If it was, they would engage. Their way of identifying a slave ship was to come up behind her. The smell of death would hang in the air as they followed its line and there would be no mistaking what was on board. No misdirection or flag swapping could mask the horrid stench of defecation and the human rotting of a slaver.

'Can we see what she is?' Regan called out

'No, sir!' The call came back from the nest.

'Let's get up behind her, then. Inform the crew to prepare the ship for battle. Signal to the *Gabriel* to fall in line behind us. She won't outrun us.'

Luke went below deck to rally the rest of the crew and prepare the ship's guns. Ben stayed on the forecastle, keeping his eye on the ship sailing across their path.

Then it hit him. His nostrils flared and his throat dried as his nose caught the unmistakable stench on the wind. A slaver.

He made his way down to the officers' quarters, where he kept a bunk and some effects. Hanging up near his bed was his cutlass, knife, two muskets, a long rifle and a small Angolan hatchet, which over the years he had found useful for cutting through ropes or a man's skull. He armed himself in routine fashion. He was used to the moments before a fight now and was ready for it. He welcomed the anticipation as he made his way back to the main deck.

'Sir, we think we know the ship.' One of the crew from the crow's nest had made his way down to the deck and was calling to Regan. 'It looks like the *Grey Cloud*, Mr Deery, sir.'

Ben looked up at Regan from the main deck. 'Are you sure, man?' he asked the sailor, keeping his eyes on his father.

'Quite certain, sir. We are now in range and able to see the crew.'

Regan had not diverted his gaze from Ben and spoke with a quiet excitement. 'Very well, then. Prepare.'

A quiet hush came over the crew and all preparations seemed to be orchestrated with a heightened purpose, for they had come across Jackson Bell's ship. Luke returned to the quarterdeck fully armed. He brought with him Regan's weapons and took over the wheel while his father armed himself.

A silence fell across the crew as they trailed the *Grey Cloud* from a safe distance, the *Gabriel* behind them, waiting for the next signal.

The stench of death filled their nostrils and it was clear that the *Grey* was carrying a full cargo of slaves.

'Engage her!' Regan ordered.

The ship erupted with cheers and the wind pushed *Ol' Charlie* and the *Gabriel* towards battle.

Chapter 38

Adder had sensed the ships coming up behind them even before he could see them. After a lifetime of being pursued, he could feel it in the same way: his senses heightened in the eerily calm moments before an incoming storm. The ships had come up too fast to be merchants. These ships wanted something else, a fight perhaps.

Damn them all to hell. They should stay out of our business.

He was the first mate on the *Grey Cloud* under Jackson Bell, who was now a commodore with three ships under his command. The *Grey Cloud* was Jackson Bell's flagship and he also commanded two galleons, the *Foca* and the *Mercader de Olas*, which they had successfully attacked and hijacked. Both had been turned into slaving ships to service the West Indies and North Americas, where the need for the black trade was still strong.

Jackson, who was not with the *Grey* on the current voyage, was waiting for Adder on the southern coast of Brazil. The Scarlets had based themselves there for years, far away from the Portuguese and British military in Rio. Over the past years, they had recruited well and now had an army behind them, all trained to fight for the revolution, waiting for the right moment to strike down their oppressors.

Adder looked back towards the approaching ships, which were now in formation to engage, and could see that he would not outrun them. Concerned, he watched the two ships riding high in the water and travelling fast, flying no navy flags – not slavers, not merchants. Were these the *Gabriel* and the *Charlotte Arms*? He had heard that the adopted Deery boy ran a crew who were as vicious and well-trained as any on the seas, but his crew were also warriors, and he would not let Jackson Bell hear the news that the great and feared Adder and the crew of *Grey Cloud* had been defeated.

'Adder, the ships are gaining. What is your command?'

Adder looked at the two ships.

Those damn Deerys.

'Prepare for a fight. Get the crew ready.'

'Sir, the ships. They fly the flags of the *Gabriel* and the *Charlotte Arms*, sir. It is the Deerys.'

'Damn them straight to hell!' Adder belted. He knew that both ships would be well armed and lighter than the *Grey*. They would be able to move past them at will and strategically take out their guns from their line formation. They would then take out the *Grey's* rudder, move in and lock the ships together, at which point the crew would spill over and the fight would begin.

There was no way to avoid it. The Deerys' ships had at least twice as many men, all trained and ready to fight. They would have by now picked up the scent of the slaves, and were coming in for the kill.

He had seen it before, when seven years ago he had been taken prisoner on the *Charlotte Arms* and transported to Rio, headed for the gallows. Only a perverse and corrupt government official on their payroll, Jasper Cole, enabled him his narrow escape.

He would not be defeated again, yet he knew that this was a fight he could not win. There was too much firepower against them, and today was not a day to die.

There had been word from Jackson Bell's camp that Jacob Stevenson himself was making the journey to Rio. They had been given another chance to finally uncover the secret of the lost Tierra Firme Fleet. Fate had allowed the revolution another opportunity to finally take what belonged to them. He would not risk this chance fighting the Deerys if he could somehow avoid it. There were far more important things to consider now.

'Nearly in range, sir.'

'Gather the women and children and bring them up to the decks.'

'Sir?'

'You heard me,' Adder said. 'Women and children only. Strip them bare and bring them up here, now!'

Chapter 39

Ben stood on the quarterdeck of *Ol' Charlie*. His father and brother were by his side and all three were now heavily armed. They had moved in towards the *Grey Cloud*, guns at the ready. First, they would take out the *Grey's* gun deck, firing above the lower deck where the slaves would be chained. The *Gabriel* would shoot first and the *Ol' Charlie* second as they passed the *Grey* in a line. They would then aim for the mainmast and, lastly, take out her rudder, leaving her floating helplessly with no way to manoeuvre or fire back on them. They would then surround the *Grey* and rope her in for a fight.

He was glaring at the broadly built man looking back at him from the *Grey's* poop deck. His frame and scarred body were unmistakable – Adder.

Ben relished the thought of fighting Adder, the man who had murdered his first crew and his first real friend. The image of Bobby's lifeless body falling over the gunwales and into the sea still visited him in his dreams and he had wished every day since for the chance to make it right.

First, he would kill Adder, sending a message to Jackson Bell that his pet beast had been put down, and then Jackson himself would know who was coming after him to close his eyes once and for all.

He wanted revenge for his friends and for his own pain. For Captain Andrews, who had taken him in and taught him in the early stages of his new life. For his crew, who had welcomed him as a merchant sailor. He wanted to kill the beast standing on the poop deck of the *Grey* looking back at him through the eyeglass.

Ben was no longer a boy. He had become a warrior in his own right and he longed for his revenge. His focus shifted to the movement on the deck of the *Grey Cloud*, when he realised Adder had not yet given the command to ready his cannons. His brother had clearly been thinking the same thing.

'Why are they not ready to fire on us?' Luke echoed Ben's thoughts.

'Look,' Regan said, peering through his eyeglass. 'They are strapping women to the masts. We would not be able to take the mast down without killing them all. Signal to the *Gabriel* to hold fire,' he yelled.

They watched in anger as the women and children were stripped naked, hands bound together and tied to the masts of the *Grey*. Their crew began tying up the children and lowering them over the gunwales, dangling them in line with their gun decks. They squirmed in pain, their naked bodies scraping against the harsh weather-beaten side of the ship.

Luke looked up at his father, surprised. 'It is the *Grey Cloud*, Father. It has been responsible for thousands of deaths. We cannot let it go or we allow thousands more to suffer the same fate. If she is here, then Jackson Bell is on her or not far away. We can finally take down the worst slaving ship on the Atlantic.'

'Don't you think I know these things, boy? Do you not think I want to see the *Grey* sink to the bottom of the Atlantic? But at what cost? We cannot fire at the mast, we cannot fire into their gun decks and we cannot sink her. If we approach and rope her in, those children will be crushed between the ships. If we defeat them, they will blow the hull and drown everyone on board. It is Adder and he will not surrender to us again. He will gladly die before that.'

Ben stood silently, staring at Adder.

'We take him on land. With stealth and with surprise. We let him reach Brazil or wherever he is heading, and we track him from there. They will be on land at least a few weeks before they embark again, and we will have our chance then. They will also lead us to Jackson, once and for all.'

'Take Jackson Bell on land?' Luke questioned. 'You do not go after Jackson Bell on land without the whole British Army at your back and God himself on your side, for he is truly the devil's spawn, some say the devil himself. Do we take down the slaver now and divide their forces? I know it will end the lives of those on board. But it will certainly save many more.'

'No!' Ben replied to his brother angrily. He looked at the young boys hanging against the outside of the ship. He had been in their place before and he would not see them without hope. 'We take them on land.'

The more he thought about it, the more it began to make sense to him. Drowning Adder would not send a strong enough message. He needed to make an example out of him, so others would know that they could easily share the same fate. Now they had finally found Adder, he would lead them to Jackson who, it seemed, was in hiding somewhere in South America.

'It will be far more difficult on land when they are scattered. We have Adder and his crew in one place, ready for the taking,' Luke continued his case.

'It is not who we are,' Ben growled again. He understood his brother's point. They had an opportunity to take out the *Grey Cloud*. Slaves would become collateral damage, but that would be nothing compared to the many who would perish should they lose her again. He knew how those slaves felt. He had been in their position before. Helpless. Desperate. He would not condemn them to die for his own cause.

'How many will die if we let them go?' Luke started again.

'It is not who we are!'

Luke stepped back when he saw the fury in his brother's eyes as Ben spun around to meet his gaze. It was a look he had seen before and he knew that he had overstepped, and that his next words would determine whether the fight would be provoked on the deck of *Ol' Charlie* and not against the slaver. He was not afraid of his adopted younger brother, but knew far better than to try and fight him.

'We give them their distance.' Regan took the opportunity to interrupt, realising the tension between his sons. 'Take a wide berth on their starboard side, out of their cannon range and move around them for Rio. There we will decide what our next actions will be.'

The *Gabriel* followed the signals from the *Ol Charlie's* bow and began sailing north, away from the *Grey Cloud*.

Ben looked through his eyeglass to see that Adder was staring back at them. His eyes stayed locked on Adder until he disappeared over the horizon.

I will find you soon Adder, and I will have my revenge.

Chapter 40

Ben had made the rest of the voyage on the *Gabriel,* where he had the privacy of his own quarters to consider the days to come. The crow's nest had sighted land some time ago and the ship made its way into Rio's harbour. He looked on in amazement each time he sailed into Rio. The small port town that he had first seen had now become a small city thriving with industry.

Many came from all over the world to find their fortunes in the mines, while others had developed businesses to service the constant traffic. This had increased trade, requiring more merchant shipping, which was good for the family business.

It seemed a lifetime ago now that he had ridden with the Couriers to follow the trails in the Brazilian mountains.

He disembarked and set off to meet Regan and Luke at The Monkey and Rat. It had been renovated a number of times over the years, and what Ben had first seen to be a simple, dingy tavern now stood as a grand hotel and popular watering hole for businessmen and travellers alike.

The streets were more crowded and the town square still thrived with the bustling of the market stalls. He walked through the swinging doors to the welcoming smell and sounds that only a busy tavern could offer.

Miners, travellers, whores, fighters, traders, merchant sailors and off-duty soldiers were enjoying the midday festivities and abundance of ale.

He saw the table where his father and brother were already

drinking and walked over to join them. A man he recognised sat with them. He had met the man many years ago when he had been invited to dine with Simon Blake.

'Ah, Ben,' Regan started, 'this is Lupe. He is the general manager of the South American section of Stevenson Transport.'

'Pleased to meet you, sir.' Ben extended his hand to meet Lupe's as he said the words.

'The pleasure is mine, Ben Deery. I have heard much about you and I have to say you are as big as the stories say.'

Ben smiled politely and pulled out one of the spare chairs. As he sat down, he caught sight of a short, fat, ugly man with beady eyes peering at them from the corner. He wore a blue broach and a peacock feather in his hat. Ben turned away from him and sat down. That stare had lasted a little longer than he had preferred but his thoughts were interrupted by the discussion at the table.

'Not everything has changed for the better around here,' Lupe said. 'The Scarlets have returned and have a strong presence south of here. They have been left alone to do as they please for far too long now. There are rumours that Jackson Bell and his pet snake Adder have also returned to this part of the world.'

'Yes, we saw the *Grey Cloud* not two days ago,' Regan answered. 'Adder was heading south of here and would have reached the Brazilian coast by now with a ship full of Africans.'

'So it is true!' Lupe exclaimed, a look of horror sweeping over his face. 'The devil has returned.'

Ben listened to the conversation but could not shake the feeling that he had been intentionally glared at by the short, fat man in the corner. He looked over his shoulder to where the man was sitting, only to see an empty chair and table. He thought it somewhat strange, but convinced himself that people come and go all the time and reminded himself that he often attracted stares due to his size, and so he let it go.

'Luke,' he said, 'we should travel down there tonight and cut their throats.'

'Easy, son,' Regan replied. 'Not without an army behind you.

Jackson has expanded the Scarlets tenfold, apparently. They have a fleet of ships. They have built their own slaving port and every raiding party and criminal in South America seems to be in allegiance with him. But I have other news.' Regan changed the subject. 'Stevenson and his family are currently en route here and should arrive at any time.'

'Yes, I know. I received the same communication. His whole family and a ship full of esteemed guests,' Lupe replied.

'That is right,' Regan went on. 'Luke is to have the choice of which daughter to marry. It will bring union to two great families and set up the future for the trade and transport business between Europe and the Americas.'

'Lucky you, son. I hear the Stevenson girls are extremely well-presented and pursued by every wealthy young suitor in Europe. Princes have tried and failed, it is said. We have been busy making sure the Government Fort and its lodgings are up to standard. Chefs, waiters, entertainers have all been engaged and are ready for a great ball to welcome the party to Rio. It will be an occasion to remember, with no expense spared.'

'Right now, all I can think about is Adder. We should seek him out, army or no.'

'Keep your voice down, Luke,' Lupe cautioned him. 'The Scarlet crew have spies everywhere now. And there is something else. There is talk that the Stevenson's arrival might draw out an old friend.'

'You don't mean…' Regan stopped and looked around to make sure no one was listening in, before lowering his voice to a whisper. 'You don't mean Simon Blake, do you Lupe?'

Lupe gave all three men a subtle nod.

'Seven years ago, I received a letter from Blake informing me that I was to take over operations in South America. He and his Couriers rode off into the shadows. I'm sure everyone here knows the rumours. Some say Jackson found and murdered him. Some say he left because he now harbours a great secret. Some say he has a map showing the location of a large amount of

Spanish bullion that was intended for the Spanish Royal Family.'

'How much are we talking?' Ben piped up.

'The Spanish Treasure Fleet's ships.' All at once, the three Deerys leant forward, fixated on Lupe's next words. 'Enough to have influence over the New World, something I am sure Bell would find interesting, especially with an army behind him. It would be reason enough for Blake to go into exile, to keep it away from Jackson. They were strange times back then. We lost the *Retribution*, all her crew, Blake and his Couriers: all in the same day.'

Ben, trying not to think of that day, shifted in his chair and ordered another three ales. Then he thought of the trail he rode seven years ago with Simon Blake. He thought of the slaver he had shot after Simon's desperate order to stop the man from escaping. He thought of a winding trail into the mountains … and a waterfall at its end.

Chapter 41

The Government Fort was a large sandstone building with three levels, each tiered backwards towards the natural incline of the mountains. On each level was a large stone courtyard providing different views and vantage points of the city and bay below.

Sasha stood at the balcony on the second level and watched the bustling markets below her. Her senses danced with the music of the market and the birds in the Brazilian rosewood trees around her. The aromas from the cooking fires, the vibrant purple of the corsage orchids and the spike of Sugar Mountain, rearing up from the waters of the bay, provided an exotic setting, one that she had dreamt of for many years.

Truly, this was a new world, and it was magical. Even though she had read stories of South America, those books had not captured the green of the mountains, the blue of the sea, the vivid red, purple and yellow of the flowers and the warmth of the salty morning breeze. She felt more alive than she ever had before. This was a world where she could be free from the distinction between poverty and station, and free to release the wild spirit within.

'It is just so exciting, Sasha,' the ever-adorable voice of her sister Penny floated on the warm morning air. 'Brenton, come quickly. Come out here with Sasha and look at this view. You can see over the whole harbour from here.'

Penny walked briskly across the courtyard, her older brother behind her. He looked comfortable in his riding pants, high leather boots and light, free-flowing white shirt. He strolled across the courtyard towards her and smiled.

'What do you think, Sasha, now that you can see properly in the daylight?' They had docked in the late afternoon the day before and the light had faded by the time her family was ashore.

'It is more beautiful than I could have ever possibly imagined. This whole trip has been, so far: Father's ship, the Atlantic and Rio. Well, just look at it, Brenton – have you ever seen so many colours?'

'It is a sight, that is for sure. Far different from London.'

'What an adventure we are all on,' Penny spoke as she wrapped her arms around Brenton's waist. He looked down at her and smiled.

'And your adventure is in no way finished. The Deerys arrived here two days ago. There will be a ball tonight to welcome everyone to Rio. I should imagine that there will be over three hundred guests.'

Penny's excitement was nearly uncontrollable. A ball was the pinnacle of social excitement for ladies as it offered the opportunity to dance, to practise conversation and, of course, to dress up.

'And this is where you will both meet Luke Deery and, I assume, where one of you will catch his eye and become his future wife.'

'I can hardly wait to meet him, Brother.' As she said it, Penny gave Sasha a sympathetic look. 'I mean, if Luke does not choose me, I will not be angry, Sister. You are the oldest and so deserve the chance more than me.'

Sasha smiled back at her sister. 'I would never let my age or position in this family get in the way of true love. I wish you the very best, little sister.'

'Well, then,' their father's voice sounded behind them as Jacob and Annette walked across the courtyard. 'We will just have to see what transpires tonight.'

'Where will the ball be held, Father?' Penny asked.

'I believe it will be held here, my child. There should be fireworks and music and a sunset that only Rio can provide. How does that sound for a romantic backdrop?'

Penny grabbed onto her father's arm, instantly bringing a smile to his face.

'Father, I can hardly contain myself. This afternoon I will find Paula and Charlotte Sheffield and work out what to wear this evening.'

'And you, Sasha?' Annette asked the less traditional of her daughters. 'Are you as excited about the prospect of this evening as the rest of your family?'

Sasha looked at her parents and older brother searching for the happiness in her eyes and, for once, decided to take the diplomatic approach.

'I do not believe I have ever been as excited as I am right now. I just hope that the feeling lasts through the night and that I shall wake tomorrow feeling the same way.'

'I am sure that you will, Sasha,' her father replied happily. 'Come, let us see the sights of the town. I would like to show you our warehouse and offices here in Rio, and on the way we can compare the Rio markets to those of London.'

Sasha walked next to her brother and sister, stopping intermittently at various stalls to meet the owners and discover their wares – silks, livestock, food, pottery, summer dresses and more. The music filled their ears as they made their way through the square, her father and mother walking in front with soldiers guarding them on both sides.

'Ah, fortune favours us, it seems.' Sasha looked over to see her father greet a group of men. 'Regan Deery, it is good to see you again.'

Sasha and Penny looked at each other sharply, the younger with excitement and the other with apprehension.

'Jacob,' the bull shaped man walked over and shook her father's hand. 'How are you, my friend? It certainly has been too long since all of us have been in Rio. Annette, it is a pleasure to see you again.' He bowed politely.

'The pleasure is ours, Mr Deery.'

'Lupe,' Jacob shook the hand of another man. 'I was just on my way to see you.'

'Excellent, Mr Stevenson, sir. We have much to discuss.'

Sasha examined the three men in front of her. Regan Deery looked like a powerful man. He was wide with broad shoulders, muscular arms and strong hands. Standing beside him, she saw a younger version of the same man, instantly realising this would undoubtedly be Luke Deery.

Across from him was another man whom her father had called Lupe. She had heard this name before and knew that he worked for her family.

'Regan,' her father began, 'I would like to introduce my son and eldest, Brenton, and my two daughters, Sasha and Penny.'

All three men bowed and nodded politely.

'It is lovely to meet you all. Please let me introduce my eldest son, Luke.'

Sasha felt a nervous tingle down her spine as she absorbed the name. She and her sister curtsied accordingly, with a synchronised, 'How do you do, Mr Deery?'

Sasha could see that Luke was indeed a handsome young man, slightly taller than his father and wearing tanned riding trousers with high leather boots, a white shirt, a dark green vest with gold stitching and a green coat that accentuated his fierce green eyes.

He walked out past his father and bowed again in front of the two girls.

'How do you do, ladies? It is an absolute pleasure to finally meet you both. Are you enjoying Rio so far?'

'Oh, it is a delightful place, Mr Deery,' Penny spoke first. 'I am not sure I should ever want to leave.'

Luke smiled at her and held her gaze before turning to Sasha. 'And you, Miss Sasha – how are you finding your trip?'

'I have to agree with my little sister, sir, as this is truly a place of wonder, and I also do not want to leave.'

'I am glad to hear it,' Luke replied politely. 'May we walk with you?'

'Absolutely,' Jacob said. 'If you are in the mood, I was going to show the family around the offices and warehouse. It is quite fortunate we have bumped into you, Lupe, so you can guide us. I have not been here often enough to take ownership of a tour.'

Lupe nodded excitedly, and the group began walking through the square together. Lupe, Jacob and Regan took the lead and Annette fell back to walk with Brenton, Luke and her two daughters.

Annette looked across at Luke. 'And, Mr Deery, I hear that you have a brother. Is that correct? Is he here in Rio as well?'

'Yes, ma'am, you are quite correct. His name is Ben and he is in Rio as we speak, though, I believe he is on his ship, the *Gabriel*, at this moment. There she is: docked next to the *Charlotte Arms*.'

Sasha followed the direction in which Luke was pointing and saw the two ships anchored at the same jetty as her father's ship, the *Mary*. These grand Man O' Wars were dwarfed by the *Mary* nearby.

'It is certainly a ship, miss.' Sasha looked back towards Luke, not hearing completely what was just said.

'Sorry?' she uttered.

'Your father's ship, the *Mary*. She is a sight to be seen, that is for sure. The biggest ship we have ever built in our docks, miss.'

For a moment Sasha had forgotten that the *Mary* was built by the Deery Shipping Company. Of course Luke could point her out by name easily.

They made their way through the square and into the Stevenson Transport building, where Lupe began his tour. The building was grand, with a large foyer leading to the offices upstairs. The rooftop allowed them to see far across the bay and out to the Atlantic beyond and all the traffic that the busy port accommodated. The warehouse was next. It was large and busy, with wagons being emptied through one door, repacked and moving out of another almost as soon as they had arrived.

She could see now how her father could afford to fund their lavish lifestyles. Stevenson Transport was a thriving, international company with all the wealth filtering up to one man: Jacob Stevenson.

Chapter 42

When the Stevenson party arrived, they saw the setting for the ball was as extravagant as it was beautiful. If the natural sunset and the shimmering light off the water from the moon was not enough, the whole fort was lit up with candles, while silk curtains swayed and danced in the warm breeze. The Government Fort had been transformed into a grand, exotic palace.

The grounds were equally as lavish and Sasha, Penny and Annette welcomed the chance to take a turn around the gardens with the Sheffields. The talk was, of course, exclusively about Luke Deery and his handsome and polite demeanour. Though Sasha could not disagree he was handsome and kind, she had not felt herself being drawn to him earlier that day in the markets. She had not felt the excitement that was needed to fall in love.

They moved inside and through to the main ballroom. It was a large hall with stone pillars and a high, painted ceiling. In the centre, people were dancing, as waiters stood around the room with their trays of cherries, wine and other local delicacies.

Sasha, growing tired of the chatter surrounding Luke Deery, saw her chance to separate herself from the other women and make her way around the main ballroom. She watched those on the dance floor, noticing that London dance trends had made their way to Brazil.

The women were dressed in silk gowns, with the men either wearing their formal waistcoats and breeches or their high leather boots, riding trousers and silk coats with matching vests.

Suddenly, a gap appeared in the crowd on the other side of the room. A man walked through it and came to a stop, surveying the scene. He was well dressed and tall with broad shoulders. He took a glass from one of the trays and nodded to thank the waiter.

Sasha looked away but could not help looking straight back at him. She tried again to look at anything else in the room but found herself staring at the man as he moved through the crowd.

He made his way from the opposite side of the hall, periodically stopping so people could shake his hand and introduce themselves. Clearly, he was a man of some importance, someone with a reputation as, even after he had shaken their hands politely and moved on, they continued to stare and whisper after him.

Sasha walked along the ballroom, following him from the opposite side. Her heart fluttered as she took each step. She stopped at one of the pillars but kept her gaze fixed on him. She could not help it. The excitement she had not felt earlier that day when she met Luke Deery was now consuming her. She was completely drawn to him.

He looked out over the crowd until his gaze reached her own. They locked eyes.

She turned away, looking to the floor, her heart thumping in her chest. It was only a second before she had to look back up, and she saw that the man had not shifted his gaze.

Embarrassed, she turned away again, sure that she had left enough time for him to lose interest, but when she looked up, he was still staring back at her. It was an unwavering, unashamed look, as if he were looking at the only person in the room.

His attention was momentarily drawn away from her as he shifted his gaze to shake the hand of an enthusiastic acquaintance. This was her chance. She moved quickly behind the crowd and made her way back to her mother and sister. As she neared them, she noticed that they had joined her father and brother as well.

She reached her mother, quickly looking back towards where

the man had been standing, only to see that he had disappeared in the crowd. A feeling of regret and sadness came over her.

'Are you all right, my dear? You look flushed. Have you been dancing?'

Sasha looked back at her mother and smiled, 'Yes. I am fine, thank you.'

Her mother looked at her, perplexed for a moment, and then glanced past her.

'Mr Deery and Mr Deery. How nice to see you both.'

Sasha turned and curtsied with her mother and sister. She noticed that Luke was looking directly at Penny and not at her. Her mother had also noticed and acted accordingly.

'Penny, were you not saying how delighted you were to meet Luke this morning?'

Penny looked up, embarrassed at her mother's forwardness. All she could do was smile until the awkwardness passed.

It had been noticeable that Penny and Luke had enjoyed their meeting earlier that day and Sasha was relieved to see that Luke seemed to have eyes only for her little sister.

Much better for everyone if he marries her and not me.

'The pleasure was entirely ours, Mrs Stevenson. I wonder, Miss Penny, if you would do me the honour of saving the next dance for me?'

Sasha looked over at her sister and saw that she was now blushing and nodding. Her heart warmed for her and, strangely, she now felt a fondness for Luke Deery; not a fondness that would create jealousy between her and her sister, but feelings that a sister and brother would feel for each other. She felt as though a weight had been lifted from her shoulders and the anxious feelings created by the prospect of an arranged marriage were now dissipating.

'Where is your other son, Regan?' Annette asked. 'We missed seeing him today.'

'Probably at the bar, I imagine,' Luke interjected. 'This sort of occasion is not really his particular forte.'

'I can understand how he feels.' Sasha realised that she had said the words out loud instead of just thinking them. Luke looked at her and smiled. It was a warm smile, friendly and unassuming.

'You do not like gala dinners and dances, miss?'

'After the first thirty, you tire of the same routine, Mr Deery.'

'Please call me Luke. And what about you, Penny?'

'I love them and never get tired.' The party all laughed together, and Luke once again fixed his gaze on the younger of the two Stevenson daughters.

Regan looked back at Annette and Jacob. 'I have told Ben that he is to be here, dressed well and clean-shaven, or I'll know the reason why, that's for sure.' He chuckled to himself as he spoke.

'Ah, speak of the devil and he shall appear.' Luke nodded behind the party and they all turned to see a large figure who had come up behind them. Sasha turned and once again the feeling of excitement consumed her when she saw that she was standing in front of the tall man she had seen across the room.

Chapter 43

Ben walked up behind the Stevensons. He had seen his father and brother approach them moments earlier and knew that he finally had to face the moment he had been dreading since he had been told the news months ago. He had shaved his beard because Regan had demanded that he and Luke be clean-shaven for the evening, but more than this, he wanted the Stevensons to see his face.

It had been seven years since they had last laid eyes on him and he had changed much in that time. But if they were to recognise him, he wanted them all to see his face – Annette, Brenton, Jacob and, of course, Sasha. Penny he could excuse from the rest.

He would look down at them as they had looked down on him when they watched him whipped almost to death. He would revel in their surprise that he was still alive and now an adopted son of a rich man with his own title and fortune. He would look into Jacob's eyes and show him a warrior's fury. He would look at Sasha and show her that he had not been discarded by the world and that he was no longer a toy to be played with.

He had seen her, moments earlier, across the ballroom. She had become a fine looking woman, although her face had stayed much the same. He was unsure if she had recognised him as there had been no look of surprise in her eyes, no look that conveyed that she thought him familiar to her.

As he walked up behind them, he saw Luke nod towards him and the group turned. He braced himself for their shocked looks, but no change registered on their faces.

'Stevensons,' Regan announced, 'I would like to introduce my adopted son, Ben Deery.'

Ben searched each face for the inevitable recognition. He expected one of them to say the name "Caleb", but none did. It had been too long, and he had changed from the boy they had known. They had been told that Caleb was dead, and in their minds, he was. As he quickly studied each of their faces, he realised that they had no idea who he really was. Suddenly, the rage within him was replaced with an unexpected calm.

'It's a pleasure to meet you all. I am Ben Deery.' His eyes shifted to Sasha as he spoke.

Annette replied first, introducing the family. He nodded and pretended to hear the names and see their faces for the first time. It was excruciating and exhilarating in the same moment.

'Nice to meet you, Brenton, and you, Miss Penny.'

As Annette introduced Sasha, he looked back at her to see that her gaze had not wavered. They locked eyes once more.

'It is a pleasure to meet you, miss.' For a long moment, neither looked away.

'I am Jacob Stevenson, Mr Deery.' Ben dragged his eyes away and looked towards Jacob, who had extended his hand. He wanted to tear Jacob's arm from his shoulder and let the man bleed out in front of all in the room. Instead, he reached out and shook Jacob's hand firmly. He looked directly into his old master's eyes and introduced himself as an equal.

'Nice to meet you, Mr Stevenson. I am Ben.'

Jacob smiled and shook Ben's hand.

'Well,' Regan began, 'we have all been introduced. Jacob, what would you say to a brandy and a cigar?'

'I would say that is a fine idea, Mr Deery. We have much to discuss with regards to the future. Let us leave the younger folk to enjoy the evening.'

The two men excused themselves and made their way to the gentlemen's room, where other businessmen and politicians were congregating.

Luke took Penny's arm and led her onto the dance floor.

Two young men about the same age as Ben walked up to the group and bowed to the ladies before linking up with Brenton. They were introduced to him as Harrold Stock and Edward Barrington, who had taken the voyage from London to be part of the festivities and to see first-hand the family plantations in Brazil.

Annette began to speak to the ladies around her. 'I do believe my Penny and young Mr Deery make a fine couple.' All agreed and began to talk of the couple's compatibility.

'And you, Ben Deery,' Annette asked. 'Don't you believe that they make a fine pair?'

'I believe they do, Mrs Stevenson.'

'Ben Deery, is it?' Ben nodded to the one he thought was Harrold, though it could have been the other. 'It is certainly a pleasure to meet you. Your reputation precedes you, sir. We would be delighted to buy you a drink and find out if the stories of adventure and heroism that are being told in London are as they say.'

Ben looked at the two boys, feeling a hint of resentment at the comment. Or was it disdain? Either way, he was not impressed. They were not men but boys. Their bodies were soft and plump after years of privilege and their minds were weak to ask such a fool's question in public. Or perhaps they lacked the courage to ask him when he was alone, afraid they might discover that the stories were real. He was thankful when Annette broke the silence.

'And what of yourself, Ben? Is there anyone here with whom you would like to dance?'

Not a question, as he had hoped, that would make the situation less awkward, and again he found that words escaped him. He knew to whom Annette was referring. He found it almost amusing that the high and mighty Annette Stevenson was encouraging him to make an advance on her daughter, the very act that had nearly had him killed in the past. This time it was Brenton who spoke up.

'I do not recommend asking my strong-headed sister, Mr Deery. Sasha just finished educating your poor brother about how much these events bore her.'

'Brenton, if you do not mind,' Annette retorted abruptly.

'I am just trying to save the man hardship when I am sure there are many others who would be more than happy to dance. No offence meant, Mr Deery, but I have had to witness far too many good men left without a partner as a result of my sister's indifference.'

'On the contrary,' Sasha interrupted, clearly embarrassed by her brother's comment. 'I have found that the visit to the New World has revitalised my enthusiasm for such occasions and I would be quite happy to dance if there was actually a gentleman present who would ask me.' She directed the comment at Brenton but looked up at Ben.

'I hope you do find a gentleman to dance with, miss,' Ben said as he looked over at the group. 'It was a pleasure to meet you all.'

He turned and walked away. He had to leave before he lost control. It was too much and he needed air before he said something he would later regret. He left the main ballroom and, taking a flask of wine, navigated his way to the courtyard, where he breathed in the fresh night air and looked up at the stars as his head tilted back to drink from the flask.

He did not wait for the wine to reach his belly before he took another gulp and another. By the fourth swig, he had drained the flask. The warmth of the wine flowed throughout his chest and up into his face. He threw the flask away and walked over to the edge of the courtyard. The breeze blew inside his shirt, cool against the sweat on his chest. He breathed deeply and forced away his anger. They had no idea who he really was. He had passed the test with Jacob, Annette, Brenton and Sasha. He was completely free now and could go where he pleased, even back to

London, without fear of being discovered as a fraud or a peasant.

'It is beautiful, isn't it?' the voice from behind him was all too familiar. It was the voice that haunted him in his dreams. He turned to see Sasha, standing in her white silk dress, with her dark hair waving in the hot breeze, her sky-blue eyes blazing back at him like blue flame. He turned away from her and looked back up at the sky.

'Yes, it is,' he replied sharply, trying not to show interest and hoping that she would either tire of the conversation or be offended and leave. It failed to deter her.

'I never thought I would see such beauty.' She stood next to him now, placing her hands on the stone railings of the courtyard. She had grown tall and strong but, though they were of similar height the last time they had been together, he was now much taller.

'I would have thought your life would be filled with many beautiful things, Miss Stevenson.'

She looked up at him, surprised by the forwardness of his comment.

'I hear you or your sister are to marry my brother.'

'Yes, that is true. However, I would not spare a thought for me. Your brother and my little sister only have eyes for each other and, as I was leaving, I believe they were having their third or fourth dance in a row. I feel that his mind is well and truly made up as to which sister he will choose.'

'And how does that make you feel?'

'I am delighted for my sister, whom I love most dearly. Would you believe I would think any differently, sir?'

It was working. He was starting to offend her and soon she would leave him be. He knew which buttons to push, even after so long. Her spirit and her freedom were her weaknesses. She would never compromise them. And why should she? Her strength of character had always been misconstrued as stubbornness. He both loved and hated her and he had learned to trust his hate, for it had kept him alive. How had love ever helped him? It had only caused him pain. Even his father and brother were kept at an emotional distance, despite all they had done for him. Love could be taken away, stripped and never given back. Hate was his and his alone to use as he pleased. His hate could not be taken from him.

'I do not presume to know what you would think, Miss Sasha. No more than you should be trying to understand my thoughts after such a short introduction.'

Sasha gave him a frustrated look. No one had ever spoken so bluntly to her. She did not know whether to be offended or intrigued. Either way, she felt invigorated standing near him in the tropical, starlit night.

A waiter moved up behind them, offering a tray of refreshments. He bowed and smiled, his teeth shining brightly through his big, dark lips.

'No, thank you,' she answered. The servant nodded and smiled and turned to Ben, who had not noticed him.

'Omiran,' the servant bowed after he had said the name. This time, the bow was much lower and slower, as if he were serving a king. Sasha looked straight at him then up at Ben with wide eyes. He looked back at her, noticing that the name had sparked an interest.

The servant did not make eye contact with him as Ben Deery took a glass of wine from the tray.

The servant looked up at him and nodded. 'God bless you, Omiran. God bless.' With that, he hurried away, offering his tray to others who had congregated near the entrance of the courtyard.

A long moment passed, until Sasha could tolerate the silence no longer.

'So, the famous and revered Ben Deery and the feared and violent Omiran are one and the same.' Her tone was not of praise but of disappointment.

Ben kept his gaze towards the bay as he replied, 'You should not believe everything you hear in your English garden parties.'

Sasha was now offended. The man in front of her had not acted in a gentlemanly manner at any time since their meeting. She had made a concerted effort to approach him, and he had not once turned to meet her as a gentleman should. He was rude and savage. Omiran was a slaver before he became an adopted Deery. How could he be anything else but a savage?

She turned to leave but stopped quickly. She would not let him offend her. She would not allow him to treat her so offhandedly.

'And what is that supposed to mean, sir?' she said with all the highbrow status she could muster, expecting an instant apology, for she was not leaving now until it was received.

'It means you should have stayed in London. This is not the place for you and your sister.'

The response filled her with rage. How dare he dismiss her in such a way? How dare he tell her what her family should and should not be doing? It was time to fight back.

'We are Stevensons and we will go where we please, sir. I was born with title. I did not adopt it.'

'So I can hear.' His reply was calm, showing no emotion in response to the conversation.

She could hardly bear it now. She wanted to hit him. She wanted to scratch her fingernails across his strong, square jaw.

'You would do well to spend some time in society, where you might learn how to speak properly to a lady, as your stepbrother does.'

'Thank you for the advice, Sasha. But I prefer my life.'

'I am sure you do. A life of fighting the slave trade does not wash away the dirt and shame of being a slaver yourself.'

This time her comment provoked him and he looked at her with steely rage that made her flinch, his blue eyes firing back at her.

She instinctively took a step backwards, realising she had gone too far. He stood in front of her now and she was able to properly appreciate his towering figure. She could hear his breathing become deeper and more intent.

She wished it was not so, but she thought him very handsome, rugged, strong, sun-kissed. She could see why they called him Omiran. His body, now close to hers, seemed to block out the world around them. He was broad and tall, with muscular shoulders, chest and arms. His long blond hair blew across his face as he stared fiercely at her, causing her skin to tingle with exhilaration.

'So, that is how you think of me, as a slaver and a murderer? Why am I not surprised? How could a Stevenson come to any other conclusion? I wish you a safe journey home, miss. Now, if you will excuse me, I would rather seek the company of a less condescending audience. Good night.'

'Good night, then, Mr Deery.' She made the words sound confident, though she was anything but. The way he looked at her had stirred something inside her. She regretted what she had said and wished she could take it back, for she did not want him to leave. Being near him had heightened her senses and she knew that there was much more to him than the label with which she had so quickly branded him. It was a reaction, and not what she truly believed. She was sorry but did not have time to apologise as he walked past her, into the ballroom and out of sight.

She squeezed her shawl in frustration and walked over to the far corner of the courtyard. It was dark, and it concealed the redness in her cheeks and her embarrassment that he had made her blush so heavily.

She waited a moment, looking up at the stars, waiting for the heat to drain from her lips. She turned to make her way back towards the ball when she was confronted by a figure she had not seen come up behind her. She doubled back in fright, grasping her chest with her hand.

'Sorry if I scared you there, miss.' The voice had an eerie chill to its tone and instantly made her feel uncomfortable. She looked at an ugly man in front of her. He was short and fat with thin, stringy, dirty hair hanging over his wart-covered face.

He looked at her, up and down, and smiled, showing off an incomplete set of yellow, rotting teeth. He looked at her as if he were picturing her naked and the noise of his desperate, aroused breathing made her skin crawl.

'Hello, miss.' His voice was quiet and threatening. It sent a shiver up her spine, and she suddenly realised that she was alone. She looked back to where she had been talking to Ben Deery, but she had walked to the other side of the courtyard and there were only her and the short man left in sight.

'Good evening, sir,' she replied quickly. 'Pardon me, but I have been away from the ball far too long and my father and brother will be searching for me.'

'Why rush off on such a beautiful evening?' he leered as he lowered his stare toward her breast. She noticed his hand move inside his trouser pocket and across his crotch. Terror began to creep through her, and she prayed desperately for Ben or one of the other men to come out looking for her.

'Excuse me, but I must be getting back. They are expecting me. My name is Sa–'

'Oh, I know who you are,' he cut her off before she could finish. 'I heard you were pretty, Miss Sasha – a true beauty – but nothing could prepare me for what I see in the flesh. You truly are a thoroughbred, aren't you?'

'You are out of line, sir, and if my father hears of this you will surely see the inside of a cell.'

She started to walk around him and back towards the lights of the entrance, but he moved into her path.

'I apologise, Miss Stevenson. I meant no disrespect. We must blame it on the wine, yes?' She was closer to him now and his nostrils flared when he caught her scent. He was not apologising, and they both knew it.

She walked around him without saying a word, watching him follow her movements with his beady eyes as she hurried away from the darkened corner of the courtyard, back towards the ball.

She dared to look back and saw him still staring at her from the darkness, his hand now out from his pocket and holding his manhood. She cringed as she made her way back into the ball, turning once more to see if he had followed her.

He had vanished

Chapter 44

The festivities of the ball could be heard faintly through the thick doors of the brandy room. Ben had been summoned to join the others and stood in the corner smoking a cheroot as Regan and Jacob, sitting in large, leather armchairs, led the conversation with the three general managers of Stevenson Transport: Lupe, William Finch and Wendell Prince.

Brenton and Luke had also been called into the room and stood behind the circle of chairs. All other occupants had been excused and had returned to the main ballroom.

'There is something stirring in these parts. I can feel it,' Regan stated. 'Something is not right here. We intercepted Adder sailing the *Grey Cloud* to the south coast. We did not see Jackson on board. Lupe, what news have you heard? Has Jackson surfaced in these parts?'

Lupe sat upright in his chair and uncrossed his legs. 'I have not been given definite news that Jackson is in Brazil. I have heard that the Scarlets have grown in numbers, yet Jackson stays closer to the Caribbean, where he is not hunted as fiercely by the British or the Portuguese.'

'Nonsense, Lupe,' Jacob cut in. 'If the Scarlets are building an army in South America, then Jackson would surely be here.'

'Unless an army is being formed to travel to North America and service his needs there,' Wendell Prince suggested.

'No,' Jacob replied, looking over at the fireplace. 'His army has business here. I am sure of it.'

A heavy silence hung over the room.

'Why are you here, Stevenson?' Regan finally asked, causing Jacob to shift his gaze from the fire and look over at him.

'We are here for the amalgamation of two great families.'

'Let's not keep secrets from each other this early in the piece, Jacob,' Regan went on. 'This meeting could have been conducted in London with far less effort. Don't tell me that you have dragged your whole family and followers across the Atlantic for an engagement party.'

Jacob looked at Regan and sat back comfortably in his chair. 'What is it you would like to ask me, Regan?'

'An old name has surfaced on people's lips. Has Simon Blake materialised? Is he alive? What happened all those years ago for him to disappear like a ghost?'

The tension in the room grew, with all eyes now fixed on Stevenson. 'I am still waiting for the question you really want to ask me, Regan,' he replied.

'Is the location of the Treasure Fleet Ships known to you?'

Regan looked over at the men in the room. There was no longer any need for lies.

'It is.' Stevenson's words hung in the air and the crackling of the fire was the only sound in the room. Ben knew the legend of the Tierra Firme Fleet. It was lost in a hurricane and an immense treasure had sunk below the Atlantic waves. All sailors had heard the tale.

'Or, at least, it was,' Jacob continued. 'I acquired this information eight years ago from a dying captain. I sent it through to Simon right away. It was not just its location but a story, a glimmer of a hint, that two or three of the treasure ships' crews had mutinied and had sailed south of the storms, keeping the hoard for themselves and hiding it somewhere in Brazil.'

Ben could feel the tension in the room rise as Jacob continued. 'I do not know the truth of it, but men have killed each other over this information and so the danger of its existence is all too real. I could not take the gamble that I was the only man privy to knowledge about its location, and so I sent it to Simon with orders that if he should discover that the legend is true. If it were found to be true, I ordered that he must keep it hidden and safe from those who would use it to rise up and terrorise the New World.

'As for Blake, I do not know if he is still alive or not, but if he has found the lost ships of the fleet, then he has done his job well. There are those who would want to create chaos with the Spanish fortune. It must be kept safe. Hidden.'

Lupe placed his glass on the table and looked at the circle of men in front of him.

'Very well, Jacob. Now that you have revealed this news, I can tell you all that Jackson knows about the fleet and about Simon's resurfacing. It was Jackson who sank the *Retribution* all those years ago. He wanted the lost fleet then and he is after it now. It is a certainty that he will return to these lands. He has heard you have come, Jacob. He has heard that Simon Blake may try and contact you. What have we all done? We have given the devil his chance to strike. You must all leave at once with your families before it is too late.'

'Calm down, man!' William Finch interrupted him, yet his voice was heavy with anxiety. Ben could sense the panic that had crept into the room. It was time to say his piece.

'What are our defences in Rio? Will the Portuguese soldiers stand with the British?'

'We are heavily armed in this city,' Wendell Prince spoke up. 'We have fortified barracks with more than enough soldiers to hold off a siege. Jackson would not be able to march his army anywhere near the city without our knowing. We have scouts along the main roads and we would know well in advance. We will have ample time to prepare our defences and send the women and children to safety. Your family is safe in Brazil; Jackson's army will not defeat us.'

'Then we need to know what his intentions are,' Ben replied. 'A small party should make its way south and find the Scarlet's army so we can understand what numbers we are dealing with.

The scouting party must remain unseen and must not engage. Luke, you should lead them.'

Luke nodded enthusiastically, as Ben knew he would. His brother was a warrior at heart and had been taught the art of militia warfare by his father from a young age.

'You will not come with me, Brother?' he asked. 'Not that I need you, of course, but I thought a mission such as this would appeal to you.'

'No,' Ben replied. 'I will travel north on the Courier paths. There will be people along the trails still loyal to the Couriers and they will be able to provide information about Simon, if he has truly resurfaced. We need to know if we will be fighting an army on two fronts. We will ride out at first light and return before the next full moon, six days from now. Father,' he looked down at Regan, 'you stay in Rio and keep the crowds amused.'

'I feel almost offended that I am being told to stay while my sons take the dangerous option.' He looked disappointed before he cracked a smile and said, 'But I guess someone needs to keep the taverns occupied.'

The air was suddenly full of laughter, though none doubted the seriousness of what had been decided.

The servants were called back into the room and all glasses were refilled as the mood relaxed, and conversations about business and future profits dominated the rest of the evening.

Chapter 45

Dawn had not yet broken through the morning darkness as Ben packed his horse. The few oil lanterns offered dim lighting as he strapped a sleeping mat onto the back of his saddle.

Musungo and his two native companions had been up earlier than the others to water and prepare the horses. They had become accustomed to travelling with Ben and the *Gabriel* and, to those who knew no better, appeared to be his servants. No one had to know that they were employees and free men. It was easier to let people assume otherwise.

'Omiran,' Musungo whispered as he walked over to Ben, his large muscular body shining like granite as the light flickered across his bare chest. 'All horses are packed and ready with many rifles. Do we ride into battle?'

Ben looked at his beaming face. There was an excitement in Musungo's eyes that he could not hide. This was why they were loyal to him, as invariably there would be a fight.

'I do not know yet,' he answered. 'Be ready to leave at a moment's notice.'

Musungo nodded and walked back to the two Gonzos.

Regan Deery walked into the stables, accompanied by Jacob Stevenson and his three general managers. He made his way over to Ben's horse and inspected the pack. Two long rifles, four muskets, a long sword, a short sword, a combination of knives, a compass, a small pot for boiling water and a spoon to go with it, a sleeping mat and an eyeglass.

He smiled, thinking about the young boy he had raised to be

a man, fearless and modest. He had found comfort in the fact that Ben loved his son Luke, and would die to protect him. Ben would protect his company and his heir.

'Is there something you need to tell me, Son?'

Ben spun around to meet him. 'Father?'

'Why do you not go with Luke? Why are you heading north? And don't tell me it is just information you are looking for.'

'It is information, but from whom is what is now important.'

'So, you think Blake is north, then?'

Ben looked at his father. He could not tell him that he had ridden north with Simon all those years ago. He could not tell him why he knew where to ride. It would be too easy to piece together his real past.

'If he is south, Luke will find him. If he is west, we will never find him in the jungles. There will be Courier trails north and we must investigate them. If there is a map, then it must be destroyed.'

'Can it possibly be true?' Luke chimed in as he walked over to them.

'Whether or not it is true is irrelevant now,' Ben stated. 'Bell and the Scarlets believe it is true and so there will be a fight regardless. It is the belief that is real, and that is the reason why his army will fight for him against whomsoever he chooses. If we can take that belief away from them, then what reason is there for them to stay loyal to him?'

'So,' Jacob Stevenson interrupted, 'we must either find it and ship it back to London ourselves or, once and for all, prove the map is false.'

He looked over at Ben and Luke. 'Boys, if you find Simon, you must tell him that I am here and that it is time to come out from the shadows. We can protect him now.'

'Omiran.' The men turned to Musungo, who was standing at the stable doors pointing out to the sky. 'First light, Omiran.'

Ben looked back to his brother and father. 'Stay safe. Information only – do not engage, no matter how tempting.

I have a feeling that there will be plenty of time for that soon enough. I'll meet you in six days on the outskirts of Rio.' He put a hand on each of their shoulders. 'Hopefully, we'll be back here for an engagement party, Brother,' he smiled as he looked at Luke.

They mounted their horses and rode out of the stables and into the breaking dawn. They rode through the main streets to the outskirts of the city until they reached the transport highway running north and south from Rio. Apart from the ten of them, there was no movement anywhere.

The two brothers nodded to one another as the Company split in two, one brother heading south to find a devil, the other heading north to raise a ghost.

Chapter 46

Ben and the Imbangalas rode hard for half a day until the sun was high and the air was humid. They reached a village that he vaguely remembered, where they stopped to eat and water their horses before continuing.

Musungo rode next to him, tall and proud in his saddle, with the other two trailing behind. Ben kept his eyes to the left of the road, searching for a familiar landmark. Another hour passed until he found a path that led them left into the hinterland. It was a small and inconspicuous trail, only wide enough to ride single file. It took them deep into the jungle before another path appeared in front of them – the Courier trails. They were still in use. It was a promising sign that the Couriers still rode. There were fresh tracks in the mud, less than a day old, heading north in the same direction as they were travelling.

They had been riding for another hour when he smelt it. The wind had changed and carried the aroma of cooking meat. He put up his hand to stop the party and the three of them dismounted and tied the horses in the scrub.

'You know these trails, Omiran?' Musungo asked quietly.

'I rode along them once as a boy.'

'I also smell the cooking,' Musungo continued. 'Is this a bad thing?'

'Only raiders or Couriers use these trails. Unpack for a fight and no more sound.' Musungo nodded and signalled to the Gonzos to unpack the rifles.

Ben was armed with his long and short swords, a bone-handled knife strapped to his chest and another in his boot. He carried two pistols, loaded and powdered, holstered on each hip, and a powder satchel attached to his belt. He had a long rifle slung across his right shoulder and carried another long rifle, which he had readied to shoot first.

He led the way off the path and into the jungle towards where he remembered there was a clearing. He moved through the undergrowth with purpose and ease despite the weight of all the weaponry he carried. It was his usual fit-out for a fight and, though the weight of the arms would be too heavy for most, he carried everything easily and found that it had never hindered his ability to move quickly or freely.

The four men moved with complete silence and precision towards the clearing. Through the foliage they could see ten men, and they were not Couriers. It was a raiding party, and yet the camp had been well-established. There were multiple tents and spare horses corralled in a pen.

This was not usual behaviour for raiders, as they rarely stayed in the same place for long periods. These men had been here for weeks, possibly months.

Useless bastards. They think they have nothing to fear out here because no one has hunted them. The Company needs to dedicate more time in this part of the world.

Raiders in Angola knew to be on their guard as the Company had made their lives perilous. Ben had been away from Brazil for a long time and the local raiders had become careless. Their camp was too established, the fire too large and their defences too weak. Their voices carried so loudly that he could have walked into the camp and sat down next to them before any of them realised what was happening.

As he listened to them, it soon became obvious that they had been drinking for hours. One of the men was talking about a slave girl and how she had screamed at the beginning but was moaning with ecstasy towards the end. The others laughed as they drank around the fire.

'I will be the judge of that,' one of them said, as he stood up and stumbled over the log towards the tents.

'He can hardly walk,' one of the others joked. 'How is he going to be able to get it up?' Another belt of laughter came from the group.

'I'll have you know that wine makes it stronger,' the stumbling drunk called out as he turned to the fire and dropped his trousers. The men cheered and clapped as the raider's exposed genitals humped the late afternoon air. He disappeared into the tent, naked from the waist down. A woman's voice cried out and the men sitting around the fire cheered once more.

Over to the left of the camp, three others were sitting at a table looking at what Ben thought had to be a map.

'Shut your mouths, you fools,' one of them hissed at the drunks around the fire. 'Do you want to let the whole country know where we are?'

'Settle, Felix,' one of them called back. 'Adder has not even landed yet. We have plenty of time to sober up, and nowhere to go until he arrives.'

Ben's gaze sharpened on them. They were Scarlets and were more than a raiding party. They were part of Jackson's army. Why had they been positioned so far north from the others?

No point guessing. I will find out the truth soon enough.

He motioned to the other men to fall back. They retreated far enough away so that they could not be heard.

'We wait till nightfall and use their fire as our light. No guns at the start. The ones near the fire first. They will be drunk and will not put up a fight. The one called Felix – I want him alive. He is in charge. Be swift with the rest.'

Concealed in the bushes, they ate their rations as they kept watch over the activities of the camp. Three hours passed before it was night and three more men had visited the tent where the slave girl had been kept. They waited until most of the men around the fire had passed out or gone to bed. Ben kept his eye on the one called Felix and waited for him to retire.

Ben moved first, jumping out from the undergrowth. With his short sword and bone knife drawn, he moved towards two men at the fire. He cut their throats with two swift strokes. Musungo and the others took his lead, making their way around the fire and slitting the throats of the sleeping men. They moved onto the tents, where they killed the others. Ben emerged from a tent, holding Felix by the neck.

'Bring the horses,' he called to one of the Gonzos. 'Nice to make your acquaintance, Felix,' Ben taunted him as he threw the man at Musungo's feet and pulled out his knife. He cut a piece of meat from the wild boar that had been left near the fire, while Musungo tied Felix against a tree with his arms behind his back.

'I have some questions to ask you.' Ben spoke with a quiet calmness as if he were giving a child instructions. He spoke slowly and clearly so as not to risk being misunderstood. 'I will only ask you each question once. If you do not answer truthfully, I will allow this man to cut away a piece of your body. I will let him choose which part. Then we will sit here and you will watch while he cooks it on the fire.'

Felix looked up in horror at the large, muscular Musungo. He needed no more motivation than the threat of being eaten alive and nodded at Ben to begin the interrogation.

'They call you Felix. Are you the leader of this party?'

Felix nodded, and Ben could see they had got off to the right start.

'Earlier, you were over at that table looking at this map.' Ben held up a map of Brazil with multiple markings and pointed to one in particular. 'I am assuming that this marker shows where we are now. What do the other markings show?' He moved his finger toward the large marker south of Rio. 'You can start by telling me about this one.'

Felix looked at the map and then over towards Musungo, who was twirling his knife in his hand. 'That marking is the main camp of the revolution.'

'The revolution. What is that?'

'It is the reckoning that is coming soon. It is coming for those who have held sway over men for too long. Men should be free and yet there is no freedom in these lands. But in the New World there is the promise of real freedom. A fight is coming to you and your people. You will all bleed soon.'

'Omiran.' Musungo raised his knife as if to ask if he could start carving. Felix looked up at Ben in surprise.

'I know who you are,' he glared up at Ben. 'You are no different to us. You kill when you need to and take what you need to.'

'You are a slaver, a murderer and a rapist,' Ben quickly interrupted him, 'and we did not ask for a sermon.'

He motioned to Musungo, who quickly moved in front of Felix and, as his knife descended, the screaming began. Felix's chokes and screams filled the air as Musungo went quickly about his work. The screaming did not stop when he moved back out of the way. Ben looked at the bloodied face before him. The left eye had been cut out of his head and now sat firmly in Musungo's hand. Blood poured out of the void, streaming down his left cheek and soaking into the shirt around his chest.

'Stop your screaming,' Ben said calmly. 'You have one eye left, Felix. I suggest you spare us from another rant or I swear to you that you will walk through the rest of your life in darkness. What do the other markings mean?'

'They are more camps, like this. We are waiting for the southern army to march north, where we will join them.'

'Where is this army headed?'

'I do not know.'

'Then if you don't know anything else and you can't show us anything else, why keep the other eye?' On command, Musungo raised his knife towards the other eye and Felix confessed in full.

'Simon Blake! Jackson Bell believes Blake is somewhere in these mountains, hidden in a secret place. He has the key to a treasure so great it will build the New World and fund our revolution. We were to set up camps and wait for Jackson and

Adder to bring the southern army to us. Jackson is going to lure Blake out of his foxhole once and for all.'

'That is why you are not trying to hide yourselves,' Ben said as Musungo sheathed his knife. 'You are not raiding along these trails. You are waiting for Adder to land and lead Jackson's war parties to the mountains. You are an army outpost.'

'What do we do, Omiran?' Musungo said as he wiped the blood from his hands with a palm leaf.

'We have their map,' Ben replied, 'and we know where their camps are now. But we must find Blake first. We will rest here till first light, then resume our search.'

Chapter 47

Luke and his five men lay on top of the ridge, looking down at the large fortress in the valley below them. They had given themselves at least ten yards between each other, thus ensuring they had better lines of sight and would be a harder target to spot. After having ridden south for three days, they had come across it – not a temporary camp, but a fortified barracks.

They had expected scouts but had not come across any. They had expected to kill silently in order to enter the barracks, but had not seen any men along the roads. They had not been stopped or questioned or followed.

This was the Scarlet's camp and they had been busy. There were towers, permanent wooden huts, crops, wells and a jetty where Luke could see three ships. One of them was the *Grey Cloud*. This was where Jackson's army was based. He had built a fortress out of sight and out of mind and had watched his numbers grow. Yet, for a fort of this size, Luke expected to see hundreds of men and a hive of activity – not the eerie silence he saw before him.

Apart from a few inhabitants, the fort was almost abandoned. There was smoke rising from a fire where a woman tended to a pot of what appeared to be breakfast for those in residence.

There were a few sailors scrubbing the decks on the ships and a few carrying wood around the camp. Luke counted twelve in total – far too few for a fort of this size.

'What is this?' whispered one of the Company men on Luke's left side. 'There is no army here. This camp was built to hold many.'

'If an army was on the march, we would have come across it or, at the very least, its tracks,' another replied softly, echoing the exact thought in Luke's head.

He looked down at the camp in the valley below them. It was true. They had not come across tracks on their way there. An army had not made its way north and the docked ships were evidence that they had not left by sea. *Where were they?*

'Luke,' the man on his far left whispered as he pointed to a side entrance of the fort. A man carrying buckets was heading down to the stream and had left himself alone and vulnerable.

Luke nodded and, without a word, the two men on his left moved quickly and silently down the slope. The man with the buckets leant down near the stream and began to fill them. It only took a moment before he was seized, bound and reefed across the stream and back into the cover of the jungle at the base of the mountain. The remaining men in the Company retreated to where they had tied the horses. They met with the others at the bank of the stream, tied their captive to one of the saddles, and rode out around the other side of the mountain. When Luke was satisfied that they could speak freely without being heard, he ordered their prisoner to be tied to the base a tree.

'We are after information. Scream and you die. Lie and you die. Don't stay on your feet and you die. Tell me what I need to know honestly, and you will live, for now. I give you my word.'

Luke pulled a knife from the front of his belt and walked closer to the man, who was old and tired and had clearly been recruited into the camp for housekeeping duties and not as a fighter. He was frightened, and Luke could see that he would not stay loyal to Jackson.

'You said I would live,' he yelped as Luke advanced with the knife in hand.

'There are many ways to live,' Luke replied quietly. 'How you decide to do it is entirely up to you, and your answers. I am a patient man and I will get the information I need one way or another. I suggest you make it easy on yourself and save a lot of pain.'

The man looked at the Company and back at Luke. His nod showed them that he understood perfectly.

'We know Jackson has built the camp to recruit an army. Where has this army marched? South? West? What are his intentions?'

The old man reeked of fear. 'There is no army that has marched anywhere that I have seen, sir.'

Luke's look turned to one of frustration. He had no time for games.

'What did I tell you about lying?'

He put his hand over the old man's mouth and slowly began to push his knife into the meat of his right shoulder. He let the point enter the flesh before he twisted the handle, making the man scream. It was a valuable lesson his father had taught him. The wound was not deep, nor crippling. It was little more than a scratch but, more often than not, the promise of pain and more to come was enough to loosen a man's tongue. Hurting a man too badly, too early, left no room for escalation and little chance of gaining coherent answers. Keeping the knife in place, and with his other hand muffling the old man's whimpers, he leant in and whispered in his ear.

'I told you I am a patient man, but I do not have time for this. There are others in the camp I can ask. If you lie again, you will die, I promise. I always hold true to my word, old man.'

He took out the knife and stepped back from the tree.

'But I do not lie,' the old man sobbed. 'The fort was holding an army. Many men, two hundred, I would say. They have been training with swords and guns, but no army marched. All left at different times, sir. No uniforms and only small numbers, six or seven at a time. No marching army, sir, I swear it.'

'Which direction?'

'On the north road, sir, towards Rio. I believe they have finished their training and have been staying in the city waiting for Jackson Bell's instructions. Jackson and Adder are there now. Somewhere in the city. That's all know. I swear it. Nobody tells me anything, sir. I just look after horses and fetch water.'

Luke looked at the others, alarmed. 'Cut him loose. We ride north immediately.'

'We are going to let him go, sir?'

'There is no one here for him to inform. Bell has built an army, but he is not marching it as one. They have been heading into the city in small groups for weeks unnoticed. That is why there are no tracks. Rio will be under attack from within.'

He leapt onto his horse and turned it northwards.

We have been fooled. Jackson and Adder are hiding in Rio, waiting for their moment to strike.

The city had defences but was in no way prepared for an ambush of this size. Jackson's men could be anywhere, even posing as servants at the ball. They may have filled his drink at the tavern or led his horse to the water trough. There was no way of truly knowing and, if they had infiltrated the barracks, it would be easy for them to disarm the soldiers and take what they wanted.

'We must warn the city forces that they are about to be attacked by organised militia groups.'

'We need to warn your brother, sir,' one of the men said.

'He is four days ride from where we are. The city could have burned down by then. No. We will have to do this without Ben. We ride fast. Cut down anything that stands in our way.'

As their horses bolted toward the northern road, a feeling of hopeless desperation overcame him. He had to warn his father. He had to make sure Penny Stevenson was safe. He had warmed to her instantly and knew now that he wanted to marry her. He wanted to kill Adder and Jackson Bell once and for all, ridding the world of their poisonous hearts.

Residing in the government buildings were women and children who had all arrived to see the Stevenson and Deery families unite and now they were all in terrible danger. He shuddered at the thought of what would happen to the women. He wished his brother was by his side. This was going to be a fierce fight and he needed the fiercest warrior with him. Luke looked at the sky as his horse galloped along the trail towards Rio.

Ben, if you can hear me, we need you now, brother. We need Omiran.

Chapter 48

Ben and his men had left their horses and had trekked inland for half a day. They moved with the silent urgency of experienced hunters. Musungo and the two Gonzo natives moved through the jungle with ease, leaving it unspoiled and intact as if the vines and branches moved for them.

Even though the four men had become proficient at not being heard or seen, Ben felt that ever since they had tethered their horses and headed into the mountains, they were being watched.

When they came across a clearing with a large stream running through it, Ben knew exactly where he was. He had been here as a boy, many years before, yet his memory of it had not diminished. There were no signs to show that anyone had been through these parts, yet he knew that this meant nothing. It was not a sign that the Couriers did not dwell in the mountains.

They were masters at covering their tracks and remaining out of sight. He crouched down on one knee and closed his eyes, concentrating on the sounds around him, listening for one noise in particular.

As he knelt there in silence, he heard it in the distance – the sound of distant thunder rumbling across the sky. But he knew it was not thunder. It was the sound of a torrent tumbling over a cliff onto water and rock.

He motioned to the other men to stay low. He disliked the idea of exposing their position in the clearing but had no choice. Someone was out there, he could feel it. He just hoped it was who he thought it was. Who he needed it to be.

'Do exactly as I do and do it slowly.' He looked over at Musungo, who nodded and signalled to the others.

Ben stood up and walked out into the middle of the clearing. The three natives followed him but looked perplexed when he began to take off his weapon belts and drop them in front of him.

'Omiran?' Musungo whispered.

'Do it.' Ben looked back impatiently.

When they were completely unarmed, Ben walked further into the clearing and out of reach of any weapon. His hands were outstretched, showing signs of surrender. Musungo and the Gonzos reluctantly did the same.

'My name is Ben Deery, son of Regan of the Deery Ship Building Company.'

They stood in the middle of the clearing in silence for what seemed like a long time. Musungo looked back at his men and around the clearing, wondering if they were all alone and making fools of themselves.

Suddenly, a group of men with long rifles aimed at their heads entered the clearing and surrounded Ben's group. They had come from behind boulders and out of foxholes. There was no escaping and Ben hoped that his gamble would pay off and he was being met by friend and not foe.

From behind a boulder, a man appeared and walked towards them. His rifle was strapped to his back. He was clearly the leader of the group and Ben recognised him instantly. He had been part of his expedition as a boy. Ben was looking at Thomas, Simon Blake's second-in-command.

Finally.

'You knew we were here.' Thomas stated. 'How? Bear in mind that the wrong words will quickly lead to your death, with the last sound you hear being the crack of the rifles surrounding you.'

Ben chose his words carefully, without having to answer the

question directly. 'We come to you for counsel, not bloodshed. I know of the Couriers and your legacy.'

'And I of yours, Mr Deery. Your slaves are loyal to you. It is very rare to see a white man turn his back on a slave with a gun, let alone three of their size.'

'They are not slaves and they come and go as they please.' Ben was tiring of the conversation moving so slowly. 'We came across a raider party half a day southeast of here. They were in position, waiting for an army led by Jackson Bell.'

'Yes. You did come across a raiding party and cut a man's eye out, apparently.'

Ben looked at Thomas in surprise. 'You knew they were there? Why did you not take them down?'

'There is nothing that happens in these mountains that we don't know about, Ben Deery. Or should I be calling you Omiran?'

There was a quiet whisper that made its way around the circle of rifles as they heard the name. Thomas realised it also.

'It seems that you are well known.' Thomas ordered his men to lower their rifles.

Ben ignored the compliment. 'Bell has raised an army. We must disarm it before he uses it for his purposes.'

'And what do you think that might be?'

'Does it matter? Any army under his command will only stop once the world has been burned to ashes. There are those who will oppose him, but we are few. You are Couriers. I ask that you fight with us and rid the world of Jackson and Adder once and for all. Their army will fall when they do.'

Thomas looked at Ben a moment and then up at the sky.

'You have come this far, Omiran. Perhaps you should come a little further. There is something you need to see.'

Chapter 49

Thomas led Ben's party away from the clearing and onto a hidden path that wound its way up into the mountain. Approximately every two hundred yards, Ben spotted men, armed and ready, posted in high vantage points. Even if someone had stumbled across this hidden path by mistake, it would be nearly impossible to lead an armed group through such a narrow passageway. They would be forced to attack in a single file and the shooters in the cliffs above could pick them off at will. The loss would be too great for any group to sustain. Ben was sure there was no shortage of weapons and ammunition on this mountain. The natural winding landscape made it an almost impenetrable fortress.

As they advanced, they could hear the roar of the waterfall ahead of them. The path stopped rising and began to descend. This was another natural advantage that protected the entrance. An enemy would become exposed on the descent and would make an easy target for men positioned on the higher sections of the mountain.

The thundering noise became louder as the waterfall finally came into view, large and powerful. The memory of Simon Blake and Thomas walking into it many years ago came flooding back to Ben. The path led to the left of the waterfall and through a group of heavy boulders where the falling water was hidden from view. As they continued down the path, it levelled out and led them back into the mountain. The water was now within view again and they moved in behind it, between the mountain wall and the falling water curtain, out of sight of the world and completely concealed by the mountain and its torrent.

They entered a sizable cave. There was a camp set up there with a fire, weapons and tents, and ten men on guard.

It was modest, damp and uncomfortable, but hidden and very well protected. Ben looked at Thomas, confused. They had come to a dead end. He waited for his eyes to adjust, wondering if he had missed something along the way. Or was this to be their end? Lured by a promise and shot dead, thrown into the wall of water and pushed into the depths of the pool below.

No. Why risk bringing us here? They could have easily killed us in the clearing.

Ben and his men looked around the small, wet space. It was not exactly worth keeping secret. What were they missing?

Thomas gestured to them to follow him as he walked over to the back wall of the cave. Ben looked at him as if he had gone mad. All that was there was a stone wall.

'Only you may continue,' Thomas said to Ben. 'Your men must stay here. This is our most secret place. You now know its location and we are trusting you all with its secrecy. It is only as a result of the situation at hand that you are here. Cross us and you are all dead men.'

Thomas moved to his right and vanished. Musungo leapt back with horror. 'Omiran, it is witchcraft! Great demons live here. Do not follow him.'

The illusion had also taken Ben by surprise, but as he moved closer he saw that the wall overlapped another. What looked like a flat solid wall from the cave entrance was actually two overlapping sections where a man could move in between, leading him into a narrow tunnel deeper into the mountain.

He followed Thomas behind the wall, down the tunnel and arrived at a wooden door. Thomas banged loudly. All the other Couriers had stayed outside to protect the entrance to the mountain and keep watch on the three Imbangala warriors.

Truly secret and impenetrable.

The iron bars on the door clanked as they slid across each other, allowing the door to swing open. Thomas looked back at Ben and smiled.

'Come,' he said and walked through.

Nothing could have prepared Ben for what was waiting as he passed through the door. From the high ledge on which they now stood, he saw an enormous cavern. The belly of the mountain was hollow and dry.

As he looked down, he saw a small but thriving village built into the mountain's inner walls. Steps led down to the permanent buildings, with rope ladders and bridges providing connections within the village, which seemed to float above the body of water at the base of the cavern.

There were dozens of people busily going about their work. A large hole in the side of the mountain allowed natural light to filter down to the village and the water, with hundreds of lanterns providing extra light.

Thomas looked at him, smiling, as Ben stared down in amazement.

'Come,' he said.

They made their way down a staircase and across a large rope bridge. At the end of the bridge stood a man Ben estimated to be about the age of fifty.

'Ben Deery, welcome to *Aldeia Escondida* … The Hidden Place.' As he spoke, Ben realised that he was standing face to face with Simon Blake.

Chapter 50

A small tavern had been built into the mountain and they sat at a table on a large deck overlooking the water below. He had been given a tour of The Hidden Place and it was truly a marvel, with natural hot springs to bathe in, fresh running water in the rock pools below, houses, a hall, a tavern, common areas, and storerooms. There were levels upon levels of small buildings, where a community had not just survived but thrived. Enough natural light shone through from the side of the mountain so that greenery could still flourish. He had been told that it was most likely a volcano, many years dormant.

He drank from the cup of wine Simon had poured him. He looked older; indeed, it had been seven years since Ben had last seen him. Much had changed in that time. Then, Ben's name had been Caleb, a boy, green and naive in the New World, and now he had to pretend that this man in front of him was someone he was meeting for the first time.

'You are not an easy man to find, Simon. I suppose that is a testament to this refuge.'

'I am happy to be able to impress the great Omiran,' Simon joked. 'Yes, son, your legend has even found ears in this secret place; and many other places that connect to the Atlantic, I imagine.'

'You have quite the reputation yourself, Simon. You look reasonably alive for a dead man.'

Simon laughed, 'Ah yes, in my situation being dead can be extremely convenient, wouldn't you say?'

Ben had to smile at the irony of Simon's comment.

'Yes, I suppose it can be,' he replied.

As Simon looked at him, Ben wondered if he had been discovered. In his haste to find Simon, he had not taken the time to wonder if he might be recognised. He tried to change the subject to conceal his worry.

'How long did this take to build? How did you even manage to get materials up here?'

'Getting materials is the easy part. I was a general manager for the largest transportation company along the Atlantic trade routes. I have a hundred different ways of getting things done. It has been built over the past seven years by the Couriers and their families who reside here. More importantly, everyone who lives here holds its location a secret. I will trust you and your men to do the same.'

'No one will know from me that it is here. I give you my word and that will also stand for my men, you can be sure of that.'

'I believe you, Mr Deery.'

Ben waited a moment and felt the pleasantries were now over and it was time to get down to business.

'We cannot stay long, Simon. Jacob Stevenson and his family landed in Rio a week ago. There are rumours that you have resurfaced to meet with him, and these rumours have found their way to the Scarlets. My brother is headed south as we speak to determine if Bell has a force large enough for a siege. Jackson still believes you were sent a map from Stevenson, showing the hidden location of the missing Spanish Treasure Fleet hoard.'

'Yes, he is a damn fool,' Simon replied.

'A fool, you say? So, the map is a lie? Why are you hiding in this place, then?'

'Do you think that if I had the location to one of the greatest hoards of Spanish bullion, I would be sitting like a prisoner in this mountain, impressive as it is?' He looked around as he spoke, as if to show pride in his work. 'The map is no lie, but it led me to nothing. It was surely conjured up by the Spanish to divert everyone's attention away from where it would really be hidden … or sunk.'

'Then, why now? Why does Stevenson bring his whole family over now?' As he asked the question, the answer came to him instantly. 'Stevenson also thinks the map is real, just as Jackson does.'

'I think it would be safe to assume that, yes. Or because he is marrying off one of his daughters to your brother, or maybe because he has not seen this part of his operation in many years, or perhaps all three. Did he come with soldiers? Protection?'

'Four warships manned with fighting men.'

'Interesting,' Simon replied. 'I suppose with his daughters in tow, he would want to be overprotective. I hear they are quite the pair, especially this Sasha. Helen of Troy reborn, so they tell me.'

'So I keep hearing.' Ben drank from his cup and refilled it with the wine.

'You don't agree?' Simon inquired. 'That is also interesting.'

'Why should it be of any interest to you what I think about Stevenson's daughter?'

There was a lengthy pause as the two men stared at each other.

Simon broke the silence. 'No reason,' he said. 'Now, about Jackson's outpost that you came across. Jackson is placing these up the coastline to help feed back information and recruit new men into his revolution. They have been filtering down south for almost a year now.'

'So you just hide away from Jackson in your mountain, Simon?' Ben said, unimpressed with the man he had so adamantly respected for many years. 'You have capable men here, so why not fight him? If we combine forces, we can take him and Adder down once and for all.'

'You do not know the whole story, Ben. It is not as simple as that.'

The conversation was interrupted by the sound of a man

running up onto the tavern deck.

'Simon, I have news.' He stopped and looked at Ben's unfamiliar face.

'Well, go on, lad,' Simon said impatiently.

'Jackson is in Rio. He and Adder both, and their army.'

'Impossible,' Ben spoke up. 'I have just come from Rio and I saw no army.'

'The information has come from one of the taverns in Port Square. They have been coming into the city in small groups, unnoticed, for the last month. They are all there now, placed and hidden. They have been waiting for Adder and Jackson to arrive. It must be to take down Stevenson, sir.'

'They are going to take over Rio. It's not a siege they are mounting – it is an attack from within!' Simon stood up and looked at Ben. 'Jackson does not want me. He wants Stevenson.'

Ben bolted across the deck, stopping at the stairs of the landing to look back at Simon.

'Will you come with us, Simon? We need you and your men.'

Simon looked at him and then over at Thomas who, having sensed the urgency of the situation, had now made his way onto the landing.

'Thomas. Gather twenty of our men and go with Mr Deery. I hope I will see you again soon, Ben. We have much to discuss, you and I.'

Ben wasted no more time with pleasantries and hurried towards the entrance behind the waterfall. He thought of Sasha and the rest who would soon be under attack from Jackson and Adder. Luke had travelled south to no avail. He would find an empty camp.

Please let me get there in time. Please don't let me be too late.

Chapter 51

Although the morning had been hot and humid, promising rain later that afternoon, the ladies had decided to take the carriage out into the town to explore the streets of Rio. Annette had noticed that Luke Deery had been attracted to her youngest, Penny, and she wanted some time with her girls to discuss the situation further.

An expedition was a good opportunity to spend time with her two daughters, alone and away from the other women, who persistently made their opinions heard and constantly interrupted the conversation.

Jacob had permitted the morning's excursion on the condition that they were accompanied by a platoon of soldiers and that they did not leave the central business district near the harbour. There were soldiers covering the perimeter of this area and roaming platoons in each section of the city. It was agreed that they would be quite safe and only out for an hour, two at the most.

Sasha sat by herself on one of the carriage seats, with her mother and Penny sitting opposite. The sounds and the smells of Rio had not lost their allure. She was consumed by this new world and did not want to leave it. The conversation was solely about Luke Deery and his suitability for Penny.

She enjoyed seeing her sister so happy and agreed that Luke and Penny were a fine match. Though she was present in the conversation, her mind constantly wandered to another name. It had surprised her how often Ben Deery had entered her thoughts since their first meeting.

Sasha remembered the excitement she had felt when she had first seen him at the ball and how he had spoken to her like no other man had before. He had not spoken with caution but with defiance and a rudeness that still infuriated her. She thought him intolerable, yet had found his physical appearance quite attractive. She felt frustrated with herself that in this new, exciting world, which she had dreamed of seeing for so long, her enjoyment was being interrupted by constant thoughts of this slaver, Ben Deery.

The coach stopped outside the markets and all three alighted to begin their walk. Sasha looked up at the sky and saw dark clouds looming. She followed the line of the storm, which stretched back behind them. Then, what she saw next made her freeze.

Sitting high on an approaching carriage, next to the driver, was a short, fat, ugly man with stringy hair and warts on his chin – the man who had approached her in the gardens during the ball. He was looking down at her, ogling her through his beady, toad-like eyes and grinning, showing his yellow, rotting teeth.

She grabbed her mother and sister.

'We must go! Something is wrong!'

But it was too late. The morning air erupted with the sound of gunfire from the market stalls and side streets. Red coats hit the ground in numbers as the British soldiers were shot down before they could react.

Men appeared out of the side alleys, swords drawn, screaming and cutting down the few soldiers that remained. A large man with scars on his face and shoulders threw soldiers aside at will, his axe crashing into their skulls, smashing them down.

The three women stood frozen as the smoke from the gunfire rose into the air. As the bodies of dying men filled the street, the rain began to fall.

'We must get back to the Government Fort,' Annette screamed to her daughters. But it was in vain – they were caught in the middle of the attack. The large man wielding the axe grabbed hold of Penny and picked her up with his spare arm. Annette launched herself at him like a lioness protecting her cub, but she was fighting a gorilla who used the handle of his axe to easily shove her aside. The women were seized and thrown back into the carriage.

To their surprise, the coach did not head out of Rio but drove towards the Government Fort.

'Mother!' Penny cried. 'What is happening?'

Suddenly, the coach doors were wrenched open and a large man climbed in. He sat on the bench opposite the three women and looked them up and down. Sasha could see that the man was strong and someone they would not be able to overpower.

'Annette Stevenson, I presume,' the man said, 'and this is young Penny and the dashing Sasha Stevenson. I have to say what a sight you three are, truly beautiful indeed.'

'Who are you and what do you want of us?' The desperation in her mother's voice was clear and unconcealed.

The man looked at her with a stare that made all three ladies sit back in in fear.

'My name is Jackson Bell, and I am here to start the revolution.'

Chapter 52

Jackson Bell. Sasha's heart skipped a beat with the sound of the name. They had been thrust into a nightmare with a mad man, and they were helpless to do anything about it.

'I am pleased to see that you have heard of me. That will save us time.'

'What do you want with us?' Annette asked, in a panic. 'Please let my daughters go. Whatever you want can be sorted out between the two of us.'

'Ah, Annette,' Jackson smiled. 'You have no idea how much sorting out you and I will be doing very soon. Oh, and you too, miss.' He looked over and smiled at Penny.

'No!' Annette screamed. 'My husband is a rich man. He will pay a great sum for our safe return.'

'Yes, Jacob will pay!' Jackson yelled back at her. 'He will pay for his sins, for turning his back on the revolution, for keeping secrets that should be set free! Yes, he will pay. First, he will see his daughters ravaged and sent back to him in pieces. Then he will pay with his life.'

As he said the words, he looked over at Sasha and smiled again.

'You are a monster.' Her voice was shaky.

Jackson continued to smile as he stared at Sasha. The coach stopped, and the noise of the gunfire diminished.

'You do not know yet the meaning of the word, Miss Stevenson, but I will make sure you do very soon.'

The coach doors opened and they came face to face with the

large man with the scars. As the three women were pulled out of the carriage, Sasha could see that they were on the road in front of the entrance to the Government Fort. Soldiers had heard the beginning of the attack and were now aiming their rifles at the carriage. Sasha looked around and saw the hopeless situation they were in.

Up on the balcony, she could see her father with Regan Deery, his general managers, and the soldiers protecting them. From where she was standing, she could see armed men lined up beside the coach, with her father in their sights.

Others had their rifles aimed in the opposite direction, towards the British soldiers who had been protecting the central business district and had followed them to the fort. It was a standoff, and no one would shoot while the Stevenson women were held captive in the middle.

'Stevenson!' Jackson yelled up to the balcony. 'I have your women! Fire on us and I will slit their throats in front of you, I swear it!'

Sasha looked at Penny, who was crying. Adder stood behind her with his arm wrapped around her and a knife to her throat. Tears welled in Sasha's eyes with the excruciating horror of it all.

'Hold fire! Hold your fire!' William Finch called out to the British soldiers surrounding the compound.

Jackson, now confident that he was safe from attack, walked out into the courtyard and climbed onto a wagon in order to be seen by all.

'I am here to declare war on the Stevenson Transport Company and all those who stand with it! Any man here who knows the feeling of oppression and indignity shall find redemption fighting for our revolution! Any who stand in our way will be cut down! Of this, I give you my word!'

Jackson Bell turned around as he spoke so that all in the town square could hear and see him. He looked up again and pointed his finger at Jacob and the many others who had now congregated on the balcony to watch the horror unfold.

'You have taken our freedom from us for too long.' He raised his other hand and pointed towards the three captured women. 'It is time we took something back.' Sasha watched her mother's head drop as the Scarlets in the courtyard cheered with excitement.

She looked up at her father and brother. She had never seen such a look on her father's face before, a look of hopelessness, desperation and terror.

Jackson raised his hand to quieten his army. 'I want the map.'

'There is no map, Bell! Please take me and let them go! I am the one you want.' Jacob's voice was filled with emotion as he spoke.

'I will take whatever I want, you bastard. You are in no position to bargain with me now. You will bring me the location of the Spanish Treasure Fleet ships. You will ride south, alone, with your map, and perhaps you will see your women again.'

On the balcony, Regan turned to Jacob and spoke quietly. 'If we let them go, you will not see them again, Jacob. We have to attack.'

'We will not attack. It is my family, God damn it!'

Jacob tried to calm himself as he made one last plea. 'Jackson, please. In the name of God, I beg you. Let them go and I will hand you all that I have, right now, right this second, in front of everyone here, if you just let them go. You will be a rich man, richer than you would ever have dreamed. Forget about this fool's quest and take the money, I beg you.'

Sasha watched as Jackson looked over at them and back towards her father.

'Tonight, I will take your handsome wife into my bed, before I share her with the rest of my two hundred men.'

Jacob looked down at Annette, who appeared to be in a state of shock, as Jackson continued. 'Tomorrow, I will send her back to you, Jacob. In twenty pieces.'

'No!' Sasha screamed as her mother began to sob. The balcony erupted with cries of anger, which mingled with the cheering from the street where the Scarlets stood. Her father was crying now. His pain could not be contained and, for the first time in her life, Sasha saw the strongest man she had ever known brought to his knees, crippled by the hopeless agony of the situation.

'If you do not come with the map in two days, your daughters will see the same fate. I swear it.'

Suddenly, Sasha felt her skirt being lifted from behind her.

She screamed for her mother, but the noise from the cheering of the army drowned out her cry.

The short, fat man was behind her, digging his knife into her ribs.

'Move and I will kill you. Make a sound and I will kill you,' he whispered. She felt his hand begin to move under her skirt, up the back of her leg and around her upper thigh.

She cried out again, trying to break free, but the point of his knife dug into her side, paralysing her and rendering her helpless.

'Put them into the coach and take them south,' Jackson yelled, looking up at Jacob once more. 'If we are followed, kill them.'

The three women were dragged and forced towards the coach. Sasha could still hear the cries from the people standing on the balcony as a Scarlet opened the coach door.

Just as the man turned around to lift Sasha into the coach, the sound of gunfire filled the air again. The Scarlet's head flew backwards as the shot hit the side of his temple, killing him at the steps of the coach.

'Incoming fire!' yelled another, as more of the Scarlets were cut down, dying on the muddy streets. Sasha turned to her mother and sister and grabbed them, pulling them down to the ground. The men around them were returning fire and no longer had hold of them.

'Hurry!' she screamed. 'Over there!' She grabbed both their hands and crawled away from the carriage and into an alleyway, out of the line of fire.

They hid behind a bundled tower of baskets and embraced each other. She wanted to be up with her father and brother in the safety of the fort. She wanted to open her eyes and wake from this horrible nightmare, but her eyes were open and she could see the men in the street dying in front of her.

Ben galloped into sight with his long sword drawn, cutting through the first line of defence before leaping off his horse and continuing on foot. He was followed by Luke and his men from the Company, alongside Thomas and twenty Royal Couriers. In the street, the gunfire continued until the Company's men were close enough to draw swords and engage with the Scarlets.

Men stabbed each other as the town square turned into a battlefield.

'Shoot at Jackson!' William Finch ordered from the balcony. The British garrison fired towards the coach beside which Jackson had been standing.

'Separate their forces!' William ordered again.

A hail of gunfire erupted from the fort, forcing Jackson and the larger part of his force to retreat from Adder and the others near the coach. The Scarlets had been split and were now taking fire on two fronts. Jackson was being attacked from the fort, as well as from the line of British soldiers who had entered from the outskirts of the city.

The Company and the Couriers fought Adder and what was left of the separated Scarlets along the western road that led out of the city.

As Ben dashed past a man, slashing his sword across his opponent's stomach and sending him to the ground, he stole a moment to assess the battle ahead. He had been the one who had fired the first shot and killed the Scarlet opening the carriage door. As he was riding into the square, Ben had seen that the Stevenson women had escaped into an alley.

He could see that the Scarlets were scattered, and his men were now dealing with a much smaller group. There were only around fifteen men to confront their thirty. Their part of the fight was over, as the Scarlets around them dropped their swords and fell to their knees. That is, all but one – Adder – who was still fighting and wielding his axe.

In the alley, Sasha held her mother and her sister tightly. The shooting seemed further away now, yet she could still hear it clearly.

'Ladies!' She heard the voice clearly but did not dare look up. 'Ladies!' Again the call came, the voice being much nearer.

'It's me, Luke.' All three of them looked up and saw Luke Deery standing there with a group of men.

'Luke,' Penny cried out and threw herself into his arms. 'Please help us. Oh God, please help us.'

'I will,' Luke said confidently. 'We will keep you safe, I promise. But you must hurry. Can you all ride?'

All three nodded and followed Luke out into the street. The other men with him surrounded the women and assisted them onto three horses.

Sasha looked around at the street, now littered with dead and dying men. She had never seen so much blood in her life and had never seen a man die until a few moments ago.

The rain continued to fall as she glanced towards the carriage that was to have been their tomb. Their assailants had surrendered and now there were far fewer of them. She could still hear gunfire further down the street. She understood Luke's urgency. Jackson's army had been isolated from them, but for how long was uncertain.

She looked down the street at the large man with the scars who was still on his feet, frothing at the mouth like a rabid dog, his axe dripping with blood.

'Luke, sir!' A man rode over to them. 'We have cleared the road but there is no safe way of getting the women back into the fort. The road is far too dangerous.'

'Understood,' replied Luke. 'We are not going to the compound. We are heading north with my brother and the

Couriers.'

'Yes, sir. We should leave now before the remaining Scarlets regroup. Where is Ben, sir?'

Luke pointed at the man standing tall further down the road. Sasha looked in that direction and saw Ben standing in the middle of the street with his men around him. He had his back to them and was facing the scarred man. Her heart began to beat faster.

Adder stood, seething with anger at the loss of his men. 'I will have those women, Deery!' he screamed at Ben. 'I will have those women! I will have them, I promise you!'

'Do you hear the shooting, Adder?' Ben called back, smiling. 'Jackson cannot reach you. You are all alone now.' Ben's smile drove Adder wild.

'Fight me, you dog!' Adder spat back at Ben. 'You will see who is alone when my axe splits your skull.'

'Come, then,' Ben replied. 'Let's get this over with.'

The two men circled each other while those around watched. Sasha's heart was in her throat now. She realised that there was more that she had wanted to say to Ben Deery. He had captivated her, and she could not bear the thought of seeing him fall. Tears started rolling down her face as she watched in horror.

Ben raised his sword with two hands as the rain washed the bloodied blade clean for the fight.

'Come then, young Deery!' Adder called as the two men continued to circle each other.

'No,' Sasha cried desperately, as Adder and Ben prepared to engage. All eyes were now on the two men in the middle of the street. Even the injured and those who had surrendered were watching in anticipation of what would happen next.

The sound of steel smashing against steel rang through the smoke and rain. Adder advanced and Ben parried. Again, Adder advanced and, again, Ben evaded him.

Adder attacked with rage and blind fury, not with the calm focus needed in a fight. Ben realised then that it was Adder's intimidating nature that had made him so dangerous for all these years. But Ben was not afraid of him. Perhaps once, but not now. Ben was exactly where he wanted to be, deep in the moment with just himself and his opponent, everything on the line, everything to lose, everything to win. This was a moment when a man's senses intensified and made him stronger, quicker and impervious to pain. He had learnt from the Imbangalas that the quality that made a great warrior was his ability to remain calm in the midst of battle.

He could see the look of uncertainty on Adder's face now. A look that told Ben he was in control of the moment and that the time to strike had come. He waited for Adder to advance. Adder's rage had no patience and his lack of focus had made him attack too often and thus tire. As Adder lunged forward, Ben stepped to the side and ducked under the swing of the axe. He jammed the hilt of his sword into Adder's ribcage and stepped past him, allowing the edge of the long blade to cut through Adder's stomach, running its course across the large man's belly.

Ben did not have to look back to know the fight was over. He had felt the blade slice deep into Adder's entrails, almost cutting him in half.

He made his way around to face the great and feared warrior, who was now on his knees trying to hold in his intestines. Ben stood in front of Adder, his sword steady in his right hand.

'It is quite a thing for a man to see his death,' Ben said calmly. 'Look at me.' Adder kept his eyes to the ground. His breathing was broken, and his shoulders began to shake. He was dying quickly.

'Look at me, Adder.' Ben spoke softly now as his anger drained from him, just as Adder's blood was draining away, gathering in a pool on the ground.

Adder mustered his strength and raised his head to look at Ben. He tried to speak but the blood curdled his words as it dribbled from his mouth.

Ben raised his sword and swung it with both hands. Adder's

eyes widened as the blade cut into the side of his neck. With a last precise blow, Adder's head separated from his body and rolled onto the ground at his knees. His headless torso fell to the street, mangled and broken. Adder was no more.

The rain intensified and the sound of gunfire grew louder. Musungo and the Gonzos ran up to Ben. Their hatchets were stained with blood.

'Omiran,' Musungo called to him. 'Jackson Bell and his men are breaking through. They head this way. No way of reaching big boss Regan.'

'We head north again,' Ben replied, still looking at Adder's dead body.

'We must leave now, Omiran, or we will be like big Adder on the ground.'

Musungo was right. The gunfire was growing increasingly louder. Jackson's troupe had made the push to connect with Adder and would be in sight at any moment now. There would be too many of them to engage and all of this would have been in vain.

'Ben!' Luke yelled from the end of the road. 'Come. The fort will hold its defences, but we must leave. There will be another time for Bell.'

Ben sheathed his sword and mounted his horse. He rode towards the others. He could see Sasha looking directly at him as he rode in to meet them. As he passed a doorway, he noticed a slight movement, but he did not stop. An innocent bystander hiding from the battle perhaps, a child even. No, neither!

He turned his horse quickly, drawing his long rifle from the saddle as he did so. He looked down at the scene where the battle had taken place. Bodies littered the street, and Adder's few remaining men stood there waiting for Jackson Bell to arrive.

Then he looked back toward the building where he had seen the movement in the doorway. He raised his rifle.

'Jasper Cole!' he called out loudly.

Sasha felt her skin crawl when she saw the toad-like figure

who had been cowering in the doorway stumble into the middle of the street with his arms in the air. The thought of her dress being lifted and the sickening feeling of his repulsive, sweaty hands on her skin forced a shiver down her back. She watched as Ben raised his rifle and aimed at Cole as the coward pleaded for his life.

'Mr Deery.' His voice was shaky and pathetic and his knees shook in the rain, 'Mr Deery, I assure you that I was not privy to…'

A cracking sound filled the air as the shot and smoke escaped from the barrel of Ben's rifle, causing his horse to rear up. A spray of red mist plumed out from behind Jasper Cole's head, leaving a black hole in the middle of his face, and the toad was dead before he hit the ground.

Ben slung his rifle over his shoulder and reined his horse to return to the group. As he neared Sasha, he heard Thomas call to him.

'Jackson will want retribution for Adder's death and he will want it swiftly. If we thought his insanity knew no bounds before, we are about to find out how far it reaches, of that we can be certain.'

Ben knew Thomas was right. There was no avoiding it now. Jackson would scorch heaven and earth to get his revenge and he, Ben, was now the prime target.

Better me than Sasha.

He looked up at Thomas and replied, 'Thomas, we must take them to the mountain. It is the only place where they will be safe until this is over.'

Sasha knew that the word "they" meant her mother and sister and herself. She looked over at the man called Thomas, who seemed to be unconvinced.

'War is upon us now,' Ben spoke to him again. 'For all of us. I must speak with Simon.' Thomas looked down the street as Jackson's men advanced. He looked back at Ben and nodded.

'North, then,' Thomas called out to the group as they turned their horses and set their course north out of the city. 'We ride to *Aldeia Escondida.*'

Chapter 53

It was dusk when they finally stopped to set up camp and rest the horses. The three natives who accompanied Ben had stayed further south on the road to make sure Jackson's army had not followed them north.

Sasha's legs were aching from the ride. She had not ridden for so long a distance since she was young, and she could see that her mother and sister were just as uncomfortable when they were assisted from their horses.

It had not stopped raining since the attack, making it impossible to start a fire. She was soaked through and was chilled in her wet clothes, even in the tropical climate.

She watched Luke as he helped them over to a large tree where there was some shelter from the rain. He wrapped sleeping blankets around them and sat next to Penny, who was more than willing to curl up beside him.

'Are you all right?' he said to all three women. They nodded in unison.

'I am not sure how to thank you, Mr Deery,' Annette sobbed. 'What would have happened if you hadn't saved us?'

'Please do not think of it again, ma'am. I will not hear of it. It is I who am filled with shame and regret that it was almost too late. I would never have forgiven myself if…'

He stopped himself, knowing that he did not have to say anymore. They all knew too well what would have been the fate of the Stevensons if the Scarlets had prevailed.

'Why do men do this to each other?' Penny asked, her voice

shaking and chilled. None of them had ever seen a battle before nor watched men kill each other. Wars and battles were a distant notion in the wealthy suburbs of London. 'Why do they hate with such fury that they can take life without mercy or regret?'

Luke looked down at her.

'Not all men are filled with hate, Miss Penny. Not all men are like them.'

Penny looked up at him and smiled. 'I hate this place, Luke,' she continued. 'Promise me that it will be over soon and you will take me back to London. Please, promise me.'

'I promise, miss.'

Annette afforded herself a moment of happiness and smiled at Sasha, who smiled back. It was now obvious that Penny and Luke loved each other and would marry. Sasha prayed now that they would make it through this ordeal alive and see their marriage come to fruition.

Her thoughts returned to the morning's events and the terror she had felt when Jackson Bell had addressed the crowded courtyard. She remembered the look on her father's face when he had been told what Jackson was going to do to them, the noise of the battle and the fight between Ben and Adder.

She had seen, in the flesh, the great warrior Omiran, and it confirmed all the stories that circled around London about this great and fearless man. She was consumed by him now, completely and utterly consumed by the thought of him, for there was no safer place in this world than by his side.

The fight with Adder was as terrifying to watch as it was exhilarating. Ben had moved with such speed and balance, not once looking as if he would be defeated by the tyrant slaver.

Ben had saved them. He had fired the first shot, which had killed the Scarlet at the door of the coach, and he had fired the last shot, sending Jasper Cole to his grave. His men followed him into battle without question, and why would they have any reason not to do so? He was a great warrior, as skilful and brave as he was handsome. She had to talk to him and was no longer concerned with coyness.

'Luke?' she asked.

'Yes, ma'am.'

'Tell me about your brother. What is the story of how he came to be in your family? Is it true he was a slaver?'

Luke smiled sympathetically and Sasha was embarrassed, having realised that she had so openly revealed her true feelings in front of everyone.

'I do not know much about his life before we crossed paths. Yes, he was part of a slaving crew on a ship that we had engaged and were trying to apprehend. Yet, I have also thought of that many times since. It did not make sense that a boy like him was a slaver, no real sense at all, miss.'

'Why do you say that?' Sasha replied.

'Well,' Luke started again, 'it was Adder's slaving ship that we attacked all those years ago. We were both much younger then, only around fourteen, or so. He is the reason both my father and I are alive today. If it were not for him coming to our aid, Adder would have killed us both.'

Sasha looked at Luke with interest. 'So, you do not believe he was a slaver?'

'I don't really know, Miss Sasha. It is not uncommon for young boys to be taken from their homes through no choice of their own and made to work on ships. Perhaps the very reason why Ben is so intent on fighting slavers is because he was made to sail with a slaver against his will. But I do not ask him about his past. I know the man he is now and I can assure you that there is no finer nor more loyal man in all the world. We have fought in many battles together and there is no one I would rather have at my side.'

Sasha felt a wave of relief wash over her. It was what her conscience had been fighting since she had first met him, torn between her feelings of attraction and the thought that he had been a slaver. She recalled the night of the ball when she had alluded that he was part of the dark trade.

You fool. No wonder he treated you will such disdain. You fool.

'What does "Omiran" mean?' she asked.

'Sasha, Mr Deery has answered enough of your questions about his brother,' Annette interrupted, clearly aware of her daughter's infatuation and lack of restraint.

'It is quite all right, ma'am,' Luke replied. 'Ben fell in love with the African continent the moment he set foot on it. He has hunted, fought and explored his way through much of it. He was once blessed by an African witch doctor, who gave him the name. It means "giant". I am not sure if it is due to his size or that he has time and time again conquered many opponents where most men would have failed. Perhaps it is both, but the name spread amongst the African tribes and has crossed the Atlantic on the tongues of slaves. He is loved and feared by many in Africa and, miss,' Luke looked at Sasha, making sure she was paying attention, 'there is much more to him than the warrior.'

Sasha nodded once and looked around for Ben. She had heard enough now. She had to speak with him. The last time they had spoken had been in anger and she, at the very least, had to make amends.

She looked around at the other men, searching for his blond hair, until she saw him sitting alone under a tree. He was facing the south, looking down the track on which they had just travelled. With rifles by his side, after everything he had already done that day, he was keeping watch. She stood up, her blanket still wrapped around her.

'Where are you going, Sasha?' Annette asked.

'I must thank him for what he has done.' It was the truth, though she wanted to talk to him for other reasons, more selfish in nature.

She walked over to the tree, immediately noticing his muscular shoulders, which were clearly visible through his soaked shirt. His blond hair was tied back behind his head, leaving only a strand of gold hanging in front of his face. She felt nervous when he looked up at her with his pale eyes. He went to stand but she shook her head at him.

'Please,' she began. 'Please don't get up. You have already done so much. Please rest.'

Ben conceded and shifted over to make more space. As she sat next to him, a strange sensation of peace came over her. She looked up at the broad leaves that protected them from the rain and waited for him to speak, but he did not. She cleared her throat whilst trying to search for the right words.

'I need to thank you for saving my mother and sister, Mr Deery,' she started, 'and for saving me. I am not as naive as you may think. I know what Jackson Bell would have done to us if you hadn't intervened.'

'You are more than welcome, Miss Stevenson.' He did not look at her as he spoke but kept his gaze firmly fixed southbound along the trail. She tried again, this time with a different approach.

'I have always wanted to go on an adventure, but I fear I should have been more careful of what I wished for.'

Ben sat there watching as the rain fell around them. He had also been replaying the day's events. One thought kept entering his mind: the image of Jasper Cole's hand up the back of Sasha's skirt and his knife in her ribs.

It was in that moment that he had charged. His men had had no choice but to follow and he could have easily killed them all if it had turned out to be the wrong decision, but he had not cared and knew now that he had never stopped loving Sasha. He knew he was still in love with her as they sat there in the rain.

'You handled it very well, miss. You took charge of your mother and sister and led them away from the battle, to safety. You have real courage.'

'I would not say "courage".' Sasha blushed at the compliment. She had no idea that a few kind words from him would affect her so greatly. 'If I am honest, I was more afraid than I could ever have imagined possible.'

'That is what courage is, miss. To stay strong and keep your nerve when you are most afraid.'

He turned to look at her now. His piercing blue eyes seemed to see through her and she felt naked as she sat with him under the tree.

'And what about you, Mr Deery?'

'Ben,' he interrupted her. 'Please, call me Ben.'

Sasha looked up in surprise. His tone was soft and caring. Until that moment, there had been resentment in his voice whenever he spoke to her, as if her very presence caused him pain. They looked at each other a moment before she turned away. She was too afraid he would see that she was falling in love.

'And what about you, Ben?' she finally spoke. 'Do you ever get frightened? Are you afraid of anything?'

She looked up at him and saw that he had not looked away from her. He gave her a sympathetic smile and she found herself smiling back at him. She wanted to touch him. She wanted him to take her in his strong arms and hold her.

'I have heard that you fight slavers, that you return those poor people back to their homes, that you are somewhat of a mystical figure to the native people in Africa.'

Ben turned away from her, his heart sinking. He could see her interest in him. They could both feel it but she wanted to know about Ben Deery and Omiran. What would happen if she ever found out that he was, in fact, Caleb, the poor stable boy who had been her servant? She would never accept it. Her family would never allow it.

'You should go back to your mother, where it is safer,' he said as he kept his eyes on the trail.

Sasha was taken aback at his sudden change. She knew that there was something happening between them and was sure that he had just felt it also.

'I could not imagine a safer place than next to you, Ben.' As she said it, they stared at each other again, and this time the attraction between them was undeniable.

'And I would not want to leave your side either, Sasha, but

you should be with your mother and sister now. We will have more time when we reach our destination tomorrow, when I know we are safe.'

She understood and nodded. She would not gain his full attention out here while they were being hunted. She was a distraction but was elated to know that she was something to him now.

She moved to stand but he rose quickly to his feet, holding out his hand to her. She put her hand in his and he helped her up.

She buckled under the soreness of her legs and began to stumble backwards, but he caught her and held her close. She could feel the warmth radiating from his body as his large hands held her waist. She held on tightly to his muscular arms to balance herself. All the world faded away as they stared into each other's eyes. Suddenly, a feeling of euphoria washed over her. As if she were in a dream where past and present were one. He felt familiar to her. The way he held her. The way their bodies seemed to match. She tried not to think of him, but his name pushed its way into her mind. Caleb. Her first love. Her only love, until now. Ben had the same eyes. The same pace of breath. He couldn't be? Impossible.

'You remind me of someone,' she whispered, not breaking her gaze. 'Tell me, how did you come to meet the Deerys?'

Ben went to move away but she held him close, pushing him back against the tree and out of sight of the others. She moved closer to him. He looked around, checking if anyone had seen them. When he looked back at her, he noticed that she had not looked away.

'You remind me very much of someone. Someone who was special to me,' she said again.

'Sasha, I would surely remember if we had met.'

'Did you know of the *Retribution*? One of my father's ships that was sunk seven years ago?' she continued.

'Yes, I have heard about that ship. Most who sail the Atlantic have. Nobody left alive.'

'So we were told. Now, I am not so sure,' Sasha said, smiling up at him.

'I wish I knew your meaning, miss,' Ben replied awkwardly. 'But we have never met before. Of that I am certain.'

Ben could see a look of great sadness and disappointment in Sasha's face. He could not tell her the truth, even though she was dangerously close to realising it. He would lose her if he did.

'I think it is time to go back to the others,' he said.

'Just a moment longer, Ben. Please?'

She wanted to stay there, in his arms, forever. She was no longer scared, cold, sore or hungry. He had made all of that disappear with one touch. She wondered if he truly was mystical.

Chapter 54

When they reached the waterfall the next morning, the sun was high in the sky. Thomas led them into the mountain behind the boulders. Ben enjoyed the look on Luke's and the women's faces when they saw Thomas vanish into the cave wall, and again when he opened the door to reveal the hidden township thriving in the hollow of the mountain.

Thomas led them to the main hall in the middle of the village. Standing on the deck outside the tavern was Simon Blake.

'Simon,' Annette called in delight, running up to greet him. 'We thought you dead. We thought we had lost you. Imagine when my husband finds out you are alive.'

Simon chuckled out loud at Annette's excitement. 'It has been a long time, Annette. Are you all right?'

'Far better now I have seen your friendly face, though I fear we would have been doomed if not for these men who came to our aid. We were separated from Jacob and the others at the fort.'

Simon looked up at Ben for an explanation.

'Jacob and my father are safe in Rio,' Ben explained. 'They are safe inside the fort, along with the British soldiers who sailed over with the Stevenson entourage. They saw us escape north. Simon, this is my brother, Luke Deery.'

'It is a pleasure to finally meet you, Mr Blake,' Luke introduced himself enthusiastically.

'The pleasure is mine,' replied Simon. 'I have fought beside your father a number of times. He is a fine man and I am sure he is proud of the man you have become.' Simon looked past Luke to the two young ladies. 'And this must be Penny and Sasha. Welcome to The Hidden Place.'

He looked back at Ben and Thomas.

'And what of Jackson?'

'He was retreating before his losses became too heavy. He will need a few days to lick his wounds before he attacks again,' Thomas answered.

'Adder will not wait,' Simon replied. 'He will already be on your trail. That animal has no patience.'

'Adder is dead, Simon,' Luke replied with a smile.

Simon stopped and looked at the men. 'You are sure of this? You saw him die?'

'I saw my brother separate his head from his shoulders.'

Simon looked over at Thomas, who nodded in agreement.

'So, Jackson's pet snake and the Scarlet's warlord has been slain. Jackson is still unaware of this place. Your families are safe in Rio for the next few days and I am reacquainted with an old friend and her family. This calls for a celebration. Come. Let us all eat and drink and talk of better things for a while.' He signalled to a woman and she came up to meet them. 'Please take the ladies to the waterholes where they can bathe. Tonight, we rest. We are safe and alive.'

'Thank you,' Annette said as she and her daughters were led off to the springs.

'Come,' Simon said to the men. 'Let us sit next to the fire and drink some ale.'

Thomas, Simon, Ben and Luke sat at a large table as jugs of ale were delivered with bread and salted pork.

'So, Luke,' Simon raised his mug of ale, 'I hear congratulations are in order. I have been informed that you are to marry one of the fine young ladies I just met. That is, if we get out of this mess in one piece.'

Luke met Simon's mug with his own and drank wholeheartedly.

'I have made my decision about which daughter to marry.'

Ben stopped drinking and looked at his brother, holding his breath.

'I have decided to marry Penny.'

Ben let out a sigh of relief. He had forgotten about the marriage and was relieved that Sasha would not be married to his brother. He knew now that he loved her, and he could not bear it if another man took her away from him.

'And what made you choose Penny?' Simon went on.

'Well, they are both fine-looking women, but when you know, you know.' He looked over at Ben. 'I love her, Brother,' he said.

'I am happy for you, Luke,' Ben replied truthfully.

'And what about you, Ben?' Luke continued.

'What do you mean?' Ben tried to mask his feelings by putting the cup back in his mouth.

'Ah, come now, I have seen the way you look at each other. She has barely taken her eyes off you since you met. It would have been awkward if I had chosen differently, yes?'

'I would not have stood in your way, Brother.'

'Well, now you don't have to, do you? But Simon makes a good point. Just make sure you don't get yourself killed before you tell her how you feel.'

'Have you told Penny?'

'Ah, well, I am waiting for the right moment.'

They all began to laugh around the table.

'So, boys,' Simon changed the tone. 'I assume you came here for more than safety. You are here to rally troops, yes?'

Luke looked up at Simon and Thomas. 'Jackson's army has been wounded but he will attack again soon. Adder is dead, which will take the wind out of their sails. If we continue to combine our forces, we can end this and bring stability to the region and start to rebuild the Atlantic trade. Don't you want to come out of hiding, Blake?'

Simon looked around him. 'Come, let us have another drink and you can tell me your plan.'

An hour passed before there was agreement at the table. It had been decided to draw Jackson out into the open and onto a field of battle. A Courier was to be dispatched to Rio with a message. Jacob and Regan were to sail north with all the British soldiers and any Portuguese who would be willing to fight by their side. They would send Jackson a message that he would have his chance for war. They estimated that the numbers for each side would be relatively even if the Couriers joined the fight, and it was decided that they would.

They stood to greet Annette, Sasha and Penny when they walked into the hall. All three looked refreshed, relaxed and beautiful. They sat down at the table and were passed wine, fresh water, fruit, bread and jam. Within minutes, the colour had returned to their faces and they were cheerful.

Sasha looked over at Ben a number of times as she tapped her feet under the table to the tune of the fiddle player. The mineral waters of the warm rock pools had revitalised her body and cleared her head and her thoughts kept returning to what Ben had said to her the day before. She wanted time to talk to him alone. She wanted to see if his feelings mirrored her own. She had fallen for him completely and there was nothing of which she was more certain.

'Simon,' Annette asked. 'What do we do now?'

Simon looked across to the others at the table.

'We are safe and protected here. Jackson Bell is not near this place nor does he know of its existence, but we cannot stay here for long. This has to end and it can only end through battle. We will call on Jackson and his army and will fight him, once and for all, on the northern beaches. Jacob, Regan and his troops will sail to meet us and that is where we will wait until the Scarlets show.'

The relaxed looks on the women's faces vanished instantly when they realised that the real battle was still to come.

'Can we not just leave?' Penny pleaded as she looked over at Luke. 'Can we not just sail back to London, where we will be safe? This is not our business.'

Luke smiled at her. 'Unfortunately, it is our business, my dear Penny. We cannot in good conscience leave and allow Jackson to take over. Rio is an important trade port for all of us. We cannot hand it over to the Scarlets.'

Sasha had been looking at Ben throughout. He could see she was upset.

'So, you will all go seeking a fight then?'

Though her words sounded as if they were meant for everyone, she had eyes only for Ben.

'It will not stop unless we stop it,' Simon replied, sensing the panic in her eyes. 'He will continue to murder and punish those in his path unless he is stopped. He knows only harm. He cannot be allowed to keep increasing the size of his army or he will take over the Atlantic and thousands will die or become slaves to him, and that would be worse than death.'

'Please,' Penny interrupted, 'can we not talk of war again. If it is in fact imminent, can we put it out of our minds for at least tonight?'

'Of course, Miss Penny,' Simon replied. 'Let us think of happier things tonight. Please everyone enjoy yourselves. Here you are safe.'

Music continued to play in the hall and the villagers moved in to join the festivities. It was a happy place, sheltered and hidden from the cruel world outside its mountain walls.

'I think it is time I cleaned myself up as well.' Ben stood up and excused himself from the group. He walked down the stairs and along the wooden jetty, which wrapped itself along the edge of the mountain walls, providing entrances to homes along the way.

He made his way past people sitting and drinking and playing cards. The village was bustling and the mood was festive in a way that only comes just before or just after a great battle has been won. As he walked towards the rock pools, people stood up and raised their glasses to him as he passed.

'To you, Omiran,' they called out to him. 'The slayer of Adder.'

He acknowledged them and continued to walk down to the rock pools that were hidden from the village. He stripped naked and walked into the water. The heat underneath the mountain kept the water warm, and the lanterns hanging around the rock walls gave off enough light for him to see clearly.

He let the water cover him completely, enjoying the feel of it around his tired eyes and matted hair. He used a cloth to clean the dirt and blood off his skin. A woman came down and cleared her throat to make him aware she was there.

'Pardon me, sir, Mr Deery. Are you happy for me to wash your clothes, sir?'

Ben nodded to her. 'Do you mind bringing me some wine, please?'

The woman smiled back at him, pleased to be able to help and, without hesitation, picked up the bundle of clothes and returned to the village.

In the hall, Sasha sat with Penny and Luke. Their cups were refilled with wine before they could finish each round, and passers-by stopped to welcome and thank them, for all had heard of Adder's death. People danced around them as the music filled their heads with cheer.

'There is so much joy among us tonight. So much happiness,' Penny said as she looked up at Luke. 'But tomorrow it will all change.'

'It will all be all right, I promise,' Luke replied, lovingly.

'How can you be so sure of the future, Mr Deery?' Sasha asked.

Luke looked at Penny and then across the table to Sasha.

'Love only needs a moment to change our world.'

Sasha's heart skipped a beat.

'What did you say?' she asked softly.

'Love only needs a moment to change our world,' repeated Penny. 'That is just beautiful, Luke.'

He smiled at them. 'Unfortunately, I am unable to take credit for such a profound and romantic statement. My brother said it to me when he found out I was to marry. I have thought much about those words since. I know now that nothing is truer. I can see the shock on your face, Sasha. I was as surprised as you to hear that from Ben.'

'From Ben,' Sasha said, almost in tears. 'And, please remind me, what age was Ben when you met him?'

'Uh, around fourteen I believe, miss,' Luke replied, confused by Sasha's sudden change in mood.

'Seven years ago, then?'

'Yes, miss. Seven. Have I said something wrong, miss Sasha?' he asked, noticing the tears well up in Sasha's eyes.

'No, Mr Deery. Please excuse me.'

Sasha backed away, her tears flowing freely down her face. She held her chest and tried to breathe. How could she not have seen it before? It was in his eyes when he held her earlier that day. It was in the way he looked at her at the ball. He was alive. All these years he had been alive.

The rock pools. Caleb is down at the rock pools.

*

Out on the balcony, Annette smiled as she watched Penny and Luke dance to the cheerful music playing in the tavern. She stood up and walked over to where Simon was smoking a cheroot. Lanterns lit up the rock walls and the moonlight and stars shining above them could be seen clearly through the hole in the side of the great mountain.

'This certainly is a magical place, Simon. As secret as it is magical. I never thought a place such as this would exist. How long have you all lived here?'

'It has been over seven years now, Annette. Seven long years. I am relieved that it may finally come to an end. There is no need to hide anymore.'

'Why, Simon? Why did you leave?'

'There are still many things that are yet to be resolved. I watched Jackson sink the *Retribution*, and I knew that the only way to prevent war was to go into exile.'

Annette looked out over the water below them.

'They were dark times,' she agreed. 'It was a shock to us to learn that all of the *Retribution's* crew had perished.'

Simon chuckled and a puff of smoke drifted into the air.

'What is funny about that?'

'Not everyone was lost on the *Retribution*, Annette. I am surprised you, Mrs Stevenson, do not recognise him. Although, I suppose, it was a long time ago.'

Annette looked at Simon, confused.

'I am sure that I do not know what you mean, Simon.'

'In seven years, not one soul has been able to discover this place without having been shown its location. Ben Deery came four days ago looking for me. He did not stumble across this place. It was memory that brought him here.'

Annette continued to look confused. 'I am not in the mood for riddles, Simon. What are you talking about? We met the Deerys for the first time in Rio. How can I know of Ben's past exploits?'

'Well, I am about to tell you, Annette,' Simon replied with a wry smile on his face.

'I met Ben Deery for the first time over seven years ago in Rio. He was young then, only thirteen or fourteen, and not yet the Ben Deery you see before you now, though he did not go by that name then either. He was placed in my charge on an expedition, during which we discovered this very place. That is how I knew who he was when he appeared only days ago.'

'I am not sure what you want me to say to you, Simon. As I said, I met Ben Deery only recently.'

'Ah, but that is where you are mistaken, Annette. You have known him far longer than that. The young boy who was delivered to me from the *Retribution* was a stableboy from the

Stevenson Estate, one who had recently been badly lashed.'

The truth hit Annette with a shock. She lost her grip on her cup of wine and it smashed onto the balcony.

'No … he can't be.'

Simon looked at her with an expression of guilt in his eyes. There was no point keeping it a secret now. He nodded and spoke calmly.

'The boy Caleb and the man you now know as Ben Deery are one and the same.'

Chapter 55

Sasha ran down the stairs and across the jetty towards the rock pools. She ignored her mother's calls from the balcony above. Her head was swimming with emotions and she had to see his face before she could believe it.

How could he not have told her? How could he not have let her know he was alive? It was almost too much for her to bear, and tears poured down her face as she ran.

She saw him as she came around the corner of the jetty to the tunnel that led down to the pools. There he was, standing naked, waist deep in the water. He was leaning against the mountain wall with his back to her. He had not heard her yet and she took a moment to process the scene in front of her. Was this really the young boy she once knew?

His muscular figure glistened in the warm light of the lanterns. His shoulders were wide across the top and his back fanned out like a butterfly, narrowing towards his waist.

His skin was bronzed all the way down to the top of his buttocks, which were just visible above the water line. As he moved in the light, she saw the scars.

She put her hands over her mouth to stop herself from crying out. They sprawled over his back like white tangles of straw. She stood at the edge of the pool and took her hand away.

She opened her mouth but could not believe the name she was about to speak.

'Caleb.' She had not uttered the name for so long. She did not dare to believe that he would turn around and that she would see the boy she had loved, the boy she had been told had perished years ago.

He turned around slowly to face her. His face was shaven clean, and his hair was slicked back. It was him.

She did not know why she had not seen it before, but she recognised the boy she loved in the man before her now.

'Excuse me, miss?' he replied.

Sasha ran into the water.

'Caleb, is it really you?' She pushed against his chest as she screamed. 'Why? Why did you not tell me? Do you know what it has been like to believe you were dead?'

Sasha pushed again but he stood unwavering, and she forced herself backwards.

She stood in front of him. The water trickled over his muscular chest and down across his chiselled stomach to the waterline, which just covered his manhood. The veins in his arms and shoulders pulsated in the flickering light of the lanterns.

'I am not sure what you are talking about, miss,' he said quietly.

'Liar!' she screamed back. Why are you lying to me? Your age! Your scars! Your eyes! I can see it in your eyes now. Please tell me you are lying,' she cried.

He looked directly at her. 'How could I possibly be this boy you once knew?'

'Love needs only a moment to change our world. And I never told you that I knew Caleb as a boy,' she said.

Ben turned his back to her and slapped his hands against the mountain wall.

'So, it is true,' she said. 'It is really you.'

'Yes,' he whispered. 'Yes, it is true.'

'Why?' she said, bewildered, her hands lying limply against the water as if she had no strength left within her. He turned back around to face her.

'Caleb was a peasant. Ben Deery is not. How could a woman like you ever marry Caleb?'

'It did not matter to me.'

'And look what happened to me as a result of your carelessness. The games that you played. Were you punished, Sasha? Tell me, were you tied to a post and lashed in front of everyone you had ever known? I was given a chance to start a new life and I took it; and, by God, I will not give it up now.'

She saw the determination in his eyes. She understood why he had done it, but it did not lessen the hurt she felt.

'Look at how much pain you have caused.' Her voice was back under control. 'And to think I once loved you. And worse, that I was falling in love with you all over again. How am I supposed to address you now? Caleb? Ben Deery? Omiran? Who are you?'

His eyes moved down below her chin and quickly back up again and she realised that her white dress was now wet, the thin cotton clinging to her body, showing her bareness underneath.

She turned and walked out of the water.

'I have always loved you, Sasha.' His words stopped her at the edge of the pool. 'Please do not cry over me anymore. I have never been able to bear to see you cry.'

He watched her standing at the edge of the pool, her dress wet and clinging to her skin, revealing her fine figure. It was stupid of him to think he could have fooled her, that he could have kept her from finding out the truth. He was relieved that she knew, that she had told him she loved him, then and now.

'Know that, whatever I have had to do to survive, you have always been in my thoughts. Please do not cry for me anymore.'

She turned to face him with a look of anger.

'Oh, I have shed my last tear for you, Caleb. I have shed far too many and I will not waste another.'

'I am sorry.' He now realised how much she had truly been hurt.

'Not good enough,' she replied.

'This must be kept a secret, and you must call me Ben. No one else can know.'

She looked at him and let out an exhausted sigh. She stared at the man in front of her, realising the truth. She could marry a Deery but not a stable boy.

'All right then, Ben Deery,' she said, defeated. Her hands moved up onto her shoulders, taking a dress strap in each. She pulled the straps aside and let them go, allowing her dress to fall over her breasts.

Ben watched speechless as she pushed her dress over her hips and let it fall to the ground. He looked at her naked body glowing in the lantern light, slender, lean and strong, her dark hair falling over her shoulders as she tilted her head to one side.

She stepped back into the pool, her long legs disappearing into the water. It crept over her smooth thighs and up to the nest of her womanhood. Her breasts swayed ever so slightly with each step as she set her course towards him.

'What are you doing, Sasha?'

'I'm going to finish what we started … Ben.'

She flung her arms around his neck and pressed her body against his. The warm wetness of her lips pressed firmly against his, taking them both back to that night in the stables.

She remembered feeling the hardness of his manhood against her body then, and the look of embarrassment on his face, but he was not embarrassed now. She could feel it pressed against her, stubborn and ready.

She moved her hand away from his neck and down into the water to meet the hardness between them. He breathed heavily, cupping her buttocks and pulling her closer into him. She wrapped her legs around his waist and lowered herself down.

Her eyes widened as she rocked her hips back and forth against him. There was pain at the beginning, but then her body began to ache in a way that she had never felt before.

She heard herself moan, trying to stay quiet but the feeling made it impossible. His breathing became faster and his muscles tensed around her. She rocked her hips against him fiercely until, with a final thrust, she felt a hot shivering sensation consume her.

The world blurred and all she could feel was the explosion happening from within. He grunted, squeezing her tight as his muscles tensed one last time.

She breathed heavily as she looked into his eyes. He smiled at her and she smiled back. In a single moment, they had become one person and in his arms she finally felt the sense of belonging for which she had been searching her whole life.

Chapter 56

Sasha needed to change her clothes before she returned to the hall, so Ben left her with the lady who had tended to his washing and made his way up to the landing to find Simon and Annette still talking on the balcony. As he walked towards them, Annette looked at him in disbelief.

She stood in front of him and cupped his face in her hands. Her face was pale, but he sensed that she was relieved to see him.

'Mrs Stevenson?' he said to her.

'It is good to see you again. You have grown into a great man.'

She moved up on her toes and kissed him on the cheek. 'I will never forget what you have done for us, especially after everything my family has put you through. I will take your secret to the grave, Caleb. I swear it,' she promised.

'Did Sasha tell you?'

'No, my dear. Simon told me.'

'I must speak with Mr Blake alone,' he replied quickly. 'I believe that Sasha needs to talk to you, also alone.'

She smiled and looked up at him. 'Yes, I would suppose that she does, Mr Deery.'

He nodded and smiled down at her, knowing that the bond with her eldest daughter would be her word. He had learned that, if anything, the Stevensons were all true to their word.

'It warms my heart to see you again, son. I am sure once Sasha is over the shock, she will feel the same way. She will be fine.' He smiled and nodded sheepishly as she left him with Simon.

Simon shot a rueful look as Ben made his way towards him.

'I hope I did not just betray your trust, Ben. It was not my intention to cause such trouble.'

'There has been no harm done. When did you realise, Simon? Was I a fool to think I could hide it?'

'It was only a week ago, when you turned up here looking for me, unannounced, that I realised who you were, and that you were about the right age. Tell me, are there any others who survived?'

Ben shook his head. 'They were all murdered. I alone was taken on board Adder's ship. Made to watch them all die. When the Deerys intervened, I tried to save them from Adder. I got in the way, and when I woke up, I was on the *Charlotte Arms.*'

'And you called yourself Ben so that there would be no ties back to the *Retribution* and Stevenson.'

Ben nodded.

'Well, then,' Simon went on. 'You have certainly kept your secret well. Ben Deery and the great Omiran are very well known. It will be more so now after Adder's death. No one knows about the boy Caleb.'

'Annette and Sasha know now. You know. That is three more than there were yesterday.'

'I have spoken to Annette and she will not tell a soul, not even her own husband.' There was a pause as Simon looked down over the balcony and into the water below them. 'So, it seems you are good at keeping a secret, Mr Deery. Would you like to keep another?'

Puzzled, Ben looked at Simon and waited for him to continue.

'This place, this hidden place, was not built by us. All those years ago when we found the tunnel behind the waterfall, the door was already there. When we opened it, much of the foundations were already built.'

'I don't understand,' Ben replied. Then he remembered Stevenson's story. He realised now that the expedition he and Bobby had been on all those years ago was always about this place.

'So, it is true then,' Ben said. 'You found the Spanish treasure.'

Simon looked at him for a second, as if he was testing him one last time, before deciding to give up his secret.

'Yes, it is true. It is below you, in the water down there, under a rock shelf: hundreds of chests. It is no wonder the rest of the fleet failed to outrun the storms. They were far too heavy and riding too low in the water. But there was mutiny pre-planned and some ships sailed south. They must have built rafts and transported the treasure inland on the river until they discovered the waterfall. The foundations you see are from one of the fleet ships itself, dismantled and rebuilt inside the mountain. Quite a feat. I imagine all those who were originally involved would be dead many years ago, perhaps from disease, natives, each other. Who knows? Only a select few here know the true secret of the mountain, but there are others who know pieces of this puzzle, secret messages passed on by the original fleet sailors. How else did Jacob come by the information? Others who live here believe that we are hiding from the Scarlets. Some live here so they are not governed by another's rule. Either way, the real secret cannot fall into the wrong hands. This includes Jacob Stevenson.'

Ben looked up, surprised. 'Why, Simon?'

'Many years ago, before you were born, Jacob Stevenson and Jackson Bell were partners of sorts, if you can believe that.'

'Impossible.' Ben looked up from the water and across at Simon, startled.

'For a long time, Stevenson's merchant ships sailed the Atlantic trade routes unscathed and untouched by the many thieves who sail this ocean. French, British, Portuguese and Spanish merchants were all attacked and all relieved of their cargoes but not one Stevenson ship. Why do you think that is, son?'

'Jacob was paying him for protection,' Ben exclaimed. 'The Scarlets were on the bastard's payroll.'

'It was more than that,' Simon continued. 'Jacob supplied Bell with the *Grey Cloud* to patrol the Atlantic on his behalf. He also knew of the slaves who were on board, though he did not share in the profits of Jackson's slaving. The ship and allowance kept Bell in operation, which made him one of the most prominent slavers and tyrants on the Atlantic.'

Ben's fingers clenched tight against the railing, causing the wood to creak inside his strong hands. 'The *Grey Cloud* was built by my father's company, owned by Stevenson and captained by Jackson Bell. Is my family also corrupt?'

'The Deerys are innocent in all of this, you will be pleased to know.' Simon's words allowed Ben to breathe freely again. 'Regan is an honourable man, though I am sure I don't need to tell you that. A shipbuilder builds ships. It is not up to him where they end up and under whose control.'

'Go on then, Simon,' Ben directed. 'What else is there to tell?'

'With free passage and struggling competition, Stevenson Transport rose well above its competitors, growing rapidly in size, operation and profits. This is the time of New Worlds. It is a dangerous and exciting era in which ambition and opportunity collide. This is a time of giants. Those who seek greatness will do everything in their power to achieve it, and with New Worlds come new kings. Both Jackson and Jacob are desperate to find this place. That is why I went into exile. That is why I have kept its whereabouts hidden all these years. Now you must also keep the secret. You must swear to keep it safe. If you give me your word, you will find us allies in your battle against Jackson.'

Ben's grip grew tighter around the railing until he thought the wood might snap in his hand. Stevenson had allied himself with a slaver and a murderer, and had reaped the rewards.

'Jacob is not here to marry off his daughters,' Ben snarled. 'He has come to lure you out of hiding, to see Jackson dead once and for all, and to seize the hoard for himself.'

'That is why you are now in charge of its keeping, son.'

'And what if I take the fortune for myself, Blake? Am I a good man? Have you heard of the things Omiran has done?'

'I could not think of anyone more deserving; but you don't want it, do you, boy? Your prize is standing in that hall.' Ben turned around to see that Sasha had changed and was now sitting with her sister and mother. She was smiling, glowing with life and excitement.

'You also have your new name and title. Just remember, Mr Deery, Spanish silver will bring you as many problems and enemies as it will riches. If it were up to me, I would see it sink to the bottom of the Atlantic.' Simon puffed the smoke from his cheeks as he spoke.

'And what about Jacob?' Ben looked over at Sasha as he spoke. 'Should we let him get away with his past sins?'

'Do not be so quick to blame Stevenson. The Scarlets were more mercenaries than murderers back then and he could not have known how far Bell would take things. In addition, you know that his family's reputation would suffer greatly if he were exposed. Sasha loves you, Ben. As sure as we are standing here now, she loves you. You are a lucky man.'

'I suppose I am,' he replied. Rarely had he ever thought of himself as a lucky man. He had loved Sasha from the first moment he had seen her and, as Ben Deery, he could now marry her. They would have wealth and position, with nothing to stand in the way of their happiness. Nothing, that is, except a war with a slaver king and his secret benefactor, who, Ben had just learned, was the father of the woman he loved. Many were going to die before he and Sasha could be together.

In the next few days, many will die. Do I still feel lucky?

Chapter 57

Almost floating with excitement, Sasha walked through the hall. The boy she had loved as a girl had become the man she had fallen in love with now. She was still quivering with the pleasure of being with him in the pool.

It had been her first time with a man. She replayed in her head how it felt to have his hands touch her bare skin and the feeling within her once the pain had subsided. A whole new world, filled with wonderful secrets and dangerous desires, had begun this night.

The wine was going to her head and she welcomed the feeling, the feeling of being truly alive. She refilled her glass and saw Simon and Ben on the deck outside the tavern. Her stomach filled with butterflies as soon as she saw him. She was in love and she knew it. She wanted to be near him, smell him, touch him and let him take her to bed. She sat down with her mother and sister.

Simon and Ben entered the tavern and sat at the table with the ladies. Luke filled their cups and sat down heavily, as a man does when the wine relaxes him.

'So, what is our plan, then?' Luke began. 'We can't hide here drinking wine for the rest of our days, as nice as that sounds right now. Should we head for the northern beaches and camp there until Bell and his army turn up? What if they do not?'

'They will,' Ben replied. 'There is too much at stake now.'

'And what of us?' Annette spoke up.

'The safest place for you is here,' Ben answered. 'Hidden,

until this is over once and for all.'

Sasha looked at him.

'I will want to be close to my future husband,' Penny spoke up.

'And I with you,' Luke smiled back at her. 'But this is not something you should witness. A battle is not the place for you, my love.'

'It is no secret now that Jackson Bell desires the Stevenson women,' Simon began. 'I agree with Luke, but I fear Bell will send part of his army to look for them and once again use them as leverage.'

'Bell will not find them here, Simon.' Thomas entered the conversation.

'That may be the case, Thomas,' Simon replied. 'But if everything Jackson wants is in the same place, he is sure to bring his whole army and focus to that place. We not only need to cut the head off the snake but burn the wriggling body as well.'

Sasha looked at Simon and Luke and then over at Ben. 'It is our decision and we have made it. Our family's safety is at stake also. We are coming with you.'

They looked at one another.

'What do you think, Ben?' asked Simon, as if he were consulting his general.

Ben looked at the three women sitting in front of him. They were almost impossible to resist, and Jackson had been so close that it may be the final push he needed to meet in open battle.

'Simon is right. They come with us. The three of you will stay on board the *Mary*, which will be manned and ready to sail to London at a moment's notice should Jackson's army prevail.'

Luke began to draw up a message for his father and Jacob Stevenson, requesting they meet them in a week at the cove on the northern beaches above Rio. They were to sail the *Mary*, its entourage, the *Charlotte* and the *Gabriel* and prepare for a battle, and they were to make no secret of their departure and intentions.

'We will send a Courier to Rio immediately,' Blake announced. 'Tomorrow, we pack for battle and take the mountain roads through the jungle up to the coastal road. Then we head east for half a day, which will take us to the northern sands. It will take Jackson at least a week to reassemble his army and meet us there once the news finds him. That will give us enough time to organise our ranks. He will want to rest his army half a day's ride from the fields. We will have scouts at the ready to let us know when he arrives.'

'I will take the message now,' Thomas stood up. 'I will see that the right preparations are made.'

Simon acknowledged his second. 'Be invisible, Thomas.'

Thomas nodded, took the note from Luke and left the table.

'It is done, then,' Simon said softly and to no one in particular. 'After all these years, it is finally upon us.'

Ben stood and excused himself. He realised that he had not slept since the Rio attack and exhaustion had hit him. He headed out of the hall and down to the lodges that had been made available to them.

The festivities were in full swing as he made his way through the village. He entered the small, modest cabin where there was a bed made up and lanterns lit. Wine had been put in a flask for him next to the bed.

He stripped himself of his clothes and lay down in the bed, thinking about how he should approach the situation with Jacob Stevenson. Part of him wanted to kill him. All of this was his doing. He had stood on the balcony during the attack in Rio, trying to negotiate his way out of a situation that he'd certainly had a hand in creating.

Suddenly, he heard a knock on the door and he quickly covered his nakedness with a sheet.

'Come,' he called out, cautiously.

As the door opened, the outside noise of the music and laughter filtered into the room and standing at its entrance was Sasha. She walked into the room and closed the door behind her.

He sat up in his bed and put one foot on the floor to stand but she put her hand out, motioning him to stay.

For the second time that night, her dress fell to the floor, revealing her nakedness in the candlelight. His tiredness faded and was instantly replaced by an uncontrollable aching in his groin. She walked over to the bed and pulled the sheet away, pleased to see that he was as eager as she was.

She straddled him and leant down to kiss him. The music outside masked their noise as they rolled around on the bed. Their intertwined positions changed time and time again, and when they were exhausted, he lay on his stomach with Sasha on his back. He found the tickling sensation wonderful as she stroked the long blond hair across the back of his neck.

'I am so sorry, Caleb,' she whispered, almost too quietly for him to hear, as if she meant to think it and not say it. 'What happened to you is all my fault, the scars on your back, my father, the *Retribution*. It is all my fault.'

He could feel her tears drop onto his back as he rolled over to face her. He knew now that his resentment was misguided, that for years he had used hate and anger against her whole family to protect himself from his true feelings for her. But there was no point hiding them now. Not after everything that had happened.

'You set me free, Sasha.' He brushed her dark hair back behind her ears and wiped the wet tracks from her cheek. 'I do not know if everything happens for a reason. A witch from Angola once told me that it did. I know now that your love freed me from poverty, freed me from a life of nothing. I know that I have never stopped loving you, that I love you now and I will love you forever.'

Her lips began to quiver, though she was smiling now. 'Why did you not come back to England? Why did you not come and find me?'

'I assumed that you would have married a lord. I did not think I could have been able to bear seeing you with another man, to see your children.'

'Well, you can see now that I am not married to a lord and that I have no children.'

'Not yet, Sasha,' he smiled up at her, as he thought how beautiful she looked in the fading light. 'I will not let you go this time.'

'Promise me, Cale ... sorry, Ben.'

'You can call me Caleb when it is just the two of us if you want. I am both Caleb and Ben.'

'I will call you Ben, but I will love you both. For the rest of my life, I will love you. Promise me we will have moments like this forever. Promise me you will live through this battle, and you will take me to the places you have been around the world.'

'I promise, Sasha.'

She leant down and kissed him passionately and they made love again before falling asleep in each other's arms, cradled safely in the bosom of the mountain.

Chapter 58

Jackson Bell held the message in one hand, a mug of ale in the other. He had not washed since the failed attack. He had dried blood on his clothes and skin, caked and black across his face. A little was his, but the rest belonged to British soldiers who had been in his way.

It had almost worked. He cursed Jacob Stevenson and his own bad luck. He'd had his daughters in his grasp, and had revelled in Annette Stevenson's terror when she had realised what was going to happen to them. The fear in her eyes filled him with excitement and he wanted to see it again. He read the message once more:

Commander Bell.
Stevenson and entourage preparing to sail north with the Mary, the Charlotte Arms and Gabriel. Three Man O War vessels in company, sir.
They have let it be known that they will wait for you to meet them at the fields behind the northern beaches.

Jacob wasn't running back to London like the cowardly dog he was. His mind had been violated by the realisation of what would happen to his women and was now calling on Jackson to fight.

Finally, the first real battle of his revolution was about to be fought. It was smart to take the fight out of the confines of the city and onto the open field – a perfect arena for great warriors to test their strength.

His thoughts moved to Ben Deery, the man who had killed Adder. Deery would pay for that. He would die slowly and painfully. The man was formidable in battle; that could not be denied. However, his weakness was the same as Jacob's. Deery would bow down before Jackson Bell if he had the Stevenson daughters under his knife. Ben Deery had fought to save them. He would have died to save them.

What a fool. All that violent talent to use against the world and he bows down to a woman. The bastard fool. He will die for that. He will die for taking my Adder.

Jackson had lost sixty men in the battle but still had over two hundred good fighters under his command. This was his chance. He had ordered his army to be ready to march north. That is where he would kill all his enemies and take Jacob and his daughters for himself. Stevenson would surely lead him to the Spanish treasure, or he would see his wife boiled and eaten in front of his eyes.

'Commander Bell, sir.' The voice came from the door of the tent. 'The army is assembled and ready to ride north when you give the word.'

Jackson threw away the rest of the ale and crushed the message in his hand.

'We leave immediately.'

Chapter 59

The ride to the cove had been swift and without any engagement. Ben, Luke and Simon walked the clearing where the battle would take place. It was good ground for a fight: even under foot and wide enough for a man to have space to move against his opponent.

The ships had anchored in the cove only a matter of minutes before the Stevenson women boarded the *Mary* and were reunited with Jacob, Brenton and the other London families who had made the journey across the Atlantic for an engagement party. They would witness an engagement, Ben thought. Just not the type they were expecting.

Regan had come ashore and walked up the sand and onto the field to meet his sons and Simon Blake.

'Well done, my boys. Well done.' He embraced them both as a proud father, before his expression turned to one of surprise. 'Dear Lord, if it isn't a ghost before my very eyes.'

'It is good to see you again, Regan,' Simon said as he extended his hand.

'And you, Blake. It has been a long time,' Regan replied as he grasped Simon's hand with his own.

'Aye, it has. You have raised two very impressive young men; I can attest to that. The Deery clan is in good hands.'

'Thanks to you, Simon. I am glad to have you and your men with us. You will be needed.'

'How many?' asked Luke, realising the meaning of his father's statement.

'We suffered a great loss in Rio. On the ships behind me, we have just over a hundred soldiers able to fight. Another forty of our own men on board the *Gabriel* and *Ol' Charlie*. How many are you?'

'We have thirty with us. With that, we are only just over one hundred and seventy men,' Simon exclaimed. 'Bell will come with well over two hundred.'

'That should be enough as long as they all hold their ground,' Ben asserted. 'The Scarlets will be weary from such a long march, and we should use this to our advantage. Jackson will want to rest his men south of here before the battle. We cannot allow that to happen. The road comes in from the west and about half a day's march from here is an area large enough for him to make camp. It is also overlooked by a wooded rise, which will make a perfect ambush site.

'We will bring powder barrels off the ships and line them up on that rise, hidden just off the road. A small team will wait for the Scarlets to set up their camp. Just as the Scarlets begin to sleep, our men will light the fuses to twenty barrels and slip back into the jungle.'

Luke nodded and laughed. 'They won't be sleeping or resting after twenty barrels of gunpowder explode above their camp.'

Ben continued. 'The Scarlets will march again at first light and be here when the sun is high and the day is warmest. They will be sluggish and weary from the heat and lack of sleep from the night before. We will set the line parallel to the beach with our backs against the shimmering of the water. That is how we will fight them. That is how we will end this.'

They all agreed it was a good strategy and scouts were sent south to watch for the expected march of the Scarlets.

The sun was fading when they returned to their camp for the night, only to see William Finch waiting to meet them.

'Mr Deery, sir. Jacob Stevenson has requested you and your sons join him and his family for dinner on board the *Mary*. We have a longboat waiting to take you once you have changed and are ready. Mr Blake, you are also eagerly awaited on board.'

It was a warm night and the men dressed in their riding trousers and boots, clean white cotton shirts and evening vests. Ben saw no need for lapels or cravats in the current climate. If he was about to charge into battle and possibly to his maker, he was going to spend what little time he may have left being comfortable in what he wore. He had no intention of pleasing Jacob Stevenson after what Simon Blake had told him.

The ship was immense, the biggest he had ever laid eyes on – a city on the water. He was the last of the four to climb over the rails of the *Mary* and was surprised to see a crowd standing on the main deck to greet them. They were not soldiers or sailors, but the wealthy London residents. As they began to clap and cheer, his first thought was that he had dressed appropriately because many of the other gentlemen were wearing similar attire.

Jacob, however, wore a full dinner jacket and cravat, formal stockings and buckled leather shoes. He walked up to Simon Blake and the Deerys with his arms held out in a welcoming gesture.

'Simon, my old friend. I have been waiting for this moment when we might see each other again after so long.'

'And I you, Jacob,' Simon replied, though not as enthusiastically, as the two men embraced.

'We have much to discuss?' Jacob whispered.

Then after a concentrated stare at Simon, Jacob turned to Luke and Ben. 'I believe I have you two young men to thank for the safe return of my family,' he said as he walked over to them and put his hand out, first to Luke. 'And I hear, Luke Deery, that you and my youngest, Penny, are going to make quite the suitable couple. The news of this fills my heart with joy beyond your comprehension.'

Luke embraced Jacob.

'Not nearly as full as my heart is at this moment, sir.'

Jacob smiled back at him and turned his gaze towards Ben.

'And the warrior we have heard so much about is here also.

Your reputation precedes you, lad. I am certain Jackson Bell and his Scarlets are not feeling so confident without their warlord Adder. Our soldiers have no doubt that victory will be ours now the great Omiran fights with us, fights for the just and the good!'

He raised his hand in the air and sang the words proudly as if he were the emperor of Rome. A resounding cheer echoed around the deck as Ben stood there, unimpressed with their ignorance. They had no idea what was coming for them, what they would have to witness in a day or so. He smiled sympathetically at the assembled crowd.

Rich, arrogant fools.

'Please,' Jacob spoke, silencing the noise around him. 'Enough of introductions. I am sure you are in need of food, wine and music. Come, see our grand cabin and dine with us. We have a feast prepared to satisfy Alexander the Great himself.'

The main cabin was more like a grand hall. It was hard to believe that they were dining on a ship. Ben was proud that the Deery family had built such a ship but was annoyed that so many trees and man hours had been used to serve one man's desire.

Stevenson was no king and even royal families would not possess such a ship. The meal was indeed a feast and the wine flowed freely at all the tables. The conversations were based on fashion, politics and business. No one spoke of what was to come and the looming battle ahead.

Rich men dine while poor men work. Rich men watch while poor men die.

Sasha sat at a table with her family, Simon and Luke. Regan and Ben sat with William Finch and Wendell Prince and various members from the London families. Through the course of the night, Ben often looked over in Sasha's direction. Each time he looked, it would only take a moment before she would meet his gaze, as if she could feel him staring at her, and it was a secret game that they were playing together.

As the meal was being cleared from the tables, Jacob asked Brenton, Simon, Regan, Luke, Ben and his general managers to accompany him into the Captain's Cabin. They lit cigars and each man poured himself a brandy.

'When will it happen?' Jacob finally asked as he stared at the men in front of him. No one answered but Ben could see them looking in his direction.

'Tomorrow or the next day at the latest.' As he finished his words, an ominous tension filled the cabin. 'It will happen around noon when neither side has to deal with the sun in their eyes.'

Ben's certainty seemed to set a resolve in the men, and no one questioned his answer. Jacob looked sternly at him now.

'Will we win?'

'We will have fewer men than Jackson, I suspect,' Ben went on. 'But we will be rested, which will help our cause. There is no question that many will die because of this. There will be substantial loss for both sides.'

'Should I set sail immediately and take my family back to London where they are safe?'

'Your family will not be safe until Bell is dead. He has it in his mind now, and he will not be able to let go of the thought. As long as he leads the Scarlets, your family will be pursued.'

Jacob nodded towards Ben to show he understood. His next words took Ben completely by surprise.

'Gentlemen, I would like private word with Ben, if I may. We will meet you back in the dining hall with our other guests in a moment.'

Ben looked over at Luke, who slightly shrugged his shoulders, clearly as surprised as everyone else by the request. As the last man left, the cabin door closed, leaving Jacob and Ben alone in the room.

Ben waited. Jacob had his back to him and was staring out through the large windows on the stern of the ship. Finally, Jacob spoke.

'You are adopted, yes?'

'I am.'

'Regan speaks very highly of you, as if he were your birth father. He mentioned that you saved him and his son during a battle against Adder himself. And yet he cannot tell me anything about you before that moment, where you came from, what your life was. Do you not think it strange that a man would adopt a son without knowing his past?'

Ben felt anger rise within him, spurred on by the warmth of the wine and brandy.

'My father knows who I am. There is no real past to talk about and so we find it just as easy not to. We do not find it unusual.'

'Mmm,' Jacob muttered as he turned around to look at him. 'I find it unusual.' He poured himself another brandy and offered the flask to Ben. He shook his head, not saying a word or averting his gaze from Jacob.

'My girls have not stopped talking about you, particularly Sasha, with whom I am unable to have a conversation without your name being mentioned.'

Ben stood there and said nothing. He knew he didn't have to.

'She is fond of you, I can see,' Jacob continued.

'And I of her.' Ben's reply rang loudly in the silent room.

'Really?' Jacob finally spoke, his tone now changed from curiosity to resentment. 'Luke Deery is to marry Penny. This will unite two great families. I am afraid it would not be suitable for a second Deery–Stevenson union.'

'Suitable or profitable?' Ben saw that his words sparked anger in Jacob, who was not used to being spoken to in such a manner, but Ben was beyond pleasantries now as his anger with Stevenson returned in full.

He felt the scars on his back tingle as he remembered Jacob's look of indifference all those years ago, when he had been paraded in front of the estate and whipped almost to death. He tried to calm himself and drain the tension from the room.

'It would not be the first time two brothers married into the same family.'

'But you're not brothers, are you? Not by birth. And I would like to know who it is that wants to marry my daughter.' Jacob had now abandoned any pretence of politeness.

The tension in the room finally boiled over and neither man had regard now for gentlemanly behaviour.

'Perhaps a Deery would not enter into the Stevenson marriage if he knew of your ties to the slave trade and to Jackson Bell himself.' Ben's words shocked Stevenson.

There was no turning away from it now. Pandora's Box had been opened and there was no return for either of them. They would never see eye to eye. They would never accept each other.

The room was silent for a long moment until Jacob gave Ben a dark smile.

'You don't like me much, do you, boy?'

'Stop calling me boy.'

'I will call you what I please. I connect the New Worlds together and I control the Atlantic in between. Me! Not you! I will do as I please, and if I need to teach you a lesson in manners, I can organise that, no matter who you think you are.'

'Yes, of that I have no doubt. What should be my punishment, Jacob? Lashes? How about fifty of them? Will you swing the whip yourself or get someone else to do your bidding as you watch on like the coward you are?'

'What the hell are you talking about, you arrogant young upstart?'

'You are a slaver, Stevenson. By keeping Jackson Bell financed all those years, you are just as much responsible for the thousands who have died on his ships.'

'I did not know Jackson was in the dark trade. I do not deal in slaves.'

'Liar! What was I, if not your slave? You worked me half to death, day after day, to line your pockets. You fed me only to make me strong enough to work the next day.'

'Who are you, boy?'

'My name was Caleb. You whipped me close to death and

329

sent me to die on the *Retribution*. Tell me, Jacob, how are your horses doing these days without my help?'

Jacob stumbled back. He bumped his glass and spilled brandy on the oak desk behind him.

'Caleb,' he whispered. 'It can't be you.'

'Jackson and Adder murdered every soul in my crew and took me as a prisoner of war, and then when the *Grey Revolt* was attacked, I was captured by Regan Deery. I should have died many times, but I have lived. I have seen places and things you have not yet imagined in your dreams. I have led battles and ended men's lives in every way possible. I am Ben Deery, and if you call me "boy" again, I swear by God I will give you the deliverance you deserve.'

'Caleb! Christ, it is you!' Jacob could hardly believe what he was seeing. Here was the peasant stable boy, now a man, standing up to him as an equal on the greatest merchant ship to have ever sailed the sea. 'So, you abandoned your previous life and became a rich man's son with land and titles. Hah. My God! It really is you!'

Ben stood there silently, relishing the moment he had made the great Jacob Stevenson stumble in disbelief.

'And what about Sasha then? Are you pursuing her to spite me? You know I can't allow it, Caleb.'

'My name is Ben Deery, and you will hold your tongue or the world will learn that Jacob Stevenson kept Jackson Bell on his payroll to attack the competition beyond the line. That the allowance you provided afforded Bell a life of slaving and merchant attacks resulting in the thousands of deaths of sailors, soldiers and innocent slaves.'

Ben knew that he had Stevenson now. Many of London's finest and most influential citizens were sitting just down in the hall, and he did not have to go far to expose Jacob, who was too weak to stop him now.

'That is the trade, Jacob. You get to keep your secret and I get to keep mine. And I will marry Sasha.'

Suddenly, the door burst open and William Finch and Brenton Stevenson entered the room. 'Excuse me, Mr Stevenson,' Finch said hesitantly. 'Is everything all right, sir? From the dining room, it sounded like yelling.'

Jacob looked over Ben's shoulder to the two men standing in the doorway.

'Yes. Everything is fine, William. Young Ben Deery and I were discussing plans for the future once everything has returned to normal.' He returned his gaze to Ben. 'I am pleased to say that Mr Deery and I find each other in agreement. Come, Mr Deery, I think I have left my guests without their host long enough.'

Ben walked through the dining room and said his goodbyes to the multitude of guests, who all wished him good fortune and held onto his hand longer than was needed, as if they were shaking it for the last time.

Perhaps they were.

He walked out onto the quarterdeck. The moon was high, and the stars were shining brightly. If this was to be his last night, he could not wish for a canvas more beautiful. As he walked down the stairs and onto the main deck, Ben saw Sasha standing near the gunwales, where the longboat was waiting to take him back to shore.

'I can't stand this,' she shivered. 'Let's set sail now and be leagues from this nonsense by morning. We can go back to London and be protected there. Please, I can't bear the thought of losing you again. I love you.'

'This will never end if we run, Sasha. We must finish it here and now. Then, and only then, can we be free. I know now more than ever that the demons of the past will always find you if you run. Sooner or later, they will find you.'

'I am coming with you tonight. I do not care what anyone says or thinks. I have to be near you.'

'No. You must stay here where you are safe. No ship will be attacked tonight. You stay here with your family.'

He climbed over the rails and down the ladder to the longboat with the other men. She watched them from the *Mary* until they were silhouettes on the shore and then she could see them no more.

Chapter 60

It was just before noon when they heard the sound of marching and saw what Ben estimated to be over two hundred men approaching from the other side of the field. As they emerged along the road, they did not look tired or worn down from the march, but he knew that it was the adrenaline from the first sight of the enemy that was giving the Scarlets their false energy.

It had still been dark when the scouts had woken him that morning. Musungo had volunteered to go with ten others responsible for placing and igniting the powder barrels along the road near the Scarlets' camp, and it had been successful – twenty large explosions erupted in quick succession on the ridge above the unsuspecting Scarlets before the men hurried back to him to report on numbers, artillery and anything else that could be used in their preparations against their enemy.

'We shook a great beehive, Omiran,' Musungo had said. 'They chased us for a while, but gave up after an hour. They will be here before the sun is highest. The fight will happen this day. You need to prepare your army.'

Immediately after hearing the report, Ben gathered Simon, Thomas, Regan and Luke together and set in motion the morning's preparations. Regan and Luke assembled the men under the Deery banner, while Simon ordered the signal be sent from the beach to the *Mary* informing Jacob, William and Wendell to assemble the British soldiers and have them make their way ashore.

They were lined up now and ready. The British regiments

led by Jacob Stevenson, William Finch and Wendell Prince, the Royal Couriers led by Thomas and Simon Blake, the Deery men led by Regan, and in the centre was the Company, with Luke and Ben standing in front. Armed and ready, they heard the roars of their enemies as they lined up on the opposite end of the field.

They waited for the Scarlets to charge but instead they saw Jackson, accompanied by four others, slowly riding into the centre of the field, a white flag raised above their heads. Simon, Jacob, Regan, Luke and Ben rode slowly out to meet them.

'Simon Blake, as I live and breathe.' Jackson's voice was filled with excitement. Simon said nothing.

'Finally, out of your foxhole and into the revolution,' Jackson continued.

'Your revolution is a fool's dream, Bell.' Jacob could not help but get involved. 'There must be order. What kind of world could anyone live in if chaos reigns? You must see that?'

'Freedom will reign!' Jackson called back. 'Men will be free to do as they please and not live by someone else's rules. Men like you, Stevenson, have poisoned the Atlantic with the rules that you, and others like you, create. You cannot control the will of free men any more than you can control the seas.'

'And what then, Jackson?' Regan spoke up. 'What happens when all men are free? Will you then decide to rule them?'

'I will give men the choice to follow, to be ruled, like the men behind me, like my Adder.' He looked at Ben as he said Adder's name. He glared with eyes as fierce as they were the day he had taken the *Retribution*.

'And when they decide to leave your rule, what will be their fate then?' Regan persisted.

'I am tired of this,' Jackson said. 'Simon and Jacob are who I want. If you come with me now, I will leave with my army and the rest of you can go.'

'The hoard is a myth, Bell. The Treasure Fleet is on in the bottom of the Atlantic Ocean, somewhere near North America.

Give up this fool's ambition and call off your army.'

'The hoard exists! You know it, Blake, and you know the location, or I wonder do all of you know by now? It will be interesting to see who lives through this day. I have more men and they are well trained; I assure you.'

'You will never be told its location. I will give up my whole family and my own life to keep it from you. Do you hear me, scum? You will never find it!' Jacob had lost his temper.

Hearing his quest confirmed after so many years, Jackson's eyes flashed.

'So, it is real. Let it begin, then.' He had no more need for talk, so turned his horse and rode towards his army.

Only a moment had passed before Jackson glanced over his shoulder to see his enemies had turned their backs to him and were riding towards their lines. He nodded to one of his men who retrieved a concealed rifle from under his horse's saddle blanket. Jackson took hold of it, turned to face the water and cocked the hammer.

'Stevenson!' His scream was heard by all on the beach. Ben had not turned his horse completely before he heard the shot ring out.

The bullet hit Jacob in the lower part of his neck, just above his breastplate. Luke grabbed the horse's reins, holding Jacob steady as they bolted back to the beach. Ben drew his long sword and moved his horse in between Jackson and those riding back to the line.

Neither Jackson nor Ben spoke as they stared at one another, before Ben abruptly turned and galloped back to his army.

By the time he had reached their line, Jacob had already been laid under one of the palm trees. Regan held his hand over the hole in Jacob's neck, but it was in vain. The colour had drained from Jacob's cheeks as he struggled to breathe and then the hollow look of a dead man's eyes stared up at them as he breathed his last breath. In the distance, Ben could hear the faint screams from those on the *Mary*. They were standing on the main deck and had a good view of the beach and field. Annette, Brenton, Penny and Sasha had seen it all.

Another much louder noise came from behind him as the Scarlets began to charge. Two hundred men ran across the field towards them, swords drawn and screaming with the excitement of battle.

Regan leapt into his saddle.

'Ready arms!' he yelled down the line. Rifles pointed at the oncoming wave of men ahead of them. 'Fire!' Regan gave the order and a line of smoke billowed from the rifles as the shots met their targets, flinging the runners onto their backs.

Ben drew his sword and walked out into the field. Cheers went up as the men saw him advance.

'Follow him and kill these bastards!' Regan shouted down the line, and again the cheers erupted as they charged out to meet their enemy.

The two armies smashed into each other, steel colliding with steel as the screams of the first men dying filled the air.

There was no use for rifles now in such close contact. Swords would be the weapons that would decide their fates. Ben had learned through his many fights that the men who swing at everything are always the first to die. He had learned to parry the first line rather than engage it, as it gave him time to get in behind his enemy's first line of attack, where it was messy and confused. He could fight from a better position behind the first wave.

Three men had fallen by Ben's sword before he had his first chance to assess the battle's progress. It was too early to tell which side was winning as men from both sides were falling, and quickly.

He checked his left flank to see Luke cutting his way through the Scarlets' defences. On his right was Musungo and the two Gonzos. Dressed only in waistcloths, they lunged their spears forward into the men around them, shouting in their native tongue with each thrust. This was a harrowing sound to any enemy, and Ben was glad that they were fighting with him.

Regan rode through the crowded field, his horse knocking men down as he swung his sword furiously.

A wall of men surrounded Jackson and instantly Ben realised why. Jackson stood and pointed his rifle. He was patient with his aim, knowing his men were protecting him for his shot. The gun fired, and Regan's horse fell to the ground.

'Father!' Luke screamed as he drove his sword through another opponent and ran off in the direction of the fallen horse. He was too late. Three Scarlets had descended on Regan, their swords stabbing his body relentlessly.

British soldiers came to his aid and fought back the attackers as Regan was dragged away from the battle. By the time Luke reached him, Regan was covered in blood and dying from his wounds.

The British soldiers created a barrier around them as Luke leant on one knee, holding his father's hand.

'Father!' he screamed. 'Hold on, Father!'

'Don't be a fool, boy.' Regan choked out the words as the blood trickled from his mouth. 'Get back in this fight.'

'I can help you.' Luke knew it was untrue, but he would try nonetheless.

'Damn you, Luke. Listen to my last words.' Regan squeezed his son's hand tightly. 'Get back into this fight. Find your brother. It is yours now, all of it. Go! Fight alongside Ben and end this.'

Luke looked down at his father's wounds and realised that there were only seconds left. He nodded to him.

'Yes, sir.'

'My boy.' Regan's grip on Luke's hand weakened and his arm dropped to the ground beside him. Luke stood up, turning in the direction from where Jackson had made the shot.

'Follow me!' he ordered the soldiers around him as he led them towards Jackson. He cut his way through the attackers and headed for the Scarlets' leader.

Crazed with the excitement of bringing down two of his

greatest enemies, Jackson was now carving his way through a sea of Redcoats. Ben and his men continued to fight their way towards Jackson from the opposite direction. From a distance, he had seen his father die. He had been helpless to stop it and now he would have his revenge.

The sound of horns erupted from behind them: the distress call from the Mary. Ben turned to see a new wave of Scarlets charge towards them from the beach. The army they had seen emerge from the trees was only half of Jackson's men. Another, large contingent of fighters had made their way around the battle once it had begun. Undetected, until they were in a position to strike from the rear. He looked around at the army against them now. At least three-to-one against his side. The Scarlets were going to defeat them.

The second wave of Scarlets had the desired impact. Surrounded and outnumbered, fighting on two fronts, red coated soldiers began falling in great numbers.

Ben frantically made his way through the battle towards William Finch, who was making a desperate attempt to reassemble what men he had left into an orderly line of defence. Their rifles were spent and those on the front lines who were trying to reload were being cut down mercilessly.

'Finch!' Ben yelled as he reached him. 'You must signal to the Man o' Wars. Use their cannons to fire at the beach.'

William Finch looked at him perplexed.

'There is no way we will be able to protect our own men,' Finch replied frantically.

'We cannot defeat them with our numbers,' Ben yelled in frustration. 'Jackson will not accept your surrender. If we do not use the cannons, we will all die here today. With the cannons, we may still have a chance. It must happen now before they clear the beach!'

Finch looked unconvinced.

'We must drive them back towards the water. When we do, order your men to retreat to the trees. They will be safe there for a moment while the Scarlets regroup for their next charge. Signal your ships to concentrate their fire towards the shoreline. Three rounds of your forty-two pounders should be enough to make many of the Scarlets run. Not all of the men who fight with Jackson are mad. They did not come here to fight against your cannons. It should be enough to break up their force.'

'All right Mr Deery,' Finch relied. 'May God have mercy on us for this.'

Ben continued to fight his way towards Simon and Luke. He turned around to see the flags signal the warships. Only a short moment later, the thunderous sound of the broadside cannons filled the air. The first round. The Scarlets on the beach had not expected it, turning in fear at the realisation what was speeding towards them. Bodies began to dematerialise as the cannons passed through the crowded beach. The ground exploded up into the air, shooting high great spurts of sand and dirt as the shots found the beach. The battle ground had turned into a dark world of soot, dust, confusion and panic as the eruptions continued down the shoreline.

'Advance!' yelled William Finch.

Redcoats pushed hard against the disorientated Scarlets, forcing them back towards the water's edge. Ben and Simon's forces created a barrier on the field between the British soldiers and Jackson Bell's smaller force.

'Wheel them to the right!' Ben yelled to his men. They concentrated their efforts towards one side of Jackson's men, steering them around the redcoats and pressing them down to the larger enemy force. Within moments, the whole fight had found its way to the beach. The Scarlets now had their backs turned to the Man o' Wars. In front of them were Ben and the allied force.

The second thunderous roar of the cannons sounded. This time many men from both sides ceased fighting immediately and plunged themselves to the ground, desperately trying to avoid the incoming terror. The second round had worked as planned.

Its aim had been corrected from the first fire and its reckoning force, burst through the Scarlets at the edge of the water. The deathly destruction was severe. Body parts separated from their origins and flew through the air, accompanied by the harrowing screams of their previous owners.

Exhaustion swept over the fighters as the battle raged on. The advancements became week and sluggish, and many men resorted to a stand-off against their opponent, facing each other, guarding, with no strength left to attack.

Finch had commanded his men well. Many of the Scarlets were attempting to flee. Some tried to escape from the sides of the battle. Some headed into the water, discarding their weapons and tempting fate as they tried to swim from the fight unarmed. The British soldiers pushed hard once more, drowning those who fled to the sea.

Jackson saw them advancing and turned towards Ben. 'Omiran!' he screamed, as he swept one of the Couriers out of his way.

They headed for each other, cutting through the last few opponents between them before they finally stood face to face. In anticipation, a ring formed around them, and the combatants stopped to watch the two warriors.

Jackson held a sword in one hand and a large knife in the other.

A smart way to fight in a crowd.

Ben, too, drew out a knife with his left hand to accompany the larger sword in his right.

The fight began with both men circling each other, looking for the weakness in their opponent. An advance and a parry, and again, and again the same, with no real result.

Jackson thrust his long sword towards Ben's face, but Ben dropped his shoulder, allowing his head to move low, to the side, and out of the direction of the blade.

Jackson's left hand swung around with his knife and Ben saw his first chance. The attack was too wide and too high. He ducked under Jackson's left arm and spun around below him, dragging his knife across the back of Jackson's left thigh.

The Scarlets' leader grimaced and fell to one knee. Ben had his chance to finish the battle. He had only to keep spinning and plunge his sword into Jackson's back, when they all heard the horrifying sound of cannon fire. The third round exploded hard into the beach. Shot landed in the sand around them and knocked Ben off his feet. Bodies collided into one another and, once again, the sky blackened. Ben lay in the darkness, motionless. He tried to recover his thoughts, tried to regain his focus, but the daze was heavy. He stared up at the sky, dreamily watching tunnels of light force their way through the cloudy smut. He tasted blood in his mouth and the pain in his body became apparent. He tried to move but the agony crippled him. He blinked hard and looked around. All who had been standing close to him were now lying on the ground. Some trying to move, many not moving at all. He looked further down the beach and saw the Redcoats chasing after fleeing Scarlets. The cannons had worked. But at what cost?

He waited a moment for the ringing in his ears to diminish. Then he heard the grunting lunge of Jackson. He turned around to see the Scarlet warlord upon him. A large bone-handled blade came stabbing down towards him. He tried shifting to avoid it piercing his chest, but the blade found its way into his flesh. He screamed with the pain as the knife dug into his shoulder. He held the weight of Jackson on top of him, but the blade began to twist, and his strength began to leave him as the knife dug deeper into his body.

'Yes, young Omiran! First your father, and now it is your turn!' Jackson whispered in Ben's ear as he pushed his weight further onto the knife, pushing it deeper into Ben's flesh.

Ben groaned from the pain. He kicked out, desperately trying to find some purchase on the ground, some foothold that might help him to escape from the pain. He felt the strength of his legs return. Aching, but enough for one last effort to save his own life.

He twisted his body towards the downslope of the beach, rolling them both on their sides. Jackson's weight was no longer above him. He could free his right hand from the knife. He punched as hard as he could into the Scarlet's jaw and felt the pressure on the knife release as the blood spurted from Jackson's mouth.

He was free. He crawled away from his attacker, the blood from his shoulder pouring onto the sand below him as he dragged his stomach across the beach and away from Jackson.

With another aching scream he pulled the blade from his left shoulder and with his right hand grabbed a handful of sand and packed it into the wound.

Both men got to their knees and made for their weapons.

Jackson was limping badly as he got to his feet. The cut across his thigh was deep and he was badly injured now. Ben lunged his right boot into Jackson's badly wounded leg and the Scarlet fell to his knees once more.

'Stand up, Bell! You are about to find out what your New World feels like.'

Jackson staggered to his feet and limped badly once more. The look in his eyes had now changed from fire to uncertainty and Ben knew he had him scared. There were groans from the crowd that had gathered to watch and, as Ben quickly glanced around, he could see that they had won.

Simon Blake stood with Luke Deery. Wendell Prince, Thomas, William Finch and the loyal Imbangalas, who had all survived the cannons and were now watching tensely.

'Do you hear that, Bell? Your army is defeated. It is over.'

Jackson looked around at the remains of his army. The ones who could still move were now fleeing into the jungle, chased by Red Coats who were shooting them down as they ran.

Jackson looked around the circle and saw only his enemies, but he would not surrender. He lunged again at Ben. He was injured and slow and his attack was weak. Ben moved to his left, parried with his right arm and drove his forehead into Jackson's nose. He heard the bone crushing against his head and as Jackson's head flew back, Ben hit him in the mouth with the handguard of his sword.

Jackson stumbled but somehow stayed on his feet, and with one last effort he lunged at Ben. Again, it was desperate, and Ben once more ducked low and to the left, slicing his long sword across Jackson's abdomen, spilling his internal organs onto the ground in front of him, as he had done with Adder. Jackson dropped his sword and fell to his knees.

Ben looked over at Luke. He lifted his sword and offered it to him.

'For our father.'

Luke took the sword and made his way over to Jackson. 'For our father and all the fathers before him.' He guided the blade into the front of Jackson's throat. Jackson's eyes widened as the blade was pushed slowly through his neck. He choked and spluttered as Luke pushed slowly all the way to the hilt, holding it there until Jackson finally fell backwards, dead before he hit the ground.

It was over. Ben looked up at the sky, shut his eyes and let out a sigh of relief. He had avenged Captain Andrews and the crew of the *Retribution*, who had been slaughtered all those years ago. He had avenged all those who had perished under Jackson Bell's tyranny, and he had avenged Bobby, who could now rest in peace, as Jackson lay motionless one on the ground. In the distance, the last sound of gunfire could be heard as the remaining Scarlets were put to rest and, as Ben collapsed on the sand, he felt the strong hands of Musungo and the Imbangalas carry him off the beach.

Chapter 61

Ben stood on the starboard side landing outside the main cabin of the *Gabriel*, looking at the city of Rio glowing in the sunset. His left arm sat in a sling and his shoulder ached badly. The surgeon had done well with the wound and it would heal in time.

The *Gabriel* and *Ol' Charlie* had joined the *Mary's* fleet and were lined up in the harbour, loaded and ready for the voyage back to England at first light.

Jacob and Regan had been buried in the gardens of the Government Fort on the hill overlooking the harbour. It had been a large ceremony with almost all of Rio's citizens attending to pay their respects to the men who had given their lives in the fight against Jackson Bell, and to those who had fought and lived. They had not afforded Bell as proper a burial. Instead, Bell and his Scarlets had been left where they had fallen.

No more than he deserved.

After the burials, another ceremony had taken place in the government hall. As the new owner of Stevenson Transport, Brenton Stevenson had signed the contract as his father's heir, the stroke of a pen making him one of the richest men on the Atlantic.

Luke had also signed a document as the new head of the Deery Shipping Company, with Ben inheriting twenty percent ownership of the company. Though he was not as rich as Brenton and Luke, he was now a very wealthy man.

'As the new owner of Stevenson Transport, I welcome the

continued partnership with Deery Shipping as were our fathers' wishes,' Brenton had said to them both. 'I hope we can continue to fulfil their dreams. With the union of Luke and my sister Penny, we will continue to bring prosperity to the Atlantic.'

Ben had been surprised when Brenton had then turned to him in front of the witnesses.

'I know how my sister feels about you, Ben. You have our family's blessing should you wish to marry Sasha. We would be proud to have such a man by her side, and with you being a leading executive in the shipping company, it seems a fitting union indeed. I love my sister and have always wished for her to find true love. I can see clearly that she has found this with you. On such a sad day, it is a joyous welcome to my heart, and I know that my father would have felt the same way.'

Sipping his wine, Ben looked over Rio and thought about the words he had heard earlier that day. Jacob would not have felt the same way, but it made little difference now.

A voice came from behind him. 'Ben, may I join you for a wine?'

He turned to see Simon standing in the doorway holding out a flask and two glasses. Ben nodded and smiled. He had always been fond of Simon and his ways. He was strong yet unassuming, fierce yet graceful and kind.

'We will be heading out with the *Mary* at first light, so I would be happy to share a final drink with you, Simon.'

'Actually,' Simon replied, 'I thought I might take a trip to London. I have not seen my home in so many years. Do you mind if I travel with you?'

Ben smiled, again welcoming the opportunity to spend a voyage with the great man he now called his friend.

'Of course, Simon.'

Simon walked out to the balcony, stood next to Ben and poured them a drink. 'A new era is upon us, it seems,' he said, raising his glass.

'So it would appear,' Ben replied, meeting Simon's glass with his own. 'What of The Hidden Place?'

'As far as I know, the only three people who know the exact location of the Fleet Treasure are Thomas, you and me. There will always be men like Jackson Bell. We cannot allow men like that to have the means to ruin the world.'

'I give you my word, Simon. As long as I live, I will do my best to keep it secret, to keep it safe.'

'That we will need to do, son, but I think, now you are a rich man, we should think about hiding it properly.'

'The Hidden Place isn't enough? What would you suggest?'

'South America is expanding. We cannot keep the mountain's secret hidden forever. I will build a town on the river next to the waterfall. The best way to keep it safe is to keep it hidden in plain sight. If you decide to, we can also build a town at the base of the mountain. Its purpose will be to mill Brazilian rosewood and create a new shipping yard for the Deery Company. It will also connect the Deerys with the northern areas of Brazil and up into North America. You do not just have to build ships for Stevenson Transport, you know. There are plenty of things you can build with wood. Look at my pipe, for example.' He puffed the smoke through his lips as he chuckled.

Ben liked the idea instantly. It would be the perfect way to mask what was inside the mountain and at the same time expand the company and give him reason to sail across the Atlantic from place to place, which he loved doing more than anything.

'I will mention it to Luke as soon as we meet again in London.'

'Ah, yes. That is right. Your ship is sailing at first light. Perhaps you should go up top to make sure you have everything you need for the voyage.'

Ben rolled his eyes. 'I am not sure I can listen to your riddles for the next eight weeks Blake, but you are right. We should make our way to the wheel. I would like to inspect her before we lose the light.'

They strolled their way up to the quarterdeck and a proud call echoed through the *Gabriel*.

'Captain at the helm!'

As Ben strode across the deck, Simon's puzzle became clear to him. Above, on the poop deck, a tall, slender figure leant over the rail. Her white dress floated in the breeze as the day's remaining sunlight silhouetted her figure and created a deep glow on her skin. She faced away from him towards the city, as if she were saying farewell.

He looked over at Simon, who stood at the wheel, smiling and motioning him to go to her.

She turned around when she heard Ben step up onto the deck. They had not seen or spoken to each other since the day before the battle a week ago. He had not thought it appropriate with everything that had happened. Everyone had a reason to mourn after the battle, and he did not know if Sasha would want to see him again so soon. He was certain that she would sail back on the *Mary* with her family, but Sasha had a way of surprising him. More than that, she knew him. She had always known him – the real him.

He would be Ben to everyone but her. To Sasha, he would be Caleb, his real self as it had been all those years ago on the Stevenson estate.

So much had happened between those days and the present, but he had always been Caleb, and he had finally made his peace with that. Sasha had loved Caleb and now loved him as Ben.

As they stared at each other in the fading light, she flashed a quick smile over the deck towards him. A distant feeling washed over him, one that he had long since forgotten. One that he had not let himself feel for many years. A feeling he had not dared to believe had ever been real.

He thought about this new world as he looked over at Sasha and, for the second time in his life, he felt hopeful.

The End

Did You Enjoy This Book?

If so, you can make a HUGE difference.

For any author, the single most important way we have of getting our books noticed is a really simple one—and one which you can help with.

Yes, you.

Us indie authors and publishers don't have the financial muscle of the big guys to take out full-page ads in the newspaper or put posters on the subway.

But we do have something much more powerful and effective than that, and it's something that those big publishers would kill to get their hands on.

A committed and loyal bunch of readers.

Honest reviews of our books help bring them to the attention of other readers.

If you've enjoyed this book I would be really grateful if you could spend just a couple of minutes leaving a review (it can be as short as you like) on this book's page on your favourite store and website.

About the Author

Mike Wardle draws inspiration from the many places he has called home. Starting his schooling in the Torres Strait Islands, located between Australia and Papua New Guinea, Mike developed a keen sense of adventure and an appreciation for cultural diversity early on in his life.

For a number of years Mike's family called Indonesia home, where they lived the expat life in North Sumatra. Mike has trekked through the jungles of Sumatra, climbed the stairs of amazing temples such as Borobudur in Java, and walked through the seemingly endless marketplaces of Southeast Asia.

Spending most of the rest of his life in rural Australia, he came to realise his love of adventure and historical fiction books. After the tragic loss of a friend, he decided life was too short not to do what he loved and so he began to write his first story.

Equally at home on a tropical island, in the jungles of Asia or in the Australian bush, Mike has an inherent love of travel, history and exotic landscapes.

He now lives on the Sunshine Coast in Queensland, Australia.

About Burning Chair

Burning Chair is an independent publishing company based in the UK, but covering readers and authors around the globe. We are passionate about both writing and reading books and, at our core, we just want to get great books out to the world.

Our aim is to offer something exciting; something innovative; something that puts the author and their book first. From first class editing to cutting edge marketing and promotion, we provide the care and attention that makes sure every book fulfils its potential.

We are:

Different

Passionate

Nimble and cutting edge

Invested in our authors' success

If you're an author and would like to know more about our submissions requirements and receive our free guide to book publishing, visit:

www.burningchairpublishing.com

If you're a reader and are interested in hearing more about our books, being the first to hear about our new releases or great offers, or becoming a beta reader for us, again please visit:

www.burningchairpublishing.com

Other Books by Burning Chair Publishing

Push Back, by James Marx

Shadow of the Knife, by Richard Ayre

A Life Eternal, by Richard Ayre

Point of Contact, by Richard Ayre

The Fall of the House of Thomas Weir, by Andrew Neil Macleod

The Curse of Becton Manor, by Patricia Ayling

The Brodick Cold War Series, by John Fullerton
    Spy Game
    Spy Dragon

Near Death, by Richard Wall

Blue Bird, by Trish Finnegan

The Tom Novak series, by Neil Lancaster
    Going Dark
    Going Rogue
    Going Back

10:59, by N R Baker

Love Is Dead(ly), by Gene Kendall

Haven Wakes, by Fi Phillips

Beyond, by Georgia Springate

Burning, An Anthology of Short Thrillers, edited by Simon Finnie and Peter Oxley

The Infernal Aether series, by Peter Oxley
    The Infernal Aether
    A Christmas Aether
    The Demon Inside
    Beyond the Aether
    The Old Lady of the Skies: 1: Plague

The Wedding Speech Manual: The Complete Guide to Preparing, Writing and Performing Your Wedding Speech, by Peter Oxley

www.burningchairpublishing.com

THE RETRIBUTION

MIKE WARDLE

Printed in Great Britain
by Amazon

45036192R00202